Up Island

Also by Anne Rivers Siddons

Up Island

A Novel by

Anne Rivers Siddons

HarperCollins*Publishers*

HarperCollins books may be purchased for educational, business, or sales promotional use. For information please write: Special Markets Department, HarperCollins Publishers, Inc., 10 East 53rd Street, New York, NY 10022.

FIRST EDITION

Designed by Alma Hochhauser Orenstein

Library of Congress Cataloging-in-Publication Data

Siddons, Anne Rivers.
   Up island / by Anne Rivers Siddons. — 1st ed.
     p. cm.
   ISBN 0-06-017615-6
   I. Title.
PS3569.I28U9   1997
813'.54—dc21   97-5849

97 98 99 00 01 ❖/RRD 20 19 18 17 16 15

This book is for Ginger Barber,
and high time

I went to the woods because I wished to live deliberately,
to front only the essential facts of life, and see if I could
not learn what it had to teach, and not, when I came to die,
discover that I had not lived.

—HENRY DAVID THOREAU, *WALDEN*

ACKNOWLEDGMENTS

Ann Nelson of The Bunch of Grapes bookstore in Vineyard Haven has probably been thanked by so many authors that she could start her own literary society, but to all that gratitude I would like to add mine. She literally gave me "her" Martha's Vineyard, that up-island world of old families and secret places, and in addition, a great deal of her time and a great many of her own treasured personal books. This book is, in a unique way, hers; its errors of fact and interpretation are strictly mine.

CHAPTER ONE

YOU KNOW HOW PEOPLE ARE ALWAYS SAYING "I knew it by the back of my neck" when they mean those occasional scalding slashes of intuition that later prove to be true? My mother was always saying it, though she was not always right. Nevertheless, in my half-Celt family, the back of one's neck is a hallowed harbinger of things to come.

I first knew my husband was being unfaithful to me, not by the back of my neck, but by the skin of my buttocks, which, given the ultimate sorry progress of things, was probably prophetic. I always thought it was grossly unfair that Tee got all the fun and I got dermatitis of the posterior, but there you are. According to my mother, again, it was a pattern we had laid down in stone in the early days of our marriage.

I had been having fierce itching and red welts off and on since Christmas, but at first I put it down to the five-pound box of candied ginger Tee's boss sent us and a savage new panty girdle that enabled me to get into my white beaded silk pantsuit. Later, when the itching and welts did not go away, I switched bath soap and body lotion, and still later had the furnace and air-conditioning unit cleaned and found some plain, unbleached cotton sheets for our bed. Still I felt as if I had been sitting in poison ivy, and often caught myself absently scratching in public as well as private. Teddy, my eighteen-year-old son, was mortified, and my best friend, Carrie Davies, asked me more than once, her elegant eyebrow raised, what

1

was wrong. Tee would have teased me mercilessly, but he was not around much that winter and spring. Coca-Cola was bringing out two new youth-oriented soft drinks, and Tee and his team were involved in the test marketing, which meant near constant travel to the designated markets across the country. I could have scratched my behind and picked my nose at the same time on the steps of St. Philips and poor Tee, jet-lagged and teen-surfeited, would not have noticed.

When I woke myself in the middle of a hot May night, clawing my skin so that the blood ran, I made an appointment with Charlie Davies, and was distressed enough so that he worked me in at lunchtime the next day.

"Well, Moonbeam, drop your britches and lay down here and let's see what we got," he roared, and I did, not really caring that the paper gown Charlie's nurse had provided me with gapped significantly when I tied it around my waist. Charlie and Tee had been roommates at the University of Georgia, and I had known Tee only two weeks longer than I had Charlie. Charlie had married Carrie Carmichael, my Tri Delta sister, a week after Tee and I had married—we had all been in each other's weddings—and we had kept the friendship going all through med school and internship and then practice for Charlie and the early and middle years at the Coca-Cola company for Tee. Charlie had probably seen my bare bottom more than once, given the house parties and vacations we four spent together.

He had called me Moonbeam after Al Capp's dark, statuesque, and gloriously messy backwoods siren, Moonbeam McSwine, since the first time we'd met. I allow no one else to do so, not even Tee.

I rolled over on to my stomach and Charlie pulled back the paper gown and gave a long, low whistle. "Shit, Molly, has Big Tee been floggin' you, or what? You look like you been diddlin' in the briar patch."

Despite his redneck patter, Charlie is a very good doctor, or he would not have any patients. Atlanta is full of crisp, no-nonsense out of towners who would draw the line, I thought, at being told to get nekkid and lay on down, unless the one saying it was supremely good at what he did. Charlie was. In time, the good-ole-boy gambit became a trademark, a trick, something people laughed indulgently about at parties. If it secretly annoyed more than amused me, I never thought to verbalize it.

"How bad does it look?" I said.

"Honey, how bad can your sweet ass look? The day Tee married you the entire Chi Phi house went into mournin' for that booty. Though now that you mention it, there seems to be a good bit more of it these days, huh?"

And he slapped me gently on the buttock. I felt it quiver like jellied consommé under his thick fingers. There was indeed more of me now than when I had married. Where once people had looked at me and seen a tall, sinewy, sun-bronzed Amazon with a shock of wild, blue-black hair and electric blue eyes, now they saw a big woman—a *really* big woman—with wild, gray-black hair, all teeth and leathery-tanned skin and swimming, myopic eyes behind outsized tortoiseshell glasses. Then, they had stared at the slapdash, coltish grace and vividness that had been mine. Now they simply stared at big.

"Christ, it's a goddamned Valkyrie," I had overheard someone say at last year's performance of *The Ring* when it came to Atlanta. Tee and I had both laughed. I seldom thought about the added pounds, since they did not for a moment inhibit my life, and Tee never seemed to notice.

"I mean the rash, or whatever it is, you horny hound," I said now to Charlie.

"Well, I've seen worse," he said. "Saw jungle rot once, when I was a resident at Grady."

"Come on, Charlie, what is it? What do I do about it? I never had anything like this before."

"I don't know yet," he said, poking and prodding. "I'd say some kind of contact dermatitis, only you don't have a history of allergies, that I remember. I'm going to give you a little cortisone by injection and some pills and ointment, and if it's not healed by the time you've finished them, I'm going to send you to Bud Allison. We need to clear this up. I don't imagine Tee is aesthetically thrilled by the state of your behind, is he?"

"I don't think he's even noticed," I said. "He's been out of town so much with these new Coke things that all we've had time to do is wave in passing. It's supposed to slack off in a couple of weeks, though, and I wish we could get rid of this by then. He'll think I *have* been rolling around in the alien corn patch."

"Gon' sting a little bit," Charlie said, and I felt the cool prick of a needle. Then Charlie said, "I thought he was back by now. I saw him the other day over at that new condominium thing in midtown, the one that looks like a cow's tit caught in a wringer, you know. I guess he was helping Caroline move in there; he was toting a palm tree so big only his beady eyes were peekin' out of it, and she was bent double laughing. She's a honey, isn't she? The image of you at that age, thank God. Y'all must be real proud of her. She working around midtown?"

He pricked me again.

"That must have been somebody else's beady eyes peeking out of that palm tree, Charlie," I said. "Ow. That does sting. Caroline is married and living in Memphis, with a brand-new baby. Honestly. You knew that; y'all sent the baby a silver cup from Tiffany's. Must have killed you to pay for it."

Charlie took his hand off my buttocks. He was silent for a space of time, then he said, "You get dressed and come on in the office, and I'll write you out those prescriptions."

I heard his heavy steps leaving the examining room. I heaved myself up off the table. It hit me as I swung my bare legs over the side. The skin of my face felt as if a silent explosion had gone off in the little room. I actually felt the wind and the percussion of it. The room brightened, as if flood lamps had been switched on, and when I took a breath there was only a stale hollowness in my lungs. A new hot, red welt sizzled across my left buttock.

"Tee has somebody else," I thought. "He has had, since Christmas, at least. That was Tee Charlie saw. He knows it was. And that was her Tee was moving into that condo."

I sat for a moment with my hands in my paper lap, one cupped on top of the other, a gesture like you make in Communion, waiting to receive the Host. I could not seem to focus my eyes. My ears rang. Through it all, the skin of my behind raged and shrieked.

I stood up, dropped my paper gown, put on my clothes, and went out of the little room and down the hall and out through the reception area to the elevator. I thought of nothing at all.

When the elevator came, I got on with a handful of lunch-bound people, some in white coats, stared vacantly at the quilted bronze doors, and thought, the family. What is this going to mean for the family?

By the time I stepped out on to the hot sidewalk running along Peachtree Street, I felt as if I were on fire from the back of my waist to my knees. I had the absurd and terrible notion that the weeping redness was sliding down to my ankles and puddling in my shoes, the visible stigmata of betrayal and foolishness.

When I was small, my grandmother Bell lived with us for a time. She was a frail, sweet-faced little woman who was afraid of many things, including my mother, whose theatrical outbursts and exaggerations made her wince and shrink. Mother caught on to that in about one minute, of course, and often set about shocking and frightening Gran just for the sport of it. I suppose it was irresistible; even I, who adored Gran and often fled to her talcumy arms when Mother trained her silver arrows on me, wondered with the unforgiving contempt of the very young why Gran stood for it. But she always did. Her way of dealing with my mother and whatever else threatened her was simply to pretend that it did not exist. The sight of her chattering cheerfully about nothing and plying her small daily rituals while literally quivering all over like a terrified rabbit used to madden me, but I do it myself now. Like a savage who will not name or acknowledge a demon lest it draw the demon's attention, I deal with awfulness by becoming a caricature of middle-aged suburban normality.

I began doing it as soon as I stepped on to the sidewalk in front of Charlie's office. I swung my bag jauntily over my shoulder, pulled my chin up and tucked in the offending fanny, and turned left down the long hill toward Peachtree Battle, finding a long, loose, city stride and swinging along with a happy-to-be-in-the-world smile on my face. I nodded to pedestrians who passed me and looked with interest and approval at the beds of impatiens and begonias in front of the Shepherd Spinal Center. I noted with another silly nod of my head the electric sign in front of the Darlington Apartments that kept track of Atlanta's population: 3.7 MILLION. That sign was a source of annoyance to me most of the time; Atlanta's mushrooming population had long since made streets and sidewalks impassable. But on this day I beamed at it with the fatuous pride that I had felt when Tee and I had lived in our first small house, in Collier Hills, and the sign meant to me that my upstart town was becoming a real contender, an honest-to-God city. Take that, New York, Chicago, L.A., I said today under my breath. I looked down at my prancing feet in approval: just the right plain, low-heeled Ferragamo walking shoes a well-grounded Atlanta woman should wear on a hot spring day. The weight of my bag thumped against my side, and I was pleased: just the right, well-worn, lustrous Coach handbag, nothing trendy or with initials on it that were not mine. All my totems were in order. But my heart was banging in slow, cold, breath-sucking beats.

My chastely Cliniqued mouth smiled wider.

I was nearly down to the entrance to Colonial Homes Drive, where for decades all the singles in my set lived until marriage and the move to Collier Hills on the way to Habersham Road or Ansley Park, when I heard a voice I knew shouting at me from the eddy of traffic.

Livvy Bowen was calling to me from her dirty old Saab, stopped beside me at a red light.

"Where on earth are you going?" she yelled in her not unpleasant New England honk. Livvy came south for the first time from a Boston suburb ten years before, when her husband, Caleb, was transferred to Coke headquarters to work on Tee's marketing team. Caleb was Harvard and Livvy was Radcliffe, and Atlanta was a thick stew of culture shock for both. Caleb had read the handwriting on the corporate walls and adjusted fast; Livvy never had. She hated the South in general, Atlanta in particular, liked Tee all right, and for some reason loved me. She had instantly, as I had her. Something in her raw bones and narrow, unmade-up face and acid tongue spoke to what my mother called the damnyankee in me. Mother spoke allegorically, of course; my parents were both Southern, back to their families' arrivals from England and Ireland, and that was more than two hundred years ago. I knew what my mother meant, though, and so, apparently, did Livvy. In her mouth, "damnyankee" was not a pejorative term.

"You're the only woman I know below the Mason-Dixon line who doesn't run by Saks on her way to the grocery store," she said in the early days of our friendship, "and the only one who doesn't own a Judith Leiber bag. Do you even know what a Judith Leiber bag is?"

I didn't then, and can't remember now.

I said nothing on this morning, only smiled brilliantly at her. I couldn't think where to put her in this teetering new scheme of things.

"You've got on lipstick and panty hose," she said and grinned, gunning the hideous Saab's engine. "Who's died?"

I continued to smile. "Hi, Livvy," I ventured as the light changed. She did not move the Saab forward. Behind her, horns began to blow.

She stared at me for another moment and then said, "Get in the car."

"Livvy—"

"I'm not moving till you get in this car," she said, with the iron of old Massachusetts money in her voice. The chorus of horns swelled. I got into the car and slammed the door and she screeched away up Peachtree Street.

We did not speak again until she swerved into the fake fifties diner that newly occupied an old car wash and stopped.

"Where's your car?" she said. "Where have you been? What's the matter with you? You've got red blotches all over your neck and chest."

"I've been to the doctor," I said in my grandmother Bell's dreadful, sunny voice. "I've got some kind of allergy; it's nothing. Charlie Davies gave me some stuff for it. My car . . . my car . . ." I looked down at my blossoming chest; my backside was indeed colonizing new flesh. I smiled at Livvy. Even I knew it was what Tee calls a shit-eating grin; I could taste it on my mouth.

"I guess I left my car in the parking lot at Charlie's."

"Uh-huh. And you were going where?"

A little lick of annoyance managed to penetrate the smog of Bell denial.

"Who are you, Joseph Mengele? 'Vee haff ways to make you talk.' I was going home, of course; where do you think I was going?"

She just looked at me. My face flamed and my chest burst into a Flanders Field of red; I could feel it. I lived in Ansley Park, in the opposite direction of the way I had been walking, and had for nearly twenty years. I had been making for my parents' old home, the one I had grown up in, on Peachtree Hills Avenue. They had not lived there for the past five years, but in a condominium behind St. Philips Episcopal Cathedral in Buckhead.

I knew that Livvy knew that. I put my face in my hands and began to cry.

"Tee is having an affair," I sobbed. "I just found out. I don't know what to do about the family."

Livvy and Caleb live in a sprawling brick house in Brookwood Hills, a leafy old family enclave across from Piedmont Hospital and its attendant doctors' buildings. I have always loved that neighborhood. I wanted to look there when we were finally able to leave the Collier Hills starter house, but Tee felt Ansley Park had a more international feeling to it, and that was the direction Coke was going in. Many of the new transferees were buying and gentrifying the old town houses there, and besides, you could walk to the Piedmont Driving Club. Tee's family had always belonged. Mine had never even been to a wedding reception there. So we found and remodeled our own tall town house with a tiny walled garden. I liked it, and had sunk a few roots and had raised my children there, but it never felt like Atlanta to me. "You can't just walk down the street on a spring evening in Ansley Park," I told Livvy once. "You have to have the right kind of suit. A jogging suit, or a cycling suit, or a Rollerblading suit, or a dog-walking suit . . . and the right kind of dog, of course. Lazarus definitely does not cut it in AP. I'm thinking of renting a dalmatian just to walk it."

"I'd be thinking of moving," Livvy snapped. "A dalmatian would be laughed out of Brookwood Hills."

We skidded through traffic and she hung a heart-stopping left across two lanes; we were in her sunny kitchen with cups of coffee before I could stop the treacherous sobs. I could not even remember the last time I had cried.

"Tell," she said, handing me a hot washcloth, and I mopped my face and told.

When I stopped talking, she snorted and said, "That's just shit, Molly. Tee's not having any affair. In the first place, you-all are joined at the hip. In the second place, when would he? Caleb's out with him when he's traveling; don't you think I'd know if Tee wasn't where . . . he said he was? Some doctor you've got. Some friend, too."

"Charlie *saw* him, Livvy—"

"Excuse me, pet, but how does Charlie know it was Tee? Every man in Atlanta in a certain class and age group looks just like Tee. Most of them work for Coke."

I had to smile, even through the thready galloping of my heart, because she was right, or partly. There is a type of wellborn Atlanta man who looks enough like Tee to be his kin, and may be: tall, lanky, blond-going-gray, hands jammed in pockets, with the shambling gait of the college athlete most of them were. Tee was the starting forward on UGA's basketball team the year we graduated and the team won the SEC championship; he still had the loose-jointed, pigeon-toed lope that went with the position. His hair was short now and gilded with gray, and fell over his forehead, and there were fine wrinkles at the corners of his blue eyes, but he was still snub-nosed and thin to the point of boniness, and his grin still charmed and warmed. We had been a stunning couple in college, a study in opposites but of nearly matched height, and we had known it then. I had long since forgotten. I wondered if Tee had.

"Charlie was Tee's roommate for four years," I said. "He'd know him if he saw him. He thought the girl—the woman—was Caroline. So she must be tall and dark and very young. And pretty, of course. Caroline is a very pretty girl."

"Crap. If the guy was hidden behind a palm tree, how could this wonderful Charlie be sure? It's not like you to jump to this kind of silly conclusion, Molly. You've never had any reason to doubt Tee's faithfulness . . . have you?"

"No," I said, and knew that it was true, knew it with the same baseless interior certainty with which I had known the truth of Charlie's words this morning. Tee had not strayed before this.

"If he was going to, don't you think he'd pick a better time?" Livvy said. "He's traveling with a team of nine people. He's almost never in the same city two nights in a row. He's in meetings from breakfast until midnight. Unless she's a stewardess with a key to the rest room, Tee's not banging anybody but you. And he's *sure* not doing it in those particular condos. Half of Coke lives there."

"But I've had this breaking out since Christmas, and that's when he started traveling . . . it's gotten really bad. It's like my body knew something that my head didn't, yet. I feel so damned sure,

Livvy . . . and Charlie said stress could do that to you."

"So can poison ivy. So can whatever you wash your underwear in. I think you've slipped a cog. What could Tee possibly want that you don't give him?"

"I've gained a lot of weight," I said in a low voice. "I don't think about it much, but I know I have. I don't take the pains with myself that I used to. You should have seen me in college, Liv. I was homecoming queen my junior year. Tee and I . . . we were something to see together."

"You still are," she said. "Don't you know people turn around on the street to look at you? You look glorious. You look like an Amazon princess, or like . . . like . . . "

"If you say Moonbeam McSwine, I'll throttle you," I said, beginning to grin in spite of myself. Some of the cold weight had lifted off my chest. The fire in my fanny and neck was cooling.

"That, too," Livvy said, and reached over and put her hands over mine. Hers were warm. I realized only then that despite the day's sullen heat, I was as cold as ice, as death.

"Listen," she said. "I don't for a minute think you've got anything to worry about, and if you look at it rationally, you'll see that I'm right. But Moll . . . what if, just what *if*, there was somebody else? What would it mean to you, what would you do?"

I stared at her. What would it mean? Why . . . the end of everything. The end of the family. God, the family . . . why didn't she see?

"What do you think it would mean?" I said. "What would it mean to you? If it was Caleb, I mean?"

She shrugged. "Depends. On whether it was serious or a fling or some kind of silly midlife thing. Depends on how sorry he was."

She smiled. Her long Back Bay teeth were the color of rich old ivory. No anxious cosmetic bonding or bleaching for Olivia Carrington Bowen; even loving Carrie Davies, who knew how close I was to Livvy, had said once that Livvy looked like a horse.

"But the thoroughest of thoroughbreds," I'd rejoined shortly. Carrie had snorted, sounding herself like a horse. I knew that she did not approve of Livvy's and my friendship.

"She's not like us, Moll," Carrie had said. "She won't ever be. She doesn't even try."

"And that's why I like her," I snapped, hoping to put an end to the subject. And I had. My old crowd did not espouse Livvy Bowen, but in my presence they no longer denigrated her, either.

"And what would you do?"

"I'd snatch him baldheaded, and then her," Livvy said. "I'd give him two hours to wind it up quietly, and if he didn't, I'd tell Coke he couldn't keep it zipped, and tell her he had a penile implant. And if he still wouldn't, I'd throw his stuff out the door and change the locks and hire the meanest lawyer this side of the Mississippi River."

She looked at me with only a half smile. I thought that she was not altogether kidding.

"What about Dana and Elizabeth?" I said, thinking of Livvy and Caleb's two daughters, both in college in the East. "What about the family?"

"Dana and Elizabeth are neither one coming back home after school," she said matter-of-factly. "I've always known that. Much as I love them, they aren't going to be a big factor in my future. They'd have to make their own separate peaces with it. Molly, that's the third time you've said 'the family.' Not 'my family,' but 'the family.' What is it with you and 'the family'? It's like you mean some kind of idea, instead of your own people . . . "

The family. The family . . .

When my mother married my father, she was nineteen years old and an actress and dancer, or at least aspiring to be one. She was, he said once, as lovely as a silver minnow in a creek. Her name was Mary Belinda Fallon, but she called herself Belle Fallon professionally. She had had unpaid parts in a number of local theatrical productions and one badly paid part in the chorus of a touring company of *Lilli* at Chastain Amphitheatre in Buckhead, and was scheduled for a far better speaking and dancing role in the next year's touring production of *West Side Story*. Her blue-black hair and milky skin had caught the eye of more than one regional producer; she had reason to think she could go as far as her lithe legs and low, purring voice could take her. But then she met and married Timothy Bell, and since she could not be billed as Belle Bell, took the fatuous stage name Tinker Bell. It was Dad's nickname for her; he'd called her Tinker from the day he'd met her. She was as erratic and glinting and shining and ethereal as the frail, jealous sprite in *Peter Pan*, and she might well have gone on to make a name for herself on the stage, for she had, in addition to her looks and a middling talent, enormous presence. Even at home she had it, even at rest. I really think she was born with it.

But she was pregnant when she married Daddy, and by the time I was born, a giant of a baby according to her—a wrecker of pelvises and stomach muscles—her trajectory was broken, and she climbed into no more rarefied air than that of local theatrical productions and later, acting and dancing lessons. My poor mother: the heart of a gypsy, the soul of a prowling tiger, forever trapped in local productions of *Showboat* and *Auntie Mame*, and once, with notable success, *Hedda Gabler*. It was a bitter loss to her, and perhaps worse for the rest of us. It was catastrophic for me. She never ceased blaming me for it.

Oh, she never would admit that she did that, and in all fairness, probably did not know it. I certainly did not. I knew only that something about my size, my very person, was unseemly and worse: damaging. Dangerous. I can remember trying to fold myself into a smaller shape when I was no more than four, and slouching like a little old osteoporosis victim when my real spurt of growth started, at nine or ten. By twelve I was five feet eleven inches, within a hair of what I am now, and felt as unclean as a leper. Of us all in the smallish house on Peachtree Hills Avenue—my mother, my father, my granny Bell, my brother, Kevin, and me—only my father seemed to know what Tinker Bell was about with her little jeweled barbs flung gracefully at me, her fastidious little shudders and drawings aside when I blundered too close to her. At those times he would hold out his arms to me, or make a dry, small joke at my mother's expense, or sometimes simply say, in his quiet voice, "Tink . . . "

My mother would run at me then, and fold me into her arms and smother me with kisses that she had to stand on tiptoe to deliver, and say, in her lovely lilt, "As if it were your fault, my darling! As if you asked to be such a nice big armful!"

And, encircled in her warm, sweet, reaching flesh, I would feel the full, ponderous weight and height of my nice big armful, and her arms would feel as cold and alien to me as marble.

It would have been impossible not to see that Kevin, my

younger brother and nearly the twin of my mother, fit with every slender, quicksilver inch of him into her arms. Flesh of her flesh might have been written for my mother and my brother.

Many years later, after a near killing loss, I found myself doubled over on my bed, arms folded across my stomach, rocking to and fro and weeping, in a kind of mindless mantra, "I want my mother! I want my mother!"

And knowing, in a terrible epiphany, that even though she was only ten or so blocks away, I had never had her, and could not now. There has never been anything in my life like that moment for sheer, monstrous aloneness. Never, not anything. I don't think there ever will be again.

It seems odd to me now that it was for her that I wept that day when, from the first moment of remembered awareness, it was to my father that I ran for comfort. But perhaps it is not so strange, after all. Any child knows, with a cell-deep certainty, when he has been given only half. Later, when that half has proved strong enough to sustain and propel, he may not miss the unproffered other half of sustenance so much, may not even remember a time when its absence starved and terrified. But the void, the abyss of its absence, is with the child always, and when great loss comes, as it so often does in the middle years, much of the attendant anguish is for that earliest loss. And so, on that hot day in a much later spring, I wailed for my mother and then got up and called my father. As he always had been, he was there, and as it always had, pain and fear shrank back. I have never been unaware as to whom I owed my life.

It used to make me wild when he would refuse to do battle with my mother, to avenge my hurt.

"I don't think ballet, darling," she said when I was six and wanted to join the magical classes she taught in our remodeled garage, where willowy little girls wore soft leather slippers and tied their hair high in severe buns and moved like wildflowers in the wind of her presence. A wall of scummed mirrors gave back their images, and a long bamboo bar was a trellis for them. It was the loveliest thing I had ever seen, and she was the mistress. If I were one of them, I would be one with her.

"Why?"

Even I could hear the whine in my voice.

"Because you are already far too big," she said coolly. She hated whining. I stopped doing it early. Now I hate it, too.

"I'll stop growing."

"You've only started growing. You'll reach the moon. You would look terribly out of place in a corps, and of course you could never hope to solo. You will be a giant, heroic woman; you must be the one who holds the ropes, not the acrobat. Whatever would the world do without its rope holders?"

"Swim," my father said when the tears overflowed my bottom lashes. "You've got just the streamlined build for it. You'll look like a mermaid in the water. I'll teach you."

And he did and signed me up for lessons at the Chastain Park pool, and cheered me on when the prowess he had predicted propelled me to victory after victory in the free stroke and relay. He took double shifts at the post office during my teenaged years to pay for my tuition at Westminster, and was always there to cheer me on when I brought home medals and cups for the school, even when Mother had a night class and could not attend. I was never popular at Westminster, not with the petite Buckhead girls whose cliques I aspired to, but I was known and applauded, and that gave me impetus enough to live with some equanimity until, in my last year of middle school, I suddenly began to come into my looks. It seemed to happen overnight; it almost drowned me at first. I was forever looking warily at the vivid image in mirrors and store windows. Who *was* that? Soon sidelong glances and a scattering of dates, usually with older (and taller) boys, followed. Miniskirts stopped looking, as my mother said, like tutus on a Clydesdale and started to showcase enough long, tanned, smooth-muscled leg to occasion whistles and calls from downtown construction crews. I began to stand to my height, and to stride instead of shuffle. I learned to smile openly and fully.

My father gave me all that.

And, when I wanted to try out for the varsity basketball team at the start of my junior year and my mother raised her silky black brows and said, "Do you really want to go lumbering around a gymnasium sweating like a draft horse with girls who have mustaches?," my father said, "You could model. There's a guy at the post office whose daughter is signed up with some model agency or something. She does fashion shows and even TV commercials. I'll find out about it."

And he did, and I signed with Peachtree Models and Talent that summer, and finished putting myself through Westminster and much of the University of Georgia on runways and in production studios. I learned to move and be comfortable with stillness, and to engage a camera with my eyes, even to lower my Amazonian bray to the clear, throaty voice I still have. Mother was proud of all that, though she could not resist giving me stilted instructions on moving and walking and stretching my neck, which had to be tossed out before the camera. And she began to shop for clothes with me, and even though she was wont to say things like, "Smocking and Twiggy baby dresses on someone your height are ludicrous, Molly. I don't even think they make them in your size," still, she steered me away from the kittenish excesses of midsixties dress that would have made me look ludicrous, indeed.

I could and did thank my father for all that, too.

But I could not make him defend me verbally to her, and that drove me early to rages of protest against the unfairness of her exquisite little sorties against me. Unfairness is the earliest and most irremedial of the world's wounds that a child encounters. It is never forgiven.

"Why don't you tell her to shut up?" I remember weeping once, when I had run to him yet again, this time over some obviously-to-me unflattering comparison to small Kevin. His natural grace and spilled-mercury vivacity, so like her own, were always being held up to me when I clumped or sulked.

"She doesn't mean to hurt you," my father said, holding me close enough to smell his familiar smell of Philip Morris cigarettes and sun-dried cotton undershirts. "She doesn't even realize she does it. It wouldn't be fair to her to yell at her."

"What about to me? What's fair to me? She's always liked Kevin more than me. He's her little boy."

"Well, you're my little girl, so we're even," he said.

And for the moment that would be enough.

It would invariably come up again, though, and I would rail at him once more: "Why won't you make her stop? I can't, but you could! You're always saying people can change if they really want to; if you told her to, she'd change."

"But I don't want her to change," he said. "If she changed, she wouldn't be her, and that would break my heart. She's the only magic I ever had in my life until you came along, Molly-o, and one day you'll see that she's the main magic in yours, too. You and I, we need magic. We're earth critters. She's our wings. Kevin has her wings, too. It balances out. All together, we make a family."

And we were at the heart of it, though I did not know it then.

Neither of my parents ever really had a family, so when they married, they simply made some rules for what they had and called it, if only in their minds, The Family. They were not the first to make living, breathing individuals fit into the iron cage of an abstraction, not by any means. *Ozzie and Harriet* and *Leave It to Beaver* probably defined family for half the baby boomers born. But it is my own family—The Family—that is finally clearest to me, and I can trace easily the steps of its peculiar, tumorlike growth.

My mother, for instance, was abandoned by her feckless teenaged father when she was an infant and raised until age ten or so by her pretty, empty-headed, Irish mother in Savannah. When her mother, still only twenty-eight, took off with a hospital supply salesman to the Florida Panhandle, little Mary Belinda Fallon was taken in by her aunt Christy O'Neill in Atlanta, and raised with the O'Neills' quarrelsome, cloddish brood of children in a clannish, dilapidated part of the city near the old Fulton Bag and Cotton Mill. Belle Fallon was all grace and moonshine and cloud shadow, profoundly unlike the O'Neills and unwanted by them, and when she graduated from Fulton High she left the mill village and crossed town, to the northside. She got a receptionist's job at the Georgia Power Company during the day, and in the evenings, she took to the stage. There were few enough struggling local theatrical groups, and she was talented enough, and above all, attractive enough, so that she made her mark quickly. Belle Fallon at eighteen was the toast of Atlanta's minuscule theater-going public.

By the time she was nineteen, she was singing and dancing and emoting in almost every production mounted within the city limits, and in some in outlying Macon, Birmingham, and Tallahassee. By twenty she had snagged her first featured part in a national touring company. At twenty-one she met and married my father, and by the time she was barely twenty-two, I was born and her career was dying, and The Family had begun to emerge as if from developing fluid. My father, himself an orphan raised in the Methodist Children's Home in Forest Park, Georgia, had his own set of rules, his own blueprint for being a responsible adult, so he was content to let my mother draft the master plan for The Family. He knew no more of how to go about it than she did.

She began by assigning us all roles. Dad would be the provider, the supporter, the fixer, the protector. Beguiled by this creature of wood smoke and wild honey who had flown into his life and alit, he dutifully left his evening law studies at Oglethorpe University and went to work at the post office, where he stayed until his retirement forty years later. He made himself into a good household manager, a banker and accountant of some asperity, a fine handyman and fixer of things broken and faulty, and a steady and constant cheerer from the sidelines for the three lives he found himself in charge of. I think that my mother chose well: Dad seemed to me, all my life and his, to be content, indeed, happy, in his appointed role. In any event, he couldn't have helped but cheer her on in whatever she chose to do; I never saw a man so quietly and totally in love with a woman.

I could hardly resent that. The love spilled over on me in full measure, and to a lesser but equally constant extent, on Kevin. But Kevin, for most of his life until he left home, wanted only Mother. If that disappointed Dad, I never saw evidence of it. It was part of the dynamics of The Family, and therefore meet and right.

Mother was the flame on our hearth, the giver of light and dazzle, the lightning rod, the visible totem of The Family. She was who we were, in our collective souls and to the world. Almost every family has one of these, but they tend to be men, or certain children of the tribe. The role of nurturing, minding, enabling does not allow for much dazzle. I think my hapless mother tried to be and do it all until I arrived, hefty and draftlike from birth, and she recognized with relief the designated giver. From the time I could toddle I was taught to accommodate, smooth over, prop up, set right. I don't ever remember really minding. I did and do it well. My role gave me status and definition; there was never a time I did not know who I was to The Family. It was only when I aspired to anything outside the cage that I came to grief. Mother never unsheathed her arrows when

I trod my road compliantly. That was when her whirling butterfly hugs and kisses were given; that was when her beautiful trained voice soothed and approved. As for those other times, I don't know what or who I might be now if it had not been for my father. As I said, his half flourished.

Kevin was our future, who we would be, how we would be known.

"Listen to him; he's already projecting," my mother gurgled with delight when Kevin howled in his ruffled bassinet. He was born graceful and pretty; he looked like her from the outset. His silky black hair was somehow hers as mine had never been, though to my eyes they were identical. His blue eyes were Fallon and not Bell, as mine were said to be. He had her delicate, porcelain features, and not the strong, carved ones I shared with my father. When he began to toddle, it was with her flat-footed, straight-spined dancer's gait. Even his tantrums were silvery and somehow theatrical. They made her laugh, as mine never did, and even my father smiled to see them. When Mother held him in her arms they seemed a Degas portrait: *Mother and Child.* Indeed, Dad once parted with a breathtaking amount of money to have a distinguished professor from the Atlanta School of Art paint them so, both of them bare-shouldered and bathed in dappled purple light from the blooming wisteria vine that sheltered our front porch. It is pure summer to look at; early summer, just before coarsening ripeness begins to swell. It hangs now in the living room of the condominium, as it did in the front room of the house on Peachtree Hills Avenue, where we sat when visitors came. Kevin and his wife wanted it when they first married, but Mother would not part with it. I knew of little else she had refused him.

So our paths were laid down from the beginning, and so we have continued since, in lockstep, four people destined and doomed to bear on our shoulders the living, holy ark of The Family. When I think of my mother's voice, it is this that I hear her say: "Family comes first, always. Blood is everything."

I told what I could of this to Livvy Bowen that morning.

"Your mother's obviously read too much William Faulkner and Tennessee Williams," Livvy said. "I can just see her in Williams. God. 'Blood is everything' my ass. Who does that make Tee and . . . what's Kevin's little wife's name again? I can't ever remember.

Chopped liver? Official consorts? Does she include them in this family stuff? Do you?"

"Sally. Her name is Sally," I said, obscurely annoyed. My attempt to explain The Family to Livvy had obviously fallen short. "Of course she includes them. Of course I do. Tee is family for me, just like Sally is for Kevin. Tee and Caroline and Teddy for me; Sally and Amanda for him. There was never any question in Mother and Daddy's minds that we would marry and have children. That's what makes family."

But did it? Mother was drawn to Tee from the beginning, I knew that; she teased and flirted with him, charmed his conservative northside parents, shone as if klieg-lit when we invited her to the driving club, was the focus of all eyes at the parties we gave in Collier Hills and later in Ansley Park. Tee gave my mother the one thing her foreshortened career had not: social status, a chance to show what she could have been if not burdened early with a gigantic daughter and dancing lessons in her garage.

But I don't think she ever approved of my marrying him. Tee should have been a woman. Then Kevin could have had him, and so had the matched consort that Mother had always envisioned for him. The only time Kevin ever really defied her was when he married Dresden-exquisite, utterly conventional Sally Hardy from below-the-salt Lakewood. Mother ceased excoriating Sally—delicately, of course—only when Kevin threatened to move with her to Nashville or Charleston or somewhere out of firing range. I don't think Mother ever saw that Kevin could not have lived with a woman who was Tee's equivalent in money, charm, and assurance. Where would he have drawn his audience then?

No, I think Mother somehow thought he would marry *her*. His mother, that oldest love. I don't think she ever forgave Kevin Sally, any more than she did me Tee Redwine. The order should have been reversed. Both of us, in our choices, threatened the sleek skin of The Family.

"Well, the pattern has held, hasn't it?" Livvy said, nuking our cooling coffee in the microwave and producing pastries from Harry's in a Hurry, just up the street on Peachtree Road. "You're still the good girl, the dutiful one. Woman of the Year in Volunteerism, or whatever, last year, right? And Kevin's still the white hope. Top local anchor in D.C., with network written all over him. And your mother is still the family star, running those recitals all over town, still looking like a gazelle and wearing those incredible hats. And your dad's still wiring lamps and making bookcases in the basement, and going to all her recitals and all Teddy's tennis matches and all your awards banquets. Does any of you know who you are? Do you know who those people who live at your house are? Jesus, no wonder your butt itches at the thought of the act breaking up!"

I have always loved Livvy's blunt pragmatism, but she can be spectacularly wrong, too, in the manner of one who has always been so sure of her blood and money and place in the world that she has never had to question it. I knew that she was wrong now. But somehow her earth-rooted words soothed the sucking terror in my stomach and eased my shallow breathing. Something in my mind moved an imperceptible fraction of an inch forward, like a gear clicking into place, my self came flooding back, and the thin, acid, starving air around me thickened into nourishing normality.

"A fine one you are to pooh-pooh blood," I said, grinning around a mouthful of apple turnover. "Yours is bluer than ink and so is Caleb's. I don't notice any transfusions of rich, rude, peasant blood in your line, on either side."

"Blood is not a policy in either of our families," she said sulkily. Livvy hates being hoisted on the petard of her lineage.

"The hell it's not. That's just what it is."

We stared at each other over the antique cherry game table that the Bowens use for family meals—Liv had once told me that George Washington was supposed to have played cards on it on his way to the Battle of Mounmouth—and then we laughed.

Later we went to lunch. I offered the club, but Livvy dislikes it. She says the people who go there, even to play savage tennis, do not sweat, they mist. So we went instead to a funky little place on Peachtree Road called R. Thomas, overflowing with lovingly tended flowers and herbs and raffish, cheerful, talking birds in cages; the last bastion, Liv claims, of the Age of Aquarius. I like it, too; the vegetarian dishes are rich and wonderful, but no one I know frequents it. Carrie Davies isn't all that sure it's clean. So I go there only with Livvy. After lunch she dropped me back at Charlie's building to pick up my car.

"So when is Tee due back?" she said, sticking her head out the Saab's window.

"Day after tomorrow. But he goes right out again Monday."

"Do me a favor. Take the two days just for yourself. Cancel all your good works and let Teddy fend for himself. He's too old for you to hover over, anyway. Spend a day at Seydell and get the works—haircut, facial, massage, makeup, all of it. Then go to Neiman Marcus and buy yourself something fabulous to sleep in. Order in Friday night. Chill the wine, light the candles. Attack Tee the minute he walks in the door; take no prisoners. Whatever it was that was terrific about your first roll in the hay, do it again. *Then* ask him if he's having an affair."

"I couldn't ask that . . . "

"*Ask* him, Moll. Jesus, you Southern belles. How do you ever find out anything you want to know if you don't ask? I'll guarantee you'll like his answer."

"Well . . . "

"*Guarantee*. By the time you two get out of bed, your butt will be as smooth as a baby's. See if it's not."

I left her laughing. I was laughing, too. In the two hours I had spent with her, Livvy had given me back my old life, my old self, my old context. I drove back down Peachtree toward Ansley Park humming "Bye, Bye, Miss American Pie" under my breath. The sun was shining and the flower borders in the midtown office buildings looked festive and European. It was, at that moment, utterly absurd to me that I had ever thought Tee was anybody but my beautiful, comfortable old Tee; that I was a cuckolded wife instead of the cherished Molly I had always been; that the family was newly and sickeningly endangered. I could not even remember how the fear had felt. I stopped at a produce truck in a parking lot and bought huge red Florida tomatoes and cucumbers and the last of the Vidalia onions. I would make gazpacho for the weekend. Both Tee and Teddy loved it. Perhaps I would go by European Gourmet and pick up something wonderful for Friday night dinner. Maybe I *would* go to Neiman Marcus; it had been a long time since I had slept in anything but an old, extra-large Black Dog T-shirt that Livvy had brought me from Martha's Vineyard, where Caleb's family had had a summer place for generations. It was so old and washed that the shiny black dog stuff had half flaked off, and the Martha's Vineyard signature labrador was a dalmatian instead. Something pale and silky, maybe, to set off the swimming tan I hardly ever lost and make my light blue eyes flame in the dark, as Tee had sworn they did when we first went to bed together. And if there was time, perhaps a good blunt haircut to tame the wild black-and-silver tangle that I never could subdue. I drew the line at dye, or even a rinse. But the other things, maybe. No. Definitely.

When I got home, still humming, and tossed the tomatoes on to the kitchen table, Teddy called to me from the rump-sprung sofa in the library that was his television lair. I walked through my Eurotech kitchen and into the book-lined cave that Tee had made for himself and that the entire family had appropriated. I could see nothing of my son but enormous feet in new Nikes hanging over the sofa's arm, but I knew how he would look: a long sprawl of tanned, sinewy arms and legs furred with the soft gold of his thick hair, dark blue eyes half closed, long, mobile mouth chewing whatever he had fished out of the refrigerator. He is Tee from the top of his head to his soles, except that Tee would die before he wore an earring. Teddy has had his for two years. So far it has not sent him spiraling into delinquency or homosexuality.

Lazarus, so named because we got him from the pound only hours before his appointment in Samarra, would be lying on the floor beside the sofa with his big, hairy muzzle on Teddy's stomach, and Teddy would be lazily scratching the top of his head. Lazarus is huge and shaggy and looks put together from leftover dog parts. We have never been sure what breeds met in him to produce such a strange animal. All of us adore him, and he us, almost embarrassingly so, but none of us is under any illusions about Lazarus. He will learn no tricks, win no ribbons, save none of us from fire or attack. Lazarus's only talent is love.

I looked over the back of the couch. There they were, as I had pictured them. Lazarus thumped his tail, and Teddy raised a hand in languid salute.

"What are you doing home?" I said. "I thought you were taking Mindy to get her driver's license."

"We had a fight. She was acting like a shit. I told her so. I said I wasn't going to be responsible for her being a shit on wheels. I think her mom is taking her," my beautiful son said, not fully opening his eyes.

"Language, sport," I said automatically. "You're going to have to apologize to her, you know."

But I was not sorry they had had a fight. Mindy Terrell is a strident, possessive girl with spectacularly disquieting looks and an obsessive attachment to Teddy. She was, I had thought, older at barely sixteen than I had been at twenty-five.

"In a pig's ass," Teddy said. "Let her call me. And she will. Speaking of calling, Dad called a few minutes ago. He's coming in tonight. He said he'd be real late, so not to wait up."

"What's the matter?" I said, my heart beginning to suck and drag again. "Why is he coming in early?"

"I don't know. Nothing's wrong. He just said he wanted to see us, just wanted to talk to us. Said we'd have a long breakfast in the morning. He sounded homesick."

I smiled. Warmth spread through the middle of me. Tee used to cut his trips short sometimes just to come home and see us, and we'd always have a long pancake and sausage and conversation breakfast the next morning. The morning after the night of his homecoming . . . my face colored at the thought of those nights. He had not done it in a long time, though. Did I have time for Neiman Marcus? No, but there was that black chiffon thing he'd ordered for me, as a joke, from Frederick's of Hollywood two Christmases back. The one with the slit in the bikini panties. I wondered if I could still get into it.

It makes no difference. I'll be out of it in no time, I thought, running up the stairs toward our bedroom with the idea of changing the sturdy, striped wash-and-wear sheets for the ivory Porthault ones my mother-in-law had given me for some unremembered anniversary. She had them even on her beds in the Redwine beach house on Sea Island. She also had Isobel to wash and iron them. I had never taken mine out of the ribbons they'd come in.

"Oh, by the way, Ma, how's your bee-hind?" Teddy called up the stairs after me, and as if on cue, the itching flame-stitched itself across my buttocks.

"Going to be fine," I called back, scratching hard. "Charlie thinks it's an allergy."

"Jeez, I hope it's not to me or Lazarus, or to Dad."

"Don't flatter yourself," I yelled, and went into the bedroom to peel off my panty hose and panties and soak my affronted rear in a warm tub.

Tee was very late coming in. I have usually fallen early into a light, waiting sleep since he has been traveling for Coke on this assignment, but this time I was awake. His step on the stairs was so familiar that I could feel it in the beat of my blood; there was the place he always broke stride, where the landing curved, and there was the next-to-top step that always creaked. I thought that there was something different about tonight, though, and then realized that his footsteps were slower, and heavier. Tired; he must be so tired. This insane traveling had gone on for far too long.

He came quietly into the bedroom, as he always did when I slept, and moved about with the ease of one who has undressed in this familiar dark many times before. I heard his shoes fall, and then the rustle that meant his pants were going down, and the little swish as he tossed them on the ottoman to the big blue easy chair under the window that looked out over the garden. The smaller swish of his shirt followed. He went into the bathroom and closed the door. I waited until I heard the toilet flush and the lavatory water stop running, and then reached for the switch on the bedside lamp. When I heard the door open again, I clicked it on.

"Hey, meester, you wan' a girl?" I called.

He froze in the flare of light, staring at me with near black, unfocused eyes. His face was emptied out and utterly still. For a moment my breath stopped. He looked mortally tired, bled white, old. His face was all angles and hollows in the shadows, and the stubble on his chin was so pronounced that I could see it from across the room. It is so fine and light a gold that you almost can never tell when he needs a shave.

"Honey?" I said tentatively, and sat up in bed in a great rustle of plastic. And then his face crumpled and he began to laugh.

Back in the silly seventies, a quintessentially silly woman named Marabelle Morgan had written a ludicrous antifeminist diatribe called *The Total Woman*. One of the husband-pleasing stratagems she had suggested was wrapping your naked self in Saran Wrap and meeting hubby at the door with a cold martini when he came home from work. Tee and I had hooted over it, and one night I had done just that, and we had ended up making love on the floor of the tiny vestibule that served the Collier Hills house as a foyer. I had had the striations of the diamond-shaped tiles on my back for days.

"Well, she's right, it works," Tee had said, panting.

Having tried and discarded the Frederick's of Hollywood ensemble as simply too sleazy to stretch over middle-aged flesh, I had remembered the Saran Wrap and done it again that night. For good measure, I had added a jumbo red velvet bow that had adorned our Christmas wreath, pulling it tautly over the worst of the weals and scratches on my bum. I was bathed, oiled, powdered, and shot all over with Sung, and my heart was galloping nearly as hard as it had on the first night Tee and I had ever gone to bed. When he began to laugh, I jumped, crackling and rattling, out of bed and ran to him and threw my arms around him. I pressed myself against him and rubbed as suggestively as I knew how; I kissed him all over his face and put my tongue in his ear. I felt his arms go around me, hard, and threw my head back and laughed aloud with joy. My clean hair swung into both our faces.

"You don' like me, I got a seester," I growled low in my throat.

Tee buried his head in my neck and scrubbed it back and forth, back and forth. He still did not speak, but I could hear his breathing thicken and deepen. I could feel him harden against my stomach, too, a ludicrous feeling muffled in plastic wrap.

"Wanna see if it still works?" I whispered into his hair.

I ripped the plastic wrap off and pulled him down on top of me on the bed. On the way down I reached over and clicked the light switch, sending the lamp rocking on its base. I gave him no quarter. I took him in my hand and guided him into me, clamping my legs around his waist and holding on as if I were in danger of falling off the rim of the world. He drove hard and deep, still not speaking, and I did not, either. Later for that. In the morning. Pancakes and sausage and Vivaldi and talk, sweet, slow hours of it. In the morning.

When we'd first made love, I was so nervous that my voice shot up an octave and I trembled all over, as if I were freezing. He was nervous, too, and half drunk; it was in our last year of school, after a Chi Phi party, in the apartment he shared with Charlie. Charlie was in Atlanta at Carrie's house; he was almost never in Athens on weekends that year. I remember that I closed my eyes and whimpered, and Tee, trying to soothe me, had whispered over and over, "It's gonna be good. It's gonna be so good, baby."

And to my immense surprise, it had been. It was so good that even before we found our rhythm, even before that first deepening and ripening, we both laughed aloud with surprise and pleasure. We were so exactly the same height and build that we fit as if we had been designed to illustrate one of the better sex manuals. There was not an inch of me, inside or out, that he did not cover exactly, fill perfectly. There was not an inch of him that I could not enclose. That had never changed, not in twenty-seven years.

And it didn't change this night. It was as good as ever. If anything, it was deeper, warmer, faster, more urgent than ever before. When we finally lay gasping aloud and tangled together, coated with sweat even in the stale chill of the air-conditioning, we still had not spoken a word. I felt as if we had passed far beyond words, into a new place where, forever after, communion would be through our skin, through our mingled heartbeats, through the very blood that pulsed in our necks and wrists and throats. I lay steeped in moonlight, pinned to the bed with the sweet, sweaty weight of him, listening to his breath soften and slow in my ear. I felt his slack mouth on my neck. I felt invincible, boneless and weightless and young. I thought it would be fine simply never to move out from under him.

But finally my legs began to prickle and go numb, and I turned my face into his neck and said into his ear, a bubble of laughter catching in my throat, "And I was actually going to ask you if you were having an affair."

He began to quiver against me, as I have felt him do before a hundred times when he laughs silently after love, and I began to laugh, too. I stretched myself as far as I could, like a cat, laughing against the side of his face, rubbing his shaking shoulders, giddy and nerveless with completion and relief.

It was not until I felt the wetness on my neck, a small rivulet of it coursing slowly down the slope of my breast, that I realized he was crying.

CHAPTER TWO

HER NAME WAS SHERI SCROGGINS. She was an assistant attorney in Coca-Cola's legal department, thirty-two years old, estranged from her viciously Pentecostal family in the Florida Panhandle, divorced seven years from her citizens' militiaman husband, childless, possessed of a naturally acute legal mind and prodigious ambition, and definitely on Coca-Cola's inside fast track.

Tee wanted to marry her.

At dawn, through a ringing in my ears that sounded as if I'd stood too near a great explosion, I heard myself say in a tinny, puzzled voice, "How on earth can you marry her, Tee? Then she'd be Sheri Redwine."

Tee turned away from the window, where he'd been watching day break over Ansley Park (But how could dawn come? How could the sun rise on such a morning as this?), and said, "I might have known you'd make a joke of this, Molly."

If I could have felt pain through the stupid numbness that enveloped me, I would have flinched at his words. I had not been making a joke. I had meant just what I'd said: It seemed to me in my craziness that Tee simply could not marry a woman whose name ever afterward would be a bibulous joke. I had thought perhaps it had not yet occurred to him.

We had talked for hours. Or rather, Tee had talked. Talked, wept, talked, wept some more, talked and talked and talked. It was as if someone had pulled a stopper out of him. He sat on the side of our bed and babbled words that had, for a long time, no meaning to me, because they were about people I did not know. I said nothing, because nothing occurred to me. I sat half shrouded in crackling plastic wrap, sensing rather than feeling the small frown between my brows, leaning closer to him every now and then so that I could hear him better, so that perhaps some of this tidal wave of urgent, tear-borne words might make some sense. Grandma Bell could not have done it better. Every now and then I could feel my head shake from side to side, no, no, in a small gesture more of incomprehensibility than anguish. Anguish was not a part of that night. Anguish presupposes understanding. I did not know this man who wept on the side of my bed, and I did not know what he was saying.

Teddy had a biology project in his freshman year at Westminster in which he studied the effect of strong emotion on the human body. I remembered that one effect of great shock and fear was the widening of the pupil to admit all possible daylight, so that the ensuing brightness could better illuminate danger. I thought now that it was true. The bedroom where we sat was very bright, even though no daylight had paled the windows on to the garden yet. I seemed smothered, and floated in a buzzing, shifting cloud of radiant mist. Sometimes I could see so clearly through it that the stubble on Tee's chin stood out like cuttings in a hay field; sometimes he all but disappeared. Occasionally I could hear words and sentences with the clarity of gunshots in a silent forest, but mostly I sat and watched his mouth move and the tears run down his face, and could not hear what he was saying.

I sat and nodded and nodded, tilting my head to hear, my hands folded in my lap, as the stray words dived out of the mist at me, pecking like scavenger birds: "Sorry . . . sorry. Never meant it to happen . . . never meant to hurt you . . . doesn't mean I didn't love you, don't love you . . . I'm an asshole, an utter jerk; don't think I don't know it. . . . Don't think I haven't gone over this a thousand times in my mind, how to tell you . . . rather die than hurt you, but can't live without her, Moll . . . the lying and the sneaking around has almost killed both of us; she feels as bad for you as I do. . . . Needs me, Molly. Needs me in a way you never did . . . never had much of a family, never any security, never any cherishing . . .

strong in a lot of ways but not in the ways you are . . . tell me what you want me to do now. Want me to move out? Want me to tell the kids? Want me to stay here with Teddy and let you go somewhere nice and think it out, Sea Island, maybe? Just tell me. . . . Not going to hurry you, not going to just leave you dangling; you'll always have what you need . . . tell me what you want me to do . . . "

Finally, after what seemed a very long time, the words stopped. The silence rang and the mist swirled. The room swam giddily. I said nothing, only sat looking at him, waiting for something else, I did not know what. But there must be something else. . . .

I blinked and the room came into focus. Tee got up and went and stood at the windows. Light was coming in now, pale, thin. That's when I said that about the name. About her being Sheri Redwine. After that, I could think of nothing else to say, so I waited some more.

Tee pulled up the slipper chair in the corner and sat facing me. I noticed that at some time he had put his clothes back on. When had he done that? All but his shoes and socks. He usually sat in the slipper chair to do that, but he did not move to do it now. He looked at me intently. I looked down at his bare feet, underwater white, and then at his face. He looked ghastly, burnt and then drowned.

"You must feel some way about this, Molly," he said finally, sounding fretful, querulous, his voice faint, like a child with fever. "There must be something you need to say. We can't not talk about it."

"It?"

"Molly . . . all of this I've been telling you. About . . . Sheri. The divorce. You've got to feel something about it. You've got to get it out . . . "

"Divorce? There's not going to be any divorce, Tee. I don't want a divorce, for heaven's sake; did you think I was going to punish you with that?"

He simply stared at me, then put his head into his hands. He laughed through his fingers, an exhausted, awful, little laugh.

"Molly, I may be a jerk and a cad and an asshole, but I am not a bigamist."

"You mean . . . you mean you want to *marry* her, Tee?"

He lifted his head and looked at me with dead, red-rimmed eyes.

"Jesus, what have I been saying to you for the past five hours?"

"Oh, Tee, why?" I whispered. There did not seem to be enough air in my lungs to speak aloud.

He closed his eyes. The endless tears began again, leaking from under his gold-tipped lashes. I had not seen Tee cry since his father's death six years before. Tears only for death, it seemed. But then, wasn't that what he was talking about? The death by murder of a marriage?

"She makes me alive again," he whispered.

"And I don't? We don't?"

"We . . . ?"

"Me. Caroline. Teddy. The family. You're talking about divorcing the *family*. How can you even think that, Tee? The family?"

"Molly . . . Caroline is gone. She has her own family now. And Teddy's going. He's going this fall. You know he isn't coming back, not to this house . . . "

"All right, then, me. What do I make you, dead? Tee, you know what we've had, what our life has been. You don't call that alive? All those years, Tee!"

He shook his head very slightly, as if the effort were almost too much. In the dim morning light he looked very young, as if he had just pulled an all-nighter at the fraternity house, studying with Charlie for finals. My heart swelled with love for him that was oddly maternal. Let him get it all out, this exhausted, fragmented boy that I loved, and then I could begin the business of soothing, sorting, mending.

"It's not the same thing," he said, his eyes still closed. "You know you and I don't have those kinds of feelings anymore. Not for a long, long time, not since . . . I don't know when. I'm not saying it's your fault, Moll. It's just . . . not like this. Not lightning, not light up the sky."

"Nobody has that forever," I said prissily, the schoolteacher I had been for a short time before Caroline was born. "That's for the beginning; you can't have it always."

"Yes," he said slowly, "I can."

"With this . . . Sheri, you mean," I said. "Does she put a little heart over the 'i', Tee?"

"Don't," he said. "Don't make fun of her name. She knows it's awful. It's her mother's idea of class, and she's too proud to change it. But she's come a very long way from that horrible family of hers. And she's done it all by herself. That's one reason . . . she's never really had a family. She doesn't even know what the word means."

"So now she wants mine."

"No," Tee said, smiling painfully. "Only me, I guess."

"Me, too," I said conversationally. "That's what I want, too. So I guess there's a little problem."

His face twisted and he stood up.

"I'll always take care of you," he said rapidly. "You'll never lack for money. You'll never have to go to work. The house will be yours for the rest of your life, if you want it. Or wherever you want to live. And school for Teddy. . . . You and Teddy will always be okay, Molly. I swear that to you. And anything Caroline wants or needs . . . "

"Tee, you don't make that kind of money," I said faintly. "Not for two . . . families. Or does she make an awful lot? Even then, it wouldn't be enough. . . . Don't you see how silly all this is?"

He looked at me for a long moment, then reached down for his shoes and put them on, standing balanced with his hand on the back of the slipper chair.

"I guess I should go on," he said, not looking at me anymore.

"Go on where?"

"Well . . . there. To her place. You can't want me to stay here."

"Your clothes . . . "

"I have some stuff there," he said, almost under his breath.

I knew that if he did, it was new. I knew all his clothes. There was nothing missing from his closet. Somehow this was dreadful beyond comprehension.

"It's that new condominium building in midtown, isn't it?" I said. "Charlie saw you moving her palm tree in. I thought he was mistaken. He thought she was Caroline. Does she look like Caroline?"

"She looks," Tee said, "a lot like you did when you were young, and don't think I don't know how that sounds. So just don't say it."

He picked up the briefcase he had put down beside the bureau the night before, a hundred years ago, but he did not move to go.

"So what about Caroline?" I said. "What about Teddy?"

"This weekend," he said. "We'll talk. I'll come over and the three of us will talk, and then we'll call Caroline. That will give you some time to digest everything, put it in perspective . . ."

I said nothing. Finally he moved to the bedroom door. He opened it and then looked back at me, over his shoulder.

"Molly. I'm sorry. I'm so sorry."

"Don't be," I said. "Nothing's changed. Nothing's going to. I'm not letting you leave the family."

He started to answer, but did not. The discarded plastic wrap clung for a moment to his feet, then he kicked it away angrily and went out the door.

The anguish came then.

I lay curled on our bed, knees drawn up to my chest, arms crossed over it, until the pale square of light on the scatter rug brightened into gold, and then the bled-out yellow of another hot day. I thought of nothing in particular, except that it was mortally important not to move, lest the agony get loose from the pit in which I had contained it, deep in my stomach, and flood over and out, and kill me. I remembered that I had lain that way twice before in my life, when severe menstrual cramps had racked me in my early teenage years, and again when I was pregnant with Caroline and Teddy. Both instances had been about containment. And then I thought, Well, of course, I lay this way before I was born. In my mother's womb. Huddled as if against cold. Even then, cold.

Sometime later in the morning I heard Teddy's TV go on and his heavy footsteps, thudding down the hall, followed by the click of Lazarus's toenails on the polished hall boards and the jingle of his tags. Before I could move, Teddy hammered on the bedroom door and called, "Ma! Ma, you up? Where's Dad? Didn't he come after all?"

I heard the knob begin to turn and found myself in our bathroom, running water loudly, before I realized I had moved. "I'm in the bathroom. Your dad's here, but he had to go back to the office until late tonight. He'll see us tomorrow for sure. He promised."

"Shit on youth brands," I heard Teddy grumble outside the door.

"Youth brands make your car payments," I said, wondering

where in my shredded depths I found the light, dry voice I habitually used with Teddy. He laughed.

"Well, then, if he's not going to be around till tomorrow, I'm going on to band practice after school, and then Eddie's. There's an Alabama concert at the Fox tonight. I thought I'd stay over at his place. That okay with you?"

"If Mrs. Cawthorne says it is."

"She does. See you in the morning sometime, huh?"

"Right."

There was a small silence and then he said, "Ma? You all right?"

"Fine," I sang out. "Just washing my hair. Listen, Teddy . . . are you taking Mindy tonight? Because if you are, you'll have to sleep at home. You know we said no all-nighters if there were girls along."

There. If that didn't sound like a normal Ansley Park mother, nothing did.

"Women, Ma. Not girls. Women. Nope. Mindy's history. Ol' Mindy's toast. Historical toast."

I felt a shocking wave of pure dislike for my son. The pain roiled and surged at its boundaries. Leaning over the washbasin, I clutched my stomach and stared blindly at the white-faced, wild-haired madwoman in the steamy mirror. Her blue eyes seemed to run like punctured egg yolks.

"It's so easy for you," I whispered to Teddy. "It's just so easy for all of you."

"Hasta la vista, baby," my unhearing son called, and thudded down the stairs and was gone.

Since I was already in the bathroom, I climbed into the shower and turned it on as hot as I could stand it, and sat down on the tile floor and turned my face up to it. The hot water was an absolute; while it pelted down on my blinded face I could not focus on anything else. I sat there until it began to go tepid, and then I climbed out and wrapped myself in Tee's white terry robe and slicked my hair back and went downstairs, leaving wet footprints on the thin, worn stair carpeting. It was stained with Teddy's teenaged years and scratched down to the matting with Lazarus's toenails; we had decided to replace it this fall, after Teddy went away to Georgia Tech. Lazarus, Tee said, was either going to have regular pedicures or get used to sleeping downstairs. Tee said . . .

The pain writhed and roared.

In the dim, silent kitchen I zapped a container of macaroni and cheese in the microwave and ate it, fed and watered Lazarus and let him out into the fenced-in backyard, got myself a diet Coke, and went into the library. Its cavelike gloom spoke to me of winter nights, with the fire snickering softly behind its screen and the television flickering. Only Teddy used it much in warm weather. I rolled the television set on its stand over to the end of the sofa, lay down full-length, covered myself with the plaid Ralph Lauren afghan Caroline and Alan had given us last Christmas, and clicked on the remote. On the screen a dark-haired, vulpine young woman coaxed hysterical tears from a black teenager and an older woman I thought might be the child's mother, and made a face of terrible, false sympathy as the tears escalated into screaming. The audience roared its approval. I turned the volume down as far as it would go, and for the rest of that day and into the evening I watched the screen as if the lives of the silent wraiths held captive within it were the only reality in the world. I found that I did not need their sound, only their movement.

At some point, in the middle of the afternoon, I think, the phone began to ring. I let the answering machine take the calls until the bell threatened to break the skin of my fugue state, then I got up and tottered on numb legs over to the phone and turned the bell off. I did not play the calls back; I knew who they would be. My mother, wanting to know if I was going to take her shopping in the morning. The ladies of the Salvation Army auxiliary committee meeting I myself had called, and had missed. Livvy, to see why I had not been at our weekly doubles match with two other Coke wives at the club. I shuffled back to the sofa and watched television some more, watched and watched. Finally, I remembered Lazarus and let him back in, fed him, and scrunched over on the sofa as he settled in beside me, sighing happily, and fell into his familiar, twitching sleep on top of the afghan. Sometime later than that, long after dark, I slept, too.

The overhead light went on deep in the timeless, thick night—hot, because I had been shaking with chills all day and had not turned on the air—and Lazarus groaned and lifted his head. I sat bolt upright, eyes blinded, heart pounding.

"Why the hell didn't you tell me?" Teddy's furious, trembling voice cried, and I scrubbed at my eyes and squinted, then saw him, standing over the sofa, his fists clenched, his face red with rage and recent crying.

"Tell you?" I said stupidly. I could not think what he meant. What time was it? Why was I down here in the library, stiff and smothering from the afghan and the weight of the dog?

"Tell me Dad had a little piece on the side," he shouted. "Tell me old Dad was playing hide the wienie with Coke's pet legal eagle . . . or would that be eagless? Goddamn, Ma, *why didn't you tell me? I'm not a fucking baby!"

"How do you know that?" I said thickly. "Who told you that?"

"You want to know who told me? *She* told me! Put her hand on my shoulder and stood there and told me like I was her goddamn little brother or something, smiling this shit-eating smile, saying she was sorry for my pain but after everything got straightened out she hoped I would one day be glad to have her in my life, like she was glad to have me in hers. Glad to have her in my life! Yeah, right, glad . . . Ma, she said you knew . . . "

"I don't understand what you're saying," I said. I did not.

"I saw them!" he shouted, beginning to cry again. "I saw them at the fucking concert! So did Eddie! So did everybody else I've ever known from school or anywhere else. And they saw me, and she gets up from her seat—they're in a box, of course, the Coke box— and comes down and puts her hand on me and says all that . . . *her*. Not Dad, her. Dad wouldn't even look at me. I had to go up there to the box . . . and even then, he wouldn't really look at me. He said he'd see us tomorrow and we'd talk it all out, and that he was sorry I found out this way; he'd really meant to tell me, but at least now we had it out in the open where we could deal with it. Deal with it! Deal with what? How long have you known about this? Why didn't you tell me?"

"Because it's not going to happen," I said, trying to push the words out on a wavering stream of breath. "This is just one of those things that happen to men your dad's age sometimes. It won't last, how could it? I didn't tell you because it's going to be okay. I didn't want you to worry. Nothing's going to happen to the family."

Teddy leaned close over me and closed his eyes and shouted,

"He's going to marry her! You call that being okay? You call that nothing happening to the family? He's going to fucking marry her!"

"Teddy, language! Did he say that?"

"No. She did. She said she thought I should know, so there weren't any false hopes and stuff. She said it needed to be out, clean and honorable. Honorable! Jesus Christ!"

"What did your dad say?" I could barely form the words with lips that had gone stiff and numb.

"Nothing," my son said. "He didn't say anything. He had his eyes closed. Mom . . . he looked *stupid*! They both did. You know what they had on? They had on bike shorts, black bike shorts that matched, and Coke T-shirts. Jesus, Mom, Dad doesn't even *have* a bike . . ."

I almost laughed around the numbness, in sheer relief. It *was* some kind of madness, then. Some kind of male climacteric thing. We could work this out, ride this out. Tee in bike shorts? The image was simply ludicrous, nothing more. Where was the danger in this?

"Sweetie, it doesn't mean anything. I promise you. You wait and see. It's certainly not a good thing, but it's not fatal, either. In six months or a year we'll have forgotten all about it—"

"*She has a ring!*"

"What are you talking about?"

"She has a ring! He gave it to her! It's this big, ugly old green thing; she wears it on her right hand, but she showed it to me and told me that it was his covenant with her, and he didn't say it wasn't. He didn't say anything more. He looked like he was going to hurl right there in the Coke box. I hope he did. All over his bike shorts. All over hers."

I could not get my mouth to move. I tried to say something into the wreckage of my son's face, but I simply could not speak.

"Goddamn you all," Teddy said in a low, terrible voice and turned and ran from the library. I heard his footsteps pound up the stairs and heard Lazarus jingling behind him, heard his door slam, heard the inevitable music start. But I heard no more from Teddy.

I rolled myself slowly and in sections off the sofa and on to the floor.

"I want my mother," I heard myself sob. And I cried and cried for the woman only ten blocks away, who could not hear me.

And then I got up and called my father, called him out of sleep, and said, "Daddy, something's happened and I need to come home."

"Come on home, baby," my father said. "I'll put some coffee on."

When two become one, as people said of a conventional Atlanta marriage of my time, everyone knows the drill and swings happily into action. There are firm rules and rituals for the treatment of the newly wedded pair, for their fêting and giftings, for their duties and responsibilities. There are even prescribed ways of thinking about the couple that go back God knows how far, especially in the South. All of this saves a great deal of time and bother.

But when one becomes two, the opposite is true and confusion reigns. More than confusion, I found. When Tee walked out, he left a kind of free-floating panic and an ensuing ostracism in his wake, only thinly veiled with sympathy. It was as if a sudden stench had settled over me, from which everyone was averting their nostrils while pretending it did not exist. Sometimes even I could smell it, lingering like body odor, and it made me feel slovenly and guilty, as if I should have bathed and so spared my friends, but had chosen not to. It was far worse because I felt in my very marrow that the same stench, if it touched Tee at all, lingered only momentarily. It was, I decided, the fatal fetor of vulnerability. No matter who was angry with him, Tee would not be perceived as vulnerable.

"It's fear, pure and simple," Livvy Bowen said, pouring a hefty slug of cognac into the coffee she had made. We were sitting in my kitchen on the third day after All That Stuff, as I thought of it, had happened. I had told no one but my parents and Caroline at the time, but in Atlanta the jungle drums are always out and poised, especially in what is fatuously called the Coca-Cola family, and I knew that almost everyone who mattered to me would know by then. Livvy, however, was the only one who had called, the only one who had come. She was ferociously angry at Tee, and smelled no stench on me. I knew she did not. I could have told if she had.

"Fear of what?" I said in my flat new voice that was as heavy as my body, my steps, my heart. Heavy and flaccid. I could not seem to shake off an endless, level white fatigue.

"Fear of it happening to them. Fear that if they get too close to you they'll catch some kind of virus and their husbands will walk out with some toots from the steno pool. Do they still have steno pools? Drink your coffee. You look like death."

"No, they have legal departments now," I said, sipping my coffee. The unstirred Hennessy puckered my mouth, but it did warm me a little, going down. In the middle of an unprecedented early heat wave, I could not seem to get warm.

"Listen, I want you to come over and stay with me for a while," Livvy said. "Caleb's going out again this weekend, and that way I'll be around if you want to start talking this out. I won't push you, I promise. But at least there'll be somebody around in your corner. You can spend the whole time sleeping if you want to. Just do it at my house, okay?"

"Oh, Livvy . . . Teddy's in my corner. Caroline is. My parents are . . ."

"Yeah, I can just hear your mother's tender words of sympathy and support now," she said and snorted. Livvy and my mother had disliked each other viscerally and instantly. "And I've already heard Teddy's. 'Goddamn you all'. . . It must have been a real Martha Stewart moment."

"He was devastated," I said defensively. "He's been a love ever since."

And so he had, my tall son, still white-faced and mute with misery and anger, but sticking to my side like a burr. Not literally . . . he did not dog me, or pressure me to talk. We did not talk much at all, in fact; had not, since he ran from the library the night of All That Stuff. But he was always in the house. School was out, and ordinarily Teddy would have vanished like a curl of smoke until September, but he did not go to the club to swim or play tennis, he did not go to band practice, and he spent little time on the telephone. The latter was the most alarming of all. Teddy's crowd, sprawling like puppies in the sun of approval and privilege since birth, checked in with one or another many times a day. The silent phone was ominous to me, and not only because Tee's call to say he was coming over to talk still had not happened. I hated the thought that my new contagion might spill out over Teddy. It seemed to me, drifting in my silent house, that nothing would or could happen until the telephone rang.

"Well, I'm sure he has, but you can hardly say what you think about Tee to him; it's the father-son thing," Livvy said. "You need to be with me. Whatever you want to say about the sonofabitch, I'll agree with you. Oh, shit, Molly, I'm just so *mad* at Tee Redwine! What a complete and utter asshole; I truly never thought it of him. And I'm just as mad at Caleb, and that whole little crowd of Coke princelings. They'll close ranks around him like the bunch of goats they are; see if they don't. Even while they're shaking their heads and doing the 'Aw, jeez' thing, they'll be covering his butt. I don't think anybody over there likes that bitch; did you know they call her the Eel Woman? Caleb says she's as slick and cold as a lamprey. But it ain't Tee who'll be cut out of the herd, oh no. Testosterone is thicker than blood or water."

I smiled at her passion, painfully but gratefully.

"You sound like you might have had a few words with Caleb about it."

"Only about five hours' worth," she said.

"Oh, Liv. I'm sorry . . . "

"Don't apologize! Don't you ever apologize for any of this," she said fiercely. "Don't you *dare* buy into that crap, that 'Somehow it must have been my fault, how did I fail him' shit. This is *Tee's* fault. This is Tee's shit. As it is, you'll end up paying the freight on it . . . "

"How? Why? Why should I pay for . . . whatever it is?"

"Oh, Molly," she said in exasperation. "You know as well as I do what happens in our crowd when a guy leaves his wife for a new toy. Haven't you seen it? For a little while it's all, 'Oh, poor thing, we must rally around her, what are friends for,' and then, after a while, after everybody gets used to him being part of a new couple, they'll begin to ask them back for dinner and little parties. You know, 'Well, of course she's awful, but after all, it's Tee!' And then it's like they don't remember who you are. Two or three times a year they'll maybe have you for the big Christmas open house—different hours from them, of course—maybe take you to the club with another of their divorced girlfriends . . . but for the big stuff, the fabric of their little lives, you're out of the loop. And she's in. They may never like her, and they'll probably despise the Eel Woman, but she'll be part of them because Tee is. This is his crowd, just like it's Caleb's now. This is guy stuff. This is the South. This is the Coke family. You think Coke is going to give a happy rat's ass about you? They're not even going to remember your name."

"They ought to fire her . . . "

"Fire her! Oh, right! What they did was promote her. Took her off Tee's team, of course; can't seem to outright condone the stuff, you know, but they transferred her to community outreach and gave her a raise. And as for Tee, I hear he's in line for Paris or London in a year or two, if he wants it. Real hardship duty."

Paris or London . . . we had talked about it. How many times? It had been something Tee was working toward, but we thought it would be much farther along, perhaps the last significant thing he did for Coke. I had loved the thought of the two of us in the blue hour, sitting on some gargoyled city terrace while the lights of Paris came on at our feet, or gardening in the long green twilight at a country house somewhere a few miles and hundreds of years out of London. Maybe, I thought, an insane giggle beginning to bubble up in my chest, they could bike in together every day in their matching latex shorts.

I snorted and Livvy looked at me.

"You don't think it's going to happen, do you?" she said slowly.

"Well, of course not," I said. "All that's if there should be a divorce, and there's not going to be any divorce. How can there be? He's . . . Livvy, we . . . Teddy and Caroline and I . . . we're what he *has*. We're what all those years have added up to for him. He can play around with having something else for a while; I mean, I hate it, of course, but in the end it's not going to matter because we're what he *has*. His whole life has been spent making what we add up to. And he's what *we* have. What would we have if . . . well, he's what we have, that's all. He's the sum of all those years and all that talk and all that laughter and all the trouble and the hard times and the . . . the . . . ordinary times, the thousands of times we brushed our teeth and . . . and rented a video, and talked on the phone to each other. All the things we've done together and planned and thought and worked for and seen happen, all the clothes that hang in our closets and the furniture we've always had . . . everything that we remember . . . who would all that belong to if we . . . didn't stay together? There's just not going to be any divorce. Let him wear bike shorts and screw her in a midtown condo; it doesn't touch who he is or who we are together. He knows that as well as I do."

"Oh, honey," she said softly.

"Why, does Caleb think Tee's . . . going to be with her now?"

"Moll . . . Tee told him that he was. He told him that back in March or April. He just didn't get around to telling you."

"Because he knows it's not going to happen," I said, and got up. "I do think Caleb might have told you, though. It would have saved all of us a lot of pain."

"No it wouldn't, love. It just would have gotten it over sooner. But you're right, he should have told me. That's one reason I'm so goddamn mad at him. Okay, enough about it. You're not ready to deal with it yet, and that's okay. It's probably too early. But I still wish you'd come stay with me next week. Teddy's old enough to be on his own; you don't want to hang on to him. Who knows, you might even have fun with me. You know what we could do? We could do four or five days at a spa, Canyon Ranch, maybe, get a complete overhaul, do some serious shopping . . . "

"And get our hair bleached, and maybe even a little liposuction, a little nip and tuck? God, Livvy, I never thought I'd hear it from you. The classic woman-scorned, feel-good routine. Such a cliché."

"Maybe that's because it works," Livvy said matter-of-factly. "Well, then, we'll watch old movies and eat pizza for six days, or get drunk, or whatever you want to do. Will you come?"

"Not right now. But I love you for thinking of it, and I may take you up on it later. Right now there's stuff that has to be settled, and it can't get done until I talk to Tee."

"Call him, then."

"It's his call to make. He'll have to do it sooner or later. He can't just pretend nothing's happened; he owes Teddy more than that, and Caroline. But it's his call."

"It's your call, of course, but I'm out of here for now," she said, getting up and hugging me. For a moment I stood loosely in her arms, feeling the strength and warmth of them, luxuriating in the simple human touch that meant love, and then I drew back and slapped her on the fanny and she turned to go. Then she looked back.

"How's your butt, by the way?" she said.

"Why . . . fine. Smooth as a baby's. Not a tingle for days," I said, realizing only then that it was true.

"Butt knows best," she said solemnly, and was out the door and gone.

CHAPTER THREE

TEE DID NOT, AFTER ALL, COME AND TALK to Teddy and me.

He faxed us.

That one thing infuriated my father more than any of the sorry flotsam and jetsam cast up by the separation. Most of the proceedings he watched with a sort of grim, detached sorrow, but when he heard about the fax he exploded.

"What kind of sorry jackass faxes his family that he doesn't want to live with them anymore?" he shouted, throwing the *Atlanta Constitution* down on the floor of the screened-in porch.

"He may be a jackass, but he's our jackass," I said, hoping to divert him with humor. It usually worked, but not this time.

"No, he's not," my father said in a low, cold voice. "That's just what he's saying, only he's not man enough to say it to your faces. Well, by God, he'll say it to mine, or I'll know the reason why."

And he got up and strode toward the hall where the downstairs telephone sat. Cellular phones were not a part of my father's ethos.

"No, wait," I called. "In all fairness, Teddy told him to fax. He wouldn't talk to Tee on the phone and he wouldn't see him."

"So what! Tee should have insisted; he should have just gone over there. This is his wife and son we're talking about. What's he going to do, E-mail Caroline?"

I said nothing. In the clear light of my father's rage, it did sound shabby and feckless. I don't know why I had not thought so earlier.

Tee had called on Sunday afternoon, late, and said that he'd like to come by and talk to both of us. I said, "Fine," as calmly and neutrally as I could, but my heart began the familiar galloping. If Tee didn't come to his senses soon, I thought, I'd simply go into cardiac arrest.

"So, okay, we'll be by in about an hour," Tee said, and I heard Teddy's voice on the upstairs extension. I had not realized he had picked up.

"What's this 'we' shit?" Teddy said coldly.

"I'm coming, too," a woman said. Her. It was her. I had imagined a silky, tongue-flickering purr, but the voice of my enemy was oddly flat and without resonance, with the nasal twang of the wire grass under it. It was, somehow, disarming.

Neither Teddy nor I said anything, and the voice went on: "It may be harder for all of us now, but it's not fair to let Tee carry this alone. I'm part of it, too. We need to know each other, you-all and I. We can build something honorable and lasting if we start out that way."

She sat beside my husband, perhaps touching him, and spoke of honor. I could not draw a breath deep enough to get a word out.

"Eat a shit sandwich," Teddy said. "If either of you's got anything to say to us, fax it."

"Teddy . . ." Tee began.

"You heard the kid," I said, and hung up. Teddy did, too. There was stillness, a silence from upstairs.

"You want to talk?" I yelled up into it.

"No," he called back.

We did not speak of the call again. I retreated into my white fugue. The fax came that evening.

It was a long one, addressed to both of us and signed by both of them. Teddy read it and crumpled it up and threw it into his wastebasket.

"I need to see it, too," I protested.

"No, you don't," he said, his back to me. "It's two pages of New Age shit that ends up saying, essentially, that he's leaving us and marrying her, and trying to make it sound like it's some kind of

43

cosmic wonderfulness that's going to lift us all straight to heaven. He says he still loves us and will forever, and then she chimes in and says we can still be a family, a new kind of family. He says he'll wait to hear from either or both of us. He can wait for me till hell freezes over. You do what you want. I hate him. I hate that fucking bitch."

He began to cry, the coarse, ragged sobs of a young man no longer a boy, and ran into the library and slammed the door.

I stood outside it, my heart wrung with pain. I could not bear the sound of his grief. But I knew that this time I could do nothing to assuage it. Only Tee could do that. Finally I went up to our bedroom—my bedroom now—and sat down to call Tee back. Then I realized I did not know his new number. And I knew that if I could help it, I never would.

I did not reply to the fax, either.

Caroline called late that night from Memphis. He had just talked to her, he and Sheri, and she was furious, wounded nearly mortally, inconsolable.

"How could he do this to me? How could you let him? My God, she's only a few years older than I am; what is he *thinking* of? Aren't you going to do something? Can't you fight a tacky little trailer park slut? If he thinks he's ever going to see his granddaughter again, he's out of his mind. Not while he's with her. My baby's not going within a hundred miles of that piece of trash. My God, she sounds like a washerwoman . . . "

Caroline was her daddy's girl, just as Teddy had always been my boy, my miniature Tee. It had always seemed natural, comfortable, an almost Wally and June Cleaver arrangement. Only then did I see what it might mean, how the crippling old patterns had repeated themselves. I stared at the phone in my hand in horror. Had I really done that to my children, perpetuated upon them the same vicious dance that I had been caught up in? If so, what else had I done, what other damage had I wrought, or let be wrought, without realizing?

"Can't you fight her? . . . "

Caroline's words stung my ears long after I had soothed her sobs with promises of a visit and hung up. Fight her? Fight who? How? I did not know how to fight anyone, certainly not this mythic creature, this arcane Sheri, without scruples or vulnerability, as intent as a young shark on the one thing she wanted: my husband. I had never known how to fight, only propitiate, only accommodate, only enable. It had always seemed enough. Poor Caroline. If anyone was going to march out and get her daddy back for her, it was not likely to be her mama.

Much later that year my father said to me, "I never could understand why you didn't get angry. If it had been me, or your mother, we'd have blown the bastard sky high. I thought for a while that you were protecting the kids, and maybe even us, but it seemed to me it went further than that. I admired you for it, but I wondered."

Anger? Dear God, of course there was anger. In those first awful days, when simply getting through one until it ended and became another was all I could seem to accomplish, I felt enough anger at Tee and Sheri Scroggins to blow the world apart. Oh, not always, by any means; there were long periods of pure, sheer pain that humbled and silenced me like a flailed ox, and there were intervals of crazy gaiety, of idiotic confidence that he would come back to us. These came mainly in the mornings when I woke, having forgotten for a few hours that catastrophe had struck, and when I first remembered it seemed simply so silly, so unimaginable, that I could only stretch and smile and think, "What have I been so worried about? Tee hasn't left us. How stupid."

And sometimes I just drifted in the soft cocoon of seductive listlessness that lay always just outside my consciousness, like a fog bank waiting to roll in. It became increasingly simple to let it.

But under it all lay the anger, red and bottomless, waiting to immolate the only world I had known. It licked at me mainly when the fact of Tee's betrayal collided with someone I loved— Teddy, Caroline, my parents. Then, I clenched and knotted everything inside me so that I could tamp it down, beat it back, chill its heat. Then is when I let the white fog come. Because I was afraid, I was terrified: I could not blow up the only world I had, the world of The Family. What would I do without it, who would I be, how would I live, who or what would provide the context for The Family?

"I guess I was afraid," I said that cold night to my father, and knew of course that I had been mortally, endlessly afraid. Naked and alone in space, no world around me? Anything was better, anything more bearable.

So in the best traditions of my grandmother Bell, I buried all of it deep. For me, that meant avoiding everyone but Teddy. I could not even see my parents after that first nighttime visit, could not run again to my father as I had then. Not yet. I gave Lilly the week off and canceled all my meetings and unplugged the phone. I stayed home and cleaned and polished silver and did endless laundry; I baked and mended and scrubbed patio furniture and cooked from-scratch meals for Teddy and me that neither of us ate. On one level it was infinitely comforting to get in touch with my house and my things again, handling them as I had not since the first days of our marriage, before we had help. I remembered how I had felt then, so full of joy that my blood prickled. Look at me, I did not think but might have, moving efficiently among the furniture of my life, what a good wife and mother I am. What a good woman. My price is above rubies. What could happen to me?

On another level, this caressing of my lares and penates put off the day when people came battering back into my life and it tumbled on again. I knew that. I figured I had about three days, four at the most, before the calls and visits began. At the end of the third day, I turned the phone back on.

The calls came, from my mother first: "Will you *please* call us? We're worried sick about you. If you don't call us today, we're coming over whether you want us or not. Do you need a doctor? Is Teddy all right? Have you talked to . . . you know, Tee, yet?"

From my father: "I trust you to let us know when you want to talk, baby. But don't shut us out much longer. There's nothing so bad we can't find an answer to it. Love you."

From Sally and Kevin in Washington, in tandem: "What's going on down there? Has Tee lost his mind? Do you need anything? Want to come up for a while? Want us to come down there and kill him? Call, Molly. We're worried."

From Caroline's husband, Alan: "When do you think you could come see us? We want to know you're okay, and I'm worried about Caroline. I've never seen her like this. You'd think her dad had died. She can hardly take care of Melissa. It would help if her father would call or come by himself; if you talk to him, will you tell him she's drowning? Or give me his number; I'll tell him myself. What a godawful thing to do . . . "

From my committees and boards and panels: "Don't worry about a thing. We're coping splendidly. Why don't you just take the summer for yourself and let us do some of the work now? Only, if you think you might want to take longer, do let us know; we'll need to make some plans for the fall."

Translation: "If you're going to be divorced by fall, maybe you'd better think about passing the torch. We love you, but you're not going to be who you were, and we need all the strength and bucks behind us we can get."

The luster and largesse of Coca-Cola rarely stands behind ex-wives. A new divorcée would be a millstone indeed.

From Livvy: "Okay. I know. Burrow in. You have two and a half more days and then I'm coming over and get you."

From Sheri Scroggins every day, on the answering machine, since I hung up whenever I heard her voice: "This is not helping anything, you know, Molly. We feel for you, but it's only making things worse, you hiding like that. We really need to talk. Tee is in terrible shape."

From Tee, once, also on the answering machine for the same reason: "Molly, please call. Please answer. This can't go on. It's not fair to any of us. Sooner or later we have to sort things out. I'll come by myself. Or meet you someplace . . . "

From Ken Rawlings, our longtime lawyer and longer-time friend: "Molly, please understand I'm not calling in any official capacity. I'm sorry as hell about this whole thing. But it would be in your best interests to talk to Tee, and the sooner the better. You can afford to be generous, babe, you're holding all the cards. I love you both, and wish to hell this hadn't happened, but since it has, be the gal I know you are and call Tee. Or me. We're going to take care of you."

"Are you going to?" Livvy said on the morning of the fourth day. True to her word, she had been on my doorstep at nine. I knew she would be.

"What, call Ken? Hell, no. Or Tee, or the Eel Woman, either. I know what they want, but it's going to be harder than that for him to . . . you know."

"Get a divorce. Say it. D-I-V-O-R-C-E. Well, if you're not going to call Ken, you better call somebody. A lawyer, I mean. If you don't know any divorce guys, I can recommend somebody who can eat Ken Rawlings for breakfast. And he doesn't have a thing in the world to do with Coke."

"Why? I'm not giving Tee a divorce. Not for that little nothing. Not for some little . . . piece of ass. He can beg until doomsday, they both can. There's not going to be any divorce, and I'm not talking to anybody."

She took a deep breath and blew it out again.

"Why would you want to hang on to somebody who's done this to you? How could a divorce be worse than this?" she said. "What are you afraid of? You're the smartest woman I know; there's nothing you can't do. You're going to have all the money you need, and the house; anything you want, if you're at all smart about it. That's where the good lawyer comes in. Tee doesn't have a leg to stand on. You must know that."

"But what if it's just a fling, what if he gets tired of her, or her of him? It's bound to happen, Liv; I can't think what on earth they could have in common but bike shorts . . . "

"It's not a fling. I've heard the talk from other people besides Caleb, Coke people. People who know them both. Tee may well indeed get sick of her, or her him, but the fool is bound and determined to marry her first. And even if they split up . . . Molly, could you live with him again after this? Could you really do that?"

I looked at her. I knew that I was never going to make her understand. And if not Livvy, certainly no one else. But, yes, I could live with Tee again after this. Because otherwise I wasn't anyone and it was too late to begin searching for another self, and what if I never did find one? You can't go through the world a spectre, so mutilated that more than half of you is gone, so lacking in substance that people can look right through you.

"You still love him that much?" she said softly.

"I have no idea if I love him at all," I said. "But there's not going to be any divorce."

She sighed, but said no more about it. We went to lunch at R. Thomas and talked to the cheerful, molting birds and drank wine and ate veggie pizzas. I felt almost normal, just a little fey and quivery, as if I were recuperating from a debilitating illness. Everything was eerily bright, and strange. But other than that, it was okay. I thought I could probably do the visits now.

As if on cue, they began that evening.

Mother and Dad rang my doorbell at six o'clock. I peered through the peephole, prepared to pretend I was not at home until whoever it was left, and saw one of my mother's flamboyant hats with my father's face looming over it, behind her. I could not see Mother's face, but Dad's was still and blank, as if he was having a passport photograph taken. My father was an essentially private and rather formal man who did not believe in dropping in on people, not even an abandoned and possibly suicidal daughter, and I felt a smile twitch at my lips. I opened the door.

Mother swooped in, carrying an armload of flowers wrapped in florists' waxed green paper. She laid the flowers on my console table and hugged me fiercely, standing on tiptoe and knocking her hat askew in the process.

"The mountains have come to Mohammed and are taking her out to dinner no matter what she says," she said into my shoulder blade. "How are you, darling? We just can't let you hide out in here any longer."

Over the waggling hat I looked at Dad. He winked, and managed a grin, more a spasm, really. I could see the worry about me in his eyes, and in the deeper lines around his mouth.

"Hi, baby," he said, and at the sound of his voice something swelled and warmed behind my eyes, and I felt tears sting in them.

"Oh, now," Dad said, trying to find a place to hug me that wasn't engaged by my mother.

I backed out of her embrace and gave a great, rattling sniff and managed to smile at them both.

"Here come the marines," I said, and we all laughed more loudly than the words deserved.

"Oh, darling, you look like death warmed over," my mother said in her throaty tremolo. "When have you washed your hair? Or had anything to eat? You run right up and shampoo and shower and put on something pretty, and we'll have a decent dinner and some wine. Dad says he'll take us to the Ritz. We'll just sit out on the patio and wait for you."

"Mother, I—"

"Let me take my girls to dinner," Dad said. "It's been a long time since I had you both to myself."

There was such a look of helpless anguish in his eyes that I gulped the stupid tears back again and said, "I'd love that," even though I could think of nothing that I wanted less to do. I knew that it would make him feel better. Forward motion was my father's antidote for all crises; stasis was the ultimate anathema to him. And who knew? It might make me feel better, too. At least the Ritz-Carlton's dim, opulent dining room was apt to be safe. It was more a corporate haven than an Atlanta couples' watering hole. The only Coke faces I was apt to see were those of clients, and they were not likely to remember me.

I installed them with drinks on the little walled patio—shabby after several days' neglect—and went upstairs to bathe and change. I shampooed and blow-dried my tangle of hair and dragged a comb through it. My mother was right. It was weeks late for a trimming. Medusa hair. My eyes in the bathroom mirror looked huge and blanched of color, as if I had bobbed for a long time beneath the surface of water. Drowned eyes. The start of a tan I had gotten a few weeks back, swimming at the club in a spell of hot spring weather, had faded. I looked pale and sodden, as if I had just been pulled from water.

I plodded into the bedroom and put on a red silk shift and high-heeled sandals, added a slash of red lipstick that made me look as if I had been eating bloody flesh, and put on and then discarded the pearl choker and earrings Tee had given me for our twentieth anniversary. I did not, somehow, want jewelry, especially not this. It seemed almost obscene. When I went back downstairs my mother pursed her lips and stared at me for a long time, and said, "Well, it's a start. A haircut and some color and a little nip through Jenny Craig will make you feel a lot better, and then your old mother is going to take you shopping. You've only let yourself go a little; there's not a thing that can't be fixed. What we need now is an agenda."

"Belle . . ." my father began.

"It's a little late to start on the outside of me," I said to my mother. "What have you got for the inside?"

"It's never too late," she said briskly. "This is not the time to be negative. And don't knock the power of appearance. I've dealt with imagery all my life. It's the most powerful force on earth sometimes. If you put your mind to it you can have that silly man back home before—"

"Mother," I said, "I'm really looking forward to having dinner with you. You're right, I've been stuck in the house too long. But I'm not going to talk about any bright little campaigns to make me over and win back my wandering husband. If you can't drop it, I'm not going."

She gave me one of her patented oblique looks from under the brim of the hat, and then dropped her feathery lashes.

"You're the boss, darling," she said, and on that note the Bell family went out to dinner.

I walked behind her up the stairs and into the dining room at the Ritz. She wore a sleeveless black linen sheath of the sort Audrey Hepburn and Givenchy had made popular in the early sixties. She had probably bought it then; she could still wear the clothes she had had as a young woman. Her arms were bare, very white in the dusky light, and even at a distance you could see the ridges of sinew and little wattled laps of flesh that hung from underneath them. But there was not an ounce of fat on them, nor on her legs, which were knotted with muscle below the knee-length skirt, and flexed sleekly as she glided through the room on her high black heels. The black straw hat sat atop her small head like a flower, but beneath it her neck was corded, and ropy, too. When had she gotten so thin? She was past leanness now, past the dancer's taut slimness I was used to, thin to chicken bone and sinew, an old woman's eggshell thinness. But she still held her head high and her spine erect, and walked like a woman who knew that every eye in the restaurant was fixed on her. And they were.

I felt the eyes slide off her and on to me, and thought how we must seem to the well-dressed, expense-accounted people at the tables around us: an exotic, somehow ossified Kabuki doll in an outrageous hat and her unwieldy offspring paddling along behind her like a gigantic duckling. Somehow I never doubted that everyone would know instantly that we were mother and daughter. Even strangers always knew that somehow. Something in my mother's pave-the-way stride, and my follow-along one, announced it. I was not unaware of that; sometimes I tried to outstride her and lead the way. My long legs should have bested hers every time. But her dancer's muscles and uncontainable presence always won. Mother led. The rest of us followed.

When we were seated, there was a solicitous business with menus and water glasses and the precise adjustment of chairs—something else that always ensued when my mother sat down to table, as she liked to say—and when she had rewarded the service with her brilliant smile and the waiters had gone away, she said, "Now. Before we have our drinks I just want to say one thing, and then we won't talk about it anymore."

I opened my mouth but she held up her fernlike claw of a hand and said, "No, let your mother have her say. I have a bit of a stake in this, too, you know."

And I was silent, because, of course, she did. She was as much a part of the corpus of The Family as any of us. I sat and waited.

"I just want to say that of course you aren't going to give that weak-witted husband of yours a divorce. We know that. We back you up a hundred percent on that, and I imagine Charlotte Redwine does, too. It's unthinkable, having some South Georgia nobody in that old family; Charlotte isn't going to permit it. The trouble is that she's permitted Tee too much over the years; nobody ever said no to him. He doesn't know the meaning of the words 'responsibility' and 'hard choices.' He's always gotten just what he wanted, even before he knew he wanted it, because he's charming and smart and a Redwine. But he's not the one who controls the Redwine purse strings and he must know it. You just hang on. You've invested too many years in that boy, and you stand to lose too much if you let that little tramp have him without a fight. I meant what I said about the hair and the spa and all that, and that's just the beginning. When we all put our minds to it, you'd be amazed at what we can—"

"Your two minutes are up," I said, around a cold knot that felt perilously like the tiresome tears. "I hear you, but I'm not going to answer you now. I want a shot of single malt and then maybe another one, and then I want to order. And I'm going to have the most fattening thing on the menu, so you may as well save your breath."

I smiled to take the sting out of it, and she looked at me with an avian sharpness, but said no more. My mother's timing is perfect. It was my father who spoke next.

"Okay, here's your old man's two cents, and then the booze will flow and that will be the end of it. Molly, you don't have to stay married to that sorry boy if you don't want to. Maybe it would be better if you don't. Your mother's wrong when she says we all think you ought to hang on to him. I, for one, don't much think you should, though if you really want to, of course I'm behind you one hundred percent. But to my mind it's Tee Redwine who stands to lose, not you. And your dear mother, of course. She's gotten right addicted to the Driving Club over the years."

"Why, Tim Bell," my mother said tremulously, allowing her great eyes to widen. He smiled at her and covered her frail hand with his.

"I can still offer the Elks," he said, and she laughed reluctantly. I sat still and looked from one to the other. I had never known him to disagree with her before on matters pertaining to The Family.

"What does Teddy think of all this?" Mother said after a moment. "I'm sorry he didn't want to come with us."

"He's badly hurt, and he's furious, and he's way, way too protective of me," I said, only then really seeing that he had been, ever since he'd found out about his father's affair.

"He bolted out of the house to go over to Eddie's the instant you got there. He hasn't seen any of his friends for days. He's been hanging around the house with me. Oh, he stays in his room most of the time, or in the library, but he always knows where I am. I've got to insist that he get out more. He can't turn into a caretaker for me. He's got a life to live; he's got college to get ready for. And you know he and Eddie and Kip Hall were planning to drive Kip's car west on Route 66 and back again in August, before they start at Tech. Now he's talking about not wanting to go. I can't have that."

"No," Dad said thoughtfully. "He's got to go on with his life. I'll have a talk with him. After all, he really isn't losing his father, though I guess it must seem to him like he is right now."

"Not losing his father . . ." I said indignantly. "Of course he is . . ."

And then I fell silent. Of course he was not. Only I was losing.

From the perfect skin of The Family, only I was being ejected. How could that be?

When I got home Teddy was in his room with the stereo booming. It was early, and I went up and knocked. It was a long time before he said, "Ma?"

"Yes."

"Come on in."

I went in. The room was in semidarkness; I could barely make out the lump under the sheet on Teddy's bed that would be Lazarus, who burrowed there habitually, as if returning to a cave. The lump stirred and a scruffy tail appeared, wagging, but Teddy lay still, on his back, staring at the ceiling.

"What's the matter? Did you-all decide not to go out after all?" I said.

"No, we went to the Hard Rock Cafe."

"It's awfully early . . . "

"I just didn't feel like hanging around there."

"What's the matter, Teddy? I know something is. Is it Dad?"

"They were laughing about it," he said in a tight, too young voice. "Oh, not at me, but about him and her. Chip Frederick and Tommy Milliken were there; both their dads are with Coke. They've both met her at some Christmas thing. Say she's hot stuff, a real babe. Said she was coming out of her dress at that party, and all the men were panting down it. Said they'd been taking bets on who finally got in her pants, but nobody ever thought it would be Dad. Eddie told Tommy he was going to knock the shit out of him if he opened his mouth one more time, and they left, but they were still laughing. I hate them. Him, too. I hope they all die."

His voice was matter-of-fact and too dry, as if the juice of life was gone from him. I would have preferred tears. Pain and anger tore through me. For that instant I wished Tee would die, too. Just die, before he could inflict any more pain on us.

"Your real friends aren't going to laugh," I said, walking over to put my hand on his head. But he flinched away from my touch, and I stood still.

"I know it," he said. "It's just that maybe I don't have as many of those as I thought."

"It will get better," I said thickly. "It really will. It's just that it's all new. People always talk about things when they're brand new. Give it all some time. I know how hard it must be—"

"I know you're hurting too, Ma, and I'm sorry, but I don't think you can possibly know how hard it is. You're not . . . you're not *kin* to him. I've got his . . . blood and his bones and his genes and stuff in me. How can he just walk away from that?"

"He isn't walking away from you, not really," I said, but he made a sharp little sound of dismissal.

"Bullshit. Listen, Ma, I just can't talk about it anymore now. I just can't. I need to get some sleep. You go on to bed and get some, too."

"Okay," I said softly, obscurely hurt, and turned to go.

"Ma?" he said after me.

"Yeah?"

"I love you."

"Me too you, Speedo," I said thickly, using for the first time in years the old nickname he had grown to hate. And I went to bed and, predictably, cried for a long time.

The next visit was from Carrie and Charlie Davies. They came by the following night about nine, in summer-dinner-at-the-club clothes: flowered sundress, blue blazer with khakis. Neither was smiling. Charlie sat in the oversized wing chair in the living room, where he always sat, his big hands dangling between his knees, looking around the room he knew as well as his own as if he had never seen it. Carrie sat next to me on the sofa and cried. She had started to speak when they first came in, and then had shaken her head and burst into tears, and I had sat beside her hugging her ever since. She could not seem to stop.

"Molly, I want you to know that I didn't know . . . that day," Charlie said heavily. "When you were at the office. I wouldn't have said anything for the world; I really didn't know . . . shit, I can't believe Tee was . . . and I didn't know it. I'd have blistered that old boy if I'd known . . . "

He fell silent. I noticed that he did not call me Moonbeam. I doubted somehow that he ever would again.

"I know," I said. "I know you didn't. Apparently not many people did, except Coke people. Tee was . . . they were . . . very dis-

creet. Don't feel bad about it, Charlie. Nothing's settled yet. I think
we can still work it out . . . "

Carrie's sobs escalated.

"I just can't believe it," she wailed. "I just can't . . . it's like it
was happening to Charlie and me. It's like a death, almost. Everybody says the same thing, nobody can believe he would . . . Everybody's just heartbroken, Molly. We all just . . . cry when we meet.
Oh, nothing is ever going to be the same again . . . "

I wondered if she had not heard what I'd said about working it
out. And I remembered what Livvy Bowen had said, about couples
feeling fearful and threatened when friends broke up, as if it were
catching.

I hugged her harder and said into her hair, "You'll see. By Sea
Island time, it'll all be behind us. Please stop crying, Carrie. You're
going to look like a Cabbage Patch doll."

But the sobs strengthened, and I looked over at Charlie for
help and read it in his miserable face.

"He's taking her to Sea Island, isn't he?" I whispered through
stiff lips. Five of us couples who had been close at school had, for
nearly twenty years, gone each summer to the Redwines' beach
house at Sea Island for a four-day weekend. Tee and I, as hosts, had,
of course, never missed it. I had only now thought of it.

"Molly," he mumbled, "there wasn't anything we could say to
him. He called day before yesterday and said it was still on, and
he'd rented the Drapers' house—I don't think his mama will let him
use hers anymore—and he expected us all just the same as usual.
Said if we still felt anything for him we'd come; he's having a bad
time, too, you know. Nobody knows quite what to do; none of us
want to go when she's there; it'll be just shitawful, but . . . well, this
is Tee. He's my oldest friend, Molly. I can't just walk away from
him. Of course, you know you'll always be our first love . . . "

I looked from his face down to Carrie's bent head.

"Carrie?" I said. "Are you really going?"

"Molly . . . I love Tee, too!" she wailed, and buried her head
back into my shoulder.

I was still numb when they left, seeming to bolt from the house
in sheer relief. I had wanted the comfort of my old friends' company, but now, I thought, I did not. What could I say to them? I

could not again hold a sobbing friend so wrapped in her sorrow that mine could not penetrate. I could not again watch the new truths written in the averted faces of Tee's boyhood friends. I knew that I would not call any of them. I also thought that Charlie and Carrie's visit was sort of an official one, that they had served as emissaries for Tee's and my old crowd, and that I would not be hearing from many of them, either. At least until after the September house party. The thought of her, moving dark and eel-like on our wide, taupe beach, dancing with Tee to our old records, helping to boil the crabs at the traditional last-night beach bonfire—or could she even cook?—going into a cool, dark bedroom with Tee and closing the door at the end of the evening, laughing, a little drunk . . . I could not bear those images, and so I shut them away and went to bed early. This time I did not cry.

Ken Rawlings came next. He came two days later, at noon, on his way to a business meeting downtown. I was working in the patio garden and Lilly, thunderous and silent since she had come back to work and found her family in shards, directed him through the house and back to where I was attacking witch grass in the flower borders.

He was immaculate in summer-weight Coca-Cola navy blue; I was sweaty and dirt-smeared in torn shorts and the old Black Dog T-shirt. He sat gingerly on a wrought-iron lawn chair and I went on jerking weeds.

"I'm here to try again, baby," he said gravely. "I'm really worried about you. The company is, too. This . . . stonewalling is hurting everybody. I want to see you get the best possible deal out of this sorry mess, and so does Coke. You'd be surprised how many good friends you've got there. So I thought I'd see if you'd feel like talking some now. Believe me, it'll go better for you if you can manage it soon."

"Did the company send you, Ken?" I said, staring down into the tangle of dreadful, pale tendrils that were strangling my delphiniums. I could almost feel the airless gasping of throttled roots beneath the earth.

"No," he said. "They didn't. I came as the friend I am. But it's no secret that the company is worried about Tee as well as you. He's not in real good shape, won't be until things are settled between you."

"And . . . this Sheri person? Are they worried about her, too? Is she in bad shape? It would be a shame if two of your star players are out of the game," I said.

"They're worried about her, sure," he said neutrally. "She's a good lawyer, Molly, no matter what else you say about her."

I was silent, and then I said, my ears ringing with the words, "Ken, if I . . . if I should ever consent to a divorce or something . . . not to say that I will, but if I did . . . would you be my lawyer? I don't know any other lawyers, not as well as I do you . . . "

He was silent, too. Then he said, "I'll be handling things for Tee, Molly. I thought you realized that. I couldn't represent you, too, though I'd like to. But I can give you a very good referral—"

"So this is official, then, huh?" I said. I was beginning to get quite angry.

"I guess it is, yes," he said unwillingly. "But I'm here because I love you, too. Believe me when I say that you need to get on with this, for your sake even more than for Tee's."

I stood up, dusting my hands on the rump of my shorts. My knees cracked audibly.

"I appreciate your concern, Ken," I said. "But I don't want any more solicitous little visits on my behalf, and I don't want a referral. Divorce is not an option."

He got up and turned to go, then looked back at me. His face was grave with what looked to be real worry, though with Ken you never knew.

"You don't want to underestimate this woman, Molly," he said. "You really don't. I know I wouldn't."

"Well, I guess that's Tee's problem now, isn't it?" I said, and he nodded and said good-bye and left. I shoved the anger deep down where all the rest of it simmered, and fell to battling witch grass again. By late that afternoon I had gotten it all.

The next week, on a Wednesday, Charlotte Redwine invited me to lunch at the Driving Club. She had, she said, just gotten back from Italy the night before, and she thought the first thing we should do was sit down over a good lunch and talk this mess out. I did not want to go; Charlotte and I have never had much to say to each other, but I'd have to talk to her sometime. Better to go on and get it over with.

I spent the night before trying to repair the gardening damage to my nails and fiddling with my hair. It was wild; there was nothing for it now but to call Karl at the salon in the morning and see what he could do with it. I hated the thought of that, too; all my friends went to Karl, and he would know as much as they did about Tee and me. Maybe I would try a new salon, a whole new look. But in the end I just telephoned the number that I could, now, dial in my sleep, and asked for an appointment.

"Come by at ten," Karl said. "I work you in. You going on to lunch? Good. We do something special for you."

I met Charlotte in the lobby of the club at twelve-thirty in a new linen shift from the Snappy Turtle—one of the few places left in Atlanta where you could get Old Atlanta clothes—and with an astonishing head of shining, jet black hair that swooped around my forehead and fell over one cheekbone, and felt silky and heavy as it swung against my neck and face. I didn't know yet if I liked the look of it, but I loved the feeling. I kept tossing my head just to feel that silken surge.

"Don't you look scrumptious?" Charlotte said, kissing my cheek and smiling her little cat's smile. She had colonized the choice umbrella table on the terrace by the pool, shaded by old trees and a wisteria vine. Her Tuscan tan made her teeth look very white, and her biscuit-colored shirtwaist fit her like her supple skin. Charlotte took exquisite care of herself. She always had. I must have been a sore trial to her at times.

It was very hot and still by the pool. Noon to one is reserved for adult swims only, and so no sleek, brown children splashed and shrieked their inevitable "Marco Polo." Only a lone swimmer cut the water lazily, swimming so skillfully that hardly a ripple broke the turquoise surface. I watched admiringly; whoever it was had superb form. His dark head barely broke the water, nor did the pistonlike brown arms.

We ordered drinks from Carlton himself, the club's longtime maître d', as formal and beautiful as a carved ebony statue and as hallowed at the club as the old orientals and the original horse brasses in the men's grill. Carlton rarely served individual tables, but he hovered over us, nodding and smiling as if we were visiting royalty. I knew that he would have heard about Tee and me; Carlton knew everything. His attention, even though it was undoubtedly directed at Charlotte, warmed me. Our daiquiris—"Let's have something fun," Charlotte had said—were at our table in record time, and Carlton had added a single anemone to each, plucked from the huge summer bouquet in the foyer.

"For the Redwine ladies," he said and smiled, bowing himself away.

"Thank God for Carlton," Charlotte said, taking a deep swallow. "At least somebody still knows how to behave. Listen, darling, we're going to go over some things today that you need to hear, about the trust fund and a few of my little investments and this and that. I've made some changes, and I want you to know about them. But we're not going to talk about them until after lunch, and we're certainly not going to talk about Theron's behavior with that unspeakable little doxy until then. So drink your drink, and maybe we'll have another and I'll tell you about Italy, then we'll have something wonderful for lunch. I think we both deserve it, don't you?"

"We do indeed," I said, liking her more at that moment than I ever had. Charlotte had quite obviously never thought me suitable for her only son and heir, but the advent of the Eel Woman must have improved me considerably in her eyes.

We sat and sipped, chatting about her trip and looking about us at the flowered terrace. The tables were filling with the lunch crowd, most of whom she knew and some of whom I did, and for once I felt languid and lulled at the club, shaded by flowers and warmed in the sun of Charlotte Redwine's presence. They all had it, the Redwines, that almost palpable aura of rightness and immutability. Tee had his share, and his father had had his, but I thought it was Charlotte from whom the aura emanated. I waved and smiled at the people I knew, feeling as secure as a tender in the lee of a great ship.

Charlotte followed my eyes to the lone swimmer in the pool.

"He's very good, isn't he?" she said. "He swims like you used to. Or maybe you still do?"

"Some," I said. "I haven't much this summer. I need to get back to it."

And I realized then how much I had missed it, that rhythmic, dreamlike gliding, that suspension in an element as pure and simple as air. Missed the effortless pumping of the arms, the kick of the legs that started high in the hips, the slow, ritualized breathing when the head turned in the water . . .

The swimmer reached the end of the pool and pulled himself out with one smooth motion, and I saw that it was not a man after all, but a woman, long and slim and brown, with seal-dark wet hair plaited into a rope that was coiled around her small head. She wore a plain black tank suit cut high on her hips and to her waist in back, and for a moment, as she walked away from us toward an empty table at the edge of the patio, I thought she was Caroline. And then I knew who she was. Charlotte saw my face and turned to look, and knew, too.

"That's her," she said in a small, brittle voice. "Isn't that her?"

"Yes," I said. The swimmer could, of course, have been anyone else at all, but I knew that she wasn't. I heard my breath whistling in my nostrils. It seemed very important not to look away from the woman in the black bathing suit, to take in that bright noon, the full and exact measure of her.

"How dare she come here?" Charlotte said in simple amazement. "Can she possibly not know this is a private club?"

I did not speak, because I could not. We watched as Sheri Scroggins held up a hand to Carlton, who was standing at the entrance to the patio, smiling benignly at his people taking their ease. He did not acknowledge her signal. No one had signaled to Carlton for service in decades.

Sheri's dark brows knit in annoyance. She snapped her fingers and called, "Waiter!" Heads turned all over the patio. Slowly and with immense dignity, Carlton moved to her table. She said something indistinguishable, studying a menu, not looking at him. He bowed slightly and turned and glided away; he might have been on wheels. Before the soft buzz of amazement and outrage could start, he was back with a frothy pink concoction thickly forested with fruit and flowers.

Sheri did look at him then.

"Did I say frozen? I did not. I said a plain daiquiri and that's what I meant. You can take this back right now and bring me another, and this time, get it right."

61

She did not raise her voice, but the flat twang reverberated around the quiet patio. I could hear indrawn breaths. Carlton's face went dead and still, and he turned and took the offending drink away. She went back to studying the menu, seemingly unaware of the hostility washing over her like surf.

"I will have her barred from this club," Charlotte said in a voice an octave higher than I had ever heard. "I will attend to it on the way out. This is outrageous. Carlton is one of us."

Despite my shock, I almost laughed. By now, I supposed, he almost was, and I wondered what that might mean to Carlton in his life outside the club, providing, of course, that he had one. Then the laughter died. Tee came on to the patio and walked over to Sheri's table, kissed her on the cheek, and sat down opposite her. His back was to us. I was glad, at least, for that.

His mother drew in her breath to speak, then let it out in a long, ragged sigh. I did not look around the patio, but I knew that a good fifty pairs of eyes were fixed, first on Tee and Sheri Scroggins, and then on Charlotte and me. Out of the corner of my eye I saw two fig-ures, women, get up and drift languidly toward the ladies' lounge. The club phones, I figured, would be tied up until two o'clock.

The two of them leaned their heads together, one dark and one fair, over the menu, and all of a sudden I was looking at Tee and myself. Tee and me, when we were young and first in love and all things seemed possible. He looked, in the dappled shade, hardly older than he had then, his snub face lit by his slow smile. And she . . . she was, in her tallness, the width of her shoulders, the sleek, wet, dark hair, the flash of blue across the pool that was her eyes, the way she tipped her head to his . . . she was me. A much younger me, so full of vitality and the nearness of him that I hummed with it. Oh, her features were different . . . there was, somehow, a sort of Toltec cast to her face, a remote, sensuous, faintly cruel bluntness. But the surface resemblance was astonishing. No wonder Charlie had thought she was Caroline. Caroline looked remarkably like I had at that age. Now, of course, few people remarked on the similarity.

"She looks like me. Like I used to, I mean," I said stupidly, as if I were remarking on the weather.

"She looks nothing at all like you," Charlotte said. There were two hectic red spots on her cheeks, and she was breathing audibly.

"She looks just like what she is, a South Georgia shantytown whore. Theron is out of his mind. I can put a stop to this, and I will. I imagine she thinks she's hooked herself a rich man; I can disabuse her of that, and him, too, with one phone call to our attorney. Which I shall make the instant I get home. Whatever happens, my dear, you and Teddy will never lack for anything. I promise you that. Are you finished? I think we've both had enough of this spectacle."

She rose, gathered up her little Chanel bag, and walked with her long, graceful, athlete's stride across the patio ahead of me, not looking to see if I followed. I did, of course. Followed blindly along in her wake with my chin held as high as I could manage, looking neither to the right or the left, conscious on every inch of me of eyes fastened on both of us like leeches. My heart was pounding so hard I could hear it. We had to pass their table to leave the patio. I thought I would die rather than do it.

I did not see him notice us, but I felt it.

"Mother," he said in a voice I did not know, a silly voice, high-pitched. "Molly . . . "

Sheri Scroggins was in front of us suddenly, barring our way. She looked like a panther who had just come out of a dark jungle river. The black suit was still damp, as was the lightless black hair, which was unplaited now and flowed over her shoulders like a cape. She smiled. She seemed to have too many teeth, all bone white in the tawny gold of her face. The eyes burned as blue as methane.

"We haven't met, but we should," she said, including Charlotte and me both in the smile. She held out her hand. I noticed that the fingers were blunt, spatulate, and the nails were bitten to the quick. I did not speak.

"You're right," Charlotte said in a voice like iced steel. "We haven't."

She walked unhurriedly around Sheri Scroggins, then paused and looked down at her son. He sat with his mouth open, simply looking at us. We might have been apparitions.

"I never thought I raised a fool, Theron," she said to Tee, and walked off the terrace and was swallowed by the huge old rose bushes, drooping with their fragrant cargo, that shielded the entrance. I could not move.

"Molly . . ." Sheri Scroggins said.

I looked at her, straight into her eyes.

"Mrs. Redwine," I said, and walked away after Charlotte.

Behind me I heard Tee call, "Molly. Mom . . . "

I shook my head without looking back. The myriad eyes seemed to leave smoking pits in the flesh of my back. I could still feel them when the attendant brought our cars around to where we waited, silent now, under the stone porte cochere.

"This will never happen to either one of us again," Charlotte said grimly as she got into her big blue Mercedes. The Redwines had a driver, but she hardly ever used him.

I smiled at her, surprised that I could make my mouth move, and got into my little Toyota wagon and drove home through the silent, snaking streets of Ansley Park, grateful for once that we lived there instead of Brookwood Hills or Buckhead. This trip took only minutes. I don't remember thinking anything at all during it.

Teddy was out when I got home, but Lazarus was there, thumping his tail from under the wrought-iron table on the patio, where he retreated in hot weather.

"Have you been out? Want to go for a walk?" I said to him, but he only thumped his tail harder and grinned at me, his tongue lolling out of his mouth and dripping. Lazarus was a sensible dog. He could not be lured out in midafternoon during a heat wave.

"Later," I said, and went up the stairs to the bedroom. My bedroom now. I closed the shutters against the hot, gray whiteness outside, took off my dress and shoes, and lay down on the bed.

I had thought perhaps that I might need to cry, or at least wrestle with feelings too powerful to permit yet. I waited. But I did not cry and I did not feel anything except the familiar sleepiness. Sleep tugged at me like an undertow, and finally I turned on my side and let myself slide down into it. It was thick and black and deep, and I don't know how long it would have held me under if the telephone had not waked me two hours later. By then the white heat was seeping out of the afternoon behind the shutters, and the idiot throbbing of the television from the downstairs library said that Teddy was home.

I fumbled with the receiver, dropped it, retrieved it, and finally put it to my ear.

"Hello," I said thickly. I sounded to my own ears as if I were drunk.

It was my mother's voice, round and full and carrying, trained. For some reason the sheer perfection of it irritated me almost beyond reason.

"Oh, I woke you, didn't I?" she said, and I thought I could hear the creamy smugness of one who never, under any circumstances, slept in the daytime.

"That's okay. What's up?" I sought to exorcize the treacly stupidity with briskness.

"I have a lovely plan," she caroled. It was the voice she had used when I was small and she wanted to motivate me to make some change in my imperfect self, to amend somehow the sheer unsuitableness that this large, square child was for a dancer, a feather, a curl of flame. The irritation mounted.

"And that is?" I said.

"That is a day of pampering just for us. Like I told you the other night at dinner. I have us an appointment at Noelle in the morning—hair, makeup, massage, nails, a salt scrub, whirlpool—and then you can take me to the club for lunch and we'll show off our fabulous new selves. And then I'm taking you shopping. To Neiman Marcus. No more of those little wrap skirt thingies. Real glamour clothes. Something you've never worn in your life. New shoes, too, with four-inch heels. And after that a little workout at Jeanne's. Don't worry. I'll do the beginner's with you this time. Once you see how good you feel, you'll want to go on with it, I know . . ."

"Mother," I said. "Just once, do you think you could take me just like I am? Could you bear to have lunch with me without the makeover and the four-inch heels? Plain old me in a little wrap skirt thingy? Just once?"

"Well, you needn't get snippy with me," she said, injured or projecting injury, I was never sure which. "Of course I'll take you like you are. You're my daughter. Only . . . well, just like you are doesn't seem to have gotten you very far, does it? Oh, darling, I didn't mean it that way . . ."

"That's just what you meant," I said, irritation suddenly flaring into rage and past that into something else entirely, a kind of wildfire that swept everything inside me away and left only surging, boiling red.

"That's just what you meant and it's what you've always meant. I've never been good enough for you; too big, too awkward, too . . . too plodding, too *earthbound* . . . "

"Darling, not at all! Forget the spa stuff and the shopping, then; we'll just go sit on the patio at the club and talk, like we haven't done in ages. Wouldn't that be fun?"

"No!" I shouted. "It would not be fun! It would not be fun at all! I did that today, Mother, with Charlotte, and you'll never guess who else was there. Tee and his new lay. Tee and the famous other woman. Tee and his little brown whore, dripping wet and falling out of her bathing suit, playing kissy-face with my husband for all of Atlanta to see. No, it was not fun and it never will be again, because I am never setting foot there again as long as I live. So if you want to go to lunch with me, you're going to have to go somewhere where you don't know the waiters and they bring you a check. Like practically everybody else in the world does. I hate to tell you this, Mother, but you can kiss the Driving Club good-bye."

My mother's voice dropped into that low, thrilling timbre that she used when she played dark, tragic heroines or did serious public service television spots.

"You mean you're going to give up your own club, give up Teddy's very birthright, just for some little tramp who isn't going to last another six months? I thought better of you. I truly did, Molly."

"No you didn't," I said, my voice shaking with fury. Where did this endless boiling redness come from? I was afraid I could not stop it, and I did not really want to.

"No you didn't. You never thought better of me in my life. You aren't even thinking of me now, you're thinking of you, and how it's you who're going to have to give up hanging around the goddamned Driving Club. Do you have any idea how it felt today? To sit there and see a woman kissing your husband, a woman who could have been you, thirty years before? To sit there and feel like a damned Clydesdale and watch a . . . a fucking water nymph sitting where you should be sitting? No. I don't think you do."

I paused for a breath, and my mother was silent. Then she said, thoughtfully, as if she were giving the matter judicious consideration, "I really should have let you study dance when you were little. I see now that it was a mistake not to let you. Dancers don't go soft and thick and puddingy when they get older. They turn into grey-hounds, not oxen."

Only someone who had known her intimately for all the scald-ing years that I had could have heard the cold, silvery desire to wound under her sorrowful words. The red rage exploded.

Through ringing ears I heard myself say, "No. Not grey-hounds. They don't turn into greyhounds. Have you looked at yourself lately, Mother? Old dancers turn into hyenas. And you know what hyenas do, don't you? They eat their young."

There was a long silence, a kind of hollow rushing, over the wire, and then she hung up. She did not slam the phone down, but replaced it with infinite gentleness. I remember thinking very clearly, sometime soon I'm going to be terribly sorry I said that. But at that moment I felt only the need, urgent and smothering, to go back to sleep. The blinding redness had faded as if it had never been, and I felt emptied out and aching to be filled with simple oblivion.

I slept until nearly midnight, when the phone rang again, and when I answered it, it was my father, telling me that my mother had had a stroke or a seizure of some sort while she was working out at her makeshift barre in the spare bedroom, and had died in the ambulance on the way to Piedmont Hospital.

CHAPTER FOUR

IN THE DAYS AFTER MY MOTHER DIED, I had the same dream over and over: I was walking down a crowded city sidewalk washed in graying late-afternoon light, and I passed one of those sets of steps leading down to basement doors that you see so often in New York and London, though not, in my experience, in any other cities. But instead of a door leading to a shop or apartment, there was a kind of grating that gave way to a subterranean tunnel, like a subway tunnel, and there, looking out through the grating along with several other people, was my mother. In the dream I stopped, though no one else around me did. It was as if I alone saw the grated window and the tunnel.

My mother looked straight ahead, not sad, not happy, not angry, not alive, not dead. She had on one of her hats, I think the black one that she had worn the last time we had had dinner, at the Ritz-Carlton. She and the others looked as if they were waiting for something, perhaps a train to somewhere.

I bent down and said to her, "What are you doing down there?" She looked at me then, and though she did not smile, I thought that she regarded me with favor, or at least not with anger. "We come here every afternoon at four to wait," she said.

I always woke up after that, my hair soaked with sweat, my heart pounding. It was a terrible dream, though I could not have told why. And indeed I did not, for I found that there was simply no one now to tell my dreams to.

Lying there in the damp, tangled bedclothes I would realize over and over again the first and realest loss that divorce brings with it. There is no longer anybody to tell your dreams to, not on the pulse of the moment, when they are most vivid and need most to be told. There is nobody to talk to about the most intimate and secret tendrils that curl through your mind, at least not at the time of their flowering. No one to laugh with, to show things to, to wish casual wishes with—not when those impulses are first born.

So the first great loss is immediacy, spontaneity. You can tell the dreams, voice the fears and longings, laugh the laughter, wish the wishes, of course, but it will be later, to someone deliberately chosen, at a remove, a considered sharing. There is no longer anyone there to be a mirror for you, so that you lose first a primal sense of yourself that has been a part of you for so long. Or, at least, I found that was so for me. Perhaps this is true of death, too, and long separations; I cannot speak to those yet. My mother had not been a mirror for me in many years. It was Tee who had listened in the nights, laughed, argued, received, given back. It was Tee who had been as there to me as I was to myself, and now he no longer was. For a long time I really hated him for that simple removal of his presence when I had something I needed to say.

I could not tell my dream to my father, who was dumb and still and leaden with loss; I could not have added my anguish to the weight he bore. I could not tell Kevin, who came immediately with Sally, nearly wild with grief for his mother. He was furious with me and would not speak to me at all; I had blurted out to him the details of my last conversation with Mother, and for months, indeed almost a year after, he was adamant in his belief that I had killed her. My father flared at him when he first voiced that sentiment, the first and last sign of animation I saw in Daddy during the whole terrible time of mother's death and funeral, and after that Kevin blamed me only with his cold silence. Telling him of the dream or anything else was out of the question. I did not know pretty, one-surfaced Sally well enough, and never would, and I could not burden Teddy with the weight of the dream. He had not been especially close to his grandmother, but loss is loss, and Teddy had had enough of that recently. Caroline, still wounded, did not come home. So finally I told Livvy.

"What do you think it means?" I said on the afternoon before Mother's funeral, while she lay in her closed coffin in the dim, tribal splendor of Patterson's and received her last homage from her students and admirers. Livvy had come with sandwiches and a bottle of cold white wine, and we sat in her car in the parking lot while we ate and drank. Kevin was doing noon chatelain duty, and would not have welcomed my presence. I knew I had an hour or so free, and the dream was a burden I desperately needed to share.

"I think it means you've got a lot of unfinished business with your mother," Livvy said. "I think *you* think your mother can't go on to her rest or whatever until you've atoned in some way for, quote, killing her, unquote, or paid some kind of stupid penance. And I think you're nuts. Your mother said something really shitty to you and when you got mad and talked back to her, she went home like a spoiled little girl and danced herself to death. I think it's just like her, and I'm pissed off at her because she's left you drowning in guilt and gone off where you can't possibly follow and make it right. And I also think that your father knows that in his heart of hearts, and who the hell cares what Kevin thinks? He'd have found a way to blame you if you'd been on Uranus when she died."

As always, Livvy was a powerful anodyne, but I had the feeling that the relief was temporary. I knew that my mother wasn't going to let me walk away that easily.

"I think I see her all the time, too," I said. "In crowds. I was walking through Saks yesterday trying to find something black for the service and I saw her so clearly in the handbag department that I started toward her before I remembered. And I thought she was on the phone this morning. I mean, I know it was Carrie Davies, but it still sounded like Mother. I'm scared to death I'm going to see her with Daddy and react, and that would just about finish him off. He's said several times that he can't see her; that it would be so much better if he could just see her. I think he means in his mind, though. Not like I'm seeing her. I almost told her in Saks to go materialize to the one who needs her."

"I think all that's probably normal," Livvy said, licking mayonnaise off her fingers. "She's always been the most powerful person in your world, and all of a sudden she's not in it anymore. How can you not see her, and dream about her? What I wish you could do is dump the guilt. Maybe the Catholics have something; you can just go to confession and get some novenas to say, or whatever they do, and be done with it. What's it going to take for you?"

"I don't really feel guilty," I said. "How come you're so much smarter than me? Why, if we're such soul mates, do you know all this stuff and I don't?"

"Because you're the one in the middle of it," she said. "If it was me stewing in all this crap and you outside it, you'd see it, too. You know it as well as I do, you just can't get to it right now."

I laughed, a ragged, thin little laugh but a laugh nevertheless, and reached over and hugged her across the waxed paper and potato chips package.

"If I were a lesbian, I'd marry you," I said.

"If you were a lesbian, you'd be a lot better off right now," she said. "Now what can we do about this Oedipal guilt of yours? Wasn't it Oedipus who killed his mother or something?"

"He killed his father and married his mother," I said. "I guess matricide by daughter is so bad they don't even have a myth for it. You think I'm just talking, but I really don't feel guilty. Maybe I will later, but right now I don't. I feel terrible for Daddy, and I think I'm going to miss Mother an awful lot when I really take it in, but right now all I feel is tired to death and kind of stunned. And I can't stop thinking about Tee. I keep waiting for him to come make all this all right. Maybe it's that I can take in either infidelity or the death of my mother, but I can't handle both at one time. Nobody was meant to get it all at once like this."

"Are you kidding? That's what middle age is," Livvy said. "One loss after another. It's hell. Didn't anybody ever tell you? And by the way, speaking of the devil, have you heard from Tee since your mama died?"

"I called him that morning," I said. "I did it totally without thinking; I just dialed his office, and when Patty answered, I said, 'Sweetie, I need to talk to Tee right now,' as if nothing had happened. I didn't even identify myself. But she knows my voice, of course; I bet she nearly dropped her teeth."

"I bet she did," Livvy agreed. "So what did he say?"

"He wasn't there. He'd gone on some kind of department retreat or something down at Callaway Gardens. From the way

Patty hemmed and hawed, I'd say the Eel Woman went with him, but I didn't ask."

Livvy started to laugh.

"Shit," she said. "Do you know where they've gone? They've gone to spend a weekend with that idiot on television who walks on fire, you know the one who's supposed to motivate people to tap their hidden powers and reach their impossible dreams? The department's got him down there teaching all the little Chi Phis to walk on fire. I told Caleb I'd build a fire of another kind entirely under him if he went. He wouldn't have, anyway. But you can bet Her Eeliness did. She's probably slithering over hot coals on her belly as we speak. Hope it fries her abs."

"Oh, God," I said, and began to laugh, helplessly, along with her. It struck me that for a woman who'd lost a husband and a mother in a matter of days, I was laughing entirely too much. But the alternative was crying, and I simply did not think I could do any more of that.

I was right. Whatever font the tears had flowed from dried up. I cried no more for my mother, or indeed for anyone or anything else, for a very long time. I sat through my mother's funeral between my father and my son, as dry-eyed as a wooden puppet, and probably resembled one. I found it hard to move my arms and legs and head, and stared at the rector of the little Episcopal church where my parents had gone for years, and where Tee and I had married, as if he alone could sustain life and breath in me. When the service was over, my muscles were sore.

I had not been in the church in a long time; Tee and I had always attended the larger and grander cathedral of St. Philip, in Buckhead, where his family had been communicants and benefactors for generations. I liked this little stone church. Its low, beamed ceilings felt enclosing and comforting, and its simple stained-glass windows, with reds and amethysts prevailing, made the interior seem awash in rosy light. Often, in the cathedral, I had the urge to look over my shoulder, to press myself into the ends of pews and the recesses of walls, to feel ridiculously as if I had come to church in my underwear, or forgotten my shoes. I often thought of *Murder in the Cathedral* when I entered. But on the day of my mother's funeral, I felt again the sense of protection and enclosure that little

St. Margaret's had always given me, and was grateful to slide into it as if into sleep.

It was very crowded. My mother was, by that time, a local legend, often referred to as "a civic treasure." Three generations of Atlantans had seen her perform, or had studied with her, and it seemed to me that most of them were in the congregation that day. The story that she had died dancing had gotten out, and both the television and news media had picked up on it, closing their brief, sound-bitten eulogies with inanities such as, "True to form, she died dancing" and "Like the trouper she was, she died with her dancing shoes on." None, of course, mentioned that it could be termed a case of death by daughter. Only Kevin had done that, and he only once.

He sat on the other side of my father in the first row of pews and cried soundlessly for his mother, Sally sniffling beside him. Because he was a rising anchor in Washington and considered one of their own, the local media all ran at least one shot of Kevin, his clever, handsome face blurred with grief and his head bowed, coming out of the church. Behind him in one or two of the shots, I looked severe and forbidding in my new Saks black, almost Medea-like. The new haircut made me someone even I hardly recognized; it was like looking at an actress impersonating me. I had my head tipped forward so that the smooth wings of hair obscured my face, but you could still tell that it was immobile, frozen. In contrast, Kevin looked vulnerable and very human, infinitely appealing. The brief television clips looked subtly wrong, skewed; it should have been I who wept for my mother, Kevin who was stalwart. Atlanta was still the Deep South, however far in spirit we believed we had left it behind. In the traditional South, women wept and men forbore.

It was a morning funeral, for the day was very hot, and Arlington Cemetery, where Mother and Daddy had their plots, broiled gently under the punishing fist of the sun. There were few family members, for the Bells did not have much family, but many others came: old friends from Peachtree Hills, friends of mine and Tee's, Daddy's lodge members, many fans of my mother. At the edge of the circle, aloof and regal in white linen that somehow looked more correct than the surrounding sea of black, Charlotte Redwine stood. I had not seen her at the church, nor at Patterson's in the days before, but she had sent a basket of delicacies and wine from her favored caterer, and an armful of flowers from her garden, to the house via Marcus, her driver, and had enclosed a note to me pledging her continuing support.

"Your darling mother, I always so admired her style and spirit," she wrote. "You must, if you can, think of me as your mother now."

She did not mention Tee. He was not at the church, nor at the cemetery. It would have been appalling taste if he had been, I suppose, but the only loss I truly felt on that hot, numbed day was that of Tee's tall body by my side. That side felt naked.

Everyone told me later what a lovely funeral and a somehow joyous graveside ceremony it was, and almost everyone mentioned the ducks. Arlington is full of little lakes and ponds, and over the years people have relocated their Easter ducklings there, so that nowadays the background accompaniment to any interment is a raucous, peevish honking. Canadian geese on their way north or south stop off to join the remittance ducks, too, and sometimes the minister or whoever is handling the interment is forced to stop and wait until a particular gaggle of ducks and geese works out a honking dispute. Everyone always smiles and looks at each other, as if to say, "Life goes on, after all. Wouldn't he/she have loved it?" The ducks added a rowdy carnival note to the going out of my mother, and it seemed to please everyone but Kevin. He glared, as if he would like to wring sixty-odd necks. For my part, I struggled so hard with the illicit, unseemly laughter that my face was red and sweating when finally we left the undertakers to their task and walked with my father back up the hill to the car. Even Daddy smiled.

"Gave her a real five-star sendoff, didn't they?" he whispered to me.

I came as close to weeping then as I ever would for my mother, except in a time and place still far distant.

We went back to my house, where Lilly and the caterers were putting the finishing touches on the tasteful little buffet lunch for family and friends that custom here dictates. Daddy had asked me to host it; he said that he could no more imagine having my mother's final festivities in the cramped condo than he could have downtown in Centennial Park. The right place would have been the old house in Peachtree Hills, where what he calls our real life was largely conducted, but that was impossible, of course. A computer salesman and his family lived there now. So I agreed, and bestirred myself with Lilly to put the house to rights and polish silver and order flowers and drag the old ivory damask that had been Tee's grandmother's out of the cedar chest. It was not lost on me that if my mother had not died, my house very well might soon have slept indefinitely beneath a coverlet of dust and lightlessness.

"It looks real pretty, baby," Daddy said when we came in from the searing brightness of the day. "Your mother would like this very much."

And it did look pretty, but I somehow doubted that my mother would have liked it at all. All told, I thought she might well have preferred Centennial Park, thronged with the thousands of people who had admired and applauded her over the years.

I am always surprised by how much I enjoy after-funeral affairs. There is sorrow, of course, the degree depending on how large a displacement the deceased will leave in the air of the various worlds represented at the feast, but it is seemly sorrow, and serves to leaven the yeasts of both hilarity and malice. There will be laughter, but it will be the laughter of loving recollection. There may be tears, but they will be the gentle tears of nostalgia and fondness. No one will vilify the absent honoree or any of the present mourners. Maybe later, after the guests have gone on to wherever they go after consuming the funeral meats, but not in the very house of mourning itself. Everyone knows everyone else almost by definition, and they are all on their best behavior, which is seldom the case when the group gathers elsewhere. There are hugs, cheek and lip kisses, comradely back claps and biceps punches, compliments and confidences.

Carrie Davies once said wistfully, at the funeral of the first of our group to die, that none of us had behaved this sweetly toward each other since the Chi Phi formal our senior year. She was right. I enjoyed my mother's funeral so much that I forgot for long stretches of time why we were gathered, and when I remembered, it seemed simply absurd that the gathering was about her death.

Her life, though, that was another matter. She was fully as present as any one of us: The talk was all of her, and her place in each of our firmaments. She might have been out in the kitchen. Surely in a moment she would sweep into the room in one of her absurd hats and kiss cheeks and pat sleeves, and her laugh would tinkle into the waiting air, and life would swirl on around her as it always had. I have never felt, before or since, quite the perfect, uncomplicated tenderness that I felt for my mother on the day that we buried her.

No one spoke of Tee, or the affair, or what I would be doing next, or what he would. They would the minute they were out the door, I believe, but not here, not on this day. Tee was, for the first time in his life, not a part of one of our gatherings. Wine and Bloody Marys flowed without his making them, shrimp salad and cheese biscuits and strawberries were eaten without his sharing them, toasts were made to which he did not raise his glass. It was, I suppose, my first party on my own in this house, and thanks to my mother, it was a roaring success. Tee should have been by my side; of course he should have. But his absence left no bruises. I was surprised at the grace of my solo effort.

Even my father felt its benison. He had a rare-for-him Bloody Mary, and smiled often and genuinely at his and Mother's last mutual guests, and once or twice I heard him laugh aloud. It did not seem strange. This final postgame party was a time and place unto itself. Only later does the real world resume itself. Then was when I would worry about my father. Then was the time in his life that would, if anything could, simply defeat him. I smiled at him and laughed with him and resolutely refused to think of what might happen to him when we closed the door on our last guests. It did not even occur to me to wonder what might happen to me.

In the end, though, Tee did come to Mother's bon voyage party. Just as the afternoon shadows were falling across the patio and the first guests were making noises about leaving, the doorbell rang and Kevin went to answer it. He came back into the living room holding an arrangement of blood-red roses so massive that only the top of his head showed over them, only the blue of his eyes glinted through them. Kevin was all pigeon-blood velvet from his waist to his crown. His arms could hardly contain the roses. There must, I thought, have been a hundred of them. All of them were perfect, breath-stopping, rococo. My first thought was that they must have cost almost as much as the party had. My second was that they were the most ostentatious things I had ever seen. I could tell by the little gasping rush of breath that swept around the room that everyone else thought so, too. Everyone present at my mother's funeral reception would talk for years about this most stunningly inappropriate of floral offerings.

My mother, I thought, would have adored them.

"Well, my goodness, who on earth?" Sally chirped, breaking the silence.

"Good lord," my father said.

"Florist's delivery," Kevin muttered from behind the juggernaut of roses. "One I didn't know."

I walked over and took the envelope that trembled, like a butterfly, on the topmost petal. It was creamy, heavy stock, and addressed to Daddy, Kevin, and me. I opened it.

"Our deepest sympathy and love," the card read.

It was signed, "Tee and Sheri." The handwriting was strong and black and slashing, not Tee's.

"Another emerging nation heard from," I said, and handed the roses to Sally and walked into the kitchen, my cheeks and chest flaming. Behind me the silence spun out. It was a full minute before the low rush of talk started.

I was in the kitchen splashing water on my face when Livvy came in.

"Christ, I thought she was the one raised in a barn," she said incredulously. "What, did somebody punch a hole in him and all his taste and manners ran out? I never saw such a vulgar bunch of flowers in my life, and I never, ever in my life heard of a guy and his mistress sending flowers to his not-even-ex-wife. They'll be lucky if Coke doesn't send them both to Edie Summers."

Edie Summers was a fiftyish, perennial debutante who taught manners and social graces to the spawn of the big houses of Buckhead. Tee had once, he had said, had an aching adolescent crush on her when he was a freshman at Westminster and she was a senior. She had since been transmogrified into such a porcelain paragon of seemliness and perfection that there seemed nothing left for her, after her banker husband died appropriately on the tennis court at the Driving Club fifteen years before, but to open a small, perfect academy dedicated to varnishing the children of her classmates with her patina. Their parents paid dearly for it, and Edie prospered, and there were few Buckhead teens who left for college who did not know how to comport themselves.

The comporting itself was another matter entirely. Tee and Charlie used to say that the wildest kids who went through Chi Phi rush all over the South were Edie's kids. I spluttered into my cupped hands at the thought of Tee and the Eel Woman in Edie's implacable clutches, and bent at the waist, laughing. Livvy laughed with me.

When we had stopped, I said, "Poor Daddy. What a stupid, awful thing for him to have to cope with. Tee ought to be shot; he ought to know better. What did Dad do with them? I ought to be ashamed of myself for running out like that."

"He didn't have to cope with them," she said. "I took them away from Sally and stuffed them in the downstairs john and locked the door. You can throw them out or send them to Piedmont or whatever after the party. I personally would take them over to Coke marketing and insert them, thorns and all, up Tee's ass, one by one, but that's up to you. Caleb got your dad another Bloody Mary and he and Charlie Davies took him out on the patio and asked him about wiring lamps. Everybody's stopped buzzing and is gearing up to leave. The great flower hoo-ha *est fini*. Crisis management is my specialty. You may kiss my ring."

And sure enough, by the time the last guest had gone and Daddy and Kevin and Sally and Teddy and I had plopped ourselves down in exhaustion on the cooling patio, Tee and his terrible roses and his awful paramour had been tucked away somewhere in our collective tribal subconscious, to be given their indignant due when we could get to them. This was it now, the time I had been dreading for days, the hour when, for all of us, but most especially for my father, the real world rocketed back into motion and the real anguish must begin.

We did not speak at first, only looked around at each other, and I had a swift, panicky moment of thinking that I honestly could not bear the pain Dad must feel. I knew by then that for myself, I could bear it with an ease that was rather appalling. I had, somehow, during the funeral and the gathering that followed, buried my mother as deeply in my own center as we had in the earth of Arlington Cemetery. Later, I thought; later, when the time is right and I can do it properly, I can think about her. There's plenty of time. This time right now is for Daddy.

Finally Dad said, "I thought it went real well, didn't you-all? I'm always surprised at how many people have seen her plays and concerts. The church was SRO. And this was nice, Molly, this little to-do this afternoon. Good food. And all those young people . . . your friends, I guess, and Kevin's. It was nice of them to come . . . "

His voice trailed off and he looked vacantly into space, his hands folded over the small melon of his stomach as if he were waiting to be called for dinner, or for the rest of his life. I thought of the awful subway dream and closed my eyes for a moment. When I opened them, he was still looking patiently into nowhere.

"It was a really pretty party, Molly," Sally said, and then winced. "Or reception, I guess. Very easy and elegant, nothing too stiff or formal. Mama Bell would have liked it."

Mama Bell wouldn't have liked it a bit more than she liked the plain little church or the loudmouthed ducks who had stolen her thunder, I thought in my new, becalmed clarity. She'd have held out for the Driving Club or nothing.

Aloud I said, "Thank you, Sally. I couldn't have done it without you. And you too, Kev. Of course."

"Of course," Kevin said. His voice was a husky rasp. Of us all, Kevin seemed the only one whose emotions were properly anchored to reality. He had lost the love of his life and he was bereft and angry. Angry mostly at me.

Another little silence spun out, and into it Teddy said, "I think I'll go make myself a sandwich, Ma. Can I fix one for anybody else?"

"There's a ton of stuff left," I said. "Didn't you get any?"

"I had peanut butter and jelly in mind," he said, and Dad and I smiled at each other. It was an instinctive smile, our old one.

"I'll see you before you go, Grampa," Teddy said, and dropped a kiss on top of my father's head as naturally as if he had done it every day for years. But Teddy had not kissed anyone in his own family since he'd turned ten. My heart squeezed with love for him.

We were drifting toward silence again. Into it I heard my own voice saying, in the tone I am told I use in my various committee meetings, "Well, I guess we need to make a few plans. Kevin, I know you and Sally will be going on back in the morning, and Teddy's getting ready for his trip west. What about you, Dad? Have you thought what you might like to do in the next few days?"

My father did not answer, only studied middle air, and Kevin and Sally looked at me in disbelief, as if I had farted loudly in some solemn, sacred ceremony. I blushed furiously. I sounded officious and insensitive and horrible even to my own ears, and could not imagine where the fluting words had come from, except that I felt a need, as strong as anything I have ever experienced, to get everyone and everything in some sort of order.

"Sorry," I whispered miserably to my father, but the need remained, pulsing like an abscessed tooth.

"Don't be, baby," he said presently, heavily and without inflection. "You're right. We do need to make some plans. Life isn't going to stop for us."

Except that, of course, for him it had.

"Come to us," Kevin said. He said it firmly and strongly, in his anchor voice. He did not often use it off the air. It always surprised me when he did, that this authority lived in Kevin.

Dad looked at him, one eyebrow raised.

"I mean it," Kevin said. "Come stay with us for a while. We'd love that, wouldn't we, Sal? You never have, not for any length of time. Mother never liked Washington. Come stay for a few weeks and get to know my world, my town. I'll take some time off, and we'll go to the National Press Club, and the White House press room, and I'll introduce you to some of the big enchiladas—Brokaw, Jennings—and we'll go down to the Eastern Shore and do some fishing, and go to the galleries and restaurants—"

"Oh, come, Daddy Bell," Sally cried. "I redecorated the guest room just for you and . . . for you. The drapes have ducks on them. Mandy would be so excited . . ."

Mandy was Kevin and Sally's eleven-year-old daughter. I did not think she had ever been excited about anything except horses.

"Just like Molly at that age," Mother used to say. "All arms and legs and feet and shoulders. Except, of course, with Molly it was swimming, not horses."

Poor Mandy. Damned by her dominant genes.

"It would be nice to spend some time with Mandy," Daddy said dutifully, but I did not think he was even aware of what he said. He seemed to me much as he always had, loose-jointed and laconic and sweet-tempered, except that there did not, now, seem to be any core to him. I thought that if the rest of us got up and left the patio, he would simply sit there until someone came to fetch him and tell him what to do. I was right, I was not going to be able to bear this . . .

"Then you'll come?" Kevin said.

"It's something to think about," Daddy said.

"No!" I cried. Again, Kevin and Sally looked at me in disapproving alarm. Daddy continued to study air.

"I mean, not right now; he needs to be here. There are all these things to be done, and then he needs time to take it in. He needs to be where he's always been; he needs quiet and familiarity to sort it all out. I'm going to help. We can be at the condo in the daytime, and at night he can come to me . . . "

I ran out of steam. The words had been a near frantic tumble. My father did look at me then.

"You've got too much on you right now, baby," he said. "I appreciate it, but I'm not going to drape myself all over you like a sack of salt. I'll holler if I think I need any help."

"No, it's only logical," I persisted. "You don't even like that stuffy little condo and I've got this whole big house, and besides, it's my job. It's what we do, us women . . . "

I smiled to let him know I was half-joking, but I could tell he saw through it.

"What's what you do?" he said mildly. I knew that he really saw me now, perhaps for the first time that day.

"Look after people," I said lamely.

Daddy sighed and looked at us, Kevin and me, before he spoke.

"What I need now is to be by myself," he said mildly. "To be alone with your mother. We haven't said good-bye, and I need to do that. She just looked at me in the ambulance; she never did say anything. I didn't either, that I can remember. We just . . . looked. She had this intent, sort of preoccupied look on her face, in her eyes, and then her face changed . . . and she died. But we never said anything to one another. That's what I've got to do next."

I felt my eyes fill, but it was Kevin who spoke. "When . . . when her face changed . . . did she look afraid?" he asked. I could scarcely hear him.

"No," Daddy said. "She looked surprised. I appreciate your asking, both of you, but I need to stick around the house until I can see her clearly again, till I can see her like she was and not like at the last . . . "

"But then you'll come," I said stubbornly. "Won't you? And we can start doing all the stuff you'll need to do. Or I could come to your house . . . "

He drew a deep breath and let it out slowly. He smiled a little.

"No. Then I'm going fishing. I'm going with Harry Florian. We've been talking about spending a couple of weeks at Homosassa for years. Now I reckon we'll do it. And then I'm going to sell that cussed condo and find another place. That's the first thing I'm going to do when I get back."

"Well, I can help there, at least," I said. "There are all kinds of nice little places around midtown, full of charm and individuality, most of them not too pricey, and they're all close to us . . . "

"Close to who?" my father said cautiously.

"Well, you know . . . to us."

"There's not any you," Kevin drawled. "Were you perhaps forgetting? What 'us' were you referring to?"

Abruptly the killing, red fury surged back, crashing down over me like a great wave. I felt myself lifted on it; I surfed on its curl. I rode it higher and higher. And, abruptly, then I pushed it down. That red wave had already taken my mother.

"I don't want to hear any more of that kind of talk," my father said to Kevin. It was nearly his old voice, out of my childhood. He looked at me with love and, I thought, a kind of weary pity.

"I'm tired of the city, Molly," he said. "I think my time in the city is just about over. The city was your mother's place. The country's mine. I thought I might look for a little place up around Jasper, or maybe even down in Lowndes County. Around home. I've still got some good friends there. I could have a garden, and a real workshop. And I wouldn't be more than a few hours away from here . . . "

His voice cracked, and I knew he meant away from the raw new mound on the shady, duck-haunted hill at Arlington.

"What would I do then?" I said desolately. "Who would I have then who's left of my family?"

"Honey, you have to start now making a life for yourself," Daddy said, as if Kevin and Sally were not on the patio with us. "And you have to make it by yourself. It can't be built around Teddy or me. Neither one of us is going to be with you that much longer. Besides that, I just can't . . . take the weight right now. And Teddy shouldn't have to."

"Then what can I do for you?"

It was a cry out of the innermost part of me, where the child he had loved and lifted up still lived.

"Well, you can come take care of her clothes, if you want to do something for me," he said, smiling a little. "I thought I could do that, but it turns out I can't seem to."

"I will," I said. "I'll start on it in the morning."

But I couldn't, either. I got up the next morning so freighted with heaviness and darkness that I could scarcely breathe; I thought I was actually sickening with some sort of virus. After breakfast I threw up, something I do so rarely that the very throat and stomach muscles involved felt alien, and I realized that I could not sort through my mother's clothes, could not touch and finger and fold away her spare little dresses and sweaters, could not handle her hats. They would smell of her and her smell would cling to me; they would swarm with memories, like bacteria. The bacilli of love and rage and hurt that they harbored would paralyze me. I rinsed out my mouth and called Carrie Davies, who had said she would do anything, anything at all that I needed. I got her answering machine.

I called Livvy.

We met at my parents' condominium. My father was not there. He had, he'd said on the phone that morning, some things he needed to pick up around town, and then he was going to lunch with Harry and a couple of his other fishing and football cronies. I knew he would be collecting things of Mother's that she had left in the various dressing rooms or offices of the theaters and auditoriums where she had acted and danced.

"If it's too hard, I can do that," I said. "But I'm glad you're going to see people. It's the way, isn't it? Just start right in? I hope it helps, Daddy."

"No, I want to do it," he said. "And I don't know if it's the way or not. Is there a way? I don't think it's going to help much, baby, but you can't sit down and die, too, can you?"

Why not? I thought suddenly.

"Of course not," I said.

So Livvy and I went into the orderly, banal rooms where my parents had lived the latter part of their lives together, and into the bedroom that my mother had used, and into her closet, and I watched as Livvy methodically folded away her things into the plastic leaf bags I had brought. Afterward we would take them to the Salvation Army. It was not so hard after all, not if I did not have to touch her clothing. I could watch. I could do that.

"Isn't there anything you want?" Livvy said as we got ready to carry the bags to my car. "Some of her things are lovely, and they're in perfect condition. You'll be sorry later if you don't keep something."

"No. Nothing would fit me. And her handbags and accessories would just look silly. They're for little people. They'd look like toys on me."

"Keep this," Livvy said. "You'll regret it terribly if you don't keep something, so keep this. It would make a terrific sun hat if you took the flower off."

She tossed the black hat my mother had worn to our last dinner, at the Ritz-Carlton, on to the bed, and I smiled in spite of myself. Livvy was right. I found that I did want it, after all. My mother would indeed follow into the rest of my life in the warp and weave of her big black hat.

"You know," she said as we trudged out with our bags, "you and that hat should just get on a plane and come up to the Vineyard in a month or so. I'm going up by myself then; Caleb isn't coming till much later. We'd have all that time together, with no obligation and no pressures, just you and me and the beach and the ocean."

"I can't be social now, Livvy," I said. I knew that she and Caleb knew half the summer population of Martha's Vineyard.

"We won't be," she said. "I don't want to, either. You'd be a great excuse. You know, you've never really been anywhere on your own, without Tee and or the children along. You ought to see how it feels. You might end up liking it very much."

"Next year, maybe . . . "

"Why 'next'?" I saw that she was going to push it. "Why, exactly?"

"Well, Teddy and school and all . . . "

She just shook her head impatiently, but she did not say anything else.

My father left two days later for Lake Homosassa with Harry and Martin Short and Philip Hines. I had been spending a good part of each day with Daddy, though he had not asked me to, and I got up very early and went over to say good-bye on the morning that they left. In the hot, colorless dawn he looked much thinner and older, and so ill and bruised that I had the sudden, panicky feeling that he would not be coming back to me. I hugged him fiercely.

"Please call me every day," I said into the shoulder that, as it always had, smelled of starch and laundry powder, clean and acid.

"I'm going to be out on the lake most days," he said. "How about once every two or three days?"

"Daddy . . . what if I need you?"

"What if you don't?" he said, and hugged me hard. I didn't say any more, and they drove away, and I stood staring in the driveway until Harry's old wagon vanished around a long curve of Peachtree Road. Then I went home and sat down on the patio and drank a cup of coffee. Teddy was spending the night at T. J. Campbell's house.

"I don't know where my folks are," I said aloud into the brightening day. Nothing in the still air responded.

In the following weeks I fussed over Teddy until he became distant and sullen with me, and after we had an out-and-out fight, ugly and flaming with accrued pain, I realized what I was doing and called Caroline and Alan and arranged for the visit that they had said they wanted. Caroline sounded distracted and dull; of course I must come immediately, she said, they'd been waiting for me to decide when. But she did not sound glad. She did not sound any way at all. The pretty lilt that had always lived in Caroline's voice, that always seemed to me so essentially Southern, was gone. Anger at Tee flared afresh, for the dying of his daughter's lilting voice.

From Tee, back from his fire-walking, I heard nothing. There were no more calls from Sheri Scroggins, either. The whole world seemed caught in a bubble of hot, stale timelessness. I was glad, finally, to board the plane that took me out of my own summer miasma and into that of Memphis.

But it was not a good visit, and I cut it short by two days. Caroline was so faded and snappish that she seemed someone I hardly knew; there was literally nothing left of the flush of easy vivacity about her that had always reminded me so of Tee. Alan was distracted and silent; he often stayed late at his office, apologizing and talking of a landmark case being readied for court. The baby slept, cried, and slept. Caroline had a cleaning woman and an afternoon sitter for the baby, and we did indeed go to lunch and shopping and around to see the sights of Memphis, but the heat and humidity were stupendous, and we did not talk much about anything of substance. Every time I ventured into her life, or spoke of mine without her father, her eyes filled with tears and she cut me off sharply and shrilly. She did not say so but I knew that she was still angry with me for not, somehow, preventing Tee from leaving her, and I knew that if I stayed much longer, the childish hurt I felt at her accusatory pain would turn to anger, and I would widen and harden the gulf between us that was, I hoped, still temporary. So on the third day of my visit, when the baby developed one of the indistinguishable thin, mewling, summer colics that the children of the South are heir to, I simply went home. Caroline wept and hugged me and promised a long Christmas visit and did not protest my leaving. I felt nothing on the trip home but fatigue and relief.

When I got out of the cab and went into the house in Ansley Park, the front door was unlocked and I heard voices on the patio. I had not expected Teddy home from Eddie's parents' summer place in Highlands until the weekend, and my heart lifted. I was finding that among the myriad small deaths surrounding this separation, one of the worst was coming home at twilight to an empty house. The thought of hugging my son and Lazarus made me as giddy as a sudden whiff of pure oxygen.

"Guess who's coming to dinner?" I called out, and ran through the dark library and out on to the sunny patio.

Instead of Teddy and Lazarus, it was Tee, who looked blankly up at me from the chaise. Sheri Scroggins, in shorts and a tank top, sat at his feet. Both were frozen in place, sweating tall glasses in hand. Both stared at me as if I were trailing tattered grave accouterments.

I felt that patio wheel around me. It was like walking into the wrong house. Tee's long body owned this patio. I had seen it stretched out there on the chaise countless times. I almost expected to see my own face on the body of the woman who sat at his feet.

"Molly—" Tee began. My heart lurched at the sound of his slow, deep voice saying my name.

"I want you to go now," I said. I sounded in my own ears like a prissy little girl mouthing words her mother had taught her.

Sheri stood up. Her body was splendid; it did not look real in the slanting afternoon light. It simply had no imperfections. She made a smile, which did not reach her eyes, of her long red mouth. After the first glance, I did not look at her.

"You had no right to come into my house when I was gone," I said to Tee. "I want you to leave, and I don't want you to come back again . . . "

But my heart shook with my wanting him to stay.

It was Sheri who answered me.

"It's his house, too, Molly," she said in the grating twang that I had come to loathe. "In fact, it's solely his house, I believe. Your name is not on the deed."

I still did not look at her.

"Why are you here?" I asked my husband.

"I wanted to see it," Sheri said again. "I wanted to see Tee's house. There was no reason for me not to. We'd have called before we came, of course, but we didn't know you'd be here. Tee's been having some ideas about it, haven't you, Teeter?"

She smiled down at him around the dreadful nickname.

Tee still did not speak. He just looked at me.

"Cat got your tongue?" I said. I knew I sounded bitchy. I could think of no right way to talk to this man who was and yet was not my husband. I wished that they would just vanish, and I could go upstairs and go to sleep.

"I've been thinking that it might be a good idea if I bought the house from you, Molly," he said finally. He looked at Sheri, not at me, and I knew whose good idea it was. This woman had come with my husband into our home, and seen it, and wanted it for herself.

"The house is not for sale," I said.

"That's really not your decision to make, is it?" Sheri Scroggins said.

"Shut up," I said to her, and to Tee, "You want my house, too?"

He looked at me then. There was something new in his eyes, a kind of edge, a thin hardness like lacquer.

"I'm prepared to make you an extremely generous offer for it," he said.

My throat thickened until I could scarcely push words past it.

"You said . . . you said it would be mine always," I said. "You *said* that. You said it the first night, when you told me about all this. You said anything I wanted or needed. I assumed you meant the place we live, the place the family lives . . . "

He looked away, and I could no longer see the new hardness.

"You assume a lot, Molly," he said in a low voice.

"When did I get to be the enemy, Tee?" I said.

He looked down at the bricks of the patio. I did, too. I thought of the autumn weekend we had laid them, he and I, an October long ago, with Teddy helping resignedly and Lazarus tracking wet grouting in and out on his big paws.

"Don't, Molly . . ." Tee said.

"You don't need this big house, Molly," Sheri Scroggins said. She spoke soothingly, as you would to a child or a demented person. "Why would you want it? A big old white elephant . . . with what we're prepared to give you, you could get yourself the most fabulous condo in Atlanta, or another, smaller house . . . anything you wanted. But we all need to be sensible now, and get down to talking about specifics. We've let this go on too long as it is. Can't you see the sense in letting Tee have it?"

"No, I cannot see the sense in it, because this is my fucking home, you idiot," I shouted at her. Her face went still and narrow.

"My life is here," I said into the fox-sharp face. "My memories are here. My history is not disposable, and if it was, it would not be to you. Do you understand me?"

She was silent, then she shrugged.

"I wouldn't be so sure of that if I were you," she said.

"Sheri," Tee said.

"No!" Her nasal voice cracked like a lash in the still, thick air. "I'm tired of placating her! I'm sick of soothing, and indulging, and waiting for her to be reasonable about all this! *I'm running out of time, Tee!*"

She turned and stormed off the patio. Her butt did not jiggle in the short, tight pants, I noticed. At the door she turned.

"You make her understand that," she said, and vanished.

I just stared at Tee. He looked back. Presently he shrugged, a tiny movement.

"You look pretty, Molly," he said. "I like your hair that way."

I turned away and stood looking over the ivy-carpeted wall at the skyscrapers of midtown. We had often stood here just so, he and I, looking at them; we were suburban enough so that their proximity still charmed and thrilled us.

"Get out of here, Tee," I said.

He went without saying anything else. In a few moments I heard the front door shut.

Teddy and Lazarus came home around dusk. I was still sitting on the patio. With his newly developed antennae for trouble, Teddy knew at once that something was wrong. I told him about finding his father and Sheri Scroggins on the patio when I got home from Memphis.

I thought that he would be outraged, but he was not surprised. My mind made one of those in-the-air connections it seems to make when pain and crisis have sharpened it.

"They've been here before, haven't they? When I've been away? Did you tell them when the coast was clear?"

It wasn't fair, but I was past that.

"They've only been here once," he said, sitting on his spine and regarding his long legs stretched out before him. Tee sat that way often. "That I know of, anyway. I didn't tell them anything. It was the afternoon you left for Caroline's. I don't know how they knew you were gone."

"And you just let them in."

He lifted his head and stared at me. There was a too-old weariness on his face.

"He holds the deed, Ma. He can come in whenever he wants to, and bring whoever he wants to," he said.

"And you were here the whole time?"

"Yep."

"With her."

"I don't even think about her."

"This is *our* house, Teddy," I said, foolish tears starting in my eyes. I struggled to keep my voice steady. "This is *our* home. This is the family place."

Suddenly he was on his feet, shouting.

"I miss him, Ma, okay? I love him and I miss him. I can't . . . just because you . . . Ma, *listen*—"

"Teddy—"

"No. Listen. Go on and do it, Ma. Just go on and do it. This way . . . it's just . . . it's not going to change anything, and I can't stand it any longer! Give him the goddamned divorce and let's get us some lives! I can't look after you anymore, Ma!"

I could not get a deep breath.

"Of course you can't," I whispered finally. "I wouldn't want you to. I've never wanted you to do that. I mean, your trip, school . . . I *want* you to do those things. You know I do, don't you?"

He scrubbed his fists angrily in his eyes.

"Ma, how can I do those things until I know you're able to . . . get on with things? That you're looking at some kind of life ahead of you? Dad isn't coming home, you know that. Don't you know that? I've tried to be around as much as I could, until maybe you do know it, but, Ma . . . I can't take his place."

"Oh, God, baby, I *never* wanted you to do that," I said in pain.

He just looked at me.

The next morning I called Livvy and got the name of the lawyer from her, the one she had said could make mincemeat of Ken Rawlings. I called and made an appointment. And then I called her back.

"Were you serious about having a guest at the beach?"

"Is the pope a Catholic?"

One month later, almost to the hour, I huddled in a bucketing seat behind a seemingly teenaged pilot on a seemingly toy Cape Air commuter plane out of Boston, peering through the open curtain over his shoulder into a wall of solid, swirling, white fog. In my cold hands I clutched my mother's big black hat. Behind me a dozen or so other passengers read or napped or fussed over children; no one but I seemed convinced that death was imminent. Just behind me two whining children accompanied by a grim-faced man unwrapped a ribbon-tied box of Godiva chocolates and began to demolish them.

"Fine," the man said. "I'll just tell Mrs. Michaels that you ate up her hostess gift."

Divorced daddy, I thought through my terror, glad to be distracted from it. "Got the kids for a week's vacation and wishes he didn't. I don't know who I pity the most."

The plane gave a great, wallowing lurch, and I stifled a small scream, and shut my eyes, and when I opened them the fog was parting and I could see, far below, the lights of a tiny runway winking steadily. The plane banked sharply and plunged toward them.

"Spencer Tracy and Van Johnson and I thank you," I said to the baby pilot, voluble with relief.

"Yeah?" he said. "Well, you're welcome. Glad to oblige."

I knew he had no idea at all who I was talking about. When he had bumped the plane down on to the tarmac and brought it to a jack-rabbiting stop, he opened the door and held his arm out to me so that I could step out on to the flimsy metal steps. Down here the fog still swirled.

"You have a nice time on the Vineyard, now," he said, and I thanked him and ducked my head and stepped out of the little plane into nothing at all.

CHAPTER FIVE

LIVVY PICKED ME UP AT THE STARK LITTLE AIRPORT that serves the Vineyard, and drove me through the stunted, fog-shrouded state forest in the middle of the island, over to Edgartown and Chappaquiddick. She drove a battered, old green Jeep Cherokee that lurched and bucketed over the pitted tarmac, and all the way to Edgartown and then to the Chappaquiddick ferry she chattered. Livvy did not chatter at home; indeed, she denigrated, in her dry, honking, rich-Yankee voice, all our friends who did. Since that included most of the women we knew jointly, Livvy honked about it quite a lot. I might have pointed this out to her in other circumstances, but on this fog-haunted drive I was so overwhelmed by the pervasive strangeness of everything that I could only sit and watch the sliding, shifting landscape lurching past outside, and listen to her tumbling spate of words.

"It's pretty, isn't it, in the fog? Well, it's pretty all the time, but I like it especially when it's foggy. It might be a hundred or two hundred years ago, any time at all, really. I miss these fogs in Atlanta. I've never seen one on a Southern beach, not in summer. The water's too warm. They're caused by warm, wet air meeting cold water, you know. Our water's pretty cold out there, especially on the Atlantic side. Look how the trees press right up to the road; what does that remind you of? Almost every part of the Vineyard reminds people of different places . . . "

"Transylvania?" I ventured. The gnarled tree trunks and dark chiaroscuro of leaves outside, seen through scarves and skeins of drifting fog, did look eerie. Anything at all might appear out of that mist; you might hear the breaths and cries of anything . . .

She grinned.

"A lot of people think it looks like the Black Forest, or the Vienna woods. I always think of Sweden when I drive through here. I spent two interminable days on a train going through Sweden, right out of college, and I swear it looked just like this. Scrub oaks and pines, with some taller pines thrown in. Endless trees, as flat as a flounder. I thought I'd die of boredom till we got to Stockholm. We played bridge all the way."

"Of course, Sweden," I said acidly. "What was I thinking of?"

I had never seen the Black Forest or the Vienna woods, nor the monotonous forests of Sweden. The traditional postgraduation European tour I might have taken was preempted by my June wedding to Tee and our Ocho Rios honeymoon. Caroline came along the summer after that, and in due time, Teddy, and then our traveling was limited to places toddlers would be tolerated. Later we traveled to Mexico and Canada and several places in the Caribbean, but these, too, were family sorties; we had been saving Europe because we knew that there was a very good possibility that Tee would be posted there. I had thought we would have ample time then to see Europe's magical places from a base in London or Paris or Rome. Now they would shed their magic on Tee and the Eel Woman. I wished, suddenly and fiercely, that I had insisted on the graduation trip my parents had offered before I rushed to the altar, and took only a modicum of comfort from the fact that the one who might most have savored saying "I told you so" was past saying anything at all.

Livvy took no notice.

"There's a part of the Vineyard that looks almost Caribbean; that's our part, with the blue, blue water and all the white sails and the flowers and the white sand. And there's a part that looks for all the world like Bermuda, right around Edgartown, and a part that looks like the English Lake District. And there are parts that could easily be the Scottish moors, up island . . . "

"Up island?" I said. Somehow the word wrapped itself around

my chilly heart like warm, cupped hands. It sounded remote and unreachable, safe above the swarming countryside, kissed by sun and air.

"Up island . . ." I repeated it.

"The west part of the island, back that way," Livvy said, gesturing. "I forget why it's called up island and the east part down island. It's mainly where the year-rounders and the old families live. There are some awfully grand summer houses up there, but mostly the summer people congregate around Edgartown and Oak Bluffs and Vineyard Haven, down island. I guess it's because there are so many good places to keep a boat. A lot of up island is wild coast and rocks. Summer people tend to be boat people."

"Are you and Caleb boat people?"

I had never heard Livvy talk much about sailing, or anything else that she and Caleb did in this chameleonlike place. It seemed a destination so apart from her life in Atlanta that I thought she simply saw no point in speaking of it. Now I wondered how we could have become so close without my knowing whether or not, in her summers, Livvy sailed a boat.

"Yep," she said. "I have a little catboat that's really the kids', but I sail it more than they do. And Caleb has a Shields. He'll take us out when he gets up here, but you'll like sailing with me in the catboat better. It won't scare the piss out of you like the Shields when he puts it on its lee rail. The cat's a nice, fat, wallowy little boat just perfect for gunk-holing."

"Gunk-holing . . ."

"I think it means just messing around. I don't hear it anywhere but up here."

"You've even got your own private language."

"Oh, you bet. For example, I'll show you some beetlebungs in a little while. And if you were here in the spring, you could hear the pinkletinks."

"I'm not going to ask. It all sounds insufferable," I said, meaning it.

"Well, I'm not going to tell you, so there," Livvy said happily, and turned right; suddenly we were out of the misty countryside and in the heart of the barely controlled chaos that is Edgartown in high summer.

"I don't think I ever saw so many people in such a small space," I said, turning my head this way and that to take in the tangle of crowded, cobbled streets and lanes that converge downtown in that primmest and prettiest of little New England towns.

"It's the rain," Livvy said. "Brings them into town in droves. Merchants love rain."

Scrimmed with mist and occasional rain showers, the cobbles gleaming wetly, the street lamps, lit against the dark day and haloed with iridescent collars, the town center might have been a slice out of another time, a preservationist's fondest dream. But the blatting, honking, barely creeping tide of automobiles jockeying for nonexistent parking spaces belied the dream, as did the well-lit shop windows displaying antiques, upscale casual clothing, fancy foodstuffs and wine, and an astronomical number of realtors' signs given the size of the town. The people hurrying through the slanting rain, their heads ducked or shielded by golf umbrellas, might have belonged to another time, though, shrouded as they were with billowing raincoats or slickers and hats—except for their feet. Surely no former citizens of Edgartown, corporeal or otherwise, ever wore deck shoes without socks. Almost every foot I saw that morning, however, was Top-Sidered and sockless. I glanced down at Livvy's feet; she, too, wore weathered brown deck shoes that left her tanned ankles bare. My sturdy navy Ferragamos almost itched with wrongness on my sodden feet.

"I don't have any deck shoes," I said. "Will I have to go home?"

"No, but you can't go out anywhere," Livvy said. "You'll embarrass your hostess beyond belief. I think there are some around the house that will fit you. They get left behind in droves."

"I could buy some."

"Oh, God, no. They can't look new. You really *couldn't* go anywhere then."

"I thought you said we weren't going anywhere anyway," I said. "That was the whole point, just to kick back with you. No social stuff."

"Well, there won't be any strictly social stuff," Livvy said, not looking at me. "Just drinks now and then with some people you'll like, and maybe some sailing, and sunning at the beach club. Real laid-back. It's just us, Molly."

I was silent. Livvy's "just us" was no one I knew. I felt a faint stirring of anxiety, down deep where the numbed rage slept. I had never considered that there was a whole other Livvy Bowen who was old-shoe familiar to people I did not and probably never would know. The anxiety stretched and flexed. What if she was another Livvy altogether? What if my Livvy, the one to whom I had fled for refuge and peace on this strange, misted island, no longer existed?

"You don't have to put your head out the door if you don't feel like it," Livvy said, waving at a couple who huddled on a street corner, laughing. "But I think it would be good for you if you did. Nobody up here knows you as the other half of Tee; they'll take you at face value, and they'll love you, and that will do more for your spirits than six months of therapy. You'll go home ready to lick your weight in tigers, not to mention the loathsome Eel Woman."

The anxiety gave a savage lunge and made it into my upper chest, almost bursting out of my mouth. Before I had come to the Vineyard I had, at Carrie and Charlie Davies's urging, had a couple of sessions with a psychiatrist who was a med school buddy of Charlie's. The doctor pointed out that the sudden wildfires of anxiety that had begun to overtake me at unpredictable moments, ever since I had called my new lawyer, were almost surely manifestations of the rage and sorrow that I could not seem to express, and that until I had worked through the original emotions, I could expect more of the outbursts of near panic. He had suggested a course of therapy beginning immediately, but I wanted, all of a sudden, nothing but to get out of Atlanta and on to Martha's Vineyard, and said that maybe I would consider it when I got back.

He did not like the idea of my running away, but did not push the therapy, and wrote me a prescription for Xanax and one for Prozac. I still had them, unfilled, in the bottom of my bag. Watching the boiling crowd of wet people on the narrow streets, some of whom I would probably have to meet and spend time with, I wished that I could swallow several of each. The anxiety was really quite uncomfortable. It rarely lasted very long, but it left my hair soaked with perspiration and my hands trembling.

"If it gets too bad, try to face it and examine it," my shrink had said. "Sometimes it will go away if you look at it and see what it really is. Of course, the best thing would be to tell your husband

and your brother and your mother just what you think of them, but you're obviously not ready to do that. So look the fear in the face and see what's there."

So I did. In the middle of teeming Edgartown, stalled in traffic by a seemingly endless line of creeping four-wheel-drive vehicles, I looked inside myself to see what it was I was so afraid of. And I saw only emptiness.

I had never been afraid of strange places before, had loved them, in fact; had been hungry to taste and explore and experience the very differences of each new place that we went. But the operative word was "we." I had never traveled without Tee. Wherever in the world I went, I went as part of a unit, part of the family of Theron Redwine, and was therefore safe because I knew precisely who and what I was. My basic self could not be changed, could not be lost.

But travel does change you. We know that instinctively; it is for that, I think, that we leave our homes and go looking for the rest of the world. Not just to see it and know it, but to be changed by it. Or, at least, the strong and healthy and safe among us do. The others— those of us who have suddenly lost ourselves or never really had them—are instinctively afraid of strange places. If the shards of self we take to them are themselves changed, what will we have left? Who, then, will we be? Will we be anyone at all?

Will we look inside and see emptiness?

I sat in Livvy's Jeep that morning and literally shook all over with the terror that I would lose the last remnants of myself on this island, and never be able to get me back. And hated myself for the fear.

"Are you okay?" Livvy said. "Your hands are shaking."

"I haven't had any breakfast or lunch," I said, forcing normalcy out between dry lips. "Are you going to feed me?"

"Chowder," Livvy said. "Made from clams I dug myself this morning, before you even thought about getting up. It's the only thing for a day like this. And first a Bloody Mary. How does that sound?"

"Like I've died and gone to heaven," I said, and it did. The anxiety went sulking back to its pit. The people on the streets looked benign and agreeable again, even their feet. Maybe I really was only hungry.

We finally inched our way on to the wallowing little On Time Ferry—"because any time it runs is on time"—and were decanted into the equally dense fog of Chappaquiddick Island, where the Bowens' summer house was. All I knew of Chappaquiddick was the painful incident of the young Massachusetts senator and the drowned secretary, and that seemed so antiquated now as to be merely quaint, an anecdote out of another time. I looked about curiously, but could make out only swirling mist and rain and the blurred shapes of low trees and scrub.

"The beach club is over there, but you can't see it," Livvy said, pointing, and I looked, and indeed could not. "We'll go swim and have lunch tomorrow. It's supposed to fair off."

Just past a phantom gas station and a community center, she swung the Jeep hard right. The fog thickened, until the yellow fog lights seemed to bounce off its solidity. I could see nothing at all. Then she turned right down a smaller lane and bumped slowly past the great masses of what I supposed to be summer homes, and pulled into a gravel and sand drive at the very end of the lane. A vast grayness loomed up before us, seeming to reach high into the sky, supposing that you could have seen the sky, and she cut the Jeep's engine and said, "We're here."

We sat silently for a moment, and by some trick of the wind off the water the fog parted for a moment, like a curtain being swished aside, and I saw a tall Victorian house dead ahead of us, shingled in dark gray-brown and girdled around with stone-pillared porches. Even here, at what was obviously its rear entrance, it looked imposing and formidable, bearing its bulbous curves and mansards and turrets upright, like an old corseted dowager. A few dark pines leaned over it, old trees by the gnarled look of them, and the latticework around the back door dripped tangled vines of old white roses. A severely clipped privet hedge ran beside it on both sides, around to the front, turning a faint sepia and russet-red with the looming autumn, and there seemed an infinity of white-shuttered windows, all blank like sightless eyes, and many chimney pots, scrabbling fingerlike at the thick sky. No lights burned.

"My lord," I breathed involuntarily, and Livvy laughed and said, "Welcome to Harbor House," then the fog swept in again and left me looking only at whiteness, though beyond the house I could sense, if not see, the immense presence of water.

"You said it was a cottage," I said, reaching into the back of the Jeep for my suitcase.

"Well, we call everything on the Vineyard a cottage if it's seasonal," she said. "It's the Old Yankee ethos, you know. Plain living and high thinking."

"You couldn't live plainly in that if you tried," I said.

She snorted. "Wait till you've seen the inside. It's falling apart, but Caleb won't let me change anything from the way it was when he was a boy unless it's rotted and fallen in under you, and then it has to be as much like the original as possible. What I wouldn't give to fill the damned thing up with Ralph Lauren and microchips."

"You do have electricity, don't you?" I said. Under my feet the porch boards creaked and yawed.

"Barely. Caleb only lets me light one room at a time, the one we're in, and even then it has to be an old forty-watt bulb like his sainted grandmother used. Sometimes he even gets out the goddamned oil lamps."

"And you with every computerized gizmo in the world in your house at home," I said, grinning. "And Caleb with Windows 95. Why don't you light it up like the Atlanta stadium when he's not here?"

"He reads the electric bill with a magnifying glass. I've long since gotten used to the idea that my husband goes a little mad when he gets up here. It's the Bowen family curse. But now that you're here, I'm going to burn every light in the house all day long, and tell him you've got seasonal affective disorder and it's doctor's orders."

She opened an ornately scrolled screened door, reached in and flicked a switch, and the living room of Harbor House bloomed into dim, yellow light. I followed her in. Even cowed by the fog and the darkness of the big house and shaken with the dregs of the anxiety, I had to laugh. It looked like a stage set for *The Addams Family*. Age-darkened vertical planking covered the walls, wainscotted halfway up with a plate rail full of mauve, floral-painted china. The dark floors were covered with thin, worn, old orientals and islands of dismal straw matting. The walls held portraits that had either faded badly or needed their glass washed; I could make out no faces. What light there was came from antiquated old wall-mounted or hanging fixtures grudgingly wired for electricity, and from a few table and bridge lamps set about. The light they gave out was the color of pale urine. The furniture was dark, ornate, antimacassared or shawled, and looked militantly unsittable. Curved and balustered stairs in a corner led up to an open upper gallery from which a series of closed doors led into what I assumed were bedrooms. In the immense, murky space above the first-floor living room hung a great, grotesque chandelier made exclusively of antlers. Looking farther, I could see that mounted heads of who knew what were hung around the room, just under the gallery. I thought you might well find a griffin up there in the gloom, or a unicorn.

"So where's the staff?" I said. "Hanging upside down from the ceiling waiting for dark?"

"Don't I wish," Livvy said, striding through the dark room toward the front of the house. I followed her.

"I'd gladly take a staff of vampires over none at all," she said over her shoulder, "but I've only got a lady who comes to clean once a week. Caleb thinks servants are ostentatious on the island. Of course his family's got about a hundred in Boston. But Mamadear, his virulent old grandmother, never had them here; said she came to rusticate, not to live like she did at home. So of course I can't have them either. Old bat. I guess it doesn't really matter. Nobody ever goes into the back drawing room unless there's a big party. We live in the front of the house and upstairs, and even Caleb is smart enough to shut up about preserving that."

We went through another dark old door and I saw what she meant. Here at the front of the house, overlooking the invisible water, were low-ceilinged, bright rooms full of shabby rugs and comfortable rump-sprung furniture, with beamed ceilings that bounced back the light. Even on this close, dark day, they glowed with warmth and use and life. A cluttered kitchen full of scarred 1950s fixtures and potted geraniums gave on to a long, window-walled room where the family obviously ate and lived: gut-spilling wicker easy chairs, cockeyed ottomans, shelves disgorging dog-eared books and games and puzzles, islands of soft faded rag rugs and one or two dingy sheepskin ones, a big trestle table surrounded with unmatched chairs, racks of sailing and tide charts, and small tables holding models of sailing vessels of every sort. Half models hung about the walls, rubber boots and sneakers and Top-Siders were scattered everywhere about the floor, and above the doors and a great, smoke-stained fireplace laid with a waiting fire hung paddles and oars and transom plates and quarter boards from vessels gone but obviously not forgotten. Beyond this room was a small paneled library so jammed with books and newspapers and magazines that only a couple of spavined morris chairs were free for sitting, and beyond all of it, outside the small-paned casement windows, the big porch held more old wicker and a hammock and a swing, and looked out into the white blankness that Livvy said was Katama Bay. I loved all of it, instantly. The knot of anxiety loosened and the cold sweat on my brow dried. I could find a lair here.

"It's perfect," I said. "I'm so relieved. I thought the whole Bowen family was richer than God, and I'd have to tiptoe around Palladian windows and gold-plated fixtures."

"Oh, they're richer than God, all right," Livvy said, touching a match to the fire. It sprang to life and began to lick at the chill with hungry little tongues. "Or we are, I guess. This is Vineyard rich. Not like Newport at all. Not even like Nantucket. No ostentation allowed. God forbid anybody add any comfort to the old places, much less luxury. The only thing that's permissible to spend money on is a fund to save the piping marsh doohickey, or one of the land trusts. And even then, you do it anonymously."

"Where's the fun in that?"

"Precisely. Oh, well. Snuggle down in that throw in front of the fire and I'll bring the Bloodies. There's lots of fun in that."

There was. We had our Bloody Marys in front of the fire, and then had seconds, and we talked and talked and talked. Or Livvy talked, of her summers here, and of the men and women and children who peopled them, and of the places on the Vineyard that were dear to her, and of the gradual rhythms that one slipped into here, if one spent a long enough time: rhythms laid down, not by a clock, but by the comings and goings of the light and the sea. I lay on the old chintz couch wrapped in damp mohair, watching the flames and listening to her spin out her fabric of summer and sky and ocean, a fabric that did not include me in its warp and woof, and so was as detachedly fascinating to watch as a movie unfolding: What would happen next? I felt mindlessly content, slung hammocklike between worlds, rocked in the rhythm of her words, lulled with fire and vodka.

We ate our chowder before the fire, too, when the pearly light went out of solid white nothingness outside and the fog was lost to larger dark. Just before we went up to bed, Livvy opened the door on to the porch and leaned her head out and sniffed.

"Wind's changed," she said. "I can smell the open ocean. It'll be fair by morning."

I got up and went and stood behind her, and took a long, deep breath, smelling it for the first time, that salt-sweet, kelp-heavy, infinitely fresh breath of the sea that I have since come to need as my own breath: the breath of Martha's Vineyard. It was like plunging your hot face into a wet, cool spray of spume. There were other notes in it, flowers, I thought. But I did not know what they were. I exhaled and drew in another breath.

"It smells heavenly, doesn't it? I've never smelled anything like it."

"There's not anything like it," Livvy said.

My room upstairs was a small, low-ceilinged cave up under the eaves, with rough, white-plaster walls and pine beams weathered the color of smoke-dark honey. A narrow iron bed was piled high with down pillows and covered with an old white pelisse spread. A mottled, ivory feather pouf lay folded at its foot. There was not much furniture, just a curly rattan writing desk and chair, a wardrobe with an organdy scarf and white china jars and bottles on it, and a ridiculous and wonderful chaise lounge made of wicker, facing the casement windows and piled with pillows and a blue plaid throw. Beside it a table held magazines and books and a rowdy bouquet of zinnias in a blue vase.

"It's a tiny little room, but it has the best view of the bay in the entire house, and I've always loved it," Livvy said. "I hide up here for hours sometimes, when the house is too full of people. And even when it's hot, it's high enough to catch any breeze that comes off the water. Open your casements tonight and pull up the pouf; it's the best sleeping in the world."

After we had hugged good night and she had gone, closing the door behind her, I did just that: I peeled out of my clothes, scrubbed my teeth in the tiny, minimal, adjoining bathroom, skinned into a long-sleeved nightgown, and opened the windows. A river of fresh sea wind flowed in. I ran across the floor and jumped into the bed, pulling up the camphor-smelling pouf and snuggling down until only my eyes peered out, gave a great sigh, and relaxed. When I was a child, I had never felt quite safe until my ears were covered with bedclothes, even if it was only a sheet on hot nights. Now I lay, covered to the ears in freshly aired old sheets and goose down smelling of sun and salt air, having only to lift my head a bit to plunge it into the great, wet-salt stream that was the living breath of the Vineyard. I lay very still, smelling it and waiting to see what would come to me, which of the old pains and sorrows I had lain with for the past weeks, which of the guilts and regrets and what-ifs. My mother: Would my mother come, in her hats and her glinting ambiguity and her disapproval? Tee, in the fresh redness of his betrayal? My father, in his quiet, inexorable grief? My needing, hurting children? Which? Who?

But no one came. I had brought none of them with me to this tall room on this fogbound island. I had landed here alone, and if I felt naked and lost to myself, I also felt lighter than I had in years. Almost—though I did not dare even think the word—free. Maybe I did not know, quite, who I was yet, and maybe no one out of my world lay beside me, but neither, so far, did pain and fear and sadness.

I can do this, I thought, and shut my eyes; when I woke, it was to the sun.

Livvy was right; there are several distinct small countries on Martha's Vineyard. From that first morning, when the sun and sea wind turned the surface of Katama Bay to blue metallic chop and Katama and Bluefish Points across it looked like a New England primitive sea scene, I could smell the separate breaths of all of them. It has been the strongest and longest held conviction of mine about the island, that when I am in one part of it I can smell the exhalations of the others.

On Chappy I can smell the peat-brown wetness of the moors of Chilmark; in Vineyard Haven I catch the loamy hot-pine-needle breath of West Tisbury. On a wild Squibnocket Beach I smell the rich, fishy exhalations of the clam flats of the Great Ponds. The rowdy scent of summer wildflowers follows me all over. The hot, dusty, tobacco-colored smell of autumn scrub oak creeps into even still, foggy spring nights in Menemsha. People talk about the great light of the Vineyard and the huge weight of the living past, but I think both are born of its disparate smells. To me, all its essential otherness is.

All this gave me, from that first day, the sense that I was in a very foreign place, separated not by seven miles but many thousand times that from the mainland. It is not for nothing that the Vineyarders say they are going to America when they mean the Cape, or perhaps to Boston beyond it.

On that first morning, I stood looking at white sails on blue water as clear and shadowless as childhood, and smelled the secret, far-dark breath of a brook that had its genesis in the high glacial moraine up island, laid down in the Pleistocene by the Buzzard's Bay lobe of the Wisconsin glacier. I did not, of course, know the facts of this, but in that smell was the dark old truth of it. Old, old . . . from the very beginning, the sheer and sentient age of the Vineyard called out to me.

"I think I'm in love," I said to Livvy, standing in my nightgown on her front porch and stretching my arms up to meet the brightening day.

"Told you," Livvy said. "So what do you want to do first? Walk? Swim? Sail?"

"Eat?"

We ate breakfast on the porch, at a small table set with a blue cloth and old Quimperware, with a mason jar full of beach roses in the center. We ate melon and sweet Portuguese bread from the farmers' market in West Tisbury, Livvy said, and beach plum jelly that she'd made herself.

"*You* made jelly? Livvy, you can't even turn the microwave on."

"Well, this is my specialty. Everybody on the Vineyard brags about their goddamned beach plum jelly; you have to learn to make it or they don't let you off the ferry. I picked the plums, too. Do you like it?"

"It's heaven. Will you give me the recipe?"

"Not on your life. Find your own beach plums. Make your own jelly. It's the law of the Vineyard."

After breakfast we took the Cherokee and went over to the ocean side of Chappy and walked on the great wind-scoured beach that stretches from Wasque Point to Cape Pogue. The glitter off the surf was relentless, and beyond it the deep blue swells of the Atlantic rolled and heaved. The wind was strong and cool, picking up the fine golden sand in little whorls here and there and tossing it high in mini-cyclones. Low dunes topped the beach, crowned with undulating green sea grass. The sand was the color of golden tea with cream, and it shone in glistening smears where the surf met its packed surface. Because of the reflections in the shining slicks, and the radiant spume that the wind blew off the tops of the breakers, nothing seemed corporeal or solid; everything was in motion, restless, breathing, murmuring, shifting. Fishermen in rubber boots stood at the edge of the surf, casting, but their reflections in the wet sand seemed at times realer than they did. It was a glorious beach, but not a soothing one, not a place where three separate great elements met in a magical stasis, as they did on our beach at Sea Island. Here everything surged and shifted, was too big, too open, too lonely. There seemed to me no human scale here.

It was beautiful though. After we had walked almost an hour we shucked off our sweatshirts and ran into the surf. After the first shock of cold, I felt as if I were swimming in champagne, or liquid diamonds. Lying in the sun afterward, feeling its red weight on my closed eyelids and shoulders and thighs, I laughed aloud in sheer well-being.

"I haven't felt this good since camp," I said to Livvy, lying beside me. I remembered it suddenly: the wonderful, weightless, washed feeling of lying under hot sun with cold water drying off your body. A young feeling, before it seemed necessary to think ahead.

"I never felt this good at camp," Livvy said. "I went to camp in northern Maine. There were maybe two days at the very end of August when human beings could swim. We swam every day from July to September. I was cold for two months."

"Did you good, didn't it? Stiffened up your spine."

"I'd rather have been spineless and warm."

We went home and showered and changed and went to the beach club for lunch. I did not want to go, but Livvy was adamant.

"You have to see somebody sometime," she said. "And if we don't go, I'll have to cook, and that means going into Edgartown for groceries, and I hadn't planned to leave Chappy for days and days. We'll just eat lunch and then go sailing. Or not, whatever you want to do."

So, because I could not gracefully refuse, I went, grumpily and defensively, in white pants and a red T-shirt and borrowed boat shoes and, as an afterthought against the sun, my mother's great floppy hat, and I had a very good time. At noon on a weekday the club was full of women and children; the few men I saw were in pairs and obviously on their way somewhere else: sailing, or golfing, or arranging hostile takeovers. The women were, on the surface, much like me and Livvy: not sleek, not coiffed, not "done." Some were young and slim and some were older and not, but none seemed unduly aware of the state of their bodies. I did not get the old Atlanta sense of body anxiety. All were tanned and many were freckled; all had well-worn, serviceably cut bathing suits or shorts or pants soft from many washings; all smiled with their unlipsticked mouths and unmascaraed eyes, displaying the sound, unbleached teeth and stubby, pale lashes of New England. All spoke in the genial honk that Livvy had. All drew me as comfortably into their ranks and their afternoon as if I had just gotten on to the island for the summer from Wellesley. Their children were like well-raised children everywhere, busy and loud and only marginally whiny. Their teenagers were remote and cool but unfailingly polite. None of either sex wore an ear or nose ring.

No one asked me what I was doing on the Vineyard. No one asked me what my husband did, or where he was. No one called my mother's hat darling or adorable, though one or two did ask me where they could get one like it.

"She inherited it from her mother," Livvy said, grinning wickedly. "It's an heirloom." I had the wit to say, "Well, she left the silver and the stock portfolio to my brother, but she knew I'd rather have something personal," and everybody laughed. It was as if I had known them a long time, these plain, solid women from the big, square houses we passed on the island, with their slightly frayed bathing suits and their open, angular smiles and their cool old family millions. I had been right the night before. I could indeed do this.

After a Bloody Mary and a wonderful baked bluefish, we went back to Livvy's house and I slept, deeply and sweatily, on the piled white bed under the rafters, and woke when the first blue of the evening was coming into the air, feeling detached and temporary, like an astral traveler accidentally parted too far from her body. The sense of being fervently alive in every cell and atom, but not having a corporeal receptacle for all this pulsing selfhood, was very strong. But it was not unpleasant. I fairly floated down the stairs to find Livvy.

We took a sunset sail in her little catboat, ghosting on the pink-mirror surface of Katama Bay as far up as the mouth of Edgartown Harbor. The harbor was full of activity: big white yachts slipping silently in past Edgartown Light, fishermen coming in with the day's bounty, launches plying to and fro, taking people to and from docks and dinner, small sailboats like ours crossing and recrossing the soft breeze. Edgartown, its lights just blooming, looked like a pointillist's painting. The afterglow from the west stained the water dappled peach. Over on Chappy the beach roses glowed on the darkening dunes, and beyond them the lights in the big houses were coming on. Smells of picnic smoke and grilling meat and fish mixed with the hundred breaths of the Vineyard. I never forgot that twilight sail. Even though we repeated it practically every night for almost two weeks, it is that first night that I remember when I look back now.

Day followed golden day, in a run of clarion-clear weather that had everyone saying, "It just doesn't seem possible that fall is right around the corner, does it? Not possible that pretty soon we'll be back home and school will have started . . . "

I shut my ears to those wistful, end-of-summer eulogies. I did not want to hear them, and somehow managed not to. Time was, for me, suspended in the amber of those perfect days, each one as same and whole and simple and seamless as an egg. Fall was not coming for me. School was not starting for me. On the top level of my mind I knew that summer was slipping by, that in a matter of days Caleb would be joining us for his annual holiday, and then he and Livvy would begin closing the house and getting the boats hauled and stored, and I would pack and take an ephemeral, jackrabbiting little airplane back to Logan and then a lumbering Delta jet on to Atlanta. But the other levels of my mind did not know this, and for long stretches at a time I forgot that I was a woman contemplating divorcing her husband for his adultery with a younger woman; a woman who had run away to an island to hide; a woman with, suddenly, a dead mother and a grieving father and an angry, heartbroken son and daughter and a puzzled, anxious dog and a medium-sized house in a silly little enclave of a big city, all to which I owed allegiance and service. I don't think any essential wounds began to heal, precisely; it was far too soon for that. But I do think that, in those long summer days, the bleeding began to stop.

"See?" Livvy said over and over. "I told you. Didn't I tell you?"

"You did," I said. "I'm sorry I ever doubted you. I'll never argue with you again."

We walked, late one night, along South Beach, with Edgartown Great Pond on our right and the star-silvered Atlantic on our left. It was the time of the Pleiades, that great, late-summer meteor shower, when the very sky above you arcs and blooms with huge, hot flowers. We had been to dinner at L'étoile, in the Charlotte Inn in Edgartown; my treat, because I wanted in some measure to repay Livvy for what her island was giving me. We wore silky, unaccustomed dresses, but no panty hose, and carried our high heels in our hands. Livvy had said we ought to see the meteor shower from the beach, away from most of the lights. It was spectacular, magical, and we oohed and ahhed with the rest of the shadowy people who were out in the soft, warm, black night to see the stars fall out of the sky.

Abruptly, my eyes pricked with tears, the first I had felt in a long time. But they were not, now, tears of hurt.

"I want to thank you," I whispered to Livvy. "I mean it. Before I came up here I didn't know if I could . . . do all this. But now I know I can. As long as you're here, I can do it."

She was silent for a time, and then she said, "This is just like school, isn't it? You and your best friend out on an adventure that doesn't have anything to do with anybody else, certainly not with any man. Or no, not school, but right after, when you're out and working and you've made your first adult best friend, and you're off doing something totally perfect that's important just because it's the two of you who want to do it, not to please any man, but just to please yourselves. I remember it from my first year working in Boston, before I met Caleb. It was very heady. Very grown-up, if that's not too silly a way of putting it. Somehow it defines you for yourself."

"Grown-up indeed," I said, and hugged her shoulders lightly. But the euphoria was gone. I really did not know what she meant. I had never done that, never had a grown-up best friend and gone off with her on an adventure designed simply to please ourselves. This was my first sense of it, that taste of liberating, solitary wine. All before had been shared with Tee.

The essential gulf between Livvy and me yawned palpably. I had not thought of it since we met. The stars seemed to dim a little in their arcs and soon stopped. We walked back to the Jeep in silence.

After that, as if the paling stars had foretold it, things changed.

CHAPTER SIX

THE NEXT MORNING I WOKE WITH MY HEAD BURIED under my pillow, a pounding sinus headache, and a dull sense that it was very late. I burrowed out from under the pouf that I had pulled up in the night and saw that though the room was filled with grayish light, as if I had waked before sunrise, the bedside clock read 9:30 A.M. I plodded heavily to the window and pulled aside the curtains. The air was opaque with slanting rain and the stunted trees along the shore were lashing in the wind.

"Shit," I said aloud to the headache and the day, and crawled back under the covers. I slept again, until Livvy's voice called me to the telephone.

I took the phone in the kitchen, where Livvy, wearing a tatty old blue sweater that looked to be Caleb's, jeans, and thick wool socks, was seated at the round oak table making lists.

"Who is it?" I said, my voice dense with sinus and sleep.

"I don't know. Some woman. Good morning to you, too," she said grumpily.

"Sorry," I muttered, feeling fussy and offended, and picked up the phone. Only then did a little knot of anxiety form in my stomach. Who could be calling me? My father was still fishing at Homosassa, Teddy was somewhere near Santa Fe with Eddie, and I knew viscerally that Tee would not call. Carrie Davies, with bad news about Lazarus, whom they were keeping? The Eel Woman?

My stomach heaved. I had all but forgotten about her; how could I have?

"Hey, sugar, how you doin'?" a sweet voice trilled. Missy Carmichael, my new lawyer. She of the Laura Ashleys, velvet headbands, and the collection of trophy testicles in formaldehyde she allegedly kept on a shelf in her office. By now I was firmly persuaded of her prowess in divorce court, but the molasses voice gave me the same shock of involuntary dismay it had when I'd first spoken with her. How could that little-girl drawl stand up against the relentless hammering of a ruthless male divorce attorney? How could it stand up to even a headstrong client, which I certainly, so far, was not?

"And those great big brown eyes and corkscrew curls," I had wailed to Livvy after she had summoned me to lunch to meet Missy. The sharklike attorney Livvy had promised had a full caseload, but recommended his young associate, Missy Carmichael, in such glowing terms that even Livvy was impressed. She met Missy before I did, on the pretext of picking something up at her shark friend's office, and had promptly arranged the luncheon. She told me, with a wicked grin, that Missy had brown doe eyes and a headful of Shirley Temple curls and stood five two in her Maud Frizons. I had called Missy, doubtfully, and the little cricket voice had done nothing to dispel my fears.

"You just wait till you see those big brown eyes narrow and hear that sugary little voice drop to a growl," Livvy said. "Carl told me she's never yet lost a case that went to court. The whole Suit Rack quails when they see her name on the docket opposite them."

"The Suit Rack" was Missy's appellation for Atlanta's corps of trial attorneys. Their name for her, Livvy said, was unspeakable. Fortunately for me, she added, she had earned it fair and square.

But the disembodied voice still sounded fey and kittenish, and my heart, already heavy with rain and a sort of premonitory dread, sank. Had Missy been the wrong choice after all?

"Reason I called is that I need a check," Missy said. She rarely minced words, I had found. "I've authorized a whole bunch of depositions and put a good private investigator on retainer, and I need to pay them up front. Stick one in priority mail to me and then I can go do my thing and you can go do yours. You wearin' your sunblock? I had a sorority sister used to go up there every summer, and she got skin cancer before she was thirty."

She named a figure that made my mouth go dry, but I promised her I'd mail the check and wear my sunblock and we hung up. It had been our agreement, the only one I thought I could live with: that she would do whatever she thought was necessary to get me the best terms possible in the divorce, and would not report to me or even contact me unless and until it was absolutely vital. The terms were mine, not hers; she disliked them intensely and, I could tell, felt contempt for me for insisting on them. She even told me that in other circumstances she would not touch a case in which she had so little contact with her client. But the partner-shark had insisted, and she was coming up for full partnership, and besides, she knew the Eel Woman from bar meetings and by reputation.

"Time somebody sank her little ship," she had said. "I'd purely love to be the one to do it. She's givin' all us girls in the bidness a bad name. And I don't have much doubt that we can mop up the floor with your honeybaby. For a big Co'Cola doowah he sho ain't playin' with a full deck. Brain has descended into his dick; I see a lot of it in guys 'bout his age. I love these cases, I really do. I might've taken this one pro bono, except you ain't poor and I ain't stupid. The one rule we got to have is when I say 'Money,' you say 'Comin' right up.'"

And I had agreed to her terms, because she had agreed to mine. I knew she would be expensive, but Tee had said anything I wanted, anything I needed, and if he were truly serious about the divorce, he would not object to the checks I wrote. I had never, in all the years of our marriage, been extravagant. The large balances he kept in our joint checking and savings accounts remained comfortable. To me, any amount seemed a fair price to pay for getting the thing done with a minimal amount of knowledge, not to mention participation. I had even left Missy a key to the house and garage, because she had wanted to get its contents catalogued and cost-estimated and I had not had the heart for that.

"Was that Missy? I thought I recognized the lisp," Livvy said when I did not speak.

"Everything okay?"

"I guess so. She needs another check. She's hiring a private investigator. God, it sounds so—squalid."

"Well, this *is* getting interesting," Livvy said. "Is she on Tee's trail, or the E.W.'s? I'd have said the latter, but you never know."

"I have no idea," I snapped, suddenly fiercely annoyed. My head hurt, and the matter-of-fact talk about the divorce made my heart flutter sickly, as it always did, and I did not like the curiosity in Livvy's voice. It sounded avaricious and mean.

"You must have some," she persisted. "Maybe Tee's got a whole string of E.W.s, everywhere there's a youth brands market. *That* ought to get you the gold watch and everything."

"Of course he doesn't!" I said. "That's not terribly funny, Livvy."

"Feeling a little snappish this morning, are we?"

"I guess we are, aren't we?"

We looked at each other, and grinned unwillingly.

"Sorry," we said together.

"It's the damned weather," Livvy said. "It looks like it might turn into a nor'easter, and that means three or four days of this shit. I hate to lose these last days to that, with Caleb coming and all."

"I don't know," I said. "It sounds okay to me. We could have fires and eat soup and read books and listen to music and drink and talk and laugh at everybody we know. You said way back that you'd like to do that."

"I didn't mean during the only time Caleb has up here," she said. "And I've hardly seen anybody yet. None of the really good parties start until the last couple of weeks."

"Who haven't you seen that you wanted to?" I said. The implication seemed clear and hurtful to me. "I certainly haven't meant to keep you from seeing your friends."

"I didn't say you had," she said, staring out at the rain. "It just sort of hasn't come up. Usually you see everybody at the end-of-summer parties, but people tend to forego those if the weather is really stinking."

"Parties . . . I didn't think there were going to be any parties."

"Well, there hardly *are* any till late summer. Oh, there are parties all over, every night if you want to go to them, but not anybody's that Chappy people usually go to. Ours are just us. You know. You've already met almost everybody."

"Not the men," I said, feeling somehow troubled and threatened by the talk of parties.

"Well, Jesus, I thought you didn't want to see any men."

"I wasn't criticizing you, Livvy," I said. "You go on to your parties; I want you to do that. I want both of you to. I'm perfectly happy staying here and reading and stuff. In fact, I'd like that."

"Well, that's going to make all these women you claim you like so much very happy. All of them have said how much they look forward to seeing you at their parties. I mean, it's just what we do up here, Molly, take ourselves to each other's parties. It's not like they're these huge social things."

"I know. It's just us. Just you," I said mulishly.

She was silent, and then turned away and gathered up her lists.

"I have to go into Edgartown," she said. "We're out of just about everything. I ought to be back before lunch, but just in case I'm not, there's some of that bluefish pâté and some crackers left, and I think some of the Greek salad. That's what I was going to fix, anyway."

"Wait a minute and let me get dressed and I'll come with you," I said, feeling contrite. I had been distinctly unpleasant to Livvy this morning. I got up and went over and put my arm around her.

"I'm sorry again," I said. "I'm being a jerk. I have the mother of all sinus headaches, and I guess I'm still not used to talking casually about all this business. Let me take you to lunch somewhere bright and warm and funky. I'd like to see the Black Dog."

She hugged me back, briefly.

"No, you wouldn't," she said. "Not in Vineyard Haven on a rainy day in August, you wouldn't. As it is I'll have to wait an hour to get on the ferry. I can promise you don't want to go out in this with sinus. Why don't you stay and make us some lunch and maybe a hot rum something or other? I do better at the A&P if I can hit it alone and work fast."

"I just thought I might find something new to read . . . "

"I'll bring you something. Really. If you get a sinus infection, I'll never forgive myself. I won't be long."

And she grabbed a yellow slicker from a peg beside the back door and was out and gone in a swirl of rain and a whoop of wind off the bay. The door slammed shut and I stood staring at it.

"Same to you, bubba," I said under my breath. But the wind

really did seem fierce, and the bay water heaved and rolled sickeningly. And the old house did indeed seem to wrap its arms around you . . .

I took a shower and washed my hair, and put on jeans and a heavy sweatshirt, then went back down to poke in the refrigerator and pantry. Livvy had, of course, only been thinking of my welfare. I felt guilty and graceless, and decided to make something hot for lunch, from scratch. The cold pâté and salad did not tempt me at all on this pelting, wind-shrieking day. And Livvy would be drenched and exhausted.

The larder really was bare, but I found some evaporated milk and two cans of clams and three ears of the native corn we had had for supper a couple of nights before. I made a kind of chowder from them, and added butter and a generous dollop of sherry. It was wonderful, hot and thick. I found cornmeal and the not-yet-washed bacon skillet, and made corn bread with the drippings. By noon I had them steaming on the countertop under cloths, and had fashioned a buttered rum thing that was so good I had one while I waited.

By one o'clock Livvy still had not come, and I had another rum. At two I put the chowder and corn bread away, and then put them back out on the kitchen table, coldly ostentatious, so that she could not miss them. Then I went upstairs and climbed into bed to sleep off the rum. For the first time since I had arrived, the house felt cold and damp.

She came in at three-thirty. When she did not come upstairs, I got out of bed and went down. She was sitting at the kitchen table, cheeks wind-flushed, drinking coffee and regarding the accusing chowder and corn bread without expression.

"I wish you hadn't bothered," she said when I came into the kitchen. "I feel like a heel. I ran into a couple of the girls in Edgartown and we decided to get some lunch. I'd have come on home if I'd known you were going to do this—"

"It's no problem," I said, magnanimous now that I had her on the defensive. "We can have it for supper."

She sighed.

"I told Gerry Edmondson we'd come for drinks and supper tonight," she said. "Peter's just gotten here, and I thought since you didn't go out today you might like a change of scene. But we surely don't have to—"

"Oh, no. I'd like to, really. I just thought, with the rain and all . . . "

For the rest of the afternoon we were unusually silent, for us, and somehow I could never seem to heave things between us back into the old, easy groove.

The evening with the Edmondsons, in a cottage half a block away and roughly the size and age of Livvy's, was not a success. I knew that this was not because of the chemistry between Livvy and Gerry and Peter Edmondson, both of whom she had gone to country day school with. So it had, by a process of elimination, to be me. I did not know what was wrong. I had laughed heartily and long with Gerry Edmondson at many of the beach club lunches and I knew that she liked me as much as I did her. You can always tell about that. And I liked chubby, sweet-faced Peter Edmondson immediately, and treated him, or tried to, with the same light badinage that I used with Caleb, or Charlie Davies. But things never jelled; Gerry's laughter was a trifle loud, and she did not often look at me but did often look at Livvy, and clung to Peter as if it had been years since she had seen him, and gradually more and more of their talk centered on people I did not know. After exclaiming and smiling until my cheeks hurt at the antics of people whose names I knew I would not remember, I gave up and went into the little library and read old copies of *Yachting* and *Audubon*. The tone of the sharp-edged, constricted talk that drifted from the kitchen softened considerably after that.

"I guess there's no sense asking you if you had a good time," Livvy said as we were getting out of the Jeep back at her house. We had not spoken until then.

"Not much," I said. I was foolishly near tears, and could not have said quite why. And then, suddenly, I did know.

"It was really true what you said to me back home, when I first told you about Tee, wasn't it?" I said thickly. "Once you're a solo act you automatically become a threat to every other woman you know. I felt about as welcome as a bastard at a family reunion! Did she think I was going to snatch Peter up to bed right before her eyes?"

"That's simply not true," Livvy said tiredly. "You're being paranoid. Gerry and Peter have one of the best marriages I know.

How could they make you feel at home? You never said anything, not a word. It's kind of hard to draw somebody out who just isn't going to be drawn."

"Be fair, Livvy," I said. "You know all you-all talked about was people I'd never heard of. What was there for me to say to that?"

She rubbed her eyes with her fists.

"We've been yanging at each other all day," she said. "Let's go to bed and when we get up, let's start over. I don't want to fight with you. I love you."

"Me, too," I said. "Let's do that."

But when I got up the next morning, to a day of wild wind and tossing gray seas but no rain, there was a note in the kitchen that said, "Gone sailing with Trish Phipps. You'd hate it in this wind. Heat up the chowder and let's have it for lunch."

And I did, and we did . . . but we shared it with Trish, who came back with Livvy. They laughed and babbled about the wildness of the wind and water, and about their ineptness, which I knew was gratuitous talk; Livvy was a good sailor and she had told me that Trish was the first woman commodore of their yacht club back home. I was silent once more. Resentment burned deep inside me like a gas flame on low.

That evening the phone rang twice, and twice Livvy said, briefly, "No, I don't think so, but thanks anyway. Maybe later."

After the second call I said, "If you're refusing things because of me, *please* don't. I'll feel awful if you do. I don't have to be with you all the time, Livvy. We're not joined at the hip."

"It's not anything I much want to do, anyway," she said. "If I really want to go somewhere and you don't, I'll go, I promise. Both of those were great, huge things for the Clintons. You knew they were on the Vineyard again this year, didn't you? They'd be terrible mob scenes, and besides, I met them last summer at the Styrons'. It's not like I'm one of his groupies."

But she was, or almost; of all my friends, Livvy was the one who, with me, not only thought Bill Clinton the better of many evils, but really liked him. I knew that she probably did want to go to his parties.

For the rest of the night I felt vaguely guilty, and could not seem to think of anything to say.

Just before bedtime, she said that she thought she might run into Boston on the early ferry with Gerry and see if her hairdresser could cut her hair.

"You're welcome to come, but you'd be bored silly," she said. "Gerry's got the dentist, and I can't think of anybody left in town who could show you around. And Gerry got the last two reservations on the ferry, though you could always try standby . . . "

"I don't think so, no," I said, knowing that she did not want me to come, or she would have insisted. "I think I might like to go and see what up island is like, though, if you don't need the car."

"By all means," she said. "But I warn you, you're probably not even going to be able to get through Edgartown. There's secret service everywhere, and Gerry says lots of the main routes are just plain blocked off."

"I think I'll try it, anyway. I love the way it sounds: up island . . . "

"Good luck," she said, smiling.

The next morning she was gone before I even stirred. Feeling like a child left behind by the adults, I got into the Jeep and clashed its gears off toward the On Time Ferry, headed up island, bound for that part of the island where, she had said, the old island people lived.

"The real people," I said aloud, not without spite.

But after all, I never got there. The harbor was so thick with boats that it looked like a field of drying laundry, and the On Time Ferry seemed permanently lodged on the Edgartown shore. After waiting in a honking, steaming line for nearly half an hour, I got out of the Jeep and walked up to the head, where a tall man in the official Vineyard men's uniform—khakis, polo shirt with an alligator on it, sunglasses—seemed to be in charge. I did not recognize him, but that meant nothing; he had the unmistakable air of one who would tell you what you could do when.

"Is there a problem with the ferry?" I said.

"It's been delayed indefinitely," he said pleasantly and neutrally. I could not see his eyes behind the black-mirror sunglasses.

"Why?" I asked, I thought reasonably enough.

Izod, or maybe Lacoste, smiled and shrugged. Neither the smile nor the shrug was large.

"Because the President is out sailing with one of the Kennedys and there's a million-to-one chance he might come into the harbor, and everybody in Massachusetts with a boat has come over to gawk," an exasperated woman behind me said. I thought I recognized her from the beach club, but if she knew me she gave no sign.

I looked back at the alligator man, who simply shrugged again. All of a sudden the whole thing made me very angry. The thought of getting out of Edgartown, of finally reaching up island, shimmered with glamour and charm.

"So we're stuck over here until he gets done with his little sail? What if there's an emergency?" I snapped.

He looked at me steadily.

"Is there?"

"No, but what if there was? There are children on this island—"

"If there's a real emergency, we can have a helicopter over here in five minutes," he said. "The ferry should be operating again in time for people to finish their errands and whatever before nightfall."

"Oh, perfect," I said, and stomped back to the Jeep and maneuvered it out of the line and turned around. I went back to Livvy's house, clashing the gears petulantly.

It was very hot and still after the two days of rain and wind, and the water looked like rippled blue silk. I thought how good it would feel, cool and tingling on hot skin, and decided that perhaps I would swim. But then I stretched out in the porch hammock and watched the boats bobbing, a solid mass stretching from shore to shore, until their motion, and that of the hammock, lulled me into a deep, thick sleep. It was not the kind that refreshes you, but the sort that imprisons and exhausts. Sometime during it I dreamed again of my mother and the barred window under the city sidewalk.

This time it was I who stared down at her silently, and she who addressed me. She still wore the black hat, the same one, I saw, that I had up in my bedroom, and I could not see her eyes under its brim, but I could see her mouth clearly, red with shiny lipstick and talking, talking. Her teeth looked bone white, perfect. Her lips moved and moved.

"You have to get up," she said. "It's very late. Why do you always do this on a school morning? You know I don't have time to keep calling you. It's the third time this week. Get up, Molly. You're sleeping your life away. Get up, get up, get up . . . "

Since I was not sleeping at all in the dream, but standing there looking down at her, I was puzzled and agitated, and tried to bend down to tell her it was not early morning back in the Peachtree Hills house and I was not in bed, but in the manner of such dreams, I could not move. The sensation of straining to do so was so strong that I could feel the ache in my arms and legs, and thought, This is no dream. But still I could not move or speak.

"Molly!" she said, loudly and sternly. "You get up this minute! I'm not going to tell you again! Getupgetupgetupgetup . . . "

She accompanied this litany by running the metal clasp of her clutch purse along the bars of the grating, making a loud burring sound. For some reason I found it nearly intolerable. I made a superhuman effort to move my muscles, and finally did, and was in the hammock again, sweat running down my neck and back, heart pounding. The burring noise turned into Livvy's kitchen phone.

I reached it on what must have been the eighth or ninth ring, stumbling and thick-tongued. It was my father. I was so stupid with sleep and the residue of the dream, so drugged with the almost palpable sense of my mother, that at first I could not think.

"Daddy, where are you? Are you here?" I said.

He laughed. "Woke you up, didn't I? No, I'm at Kevin's. That's one reason I called. I wanted to let you know I'll be here for a while."

"At Kevin's . . . what for? Are they okay?"

"They're fine. I just thought it was time I came to visit. I never really have, you know, not for any length of time. And Kevin had a little vacation time left, and we thought we might take Mandy to Jamestown and Williamsburg and maybe do a little fishing in the tidewater. Sally's doing the decorations for some kind of charity thing and this is a good time to get out from under her feet . . . "

He fell silent. For a moment I could not think of anything to say. Certainly there was no reason why my father should not visit his son and his family; but still I felt uneasy about it, as if he were play-acting his enthusiasm, talking too volubly about it. I also felt a small, unmistakable curl of what could only be jealousy, and under all of it was the formless but nevertheless firm certainty that there was something wrong with his voice. For the first time I could ever remember, even in the days just after Mother's death, my father sounded tentative, almost frail.

"Are you all right?" I asked.

"Sure I am. Can't I go visit your brother for a couple of weeks without you thinking something's wrong?"

"Of course. But . . . two weeks? You've never stayed away from home that long . . . "

After a pause he said, "Well, baby, your mother never could seem to get away for very long. Now I've got the time and nothing to keep me here. You'll be up there for another two weeks or so, won't you? And Teddy's not going to be around. I'm finding . . . I'm finding that I don't think I can stay in the condo, Molly. It didn't bother me when she was . . . you know, alive, but somehow I just can't stay there now. I'm going to stay up here awhile, I think, and Ralph's going to look for a little apartment for me—he knows what I want—until I decide where to light. Don't you worry about me. This is just what I want to do."

"Oh, Daddy, you know you can stay with us! With me—you know we've got all that room, and you'd be near everything; you could walk wherever you wanted to—"

"We've been over that, baby. I'm not going to live with you and Teddy. It's not right, and neither of us would enjoy it. I'm not at all sure you ought to stay in that house, come to that—maybe you're the one who ought to be looking for a smaller place, that you can handle alone—but at any rate, it's done. I've put the condo on the market. Ralph's doing that, too. It ought to move pretty fast. With any luck I'll have a new place before I wear out my welcome here."

"Daddy . . . oh, Daddy . . ." I said, tears near the surface, though I couldn't have said why. It was only that always before, I'd known where to find him, had a place where he was to run to, if I should need it. But I could not run to him in Kevin's house.

"Well, will you stay with us some this fall? Maybe on weekends, when Teddy's home? Will you do that?"

"Well . . . another reason I called, Molly, is about Teddy. He called last night, and asked me to talk to you about this before he called you. I didn't want to at first; he needs to fight his own battles, but after I heard, I think it makes some sense. So I said I'd put my stamp of approval on it, for what it's worth, and then he'll call you. He'll probably do that tonight . . . "

"My God, what is it?"

"Relax, it's nothing dire. Pretty good plan, in fact, I think. Molly, you know they stopped in Phoenix? Spent a couple of days there with that friend of Eddie's? Well, while they were there they went to a party given by some friend of the friend who's studying architecture at the University of Arizona, and he and Teddy clicked, and the next couple of days Teddy went around with the friend of the friend, seeing the department and the work they were doing, and some of the new stuff going up in the Southwest, and the countryside, and the upshot is that Teddy is on fire to stay out there and study architecture. I never heard him this excited about anything, Molly. I've always sort of worried because he's been so cool about everything, but he's just eaten up with this. Not just the field, but the country, the Southwest . . . he wants to design for the high desert, as he calls it; I think he really does want to do that. In fact, I think he'll find a way to do it whether or not any of us approve. So I thought I'd see if I could smooth the way a little with you, because I know you were counting on having him around the next few years . . . "

I took a deep breath while I tried to assimilate this. Teddy? Studying in Arizona? In love with the high fawn and purple cliffs of a place utterly alien to the country of his home? Building houses for that strange, inhospitable land; perhaps staying to live among its people? What on earth was he thinking; what was my father thinking, to give his approbation?

I let the breath out in a low, controlled stream, and said, "Well, he can think again. I never heard of such a thing. He's all set at Tech; I've paid the tuition, he's got a room and a roommate, he's signed up for rush . . . if he has to study architecture, and this is the first I've heard of it, he can do it just as well or better at Tech. They've got a world-class department. And besides, it would cost at least twice as much to go to school out of state, and I think architecture's a five-year course . . . I don't think his father would ever agree to that."

"He has agreed to it," my father said. "Teddy called him first. Tee thinks it's a great idea. He's already said he'd be glad to handle the cost—"

"Well, goddamn him!" I cried, rage swamping me. "Of course he said that! Anything to get back on Teddy's good side after what he's done! And besides, it'll get Teddy off his back, won't it? He won't have Teddy's accusing eyes on him everywhere he turns with that snaky bitch . . . "

"Another reason I said I'd tell you first was so that you could get this out of your system before you talk to him," my father said. "I know how hurt and angry you are at Tee. So am I. But I hope you're not going to let that interfere with Teddy's welfare. Molly, he sounded so happy. Happy like a man is happy, not like a teenager being giddy. I hope you'll think about that before tonight, when he calls. He needs to make a separate life with his father, no matter how you and Tee resolve it. And frankly, if it's going to be a long, messy process, I'd think he might be better a little apart from it. I know how you'll miss him, but this way you can plan what's right for you, without having to factor in Teddy's immediate welfare—"

"Teddy is my family! You are my family! Both of you are . . . and both of you want to leave me! What have I *done*?"

I could hardly see for the fog of red that danced in front of my eyes.

"Honey, you think about it, and you talk to Teddy, and then you call me back here in the morning. Nobody's leaving you, not really. I think of it more as maybe freeing you to look after yourself. You've never really been able to do that before. Here's your chance—"

"I don't want to be free!"

I shouted so loudly that I could hear my own voice reverberating in the still, hot kitchen. I wondered, in the ringing silence that followed my outburst, precisely where my father was calling from. I realized that I could not remember all the nooks and crannies of Kevin and Sally's elegant Georgetown row house, the one that so suited a going-places TV anchor and his perfect wife and child. Wherever he was, I knew Daddy would be alone, that he would not risk anyone else overhearing what he had to say to me. Alone in a strange house, by himself in an overdecorated corner of his son's home, reaching out in his solitude to smooth things over for me . . .

"I'm sorry I shouted," I said in a low voice. "I must sound like a spoiled brat. I think it's an awful idea, but of course I'll listen to Teddy when he calls. It's just that . . . I feel so alone, Daddy. From . . . being connected to everybody to all by myself in one summer . . . "

"I know."

I winced. He did know.

We said our good-byes and I went back out on the porch and sat down in a wicker rocking chair to think about it. I knew I would not get back into the hammock.

Daddy must have called Teddy in Phoenix immediately, because I had not sat there for more than half an hour before my son called.

"You having a good time?" he said. He sounded as if he were in the next room, and suddenly I missed him with a pull I could feel in my very womb.

"Yeah, but I miss you," I said, determined not to whine, weep, or lay any other burden on him.

"Miss you, too. Listen, I know you've talked to Granddaddy, and I know you're not too red hot on my staying out here. I just wanted to try to tell you how it is, what it means to me. It was so sudden, Ma, and I guess it sounds hasty and un-thought-out to you. But it's . . . I can't explain it right. It's like all of a sudden I literally saw the thing I was supposed to do with my life. Everything from here on out fits. It's like I was just born, somehow . . . "

My father was right. Somehow Teddy did sound, not like a boy, but a man, a man newly confronted with a passion that he knows is going to change his life. His voice made the fine hairs on the back of my neck stand up. I remembered his anguish the night I came home to find Tee and Sheri Scroggins in my house, the night I had accused him of letting them in; I remembered the cry that had seemed literally torn out of him: "Let's get us some lives! I can't look after you anymore!"

"Teddy," I said, "if that's really what you want to do, then you must do it. I only . . . I just don't know about the expenses, for one thing. Your dad says he'll be glad to handle them, I know, but he could change his mind and then where would you be? I don't know what I'm going to have in the way of money, exactly; and it might be that . . . Sheri . . . won't want him to spend the extra money, and then you'd be out there and have to come back, and that would be *so* hard . . . "

"No, Ma, she's all for it. She got on the phone when I called Dad—I guess she was listening in—and she said by all means, I should follow my bliss. She's talking about this TV thing she saw, about this guy Joseph Campbell—"

"I watch PBS too, Teddy," I said, hating Sheri Scroggins even more for making New Age twaddle out of something that had moved me deeply. "Well, I'm not surprised. That's one less of us for her to have to contend with . . . "

He was silent, and then he said, "Ma, the only reason I called Dad first was because I didn't know who would be, you know, handling the money and stuff, and I figured he probably would, and I wanted to get it all arranged without having you worry about it. I didn't want to talk to her, and I wouldn't have if she hadn't gotten on the phone. But she was decent about it, Ma. I still think she's a bitch, and I always will, but she was . . . not bad about this."

"Well, then, so be it," I said, my head literally spinning, as if with vertigo. I put out my hand to the kitchen table, to steady myself. "I guess I'm going to have another Philip Johnson on my hands. You are coming back before you start out there, aren't you? To get your clothes and things?"

"Well, I'm coming back, sure, but probably not for a while," he said. "School starts sooner out here. I'm already registered, and I'm staying with this guy I met, Grady McPherson, until Dad's check comes and I can get a place and some stuff for it. I had enough to cover registration. I've got a lot of work to make up. So it'll probably be nearer Thanksgiving. Listen, Ma . . . I can't tell you . . . I mean, I need for you to know what this means, this country and all. Ma, I want you to be okay, too. I'll probably see almost as much of you as I would have at Tech. And if you really need for me to, I can always come home . . . "

"I'm perfectly okay, baby," I said. "I'll miss you, but I'd miss you at Tech, too. We'll do fine, me and Lazarus. And Granddaddy will be around . . . "

But where will he be? And who?

"I love you, Mom. You know that, don't you?"

"I love you, too, Teddy."

I was still sitting at the kitchen table, staring at nothing at all, when Livvy and Gerry Edmondson came in from Boston, laughing and griping good-naturedly about the traffic in Edgartown and on the ferry.

"My God, what happened to you?" I said, looking at Gerry. Her left wrist was in a cast.

"I've been swanned," she said and grimaced, laughing a little.

"Swanned?"

"Yeah, and I know better, so I got what I deserved. There's a pair of swans on the Mill Pond, they've been there forever, and everybody feeds them, including me, so they're not really wild. I was up there yesterday to get some stuff at one of the roadside vegetable stands and stopped for lunch at Alley's and after lunch I took my leftover sandwich down to the pond for the swans, and there were some of the babies right up on the bank, and they came running and I started to feed them, and all of a sudden the old cob was on me like a duck on a june bug, flapping his wings and hissing. He literally broke a little bone in my wrist before I could get out of there. I forgot how fierce they are about their families. You think swans are so graceful and serene and noble, but they're meaner than hell when somebody threatens the nest or one of the babies. They mate for life, you know. You'd think I was going to swan-nap those babies . . . "

"God, that's just wonderful," I breathed. "About the way they feel about their families, not about your wrist. Lord, that must have hurt. I had no idea they were so strong. I'd love to see them sometime. Where did you say they were?"

"They're all over the Vineyard, but this particular pair are in West Tisbury, up island, and I wouldn't recommend it unless you know judo."

Up island again. Up island, where the roots of the old families went three hundred years and more deep, where the last glacier had left a near impregnable fortress, where stone walls and old forests gave order and shelter.

Where even the swans fought savagely to keep their families intact.

The tears that I could not seem to shed prickled in my eyes and nose, and I turned away so that Gerry and Livvy would not see them.

"I'd love to see those swans," I said again. "I tried to get up island today, but Clinton was out sailing and the ferry wasn't running. Nobody could get off Chappy. How long is he going to be here, anyway?"

"Through the weekend," Livvy said. "He leaves the day Caleb gets here. Listen, if you really want to see swans, I can show you those and twenty more besides. And the prettiest part of up island, to boot. It'll mean going to a party, though."

"It might be worth it to see the swans," I said. "What kind of party?"

"Well, a pretty big one, I'm afraid. But nice people. Really interesting. It's for the Clintons, as a matter of fact, the night before they leave. A thing at the Hartnells' in Chilmark. You know, he's the historian and she's the one with the fabulous gardens that've been in every magazine in the world? I think he was a Rhodes scholar too, though it would have been before Clinton. Their house is supposed to be incredible and, of course, her gardens. I've never seen them. We got invited because I was on a committee with her last summer for a literacy action thing to benefit the Tisbury Senior Center. The invitation is for me and Caleb, and since he won't be here, you've just got to come with me. That's one house I'm not about to walk into by myself. Will you, Moll? I promise we won't stay long, and I won't leave your side, and we'll stop and see the Tisbury swans and then I'll take you down to see hers. Their house is right on Chilmark Pond, and there are lots of them down there. Come on. You don't have to speak to another soul but me if you don't want to."

"Please come, Molly," Gerry said. "You'll be the one other person there Peter and I know besides Livvy."

I doubted that, but I thought suddenly how ridiculous I must seem to them, hiding in Gerry and Peter's den because they were talking of people I did not know, having to be coaxed with swans and gardens and the promise that I would have to speak to no one at a party for the President of the United States.

"I'd love to go," I said. "I don't suppose there's a chance in the world I've got the right thing to wear, but I'd love to go anyway."

"Wonderful," they cried together, and we all laughed. Soon after that Gerry left, and Livvy and I spent the best night we'd had together since the one on South Beach, drinking Merlot and eating linguica and pasta and talking of everything in the world except the fact that come autumn, Teddy as well as Tee would be gone. Somehow I never got around to telling Livvy that.

So far as the swan situation went, the trip up island was a disappointment. The fabled pair that inhabited the pond in West Tisbury was nowhere to be seen, though Livvy did point out to me the big mound of dried grass and straw on the far shore that was their nest.

"Probably out maiming small children," Gerry said sourly. She looked wonderful in a white linen sundress, her brown shoulders shining in the last of the light over the pond. She wore high-heeled sandals and had a rich paisley shawl thrown over her arm. She was, suddenly, a different woman from the one in the faded bathing suit I had laughed with at the beach club for many days. I did not know this woman. Livvy, in black silk palazzo pants and a silk halter, was more familiar; I had seen her dressed for a party many times before. But somehow, standing here on the verge of this old village pond, with a scattering of tall white houses and village buildings behind her, she was different, too. There were shadows about her that were of otherness as well as twilight and old trees.

Even without the swans, I loved up island. It was exactly right, just as I had imagined, had somehow known it would be. Traffic here was sparse. It was still and silent in the sunset light from Vineyard Sound to the west; the land gave away none of its old secrets, but it reached out for you, too, took you in. Something inside me that had been clenched and anxious, though I had not known it, relaxed. I took a deep breath and smelled rich earth and wood smoke from somewhere, and flowers drying in the sun, and somehow the earthy musk of animals. The sense of the sea was far away here. West Tisbury might be a small New England village hundreds of miles inland.

We had come across the island on the same road I had come in on, past the airport, through the state forest. Even in the fading light, the scrub oak and pines seemed dark, dwarfed, exaggerated, an operetta forest. Breaking out into the village, I seemed to breathe easier. The orderly old white farmhouses, the Congregational church and the post office and police station and town hall all spoke of a real and ongoing life, of work done and rest taken, of families who lived on the land as well as played on it.

"It's charming," I said. "It looks like everybody's dream village, the way you imagine perfect, old-fashioned life to be. Is it mostly farms around here, or what?"

"It was once, I think," Livvy said. "Not so many people farm or raise sheep anymore; to own a lot of land up here now is to be taxed to death. Lots of the old families have sold off most of their land to off-islanders and summer people. People do carpentry and plumbing and building and whatever, or have regular jobs in Vineyard Haven or maybe Edgartown and Oak Bluffs. It's not exactly idyllic. There's a lot of outright poverty on the Vineyard. Winters up here are killers. There's some money, of course; some of the old families are land rich still, if nothing else, and some of them have a lot of summer rental property. The Ponders—they're the island's oldest family, came here on a Crown grant in the middle 1600s—have about fifteen houses they rent out, I've heard, and about nine more in the family compound. You'll see and hear Ponder all over the Vineyard. The first ten generations of them were preachers, I think, and every one of them seems to have been a selectman at one time or another."

"Will any of them be at the party?" I asked.

"I doubt it," Livvy said. "I don't think they're very interested in the goings-on of the new people, even though the Hartnells have been here since the mid-fifties. I've never met one of them in all the summers we've been coming here."

Which meant, I knew, that the old families had never been asked to the parties on Chappy and most probably vice versa. That knowledge made me obscurely happy.

"What about the Portuguese? Do they mingle?"

"No. Not with us and not with the old Vineyarders. Not much, anyway, that I know of. It really is a pretty striated little island, when you come right down to it."

"Awfully small not to know your neighbors," I agreed.

"Well, that's true anywhere, don't you think?" Gerry said, rather sharply, and I realized she must have thought I was criticizing the Vineyard as a place where prejudice ruled.

"Of course," Livvy said. "You know it is at home, Molly. How many times do you go to parties in Vine City, or vice versa?"

I was annoyed, even though I knew they were both right.

"I don't think they have many parties in Vine City," I said.

There was a crisp little silence, and I retreated under the shade of my mother's hat brim. The hat was, after all, a mistake; perhaps the entire evening was. Somehow I could not seem to put a foot right these last few days. I did not know if the fault lay with me or them, but assumed, as I always had, that it was mine. In strange country, I always seemed to defer to those who were not strangers.

Like the hat.

"Oh, wear the hat," Livvy had caroled when I had come downstairs in the only fairly dressy thing I had brought, a black-silk knit pants suit in which I traveled, that showed no wrinkles even if I slept in it. It was serviceable and respectable, but not much else. The only dress I had brought was denim. The black did need something to give it panache.

"Do, it's wonderful," Gerry had agreed. "So go to hell. You'll be a sensation."

So I had put the hat on, and unbuttoned the jacket a couple of buttons to show off the chunky gold necklace I had borrowed from Livvy, and did indeed look, at least in the watery old mirror upstairs, like a carefree woman going to a big party on a summer night. I had gotten my tan back during the long beach club mornings, and it and the shadow of the hat made my eyes burn blue and my teeth flash white.

"Not bad, for an abandoned wife," I said to myself, leaning over to see if the cleavage the neckline revealed was too . . . cleaved. It looked pretty good to me, for a party. I had never lacked ample cleavage.

But now, in the silence and shadows of up island, I felt that the swooping hat was silly and theatrical, and the unbuttoned suit jacket just plain tacky. I hitched at the jacket to pull it higher, and started to button it up again, then stopped. I had meant no criticism, and I wasn't going to let Gerry Edmondson's touchiness intimidate me. She had been dour from the beginning of the evening; Peter, she said, had gotten tied up in Boston and couldn't make the party. We were, this night, three women without men. I knew that Livvy and Gerry felt the absence, but I liked it. It rather leveled the playing field.

"Let's go find some more swans," I said.

Out of West Tisbury the countryside changed again. It became wild and craggy and sweeping, a place of salt meadows and stone walls and great glacial boulders, bare and wind scoured and beautiful. Like Scotland must be, I thought. Here along South Road you could see the old houses, crowning the moors or nestled into the folds of the cliffs to the east that gentled themselves down to the ponds and overlooked the wild beaches and the sea. In the center of the island, around West Tisbury, you could see only the little over-grown lanes that led to the houses. I liked this land of gnarled open-ness, but it was the little hidden forest roads that seemed to call out to me. If I lived here, I knew that I would make for the forest like a captive wild creature finally released.

Just before we reached the turnoff for the Hartnells' house on Chilmark Pond, just past the cemetery where, Gerry said, John Belushi was buried, there was a long driveway on the right, leading up to a tall, gray-shingled house near the top of the glacial ridge. It sat alone in a cluster of leaning outbuildings, and you could tell, even from the road, that it was very old. At the roadside, beside the driveway, a hand-lettered sign read, "Furnished camp available, free in exchange for caretaking and light swan-tending duties. Win-terized. Call," and it finished with a telephone number.

I was enchanted. "Swan-tending! What a magical come-on; who wouldn't want to spend a winter tending swans? How do you tend swans, anyway? What's a camp?"

"You tend them with a lot of respect and an AK–47," Gerry said, but she was smiling, good humor restored. "Camps, I think, are these really rustic little shacks or something that some of the year-rounders have, mostly around Menemsha, where they go to rough it beside the water and fish and stuff. I think a lot of them live in their camps when they rent out their houses in the summer. That's a Ponder house, so it must be a Ponder camp. I've never heard of one being winterized. And I don't think I've ever seen one. Peter says they're neat, like a boy's playhouse or tree house or something, but I don't think I'd want to spend a Vineyard winter in one. And I don't know why you'd be tending swans; they usually spend the winters in the saltwater ponds along the shores, where they're protected from the wind and the water doesn't freeze. If they don't migrate. I think a lot of them do."

"A man could do worse than be a tender of swans," I said, paraphrasing Robert Frost.

"Not much," Gerry said.

A cluster of balloons fastened to an inconspicuous mailbox on our left marked the entrance to the Hartnells' road, and we turned in and followed the bumping dirt lane down toward a thick fringe of trees. Beyond them I caught the glitter of water, and beyond that the dark blue line that was the Atlantic. Unlike most of the other up-island houses, I could not see this one, and realized that it must be a low house, built to nestle in the trees.

"Have we got the right night?" I said. There was no sign of life from the twisting lane.

Then we turned the last sharp curve and there was a meadow with perhaps a hundred or more cars parked in it, being guided in by young men in dark pants and white shirts, carrying walkie-talkies. Beyond the meadow, out of a nest of old shrubbery and stunted waterside trees, the tiled roof of a long, low house raised its peaked head. Even from here I could hear the soft boom of percussion, and a low hum that must be conversation, spiked every now and then with laughter. Without any warning at all my mouth went dry, and my heart began to pound.

"I think I'd do better with swans," I said faintly.

"Don't be silly. It's the party of the year. Come on, you'll know all the Chappy people," Livvy said, and took my arm and marched me across the meadow toward the house. On my head my mother's hat flopped uncomfortably, as if a large black bird were perched there, deciding whether or not to take off.

We walked through a hedge of dark old rhododendrons and the house came in sight. It was a replica of an English stone cottage, I saw, or what might pass for one: mossy gray walls, tiled roof with more moss growing from it, mullioned and leaded windows, small cottage gardens rioting with perennials. I saw that the gardens sloped down to the shore of the pond in a series of small, roomlike spaces enclosed by stone walls and arbors thick with vines and tall hollyhock and sunflower fences. There must have been half a dozen of them. The last few were out of sight below the trees that fringed the pond. Benches and garden lights and bits of old statuary and birdbaths sat about, looking not at all like the miniature golf courses Livvy had said she bet they did.

"Trolls," she had said. "I hear she has garden trolls beside her koi pond. Too twee for words."

But there was nothing twee about these gardens, or the house they surrounded. Both were absolutely charming in the light off the twilit sea, looking more like a painting or a dream than a place where people lived and worked and spread manure and swatted mosquitoes.

In and about the gardens and on the wide terrace that fringed the house on all sides there must have been three hundred people. At one end a small orchestra played. Old-fashioned Japanese lanterns glowed in the arbors and trees that hung over the terrace. I could see another knot of people gathered around what must be the bar, at the other end of the terrace. White-coated waiters floated through the crowd like butterflies, bearing trays of drinks and hors d'oeuvres.

"I think I'll walk down to the water and see if the swans are around first," I said through the cotton in my mouth. "Anybody want to come with me?"

"Molly, what on earth has gotten into you this summer? At least come and meet your hostess . . . oh, all right," Livvy said and sighed. "Come on. I'll walk down with you. Then you're going to have to mingle. I said I wouldn't leave you, didn't I?"

But she did leave me. The words weren't out of her mouth before a swarm of women in bright silks and cottons detached themselves from the crowd and bore down on us, chattering and peeping like birds. Before I could blink my eyes they had surrounded Livvy and were bearing her away.

"Where have you *been* all summer?" they trilled. "We've been looking all over for you! Do you realize it's almost time to go home and we haven't even had lunch? I heard you had a guest; has she been ill, or what? Has she gone? Come talk to Dink. Toby . . . Stuart . . . Potter . . . they've been asking all summer where you and Caleb were . . . "

Over their heads I saw Livvy looking back at me, her mouth making sounds.

"Come on, keep up with us," I thought she said, but could not be sure. I turned to Gerry, but she was no longer there. I started after them like a clumsy duckling trying to keep up with a flock of—yes, swans—but a waiter with a tray backed into me, and by the time he had apologized and brushed the white wine off my black lapels, the swan pack had disappeared into the general maw of the crowd. Pure terror pinned me suddenly to the terrace, where

I stood. I took a glass of wine from the waiter and drank it down and looked about me, smiling broadly, like a woman who will soon be joined by a hundred incomparably chic and interesting friends, and waited. Surely when the tide cast Livvy up, she would come back for me.

When she hadn't, perhaps half an hour later, I found a waiter and swiped another glass of wine and slipped off the terrace and down the path into the darkening garden. To the west, the sky over Menemsha was vermilion and purple and pink and gold, but down here on the opposite shore, the soft, thick night was falling fast. By the time I had stumbled through three or four garden "rooms" it was completely dark, and all the little ground lights had come on. Stars chipped the sky, but there was no moon yet. I remembered that it had risen late these past few nights. As soon as I reached the fourth garden room, the crowd of strollers had thinned, until I was alone. Only then did I slow down and take a deep breath. The path made a sharp turn and went down a flight of shallow stone steps, and I was in the last space, a trellised square with vines hanging low over a small pond, and an incredible smell of earth and dampness and flowers. Something like jasmine scented the night, but I did not think jasmine grew this far north. Whatever it was, it soothed my pounding heart and hot face like cool water. There were stone benches encircling the trees nearest the pond, and I sat down on one that girdled a huge old oak, so thick that I could not have put my two arms around it. Letting my breath out in a long sigh, I drained my glass and put it down on the bench, and stared at the dark water. Dark shapes and flashes of gold and orange wheeled and darted in its depths: the famous koi. Where were the trolls?

"Hey, you stupid fish," I said aloud. "I don't like your party. I want to go home."

And I did, wanted it with the simple, consuming, one-pointed misery that I had felt as a child the first time I was sent to Camp Greystone, homesick and too big and knowing no one among the flock of girls my mother had decreed I share my summer with. I purely and simply wanted to go home. To whom was not, at that moment, important. I did not think that far ahead. Later I loved camp, but not that first time.

As clearly and grotesquely as if the koi had answered, I heard my mother's voice. It was not the impatient one, but the lazy, indulgently amused one that stung infinitely worse.

"You're hiding again, aren't you, Molly? How many times have we talked about that? *Never* run. *Never* hide. It looks so craven, darling. You are just plain too big to shrink away from things. Even small women should never do it. I would not dream of it. Now get up and go back up there and show those tacky women what your mama taught you."

I sat still for a moment, pinned to the bench with shock and anger. And then I got up and tossed my glass into the lush plantings around the pond. The koi roiled and splashed.

"You shut up," I whispered, and then said aloud, "you just shut the shit up."

By the time I reached the terrace again, I was trotting smartly.

I was almost back to the first garden room when I heard Livvy's voice. It was sharp with annoyance and, I thought, worry.

"I can't imagine where she's gotten to. I never saw her after you-all shanghaied me. Are you sure none of you did?"

I opened my mouth to call out to them in the darkness. But then Gerry Edmondson's voice said, "Are you kidding? In that hat? If we'd seen her, we'd know. So would everybody else. They'd still be laughing."

Once again I froze. I felt as if I'd been struck in the stomach. It had been Gerry who had urged me, along with Livvy, to wear my mother's hat. It suddenly burned my forehead as if it had been set alight. I shrank back into the shadows of a group of slender poplars. I stood in the Italian garden room, screened from their view by poplars and tall urns.

"I wouldn't know her if I saw her," said a voice I did not recognize. "What does she look like?"

"Like Jane Russell in *The Outlaw* from the neck down. From the neck up she looks like Auntie Mame."

Trish Phipps. Livvy's sailing partner. My face flamed.

"Not *the* hat!"

Corky Fredericks, Livvy's first Radcliffe roommate. I knew her from the beach club, too.

"Yep. The famous hat. Mawmaw's hat, as y'all undoubtedly

know. I think it's an old Southren custom, to wear your dead mama's hat."

Gerry again, aping my accent expertly.

"Shut up, all of you," Livvy said. "She's my best friend, and she's going through an awful time. You know that."

Oh, bless you, Livvy!

"Well, what the hell am I, chopped liver?" Gerry. "I've known you since we were six years old."

Jealous, then. I felt obscurely better.

"My best Atlanta friend, idiot," Livvy said. "And I'll admit she's been acting a little odd. She's not normally like this. But then she's not normally being divorced for a thirty-year-old Coca-Cola lawyer who looks like Angelica Huston, either."

"Ah jus' knew Co'Cola would be involved in it somehow," Trish Phipps said, picking up Gerry's thick accent. "When is honeychile goin' home, then? Or is she gon' stay with you and Caleb forever? I hear those unattached Southren belles are real big on livin' with other folks. Shoot, I don't reckon it would be so bad. She could take in y'all's washin'. Look after ol' Caleb, doncha know. Wonder if she wears the hat to bed?"

There was a soft explosion of laughter. Most of it I recognized from the beach club mornings.

Livvy's rose over it, reluctant but clear.

"Shut up, everybody. Help me look. She might be sick."

I slipped through the line of poplars and hurried down through the floodlit meadow until I found one of the parking attendants. I asked for Livvy's Cherokee. When he had consulted a list on a clipboard, he walked me there, shining his flashlight on the flattened grass.

I got into the backseat and curled up in as small a ball as I could make of myself, and closed my eyes, but not before I had torn off the hat and flung it to the floor. I should have been angry, but I was not. I felt nothing but a terrible mortification, and a profound desire not to talk, to Livvy or anyone else.

When they finally found me, I kept my eyes closed and muttered, "I'm sick. Leave me alone," and they did. We made the long, dark ride down island and across to Chappy in silence. Once Gerry started to say something, but Livvy cut her off.

"Save it," she said shortly.

When we had dropped Gerry off and parked outside Livvy's cottage, I sat up and said, "I'm going to run on in. I must have eaten something that disagreed with me. I feel awful."

"I'm sorry," she said in a distant voice, and I knew that she did not believe me. I could not even imagine what she thought I had been doing during the party. Crouching and shivering in the Jeep, probably.

I got out in silence and hurried upstairs to my room and closed the door.

"In the morning," I thought. "In the morning I'm going to call and change my reservation and go home as soon as I can. I don't have to see any of those women again. I don't even have to see much of Livvy."

But she defended you, the rational part of my mind pointed out.

But she laughed, said the other part, the larger and older part.

I thought I would not sleep, but I was asleep before I could turn over. I had the subway dream again; in it my mother said, in the strange, hollow, mechanical drone, "Hold your shoulders up. It just makes you look bigger when you slump. Hold your shoulders upupupupupupupupup . . . "

I woke very early and went downstairs and called Missy Carmichael at home, to tell her to have the house opened for me.

"Hey, I was gon' call you when I got to work," she said. "Something's come up. Two somethings, in fact. Bad news short-term, real good news long-term."

"Why am I not surprised? Shoot," I said tiredly.

"Well, the worst of it, but maybe the best in the long run, is that Tee's closed your joint checking and savings accounts and opened another one in your name. It's got five thousand dollars in it. There'll be another five thousand deposited every month. I called that Lorna woman you said you'd told about me, because our private eye needed another little shot of moola, and she told me. She didn't have your number up there or she'd have let you know directly."

When I didn't reply, she said, "I know. It's a shitty thing to do, but it's not illegal. You'll have enough money to cover your and

Teddy's living expenses fairly comfortably, but you won't ever have any reserves unless you've got some stashed I don't know about. I assume you don't."

"No."

"Well, don't worry about my fees for the time being. This is going to look so godawful to a jury that we'll probably get every red cent he's got, so if you can tough it out for a while, it'll be a real bonus. Of course it's her, but it's going to look like he's the heartless jackass instead of just being pussy-whipped."

I took a deep breath. "What's the second thing?"

She fairly crowed. "This is going to be the kicker. This is going to set you up for life. Now he wants the house, or rather, she wants to live in it, so he's saying, or his lawyer is, that since it's legally his, he's just going to keep it and move you somewhere else, or, and I quote, 'Provide adequate housing for you.' Adequate, my ass. He is flat-out teetotally stupid, thank God for our side. Cuts off your money and then tries to throw you out of the home you've lived in for twenty years? I don't think so."

My heart began the familiar dragging thunder again.

"When will that happen? Surely not for a long time? I was going to ask you to get the house opened for me. I'm coming home as soon as I can . . . "

"Oh. That could be a problem," she said slowly. "Of course you've got the right to live in it until he gets a court order for you to vacate, or you settle it privately, and that could take some time. But the thing is, it would look *much* better to a jury if it looked as though you were being super-cooperative, that you moved out the minute you heard he wanted it. I was hoping you wouldn't come back to the house. I was thinking you might rent something short-term; I could have found something for you, but of course you couldn't manage a decent deposit now. . . . Shit. Isn't there somebody you could get a short-term loan from? You said Mrs. Redwine was solidly in your corner . . . "

"I won't do that. I'll never do that," I said.

"Well, could you stay up there for a while, another month or two, maybe?"

"Absolutely not. It's out of the question."

"Molly . . . this is not the time to hang tough about this. This is the time to be so cooperative your shit don't stink. Later, *then* you can play hardball . . . "

The strength ran out of my legs abruptly. I sat down on the edge of the kitchen table.

"I'll call you back, Missy," I said. "I just can't talk any more right now."

"Okay," she said reluctantly. "I know this is tough. I told you it would be, with that trailer trash involved. But try to think of something soon. I've got to get back to Tee's asshole lawyer before long."

I hung up and rose and went out on the porch that overlooked Katama Bay. It was so early that the water was still and flat and pink-stained, a mirror for sunrise. Only a few white sails ghosted slowly over the surface. For the first time, the high white light of summer seemed to have given way to the lower, golden slant of coming autumn. It was warm, nearly hot, but I could almost feel the still white chill of the first frosted mornings here. I sat down on the chaise and put my face in my hands and closed my eyes.

"Feeling better, I trust?" Livvy said behind me. Her voice was high and sharp. She wasn't going to let last night go.

"Yes, thank you," I said formally, not turning.

"You want to tell me the nature of your sudden malady?" she said. "Just so I can explain to all the people who wanted to meet you, of course."

"I'd have thought they were too busy laughing at my hat to worry about it," I said. My voice sounded prissy in my own ears, snippy and aggrieved.

She sighed, a long sigh. "I'm sorry you heard that. They were acting like shits. Women in groups like that are bad about ganging up on other women, especially outsiders. I guess we do it at home, too. It isn't that they don't like you . . . "

"Oh, of course not. I could tell that."

"Look, I'm sorry I snapped at you," she said. "There was a call on the machine from Caleb last night. He can't come. Youth brands has got some new crisis in Chicago or somewhere, and he's having to go there for at least two weeks. I'm devastated; it's the first time he's ever missed the Vineyard. But I shouldn't take it out on you."

Two weeks. Her husband is going to be away from her for two

weeks and she's devastated. Try two months, or two years, or forever, toots, and then tell me about devastation, I thought.

"You better make real sure he hasn't got a little action going in Chicago," I said meanly, out of my pain and humiliation from last night. "There's a lot of that going around Coke, you know."

There was a silence, and then she said, "That was the rottenest thing you've ever said to me. Just because you can't hold on to your husband, doesn't mean I can't mine . . . "

I wheeled around to face her.

"Livvy . . . I'm sorry," I said. "It's just that . . . last night . . . I heard you laughing, too."

"Well, Jesus Christ, excuse me for being human," she cried. "You know, Molly, it hasn't been the easiest thing for me, trying to cuddle and cajole you along, trying to read your moods and find things to take your mind off Tee. I'm sorry I laughed, but if you heard that, you heard me defending you, too. It seems like that's all I've done for the last two weeks."

"Well, don't worry about it, because I'm going home as soon as I can," I said, and then I remembered.

She read my face.

"What is it?" she whispered, the quarrel forgotten. Livvy could always tell when things were really dire with me.

I told her, trying to keep my voice matter-of-fact and level, trying not to cry.

"Oh, baby," she said, hurrying toward me. "That complete and utter turd. That bitch. What are you going to do?"

"I guess . . . call Mrs. Redwine," I said. "See what she's willing to do."

"No, God!" she cried, involuntarily, and I smiled at her in spite of the pain in my chest. "You can't do that! You must never do that! You'll never be free of her. Listen—stay here. Stay here as long as you want to. You can close off the upstairs and keep the house reasonably warm with the fireplace and space heaters till almost December. Take all the time you need; surely Missy will have it worked out by then. You said you loved the Vineyard, and I'm going back home as soon as I can get a plane. You'll be able to spread out and relax and think."

"Oh, Livvy . . ." Pain twisted my heart. My spiteful words

about Caleb were driving her home; how could I have planted that poison seed in her heart? Sickened by my own bacilli, I was spreading them now to Livvy, the person, besides my father and children, and, once, Tee, I loved most. Had loved . . .

She shook her head impatiently.

"No. It wasn't you. I decided that last night. I don't know why, but I just can't stay up here any longer without him. I need to at least see him before he goes off to Chicago or wherever. Stay, Molly. At least let me make up a little bit for last night, and for the other times. I love you, and I certainly haven't acted much like it."

"I love you, too," I said, choked, and we hugged for a long time.

She left two days later. When I got back from the airport, in the Cherokee, I came into the empty cottage and sat down, waiting for the warmth and peace I had felt when I had first come here to flood over me. Instead, what came was anxiety so strong it was almost real fear. I got up and walked out on to the deck and looked at Katama Bay, and all of a sudden I knew that I could not stay here, in this house, on this beach, on this little island, alone in this huge, wide, shelterless, shadowless seascape. I knew that I would die here, alone, of fear and loneliness and loss and pure exposure.

I got into the Jeep and drove through the teeming mess that was Edgartown in late August, up Edgartown–West Tisbury Road through the stage-set forest to South Road, up island. Up island. . . . The trip felt as inevitable and right as my own heartbeat.

When I reached the big shingled house on the crown of the glacial ridge, I looked to see if the sign was still there, on the road beside the mailbox. It was. "Furnished camp available . . . light swan-tending . . ."

I turned in so quickly that the Jeep bucked like a wild thing, and I did not slow down as I climbed the long hill.

CHAPTER SEVEN

THE HOUSE STOOD IN FULL SUN on the slope of a ridge that seemed to sweep directly up into the steel-blue sky. Below it, the lane I had just driven on wound through low, dense woodlands, where the Jeep had plunged in and out of dark shade. But up here there was nothing around the house except a sparse stand of wind-stunted oaks, several near-to-collapsing outbuildings, and two or three huge, freestanding boulders left, I knew, by the receding glacier that had formed this island. Above the house, the ridge beetled like a furrowed brow, matted with low-growing blueberry and huckleberry bushes. At the very top, no trees grew at all. I looked back and down and caught my breath at the panorama of Chilmark Pond and the Atlantic Ocean. It was a day of strange, erratic winds and running cloud shadow, and the patchwork vista below me seemed alive, pulsing with shadow and sun, trees and ocean moving restlessly in the wind. Somehow it disquieted me so that I had to turn and face the closed door of the big, old house. I had come here seeking the shelter of the up-island woods, but this tall, blind house, alone in its ocean of space and dazzle of hard, shifting light, offered me no place to hide.

I was about to turn away, my raised fist not, after all, having knocked, when a voice from inside called, "Who's there? I know somebody's there."

I sighed. After that I could not simply drive away.

"I've come about the sign down on the road," I called. My voice sounded huge and hollow in the vast, windy silence.

"Oh, how lovely," the voice called back, and I smiled in spite of myself. It was a sweet, high voice, like a child's, but there was something unchildlike in it, too, a kind of timorous fragility that you hear only in the voices of the very old or the ill.

"Push the door open, it sticks. I can't come to you," the voice said, and I did, and stood in the cavelike darkness of a room that seemed enormous and smelled of camphor and dust and trapped summer heat. After the dazzle of the hillside, I could see nothing, and stood blinking for a moment.

"Are you in? I can't see you for the glare. Come over here where I can see you," the voice said, and I walked slowly toward it, feeling my way and bumping into looming, clifflike pieces of furniture. In the middle of the room I stopped, as blind as if I were an eyeless cave creature, and then a dim yellow light came on in the far corner, and I could see again.

I stood in the middle of what must have been a living or drawing room once, but now was a sickroom, or at least the corner I could see was. A hospital bed stood there, beside a round table spilling over with books and magazines and glasses and saucers and spoons, and in the bed a tiny woman lay, propped up on piled pillows of linen so old they were ivory yellow, like old teeth. On the other side of the bed, a tall window looked out on to what must be the backyard, but an old-fashioned roller shade was pulled down so that no one could see in or out. On a table, a small lamp was lit. There were vases and glasses and jars full of flowers everywhere, some fresh, some drooping, some completely brown and dry. Among them, under the yellow covers and against the yellow pillows, the little woman looked as tiny and sere as the mummy of a child, and as yellow, almost, as the bedclothes.

Her tiny face was crosshatched with delicate, fine lines and wrinkles, the skin a polished ocher against which wisps of silvery white hair stood out like dandelion fuzz. Lord, she was old; she looked too old to be alive, almost, in her high-buttoned white nightgown and the sparse nimbus of hair. But her black-dark eyes burned with joy, and her smile was as white and delighted as a young child's. I smiled back; it was impossible not to.

"The swans? You've come about the swans?" she said.

"Well, I saw the sign and I was curious . . . "

"Would you come a little closer? I can't find my glasses and I don't see well anymore . . . "

I walked forward, into the circle of light from the painted china lamp. She drew in a breath, and her face seemed to flame with a kind of rapture.

"*Portugués*?" she whispered. "You are *Portugués*?"

Before I could answer, another voice called from the back of the house, "*Ingles, Luzia, se faz favor*. Speak English."

It was such a deep voice that I thought at first it was a man's, but there was something feminine in it, something fruitful and dark in its depths.

"But, Bella, she is *Portugués* and she has come for the *cisnes*. The swans, I mean . . . "

"I'm afraid I'm not Portuguese," I said hesitantly, for it seemed of enormous import to her that I was. "But I did want to know more about the swans, and the camp . . . "

She peered up at me and then shook her head.

"I see now that you aren't. Your eyes are blue, of course . . . it's just that you are so big and so dark, and your teeth are so white. There are a lot of Portuguese women who look like you. But never mind, you're here about the swans and that's all that matters."

There was the sound of heavy feet and an enormous woman came into the room from somewhere back in the house. I gaped; at first she seemed to me simply a mountainous black shape looming over me, a creature as much of the dark as the other little woman was, somehow, of the light. But at second glance I could see that she was simply a painfully obese, very tall old woman dressed in black stretch pants and a black overshirt, with her dark hair wound in braids around her head and black, soft shoes on her feet. She leaned on a cane and smiled at the little woman and at me, and the impression of menace faded, though her smile was chilly and formal.

"I am Isabel Ponder, and this is my cousin, Luzia Ferreira. I'm sorry I didn't hear you knock. Luzia must have given you a turn, crouching in here in the dark like a little old toad."

The smile widened and sweetened for a moment, then melted back into its polite chilliness.

"No, it's all right. I really hadn't knocked yet. I saw ... I saw your sign a few nights ago, and I thought I'd come and see about the camp. I think I might be staying on the Vineyard for a while, and it sounded ... it sounded charming. I mean, the bit about tending the swans ... "

I knew I was babbling, and fell silent under the weight of that fixed smile and the still, dark eyes.

"I thought that up! That's my line! I said it and Bella wrote it down," the little woman bubbled, and this time we both smiled at her.

"It's a nice line. It's the reason I stopped," I said, as you would to a child, and she clapped her hands. What was it, I thought, early Alzheimer's? Illness and weakness? Just the onset of extreme old age?

"Yes. It is," Isabel Ponder said. "Well. So you're interested in the camp? Please sit down and tell me why you are. It's terribly isolated and the winters can be very hard here, and I can tell you aren't an islander. You're not even a Northerner, are you?"

We sat down on a sagging sofa in front of the hospital bed. I clasped my hands together in my lap and faced her as you would a headmistress, or one to whom you were applying for a job. She was panting for breath by the time she had settled herself, drawing great, hoarse, laboring breaths that whistled in her chest, but she was still formidable.

"I'm not a Northerner, no," I said with as much composure as I could muster. "I'm a Southerner. From Atlanta. I came up to visit friends and I ... I thought I might stay for a while, and I didn't want to impose on them; they're over on Chappaquiddick, and they need to close the house ... and when I saw your sign it just seemed to be ... I thought ... I liked the look of it."

What was the matter with me? This woman needed to know nothing except that I was interested in looking at her camp. I owed her nothing else but my name and my interest. But I found myself anxious to please her.

"My mother's name is Belle, too. Was, rather," I said.

"Ah. She is not alive, then?"

"No. She died ... not long ago. ... "

How can that be? Mother, where are you?

145

"Oh. And you are alone now."

"No. I have a son and a daughter and a husband . . . well, not exactly a husband, not for long . . . and my father is still alive, and I have a brother in Washington . . ."

"But you still want to spend the winter in a camp on Martha's Vineyard," Isabel Ponder said. Her words seemed to mock me, if not her tone, which was perfectly neutral.

"I . . . yes. I think I do," I said crisply. "Depending on its suitability, of course."

"It is quite suitable," she said, unsmiling. "You said you don't exactly have a husband, or won't have for long. You're separated, then? You're being divorced?"

"I'm doing the divorcing, actually," I said lightly and desperately. Why could I not just stand up and go? This inquisition was unthinkable.

"Ah. Was he cheating on you?"

This time I did stand up.

"I'm sorry to have taken your time—"

"Bella! You say you're sorry right now!" the little old woman in the bed cried out in such anguish that I turned to her instinctively. "It's all right," I said softly.

"Luzia is right. I'm being terribly nosy and impolite," Bella Ponder said, but she said it heavily and roughly, as one would who was not used to apologizing.

"It's just that . . . I sympathize, you see," she went on. "My husband left me, too, when my son was only a baby. That's when Luzia came to help us out. I know how hard it is. I didn't mean to offend you."

"No, she didn't. She really, really didn't," Luzia Ferreira said from her bed. She was actually wringing her hands together. It was for her that I sat back down and said to Bella Ponder, "It's very recent. I'm still having a hard time getting used to it. But it's the main reason I might like to stay on here for a while. My father is with my brother in Washington, and my daughter lives in Memphis with her husband and baby, and my son is at school out West. I just didn't feel like going home yet, somehow."

She nodded, studying me.

"So . . . no family at home. You thought you might have a little adventure in a different place, get your head straight, all that. Tell me, are you tough? Can you take bitter cold weather? Can you take isolation? Can you cope with being snowed in, and power failures, and weeks and weeks without the sun, and mud up to your knees, and spring looking like it will never come?"

"I'm tough," I said, a pallid anger stirring at last, deep down inside me. "I can't think of anything this island can hand me that I can't take. But I don't see any point in talking about it anymore. You've obviously got serious doubts about me. I think you'd be much happier with someone from the island. Surely there's someone, a member of your family, who could tend your swans. My friend says yours is the oldest family on the island, and that there are lots of you around—"

"We can't have anybody from the island," Luzia wailed, and I turned to look at her. Great tears were sliding slowly down her little brown walnut of a face. I stared in surprise and pity.

"I am not close to my husband's family," Bella Ponder said. "I will not ask them for help. Whoever takes the camp is going to have to do some things for Luzia and me, too, and there are other caretaking duties that will be involved. I need to know that whoever is in the camp is strong and capable, and will stay for . . . as long as I need them. Several months, at least. How do I know that you won't get homesick for your family, or that you won't go back to your husband in a month or two? It's not going to do me any good if you are going to do that."

"I can't promise that," I said. "I don't have any idea how long I want to stay. I'd thought I'd try it a month at a time, and just go from there. Of course, if I did agree to take it and I'd promised to do specific things for you, I wouldn't just go off and leave you in the lurch. I'd wait until you got someone else, if I decided to go back home . . ."

"We can't do that," Luzia cried. "Don't you understand?"

"Hush," Bella Ponder said to her cousin without looking at her. "I guess that's fair enough. There wouldn't be much work involved in helping us out, just a few groceries gotten in once or twice a week, and driving us to the doctor when we have to go. Luz has been in bed since she broke her hip three years ago; got osteoporosis, too. And my heart doesn't seem to want to go like it once did. Too damned fat, that's for sure. I can't walk much. Can't do stairs, can't carry things. But we never did go out much. You wouldn't be burdened by us. And those sorry swans; well, mainly they have to be fed, and the water in the pond has to be broken up twice a day so it doesn't freeze up on them. Spoiled old fools won't leave that pond, not even in winter when all the others are down on the deep salt ponds where it doesn't freeze. Won't even go back to wherever it is that they belong in the summer like they're supposed to. Luzia has spoiled them to death, and now she can't take care of them, and I can't either . . . "

"Please look after Charles and Di," Luzia said in her sick child's voice. "It isn't their fault I spoiled them so. I never thought about making them dependent on me; I just thought it was so nice that they wanted to spend their time on the pond with us . . . well, you're a mother. You understand how it is to worry about what happens to your children when you can't take care of them any longer . . . "

I looked over at Bella Ponder, a quick, alarmed glance. Surely this crippled old woman did not think of the swans as her children?

I caught a fleeting expression of what, amazingly, looked to be anguish in Bella's dark eyes before she sensed me looking at her and rolled them indulgently.

"Luz never had children of her own, and that's hard for a good Portuguese girl," she said, smiling her wintry smile. "She loved my little son, and when he went off island to school she missed him terribly, so when these two took up with us down at the camp, she just adopted them. Miserable, overgrown turkeys, it was like having two devil-possessed toddlers around the house, only these never grew up. They're still as cantankerous today as the day they flew in. But they'll come running for Luz like lost children; I try to take her down to the camp a few times during the summers. It's been three years since we spent much time down there, but they don't forget."

"Well, of course they don't," Luzia Ferreira said. "Have you forgotten *your* mama?"

"Charles and Di," I said. "Are they royalty?"

In the yellow bed, the tiny woman beamed. "They are, sort of. They came the summer of the royal wedding, and since they were still youngsters then, and a new couple—you could tell that—I named them Charles and Diana. They're devoted to one another. You should see the way he hovers over her, and brings her the best food, and hisses and beats his wings when he thinks anybody is too close to her. Still in love after all these years . . . "

"Not like their namesakes," I said, smiling. "You aren't afraid they'll have a scandalous breakup one day?"

"No," she said seriously. "Swans mate for life. They're not like us about that. Loyalty and faithfulness mean everything to them."

"Not to mention biology," snorted Bella Ponder, but she was still smiling.

"Are there others?" I said. "Do they have children? What do you call them . . . cygnets, isn't it?"

"They had babies the first spring," Luzia said. "But something got them . . . a fox, or snapping turtles, or maybe a dog. After that they never did again, that we knew of. I think . . . I think they just decided that each other was enough for them. It's quite unusual, I understand. You'll see for yourself, when you get down there. You're going to like them, and I do believe you're the one they're going to choose to take my place. I can just tell. I don't think foolishness bothers you, does it?"

Somehow that touched me to the core. I felt tears prickle in my eyes.

"I guess it doesn't," I said. "I've lived with it a long time."

"Well, then." She slumped back against the pillows, obviously exhausted. "You go with Bella and see for yourself. It's just the right thing; I could tell when you rang the doorbell. But then, you didn't ring, did you? I just knew you were there; that's even better. I am so grateful."

And she closed her eyes. The lids were blue and papery and veined, but the lashes lay sweetly on the old cheek. I looked at Bella.

"Can we see the house?"

"Of course. Just let me get my things," she said.

Her things were a huge canvas boat tote crammed with paper bags and a beautiful old silver-headed cane. Even with the cane, it took me a very long time to get her out to the Cherokee and into it. When we finally achieved it, she was white and sweating and gasping alarmingly for breath, and I was soaked with nervous perspiration. What would I do if this old woman had a serious, or even fatal, heart attack in the Jeep? I did not know where the nearest hospital was, nor the nearest fire station. Was there even a phone in the big house? Yes, wires were stark against the blue sky. But I couldn't possibly lift her . . .

She soon got control of her breath, though.

"Damned flabby heart," she said calmly. "You can see why we need a little help. It's funny, isn't it? You never think it's going to happen to you. When I first came to this island I was as strong as any man, and for more years than I can remember I took care of myself and my boy and Luzia, and that big old house, and the camps . . . and Luzia, well, you should have seen her when she came. You'd never have known she's older than me. She was like a little lick of flame, or a piece of the wind, always moving, always running and singing and laughing. We used to run all over those woods, and swam in the pond . . . No, you never really do think it's going to happen to you."

I looked over at the wrecked old gargoyle under my lashes. I could no more imagine her and the frail little old mummy in the big yellow bed running like puppies through the woods and in and out of the bright, cold water than I could imagine elephants, or monuments, dancing. Pity tore at my heart.

"Where did Luzia come here from?" I said.

"From West Bedford, just outside Boston," she said. "A lot of my people and hers lived there when she and I were young. There was a regular colony of Portuguese for a while; some of the men were at the Hanscomb Air Force Base, and others worked in Cambridge and Boston. Luzia and I were both born there, and we went to high school there. I was working in a restaurant in Cambridge when I met my husband; he was at Harvard then. When he . . . left us, my son and I, I needed help, and Luzia's parents were about to move back to Portugal, so I asked her to come here, and she's been here ever since. She's all I have of family now . . . "

"Your son . . . is he . . . not alive?" I said hesitantly. I had not gotten the sense of tragedy from her, only bitterness, a formless anger.

"Oh, yes. I meant family here. My son just . . . doesn't come here anymore. He has no more use for his father's people than I do, and apparently they have none for him. None of them have ever made a move to contact him. None of them made a move to see him when he was here, when he was just a little boy. That's why I sent him off island, so he could grow up and go to school among his own people, in West Bedford. He's come back very few times since."

"How old was he when he went away?" I said.

"Eight. He was eight."

Eight years old. My God, poor little boy. To lose his father at two, and then his mother and his aunt and his very world at eight . . . no wonder he did not come back to this island.

"Where is he now?" I asked. "What does he do?"

"He's a schoolteacher. He teaches in a private school in Washington State," she said. Her voice was flat. "He teaches English literature, I believe, somewhere just outside Seattle."

The "I believe" spoke of distance and pain, and I did not pursue it, except to say, mildly, "That's a long way away."

"Yes," she said. "That's a pretty hat."

I saw that she was looking at my mother's hat in the backseat, and I accepted the change of subject.

"It was my mother's."

"She had good taste. I'll bet she was a pretty woman."

"Yes, she was," I said.

She directed me back to the right, where we bumped in silence along the deserted, close-grown road, and then left on to Middle Road, which bisects the up island landscape, between South Road and North Road. We were driving along the glacial spine of the island now, and I did not try to converse with her; the sweeping vistas of meadows and boulders and moors and ponds and the great silver sea beyond claimed my eyes. Up island, in that moment, seemed as remote and empty of humanity to me as the Scottish moors it resembled. It was crisscrossed with beautiful old piled-stone walls that, now, seemed to define nothing at all, and here and there a great piled old house, or an obviously new and opulent one, dotted the green and gray, or broke the racing cloud scud from the tops of the ridges. And then, abruptly, we were in the little town of Chilmark, with its community center and firehouse and huddle of stores and church and schoolhouse. I drew a breath of relief; here were life and the living. Men and women ambled about the crossroads or proceeded in trucks and Jeeps through the intersection where the famous beetlebung trees loomed, beginning now to be tinged with promissory scarlet. It was near noon, and children ran in and out of the old shingled two-room school. It was such a classic, pastoral village scene that I grinned to myself, thinking what Tee would have said about it, and then, remembering, amended the thought to what Livvy would have. I did not mind the Disneyesque quality of it, though; this was real, and powerfully endearing, somehow touching a chord deep within me. Wasn't it, after all, like this that people were meant to live? In villages, as neighbors, wrapped in water and hills? I smiled at Bella Ponder.

"So pretty," I said.

"Pretty is as pretty does," she said, and pointed right, and I turned on to Menemsha Cross Road.

The two old Ponder camps lay across North Road, at the end of one of a nameless warren of small, wild lanes that eventually led down to the waters of Vineyard Sound, near Menemsha Bight. It seemed to me that we bumped through the low-growing, close-pressing forest interminably, seeing nothing but overhanging branches and undergrowth—ferns and vines and the stunted trunks of trees—only occasionally catching a glimpse ahead of silver-gray, which spoke of open water and the sky. At the head of each tiny lane a ramshackle mailbox leaned, or sometimes a weathered, falling-down wooden gate that could have deterred no one. I asked Bella if any of the lanes had names, and she said that a few did: She could remember Prospect Hill Road, and Cranberry Road, and Beetlebung and Kapigan Roads, and, of course, Pinkletink.

"But," she added," I don't think our road ever had a name. People just call it Ponder Camp Road. That's as good as any, I guess."

She pointed again, and I swung the Jeep on to an even tinier, more green-choked road, and slowed to a snail's pace as I felt my way through the ruts and vegetation. There was no glimpse of sea or sky now, only the relentless, scratching, pressing green. The roadbed was appalling.

"This must be impossible in winter," I said.

"Not if you've got four-wheel drive," she said. "I can't remember ever being stuck in here."

Of course not, I said to myself, chastened.

I followed a sharp turn to the left, then stopped the Jeep abruptly with a soft gasp. In a clearing just ahead sat a small, shingled, two-story cottage, gone dark brown now with age and weather. To one side of it, and a bit in front, a larger cottage stood, this one all on one level and shrouded with some sort of creeper going scarlet. Like the first, its trim and shutters were white, this one's seeming new-painted and glistening in the unaccustomed sunlight of the clearing. From its mossy stone chimney a wisp of ghostlike smoke curled. Flowers in window boxes rioted red and yellow and peach and pink against the old shingles: tuberous begonias, I saw. We could not grow them in this vivid perfection at home, though I had tried. The windowpanes shone. Behind and above it, the little two-story cottage looked dim and shabby and unloved, its chimney cold, its windows scummed and opaque with spiderwebs. Beyond both the still, dark water of a little pond gleamed, ringed with emerald water weeds and rushes and small, wind-shaped trees. One end of it was thick with leathery-green water lilies. At its near edge, beside a listing little gray dock, a half-beached skiff lay, its faded red paint obscured in patches by the relentless vines. Beyond all of it, the silver of the sea tossed and flashed.

It was so utterly, picturesquely lovely, so somehow ridiculously operettalike, that I simply laughed. My heart squeezed with enchantment.

"Where are Hansel and Gretel?" I said. "Surely no self-respecting witch would eat them up in this place."

"It's right nice, isn't it?" she said complacently, knowing of course how it looked; hadn't she said she and Luzia had spent most of their summers here? I could see, suddenly, what a bitter loss this place must be to both of them. The old farmhouse on its wind-scoured hill was beautiful, in a stark and lordly way, but this secret glade, with its sunlit pond and the promise of the sea always before it, was sustenance and shelter. I could literally see it frilled in the first tender pink and green of spring; see it wrapped in silent, succoring snow; see it, as I would soon, licked by the fire of autumn. I had been right in what I sensed: This is what had waited for me up island. I knew before I got out of the car that I would take the camp.

"May I go in?" I said eagerly, turning to her.

"Why don't you go see the swans first?" she said. "Take them a little bite and get acquainted, give me time to get myself up for walking some more. Then I'll show it to you."

"I can go in by myself; I don't want you to make yourself ill," I said.

"No. There are things I want to tell you about the house. Take that top paper bag and go scatter some of that barley on the edge of the water and some right in it. They'll be along; they don't go far from the water."

I dug the first paper bag out of her tote and got out of the Jeep and walked across the glade to the pond's edge. The air smelled of pine and sun-sweetened grass, of the clean, fishy smell I associated with childhood lakes and creeks. There was, under the deep silence, a kind of hum that might be insects or just the living heart of the wood itself. I stretched and smiled, and walked carefully out on to the old dock, feeling it sway and hold, and tossed handfuls of the cracked barley she had given me into the water, and more behind me on to the grassy fringe of the pond. For a moment there was only the silence and then there was a kind of liquid rustle, and the sound of moving water, and a great white bird came gliding through the rushes toward me.

It was a mottled gray-white, as though years of wear and winters had dimmed the luster of its feathers, and its bill was bright red-orange, with a black mask above it and a black knob jutting over the bill from its forehead. Its neck was curved in the beautiful, tender S curve that I associated with fairy-tale books and old engravings. It was enormous; I was shocked at its size. It must have weighed a good sixteen or seventeen pounds. I don't know why I was surprised; I had seen swans before, in zoos and botanical gardens. But somehow, here in this wild place, with nothing but quiet water between me and it, it looked large indeed, and formidable.

It stopped in the water and looked at me, tilting its head to one side. Then it raised its wings over its back so that it was one huge, ruffled puff of white: lovely. I was captivated. I knelt and reached my hand out to it, offering barley.

"Hello, you pretty thing," I said. "Are you Charles, or Di? Want a little nibble of brunch?"

From around a clump of reeds a white tornado erupted, rushing awkwardly at me, hissing and grunting. I had heard grunts like that from alligators on television nature shows: I jumped back reflexively, but not before the wind of great, flailing wings brushed my bare arms and face. It seemed that the whole glade, and the air over the pond, were filled with whirling, whistling wings.

I cowered on the dock, covering my head and face with my arms; the wings slowed and stopped, and I risked a look. A second swan, much larger than the one who still lingered in the water, was waddling angrily back and forth along the bank under the dock, looking up at me and darting its big head, on the end of its serpentine neck, like a snake. Charles, no doubt of that. I had, I supposed, threatened Diana.

I stood frozen, effectively treed on the dock by the absurd swan, remembering the cast on Gerry Edmondson's wrist, put there by a swan in a West Tisbury pond. Staying here was out of the question, I thought: I couldn't go through this twice a day indefinitely. What if one of them broke *my* wrist; I wouldn't even be able to drive. I felt a deep, childish sorrow start in my stomach: This place had spoken so clearly to me of something I had not even known I needed.

The Jeep horn began to blare, and I looked back. Bella Ponder's black head was thrust out the window.

"Stand your ground!" she rasped. "Don't run. He'll stop in a minute. It's all show."

I stood still, and soon the marauding cob stopped his furious lunging and hissing, and settled his great wings to his side again. With a final, baleful glare at me, he turned and waddled awkwardly back to the water and glided silently across it to where the barley lay on the bank. The pen followed him, serene in her settling white feathers. When she began to peck at the grain, he did, too, and soon both were feeding greedily, backs to me. I tiptoed off the dock and back to the Jeep, feeling sheepish and cowardly. In my head I could hear Livvy: "You didn't take it because a *swan* chased you?"

"I didn't realize they were so big," I said aloud in a small voice.

Bella was panting from the effort of shouting.

"I should have brought the swan stick. It's an old walking cane of my husband's grandfather's, made of black oak, as hard as iron. I never feed those savages that I don't bring it along. Luzia hates it, but it works like a charm."

"You don't hit them?" I said, horrified.

"Of course not. Luzia would leave on the next ferry. I just shake it at them. At him, really. They may be mean, but they're not stupid. They'll back off every time. Like I said, it's all show. They know where their meals come from. Lord, but I'll be glad when somebody can take over for me. I don't know if I can keep up the room service much longer."

"Is that what they eat, grain?"

"No. They eat submerged water plants and sometimes the gleanings left in the fields. Barley is what the royal Europeans used to feed them to fatten them for the table. If one of them ever gets too far out of line, at least he won't taste like old shoe leather."

I laughed, and she grinned fleetingly. I found myself liking this rude old woman without quite knowing why.

"So shall we do the cottage now?" I said.

"I think I'll send you ahead after all," she said, "and tell you what you need to know after you've seen it. My heart's still fluttering a little."

She did look white and tired, and so I nodded. "Will I need a key?"

"No. They're never locked," she said, and I started off toward the larger cabin.

"No," she said. "That's not for let. It's the other one, the smaller one."

"I'm sorry," I said. "I just thought, with the fire lit and the windows and the flowers and all . . . "

"I'll tell you about that one when you get back. The little one is cozier in the winter, and it needs a lot less care. It's a little out of shape right now, but I can get it ready for you at a moment's notice, if you like it. It's where Luz and I always stayed."

So I walked past the Hansel and Gretel cottage and went up the stone steps of the little two-story cottage and across the sagging porch and pushed the ancient white-painted door open.

The little house was indeed little; it was tiny. The downstairs consisted of one large room with tiny, diamond-paned windows so scrimmed with dirt and overgrown with outside vines that it was nearly impossible to see; when I flicked on a lone brass lamp on a rickety table, nothing happened. I made out a huge, age-and-smoke-blackened fireplace that dominated one wall, and a spavined old sofa covered with a filthy quilt facing it, and a couple of what looked like wooden kitchen chairs circa 1900. The ceiling was low and beamed and black with the smoke of years, and at one end a faded cretonne curtain was drawn back to expose a kitchen so rudimentary that I literally shuddered at the thought of trying to put a meal together in it. There was an iron stove with the flue leading out a tiny, high window; a pitted, old, white gas range; a sink on pipe legs; and a refrigerator that had its motor sitting sadly atop it. There was one linoleum-covered counter, and open shelves above it held a few tins so weary and dim that it was impossible to tell what they contained.

At the other end of the room, a cramped staircase rose into the gloom of the second floor. I climbed it, my heart sinking steadily toward my stomach. The risers were so narrow that I had to go up sideways, and the pitch was so steep that I clung to the rough pine wall as I climbed. I did not think I would spend a week here before I tumbled down it and broke something vital to my well-being. Up here were two cubicles obviously used as bedrooms, one slightly larger than the other, with tiny closets closed off by curtains and narrow iron bedsteads in each. Thin, stained mattresses sat atop them. Both had dirty old footlockers, chests of drawers that might have housed a Barbie doll's wardrobe, and a straight chair apiece. Both had long, floor-to-ceiling windows scummed with grime and cobwebs, but when I went to one and rubbed a space in the dirt, I saw that they overlooked the whole sweep of glade and pond and the sea beyond, and that from up here you had a panoramic view of Vineyard Sound. It was blue now instead of the morning's restless pewter, and dotted with white sails. It was lovely: This vast seascape would be the first thing you saw when you raised your head from your pillow, providing you kept the windows clean. I thought of the dancing stipple of sea light on the ceiling in the summer, and the flickering white snow light of winter. I thought of curtains and deep comforters and plaids and copper lamps and banked fires, and piles of books on bedside tables, and pottery bowls of apples, and maybe a little radio spilling out Brahms. . . .

You would not be cold here. Each bedroom had an iron stove

like the kitchen's, with a solid wooden box to hold wood or whatever they burned, and I had noticed that in a corner of the dim kitchen a big, if ancient, hot-water heater held court. There was a tiny bathroom opposite the bedrooms, but I had not yet had the heart to look in it. When I did, I winced at the dirt, but saw that it had a big, old-fashioned clawfoot bathtub with a shower curtain, so there must be a shower, and a bulbous toilet and washbasin that spoke of 1920s Sears Roebuck. The floor was wide-planked wood, and I pictured rag rugs and copper pots of chrysanthemums, even though it was now an inch deep in grime and had the leprous remnants of old linoleum in peeling patches across it.

I thought, also, of my huge sea-green bathroom at home, of the shining glass blocks and hanging plants and the Jacuzzi we had put in two years before, and the soft, incandescent lighting, and the double sinks and view of the park, of the bentwood rocker where I sometimes sat with a glass of wine while Tee bathed. . . .

I shook my head briskly and felt my way back downstairs and across the dark living room and porch, back to the Jeep. She sat looking at me stolidly, and said nothing.

"I'm afraid it's out of the question," I said rapidly. "It's just too . . . primitive. I mean, I've never even tried to start a woodstove before, and if one of the appliances broke down I wouldn't know what to do, and then if anyone should want to visit me, I have no idea where I'd put them, and it's just so far away from everything . . . and I do have to take the Jeep back to my friend's house; I'd have to buy a car, and I didn't see a phone . . . "

She took a deep breath.

"I apologize for the shape it's in. I don't blame you for worrying about that. I thought it would be the bigger one that I'd be offering, but . . . it didn't turn out that I could, and I didn't have enough notice to get this one cleaned up. But I promise you that I can have it shining for you whenever you'd like me to, and as for the phone, I'll be glad to have one put in; there's a line in here anyway, for the other one. And there's an old four-wheel-drive truck in my shed you could use; I'll never drive it again, nor will Luzia. You know, when it's all clean, and the sheets and curtains are fresh and up, and there's a fire in the fireplace and something cooking on the stove and music playing—I've got an old radio you can have, too, and a

158

little TV set we've never even watched—it's one of the coziest places you'll ever see. And the sunsets ... well, the Menemsha sunsets are famous all over the world, and from the porch of this one you have the best view of the sunsets on the entire island. On a fall or winter night it's really something special. We used to stay down here until the snow literally ran us out, Luz and I; I put in the stoves so we could stay on in the winters, and we did that until she fell. Those were good nights, I can tell you. Once or twice we saw the northern lights out over the water ... "

Her voice was hypnotic. I saw them, too.

"Why don't you try it and see, oh, until April, maybe?" she said. "If you really wanted to go home for a little while over Christmas or something, I could always find somebody to do for us for a few days, I guess. Of course, you'd be surprised how nice Christmas is out here in the woods. We spent several here before Luz fell, once with company, and it was like an old-fashioned Christmas out of a picture book. There was fresh snow, and the deer came right up to be fed, and the birds all came for the suet, and there's all kinds of wild holly around, and we put us up a little spruce from the woods, and cooked a turkey ... we both still talk about that Christmas. I'll bet your boy would get a kick out of an old-fashioned New England Christmas like that, and your dad and your daughter and her family, too. I've got several single beds in the barn I could move in, and there's a sleeping alcove under the stairs that'll hold a double. If you could see your way to stay through the winter and help us out, I can get this place fixed up so you won't know it in no time at all."

Snow, holly, deer, a fire, a little tree beside the fireplace—the scene unrolled in my head like a home movie, a happy one. And the money ... Until April. Eight months. Forty thousand dollars saved ... I could live a very good while indeed on that, back in Atlanta. I could plan a life in that amount of time.

I turned to her. "Why aren't you talking to your family?" I said. "I don't want to pry, but I don't understand why you want me so badly. There must be so many of you ... "

"Like I said. I won't ask them for help," she said. "I don't need to bore and burden you with the reasons. If you really can't see your way clear to do it, I can find somebody else. I don't mean to distress you by appearing to beg."

She looked defeated. Simply that. Proud, old, sour—and defeated. Her life in this enchanted wood was already over, and soon it would be over entirely. I, on the other hand, was seeking a place to plan the rest of mine. I felt a powerful turn of empathy and remorse. It could so easily be me in a few years, trying in the midst of the wreckage of a failing body to secure a future for myself and perhaps some faithful, ailing companion. What, to me, were a few months? What waited at home for me, anyway?

"If you can really get it livable, I'll stay until April," I heard myself say. My voice rang in my own ears.

"Thank you," she said, and dropped her eyelashes, but not before I saw the wash of tears there. They were gone when she raised her head, though.

"When would you like to come?"

"Well . . . when could you get it ready?"

"Day after tomorrow?" she said.

"Really? So soon?"

"There'll be no problem. You'll see," she said strongly.

"Would you want me to sign anything? A letter of agreement, or something?"

"No. I think you honor your word," she said.

"Well, then . . . it's a deal," I said, and gave her my hand, wondering if I had truly lost my mind. Probably. But, on the other hand, if I had signed nothing and it turned out that she could not, after all, get the camp livable, there was surely nothing to prevent me from going elsewhere. What could I lose?

She took my hand in her large old one. It felt cold and dry and rough, like the skin of a long-dead animal. I knew that hand; I had held others like it in my days as a volunteer at Grady Hospital, Atlanta's huge charity medical facility. It was the feeling of failing life systems: heart, lungs, circulation. I knew that I was holding mortality in my hand.

"Deal," she said.

I got into the Jeep and put the key in the ignition, and she said, "There's something else."

I turned to look at her. She was looking over at the other house. I don't know why, but the hair on the back of my neck stood up.

"What?"

She spoke without looking at me.

"It's my son. He's had to come home for a little while; he had an operation on his leg, and he needed somewhere to convalesce, and he asked if he could come here. It used to be his favorite place in the world, these old camps. I couldn't say no. It happened after I'd put the notice up on the road, and I just didn't get around to taking it down. I'd have put him in the smaller one, but he can't manage the stairs yet, and somehow I just didn't think anybody would really ask about the camps. We can't have him at the big house; I can't even take good care of Luz. Of course she'd want him; she'd cry and tease for him to come up there until she drove me crazy, so I just haven't told her he's here yet. He only came a couple of days ago; a friend from his school brought him, and he won't be here long, I don't think. Just maybe till late winter. It shouldn't take a lot of time. But he's going to need just a little bit of looking after . . . "

"And you want me to do a little bit of caretaking for him, too," I said, my heart sinking again. "Mrs. Ponder, I'm not a nurse. I can't take care of an invalid . . . "

"He doesn't need a nurse," she said. "He wouldn't have a nurse. He insists on doing for himself, and he's such a contrary loner, he wouldn't want anybody around helping him even if he needed it. All he needs is for somebody to get him in some groceries a couple of times a week, and maybe take him over to the hospital in Oak Bluffs once a month or so for the doctor to see how he's coming along. I don't think you'd be seeing enough of him to even know he was over there. He's got trunks and trunks full of books, and he had his big old stereo shipped over, and he's working on some kind of book of his own. You wouldn't have to go in, even, just leave the groceries on the porch. He could put you out a list . . . "

"It's just that I didn't count on having anybody so near . . . "

"Well, he's a nice boy. He wouldn't be a bad neighbor to have, even if you had to see him every now and then; he really minds his own business, always has. Real polite, though. Listen, I've brought him a few things to tide him over; I've got them in the tote. Why don't you just take them in to him, and meet him, and tell him who you are? See for yourself how easy it would be. He knows somebody will likely be coming . . . "

I wondered how he could possibly know that unless she had called him from the big house before we had left. But I said nothing, only looked at her helplessly. It did not, in fact, seem like a great deal to ask; I could get his groceries on the same days that I did Bella and Luzia's, and maybe even take him to his doctor's appointments at the same time they had theirs. And it might, after all, be rather nice to look out into the winter nights and see the warm yellow of a lit lamp, smell the smoke of a fire nearby.

"Well . . . all right," I said. "If you're sure he knows I'm coming."

"He knows," she said.

I started toward the larger camp and then stopped and looked back. She had her head in her hands, but she lifted it and looked at me, perhaps feeling my eyes on her.

"What's his name?" I called.

"Dennis," she called back. "I call him Denny."

I went on up the path and the steps, gray stone like the smaller one's, but scrubbed and lined with late geraniums in pots. The porch floor had been scrubbed, too, and big earthenware jugs of chrysanthemums sat on either side of the door. In spite of the smoke coming from the chimney the day was warm, and the white front door was ajar so that only a screened door separated the inside from the out. I peered in, but could see nothing for the dazzle of sunlight behind me. There was no sound. I rapped my knuckles lightly and waited.

No one answered, so I rapped again, and then called out, "Hello? Is anyone here? I've brought some things from Mrs. Ponder . . . "

There was still no response, and so, tentatively, I pushed the screen open and went in. Like the living room in the big farmhouse, this one was all murk and shadows, but it smelled of lemon polish and freshly ironed linen. I stood, waiting for my eyes to adjust. When they did, I saw first that a large chair was overturned and lay in the middle of the wooden floor, and then that beside it a little table was upended, and had spilled books and a pitcher holding wildflowers down beside the chair. Wrongness flooded the room and lifted the hairs at my nape again, and I began to back out on to the porch. And then I saw the man who lay behind the chair, and my heart and breath stopped.

I had no doubt in that instant that he was dead. His face had the silvery-yellow sheen of the few dead I had seen, and he lay utterly, totally still, on his back, with his arms flung out to his sides. His eyes were closed and looked as if they had been closed for hours; their lids were dark and bruised-looking, and in the pallor of his face the circles under them stood out like paint smudges. His hair was a dusty, lightless black streaked with iron gray and fell over his forehead, and he had that pinched and shrunken look at the base of his nostrils that I had noticed during my duties in the oncology ward at Grady: the look of a tool that is no longer needed. His mouth was bloodless and a little open. Even in my shock and fright I could have told that he was Bella Ponder's son. The carved, attenuated features were the same, except that his were no longer informed by life.

I made a small, strangled sound and took as deep a breath as I could manage, and my heart lurched forward. How could I go out and tell that old woman that her son was dead? Perhaps I should call someone else, a hospital, the rescue squad; hadn't she said there was a phone in this cottage? I took a tentative step farther and looked around for it.

"And who the fuck might you be?" a voice said, with no force behind it, but clear nevertheless, and deep.

I gave a small scream and looked again: His eyes were open and his head was turned toward me. His eyes were a strange light gray, the color of clear winter ice, and I saw that his face was so thin that the ridges of his brow and cheekbones stood out like rock under depleted soil. He still had no color but the dreadful, translucent ivory.

"Lie still," I whispered. "I'm going to call someone to help you, and then I'll get your mother . . . "

"You'll call nobody and you will not get my mother," he said, and his voice grew a bit stronger. He was struggling to sit up. I started toward him to help and he made a violent gesture at me: Get back. I stopped. It was only then that I noticed that he had only one leg. He was wearing khaki knee-length shorts, and one long, spidery leg was stretched out before him. The other shorts leg was empty. Whatever had happened to him had taken it at least at midthigh.

"I guess you're the handmaiden my mother has hired or bribed or otherwise charmed to look after me," he said, and his voice was cold and level, though still weak. "Who are you? Another royal Coimbran cousin-in-exile? Or is your name maybe Rakestraw or Fowler or Phipps? Or even Ponder? If so, how much did she pay you? If not, are you a bona-fide, official sister of charity come to fill your quota of one-legged gimps? Do tell, pray do, and end my poor befuddlement."

There was such venom in his voice that I could not think of anything to say. He was obviously not in immediate extremis and even more obviously did not want me in his house, but on the other hand, his pallor was truly appalling and I *had* found him lying on the floor, looking quite dead. And he did indeed have, as he himself said, only one leg. Conditioned by years of volunteer work and even more years of my mother's maxims about my place in the world, I went over to him and held out my hand.

"My name is Molly Redwine," I said. "I'm not anybody's handmaiden. I came about the camp your mother advertised, and she just now told me about you, and asked me if I'd consider doing a few errands for you until you recuperated, and if I'd come bring you some things she has for you. She can't walk far herself; I'm sure you know that. She said nothing at all about your having . . . about the seriousness of your illness or your operation or whatever it is, and she has offered me no money at all, nor would I take any if she had. I'm sorry if I startled you. You scared me to death. I thought you were dead. I have no intention of bothering you and I will leave the instant I can get you on your feet again, or whatever it is that you need, but I'm not going to leave until then because your mother can't help you and it doesn't look to me as if you can help yourself."

He looked away, lying still, and then said, "I'd appreciate it if you'd help me up. I was trying to get situated in the chair and I missed it and fell. I still can't get up very well when I fall. I've been taking . . . treatments that make me weak. I shouldn't have talked to you like that. But I don't need any help, and she knows that I don't want any, and still she . . . Well. If you'll give me a hand you can be on your way, and I hope you'll tell her for me to stay the fuck out of my business and my house. No offense, of course."

I tightened my mouth and went over and held my hand down

to him. Leaning on me heavily, and with me pulling, he eventually made it to his feet—or, rather, his foot—and I pulled the chair up behind him and he sank into it, whiter than ever and breathing shallowly.

When he did not speak, I said, "You've been taking chemo, haven't you? I've done a lot of work with oncology patients. I know the look. It's none of my business, but it doesn't look to me as if you're nearly ready to be out of the hospital, to say nothing of way out here, without anyone with you full-time. I don't want it to be me any more than you do, but you really do need somebody. I'm going back and tell your mother that, and tell her to go on back home and call you and work it out with you if she can't get up here herself. It's suicidal for you to be here like this by yourself."

I turned to go, and he said after me, "You're right. It's none of your business. Tell her whatever you like; I'm not talking to her and I'm not having anybody gawking and groping around here every day, helping me pee and wash myself and eat. You can tell her that, as long as you're telling her things. Oh, and thank you very much for your concern, Molly . . . ah, Redwine, was it? You're not from around here, are you, Molly? I have to hand it to her; I never thought she'd try it with somebody from America."

He closed his eyes and turned his head away, looking dead once more. I stood still, my heart hammering with the malice and sheer sickness of him, and then I turned and strode toward the Jeep to tell Bella Ponder that I would not, after all, be taking her up on her offer.

CHAPTER EIGHT

I T COULDN'T HAVE BEEN MORE THAN A MINUTE'S WALK back to the smaller camp and the Cherokee, but it felt as if it took a very long time. I seemed to be walking in slow motion, as against a heavy current. There was a clarity to the air that snapped details into sharp focus, as if every leaf, blade of grass, stone, glimpse of water had been edged in light. I could see a ladybug on a leaf, a scaldingly red miniature, and make out the whorls and slivers, the velvety green algae beard, of the pilings of the old dock. I felt dully sad and terribly tired. I had been up and down with this place so often in this short morning, so suffused with hope and rightness one moment and doubt and regret the next. But now there was only the sense of possibilities lost to me.

For this situation was impossible. I could not care for the sick and virulent man in the larger cabin and I could not accommodate the sly old colossus who sought to bring us together. I was repelled by the one and mortally weary of the other. I could, I knew, look for a house somewhere else up island, but I knew also that none would ever suit me after this one. Anything else would have holes in its magic, belong to a duller and more dangerous world.

I thought that I would simply go home. There would, surely, be apartments that did not require enormous deposits. I might not like them, but I could manage. Nothing, as my mother used to say, is cast in stone.

But anger at the old woman and her son lay deep under grief for the haven that had been dangled and then snatched back.

I did not look at Bella Ponder until I reached the Jeep. When I did, she was smiling at me, a smile that exposed her pale gums and was somehow unpleasantly false and slyly propitiatory. I would have bet a lot that this old woman did not often propitiate. I knew that she knew I was angry with her; how could she not?

"I hung your mother's pretty hat on your door," she said, pointing, and I looked; it was there. I looked back, saying nothing, waiting.

"People seem to be doing that all over the place these days," she said chattily. "Down island, I mean. Only hats you see much up here are Landry's Fish Camp hats and a few Red Sox things. Look kind of silly on your front door, wouldn't they? But I thought it might be sort of nice for you, to have your mama's hat hanging on your own new door. It looks pretty against that white, don't you think?"

I did not look at the hat on the door again. I took a deep breath.

"Mrs. Ponder," I said, "you have not been straight with me from the very beginning. Everything, all the stuff about fixing up the camp and putting in a phone and giving me a car and a TV . . . it was all for that, wasn't it? That back there?"

I gestured toward the larger camp. She did not speak. She dropped the brilliant black eyes and looked at her lap.

"You knew your son had more wrong with him than just a little operation on his leg; you knew he was an amputee, and that he had . . . a malignancy. I've done volunteer work with cancer patients for half my life; I know what it looks like. I know what it *is* like. I know what it requires in the way of caretaking. Your son was lying on the floor stock-still and as white as a sheet; I thought he was dead. He'd been trying to sit in a chair, and fell and couldn't get up. Just trying to sit in a chair. When I tried to get help for him, he said . . . well, you wouldn't believe what he said. Or maybe you would. I can't and won't take care of a man in the shape he's in, and I can't and won't have anyone talking to me like that. He should be in a hospital or a rehabilitation facility, or maybe even a hospice; at the very least he needs a full-time nurse with him. If he won't see you, surely you should be looking for somebody who could live in and take proper professional care of him. It's absolutely suicidal for

167

him to stay alone, and it's absolutely out of the question for me to look after him."

I had been looking at the ground while I delivered myself of the speech; I have always had a hard time with confrontation and ultimatums. When there was no answer, I looked into the Jeep at Bella Ponder.

She was crying. Incredibly, her eyes closed and her mouth struggling with itself not to distort, Bella Ponder sat in Livvy's Cherokee and wept. I knew that they were not crocodile tears; they were as grudging and painful to her as if she wept blood. It was like watching a monolith, a great statue, suddenly begin to cry. I knew that it would be nearly unbearable to her; she might inveigle and cajole and lie and even, ponderously, flirt, but to weep in front of a stranger would be more than her awful dignity would permit her.

Under my righteous little spurt of anger I felt embarrassment and a sympathy that was entirely unwanted and nearly excruciating. I turned away so that she could compose herself, my heart pounding, tears stinging my own eyes, hating both the heartbeat and the easy wetness.

Behind me, Bella Ponder's heavy, defeated voice said, "He won't let me help him. He hasn't spoken to me since he left this island, practically. He said he'd shoot at the visiting nurse if I sent her. He won't have his Ponder kin, not that they'd come if I asked them, which I wouldn't. He'd only agree to have somebody who didn't know any of us, somebody from off island, and then only if he could pay them. I couldn't find anybody like that; there's not anybody like that up island in the winter. And then you came along and it was like somebody sent you to us; you were all those things he said, and you even looked like . . . you seemed kind of like one of us in the bargain. Luz was right; you have the look of a Portuguese about you, somehow. She thought it was a sign, and I didn't know but what it was, too. I knew you wouldn't take any money to look after Denny, so I offered you everything else I had, that I could think of. I was going to let him think I was giving you his money, not that he's got much. His wife and his girl get most of it, I hear, and he'll have had to quit his job. He couldn't have anything to speak of or he wouldn't have come out here. I didn't . . . I haven't seen him in over forty years. I knew it was cancer, but I guess I didn't know it was so bad. He said . . . the only thing he said on the phone was that he thought he wouldn't need anybody past March or April. I thought he meant he'd be well by then, and he'd leave, but I guess maybe that wasn't what he meant . . . "

Her voice, suddenly frail and old, trailed off, but when I looked at her I saw that the tears had not stopped. They slid silently down the big, seamed, brown face, leaving trails like a snail's on earth.

I looked over at the door of the smaller camp. My mother's lacy black hat stood out against the pocked white like a spider on old snow. It looked fixed, inexorable. This is my outpost in this place, it said. Here I live. Get in here and start doing what you know you should be doing.

I took another deep breath, feeling it shake in my lungs.

"Mrs. Ponder," I said again, "I'm never going to ask you what's wrong between you and your son. I don't even want to know. But if I should stay and try to do some things for him—and I said *if*—he'll have to stop talking to me like he just did. I really can't have that. And you'll have to stop trying to manipulate me. *And* I insist on at least having the visiting nurse; why couldn't he just pay her if he wants to pay somebody?"

"She doesn't take pay. She's a county service," Bella said. Her voice was still soft and even deferential, but it was two decades younger. "Denny wouldn't take county help, and I wouldn't ask for it. My God, our people come from royalty back in Portugal, ours and his; he's named for King Dinis, who was a direct forebear. Everybody who knows anything at all about the Portuguese knows about King Dinis. He was called the troubadour king, the poet king. He built more than a hundred castles in Portugal in the twelfth century. I think Denny gets his talent from him; he writes beautiful poetry. Some of it's been published. You think a Miara from Coimbra is going to take charity?"

Oh, God, I thought, nearly overcome with a great, helpless, white fatigue. This poor, awful, grotesque, proud, silly old woman. She would have recognized my mother in a nanosecond. They're the same person. Who on earth would bother with her and her awful, dying son?

But I knew who was probably going to bother.

I reached across her into the glove compartment of the Cherokee and pulled out the pad and ballpoint pen that Livvy kept there. I wrote on it; I scribbled for quite a long time. Then I jerked the sheet from the pad and gave it to her. She read it carefully, her face impassive but still tear-stained, and gave it back to me and nodded. I folded the sheet small and took it up on the front porch of the larger camp and pushed it under the closed door and came back to the Jeep.

"Get somebody to come get his answer in the morning, and call me and tell me what it is," I said. "I want him to sign it, too. If he agrees to it—*all* of it, everything—I'll take the camp. I'll try to keep it and look after him a little, with some outside help when I think I need it, if and until he gets so he needs hospitalizing. I'm out of it then, no questions asked. I may stay on after that, or I may not. I'll try to let you know as far ahead as possible if I don't. And I'll only do this if you agree not to put me in the middle of whatever this mess between you is, and if you both agree that I can call the visiting nurse or somebody whenever I think it's necessary. That's it. No more talking."

Bella smiled. It tried its best to be a humble smile, but triumph oozed from it like sap from a maple tree. For some reason, that came near to amusing me. I would have been somehow disappointed if I could so easily bring this elemental force to her knees, I knew. Disappointed and perhaps just a bit frightened of my own power. I had never been able to do that with my own mother. It would have been disconcerting, to say the least, to be able to do it with anyone else's.

We did not speak again until I had reached the farmhouse and opened the door on her side to help her get out and make her way up the steps. After I had hauled her to her feet, she put her hand on my arm and looked down into my face. Few people are able to do that. It was an odd sensation.

"I want to thank you for what you're doing," she said, and shook her head impatiently as I started to speak. "I don't mean about Denny; there's no way I can thank you for that. I mean what you're doing for Luz. I was about one day from having to call somebody about those swans. The last two times I've gone down to feed them, I thought I wouldn't get back. And I couldn't let them starve. And I sure couldn't ask anybody else to feed them and bust up that ice all winter. They'd laugh in my face. Not that folks around here are mean to animals, I'll give you that, but they've got other things on their minds, and they sure aren't sentimental about swans. There's too many of them pecking around up here, and they do too much damage. Somebody would have just shot them and that would have been that. It would have killed Luz. So I thank you."

Then she took my arm and, leaning heavily on it, made her way back up the steps and into the old house, stopping every few seconds so she could gulp in air. When we finally got inside, her face was nearly purple, and sweat ran down it like rain. I put her into a chair beside Luz's bed and got a glass of water from the dark old kitchen. It smelled of spices and tomatoes and illness.

She sipped the water, and Luz smiled at us, an irresistible smile, full of joy and gaiety. It moved me even more than Bella's tears had.

"I knew you were going to save the swans," she said. "I said so before you left for the camp. Didn't I, Bella? I said, 'Bella, this is our *Santa Cisna*, who's going to take care of Charles and Di for us. I've prayed every night to the Virgin to send her. And here she is.' I said that."

As soon as I satisfied myself that Bella Ponder could breathe again, I left and went out to the Cherokee. I drove back to Chappaquiddick with the radio tuned to a Boston FM station playing Baroque music. Halfway between West Tisbury and Edgartown *The Water Music* began, spilling its liquid notes out into the car, and I grinned at the radio.

"Okay," I said aloud. "I know a conspiracy when I hear one."

I knew that Dennis Ponder would agree to my terms. I could not have said how, but I knew it as certainly as I knew that it was the On Time Ferry whose deck wallowed beneath my tires, and not the QE2. Everything about this strange, freighted morning was bright with portent. And though I had no wish at all to be anyone's *santa*, of the swans or anything else, I was glad of the knowledge. The song of the little camp and the glade and the pond was loud in my ears; it swam in and out among Handel's silvery notes, playing with them, vaulting over them. I knew I had been right about up island.

I felt almost manic with anticipation, as gleeful as a child with a daring, secret plan, when I went into the old house on Katama

Bay. But I had no sooner sat down at the kitchen desk and pulled the telephone to me to begin the series of calls I had to make than the great, glittering brightness outside curled into the kitchen like smoke and wrapped around me, and the elation left. In its place was the crawling unease I had felt here for the last two days. I got up and went to the porch door and looked out, looking both ways and up into the sky to see whose prowling shape I seemed to almost catch from the corner of my eye. But there was nothing, only the fractured diamond surface of the dancing bay, and the late summer light playing in the trees and grasses that bent in the wind, and the shadows of the small clouds that rocketed across the afternoon sky. The wind was hard; I could hear it making a crooning sound that had little to do with summer and soft, golden light; it prowled in my blood and bones. The vista from the porch was too big by far, too exposed. I pulled the curtains and sat back down. The restlessness in me that wind and space called up came very near to fear. But with the curtains drawn and the lamps lit, I felt better.

I did not think I could stay much longer in the house on the water, though. Not this house. Not this water.

First I called Teddy at school and, miraculously, reached him at his apartment. He was home for lunch, he said, and I smiled, seeing in my mind as well as hearing the sandwich that bulged in his cheek as he spoke. It struck me that I would love little more right then than to make a sandwich for my son, and I played the scene out in my mind, and found to my amazement I could not picture my own kitchen. Instead, I saw myself slicing bread and spreading mayonnaise in the cramped kitchen of the camp in the glade, scrubbed now and bright with fall flowers and noon light.

I told him what I was going to do, and he nearly choked on the sandwich and then laughed aloud.

"Way to go, Ma," he crowed. "My Robinson Crusoe mom! What brought this on, as if I didn't know?"

Suddenly I did not want to tell him that my house was, in effect, not mine anymore. It sounded impossibly theatrical, nauseatingly poor me. It was, after all, Teddy's house, too; why had I not considered where he would go if he wanted to come home? This separation was, after all, about other people as well as me. It had been that that had outraged me from the beginning, and yet in all the time I was falling in love with the camp, I had not thought of Teddy.

"It's not a sure thing yet," I said, feeling my grand adventure deflate like a circus balloon. "I wasn't going to do it without consulting you . . ."

"Well, I think it's cool," he said. "How long do you think you'll stay? A month? Two?"

"Well . . . actually, I thought longer than that. Through the winter, at least. Teddy . . . there are some reasons I don't feel I can come back to Atlanta for a while. Missy thinks it's best, too. I can't . . . it's probably not a good idea for me to live in the house for a while, and money's going to be a little tight, not that that's anything for you to worry about. It won't affect you . . ."

"Is he cutting off your money?" my son said, and there was ice and pain in his voice.

"No," I said. "It's my own decision. As I said, it's not going to affect you. But listen, I thought you might like to come spend Thanksgiving with me up here. We can have a real, old-fashioned New England Thanksgiving. Maybe Grandpop can come, too. It's really very beautiful up here. I'd love to show it to you . . ."

There was a silence, and then he said, "Ma, since you aren't going to be home anyway—in Atlanta, I mean—would you care if I went camping with some of the guys? There's a guy in my structures class who lives near the Anasazi ruins in Arizona, and a bunch are going. I'd give my eyeteeth to see that. But listen, if you're going to be up there by yourself—"

"I'm not going to be by myself," I said hastily. "The Anasazi, wow! I'd kill you if you *didn't* go. I'll call Grandpop. I bet he'd love to rough it in the woods . . ."

"Mom, he's going to Aunt Sally's folks' with them. I talked to him the other night. Listen, why don't you call Caroline? What better company for Thanksgiving than a new baby? In Tennessee, if not up there . . ."

"Well, that's just what I'll do," I said heartily, knowing that I would not. Caroline had not yet mustered the nerve to take the baby to the park by herself. She would faint at the very thought of up island. My throat closed up; I had had no idea how much I missed Teddy until I heard his voice. Missed and loved him; loved him enough to insist that he try his new wings.

"If they can't come or you can't go there, just call me. I'll be there with bells on," he said.

"No need, I've met a lot of people up here who're looking out for me," I said lightly. "I'm the belle of the bay."

"I'll bet. Any interesting guys? Any action?"

"Only one," I said. "And he's as mean as a snake and one-legged besides."

Forgive me, Dennis, I said to myself. But right now you're more use to me as fodder to amuse my son than anything else. And besides, you owe me.

"Just your speed," Teddy said, and we laughed together. Even over the telephone, even with the disappointment and the missing, it felt good.

I meant to call my father next, but instead I stretched out on the sofa, and slid instantly into a long and vivid dream about my mother. It was not the usual dream about the grated subterranean window, or at least not just that. It began in the same way, but it went farther into the country of nightmare and panic than I had ever been in my dreams before, and I know that I will remember the precise, sweating texture of that dream until the day that I die.

It started out the same: with me on the city street looking down to see the barred subterranean window where my mother always sat in the black hat, waiting. But this time the window was empty, and I turned to my father, who stood beside me in the crowd, and said, "She's not there."

"Maybe she's found what she was waiting for," my father said, looking around. I looked around, too, and saw my mother standing ahead of us on the sidewalk, facing backward in the crowd so that she looked at us. She wore the hat, and she was smiling with pleasure and sweetness. In my dream my heart gave a great fish leap of joy. I knew that she was dead, but nevertheless, there she was, smiling her approval at me. I did not point her out to my father, who was still looking about eagerly, or any of the crowd going past, lest they become aware of her suddenly, and somehow frighten her away. It seemed, with the senseless sense of dreams, entirely possible for my dead mother to be with me as long as I did not call attention to her. I did not understand why my father could not see her, though.

I went close to her and whispered, "I'm so glad to see you. You look so pretty in that hat."

I did not point out to her that I knew she was dead. It was as if she herself did not know, that for her to know would be to lose her.

"I've always liked this hat," she said. It was her voice, no doubt of that, low and full and with that hint of husky theatricality that I had always so envied. "I don't think there's anything like a big hat to play up a woman's eyes. I'd give it to you, but it's meant for somebody else."

I could not say, No, it's not, I have it, so I just nodded and said, politely, "Oh? Who?"

"Your father," she said. "This hat is for your father. Can you find him for me?"

"I don't know where he is," I said in the dream, but my eyes flicked to my father of their own volition, and I saw her see him, and start toward him in a little rush of joy. She took the hat off and her hair flew free around her pretty head, and she held it out and called, "Darling! Come and get your hat!"

I turned, and behind me my father had seen her, and was starting toward her, his whole heart and soul in his eyes. He reached out for her hand and the black hat.

In that instant I knew that if he touched the hat he would be dead, too, and gone with her, and after that I would see them both in the terrible window, waiting for whatever it is the dead wait for.

"NOOOO!" I screamed, and woke myself up.

It was a full five minutes before I could stop shaking, stop the cold sweat that ran down my face and neck. My heart pounded for long after that. I looked at my watch and saw that I had slept for nearly two hours. Outside the drawn curtains, the sun would be setting. Blackness would be coming across the water from Nantucket.

I went to the phone and called Kevin's house in Washington. Kevin answered; he sounded as he did on the air. I wondered if he put his coat and tie on when he answered his telephone; he sounded as if he did.

"How is Daddy?" I said without preamble.

"Daddy's awful," Kevin said, and my galloping heart raced faster.

"What?"

"Depression," Kevin said. "Full-blown clinical depression. No doubt about it. We did a special on it a couple of months ago. It's all there, the lethargy, the sleeping, the lack of interest in everything, the loss of appetite, even the sloppy personal habits. It's a delayed reaction to Mother, I know. He's been in denial ever since she died, and now it's caught up with him."

"Have you had him to a doctor?" I said, pain for my father all but drowning me.

"He won't go, but I've talked with a shrink friend of ours, and he says there's no doubt of the diagnosis. He gave us a prescription for Prozac, but I don't think Dad's taking it. Sally doesn't want to monitor him, and I can't stay home and see that he does. Listen, Molly, I'm glad you called. I've been meaning to call you. You're just going to have to take over now. He's making no plans to go back to the condo, and we've decided that he ought to move in with you. It's the obvious solution, and it could be a help to you, too. But I know he'd take it better if the suggestion came from you."

I told him then about Tee and Sheri and the house in Ansley Park, and why Missy thought I should not live in it, and about the money, and then about the camp on the pond and the plans I had made.

"Well, if that's not the most harebrained, selfish thing I've ever heard in my life," Kevin exploded. "And the most typical. Get it all worked out for little Molly and let everybody else go hang. I guess it doesn't matter to you that Sally cries herself to sleep at night, and Mandy can't have any of her friends over anymore. Dad just sits there. He just sits there in the living room with the TV set on, not watching, not talking, just sitting there . . . "

I took a deep breath. It shook as I exhaled.

"Kevin, you know that never once in my life have I worked things out for myself and let everybody else go hang. You know that. That was unfair and untrue. If anybody in this family works things out for themselves and lets everybody else . . . "

I let it trail off. I did not want to fight with him. I never won.

"Okay, okay, I know," my brother said, and let his breath out on a long sigh. "That was below the belt. But we're all near to cracking. Look, if you can't go back to your house, and I think your lawyer is wrong, by the way, maybe you could go live with Dad, in the condo. He's not even trying to sell it anymore. It would solve all your problems, and he'd have somebody with him. I think he has to have that. Maybe you could get him to go for some help; we sure can't. I don't know but what he's not suicidal."

"Kevin! *Daddy?*"

"You haven't seen him, Molly."

"Let me talk to him."

After a bit my father came on the line. I listened very carefully, but to me he sounded just as he always had; the slow, mild voice was the father's that I knew and none other.

"Hey, baby, they lynched you yet?" he asked, and I laughed. It was an old joke of ours, that I tanned as darkly as an African-American in the sun.

I told him about the camp, and about the old ladies and Dennis Ponder, though I softened that considerably, saying only that Dennis was recuperating from leg surgery, and I tried to make the plight of the old ladies merely funny and crotchety. I said nothing about my reasons for not coming home or about my severely curtailed financial circumstances; no reason to burden him with that. But I dwelt at length on Charles and Diana, and was rewarded with his old, rich chuckle.

"That must be a sight to see," he said. "I'm going to read up on swans. Maybe I can find some arcane tidbit of swan psychology that will help you with the old man. Well, babe, good for you and all your plans. Sounds to me that you've gone from the frying pan into the fire, though; from looking after one family to looking after another, with an ornery feathered family thrown in."

I had not thought of it that way, and was not sure I liked the implications.

"Well, they're not my family," I said lightly. "That's why I can do it, I think. There's really not much to it, and I'm not emotionally involved with anybody. That's the killer. That's not going to happen again."

He laughed again, but comfortably.

"So you say."

I asked about Thanksgiving and he said yes, he had indeed committed to Sally's parents.

"Would you come for Christmas?" I said hesitantly. All of a sudden it was very important to me that he say yes.

"Well, that would be fun, wouldn't it? Snow and swans and all that? Sure, if you're still up there," my father said.

I got Kevin back on the line.

"He sounds okay to me," I said.

"He's trying to spare you," Kevin said. I could tell by his voice that he was angry again.

"I don't think so . . . "

"Shit, Molly, it's what he's always done. You were always his baby."

And you were always Mother's, and now you're not anybody's, and that's what all this is about, I did not say. I waited. There was a silence. Then he said, "Molly, you go on home and take care of him. Enough is enough. You're the only one who can do anything with him."

"I can't do that," I said.

"What is it, you want to kill him, too?" Kevin said, and I hung up on him, shaking. But I was not surprised. I knew that he would always feel that I had killed our mother. Whether or not he was right, he had the power of his cherished conviction about that. It would always be his best weapon against me.

I got up from the desk and poured myself a small glass of the lovely, thick, tawny port that Livvy had brought over from Boston; Portuguese port from the Duoro River region, she had told me. It tasted like smoke and honey going down. I brought the glass back to the desk and sipped at it as I dialed Missy Carmichael.

Missy hooted at the idea of me in the cabin on the pond all winter, with my ill and eccentric entourage, but she favored the idea all the same.

"It'll sound divine to a jury," she purred. "You living in a freezing hovel far away because you can't afford to come home, especially at Christmas. I can make hell's own amount of hay with that."

The trial. How could I have forgotten about the trial? It did not seem real at all.

"Any idea when that will be?" I said. The whole notion made me more tired than I thought possible. I slumped in my chair.

"Well, it's funny," Missy said. "Tee's beating around the bush about the trial. He's missed the last two meetings with us; she's always there, breathing fire and brimstone, but he just . . . hasn't shown. I don't know why, and I don't think she does, either. It sounds to me as if she doesn't know where he is a good bit of the time. He sure ain't taking my calls. I finally called the Eel Woman at the office to try to get some answers. She blew me right out of the water. Meaner than fresh cat shit these days, no doubt about that. But it doesn't look like she can do anything with him any more than we can. I can't help but wonder if he's having second thoughts. If I were him, I'd be afraid to tell that woman I had any doubts, either; hand you your balls back, she would. So the answer to your question is, I don't know. You'll eventually have to come home, but not for a while at this rate. You'll stay with me when you do, of course. Oh, and that little geisha at your bank called and Tee's first payment to your new account has come in. She didn't know how to call you, so she asked me to let you know. You can draw on it whenever you want to. You probably ought to open yourself an account up there, if you're serious about staying. It would show good intent if you did."

I did not know how I felt about Tee's wishy-washiness. I found that I could not fit any possible change of heart on his part into any scenario for the future I could imagine, so I dealt with it by simply not thinking about it. I buried it deep, along with all the other flotsam and jetsam of this awful summer. I would take it out and look at it later, when it might make more sense. I asked Missy to send some of my winter clothes, and hung up, feeling more rootless and suspended than ever. I took an apple and went over and walked on South Beach, thinking the sunset and the fresh wind might dispel some of the murk in my head. But the sun had slipped behind a great bank of silver-shot gray clouds in the southwest to die, and the sea had turned a terrible, beautiful, flashing pewter, all motion and coldness. When the lone family left on the beach packed up their things and disappeared over the dunes to their car, I fairly flew to the Jeep and drove back to Livvy's. Aloneness had turned into a great, personal thing that stalked me like a panther.

The phone was ringing as I came into the kitchen, and I grabbed it up as if it were a lifeline thrown into black water. Any voice, any voice at all . . .

It was Livvy. Caleb was working late and she wanted to talk. I could tell that she had had one and perhaps more of her sundown glasses of wine. I poured myself more of her port and settled in to listen. Her voice warmed me, like the liquor going down. In all the strangeness around me, Livvy seemed as palpable as if she sat in the room. She told me the news of our set, which made no more sense to me than if she spoke of a group of aborigines she had read about, and then said that Caleb had told her that the gossip around the office was that Sheri Scroggins was living in my house in Ansley Park. Tee, she said, was almost never in town anymore, but she supposed that he had installed her there.

"Even she wouldn't dare, unless he had," Livvy said. "You'll probably have to pry her off your rug like a tick. I wonder if they plan on just letting you find her there when you come home? Speaking of which, have you made any plans yet? I don't care how long you stay up there, but the pipes will freeze eventually, and people are asking me. Carrie Davies, that chalice of all that is fine and fair in Southern womanhood—oh, all right, I know she was your sainted roommate—called me last night wanting to know. She hemmed and hawed and finally let drop that poor old Lazarus is driving her crazy. Says he has a certain doggy odor, and I gather he licks his balls—not that Carrie would say so, of course. I'd take him but I'm going with Caleb to Chicago for a youth brands conference, and then we thought we might go up to Mackinac Island for a week or ten days. Kind of a second honeymoon."

She giggled, and I smiled into the empty room. I was glad things were still good with Livvy and Caleb. My poison hadn't found its mark, then.

It was only after I hung up that I realized I had not told her of my decision to stay here. I could not think why I had not.

I called Carrie Davies. Listening to her piping treble chiming through its scale, I wondered why I had never noticed what a shrill voice she had. Livvy had once said Carrie sounded like a hedgehog looked like it ought to sound, "all tiggywinklish." I had defended Carrie, but now I saw what Livvy had meant. Carrie and Atlanta seemed as far away as the dark side of Uranus.

"It might be a while before I can get back," I said to her finally, when she had run down. I had no intention of telling her my plans yet. "I know Lazarus can be a little much. Could you or Charlie take him to the Ansley Animal Clinic until Dad or I get home? Dr. Newman knows him. He's boarded him before."

"Well, of course," Carrie said, the alacrity of deliverance clear in her voice. "Maybe that would be better. He's really pining for you, I think. He howls a lot. Oh, here he comes; listen, Lazarus, here's your mommy. Say something, Molly . . . "

"Hey, big dog," I said into the telephone, feeling foolish, and was rewarded with a long, mournful howl.

My heart literally cramped with pain and homesickness for him. Here at last was reality.

"Carrie, do you think Charlie could possibly put him on a plane up here for me?" I said, wondering why I had not thought of it until now. Of course, that was what the camp and the glade called out for: Lazarus. Big, goofy, clumsy, loving Lazarus. The swans would just have to work it out.

"I guess so," she said doubtfully, seeing her imminent deliverance seeping away. "Ah . . . when would you want him?"

"Can you give me a week?"

There was a silence, and then she said, warmly, "Sure. What's a week between me and this old guy? You know, it's Tee who really ought to be taking care of him, but the way he's acting, I wouldn't let him take care of an iguana. Did anybody tell you that he's moved that little hussy into your house? I guess I shouldn't tell you, but I think you've got the right to know . . . "

"I heard," I said. "It's okay. Little does she know that there's colorless, odorless, death-dealing radon seeping from the basement as we speak. Asbestos, too. She'll be toast in a month."

"Really?" gasped Carrie.

"Why do you think I'm not coming home yet?" I said, knowing that she would take it literally, and that it would be all over Buckhead by this time tomorrow.

I thanked her again for sitting Lazarus and hung up. My good humor was restored enough so that the rising wind outside did not really bother me, and when I finally crept upstairs to sleep, I dreamed, not of my mother in her haunted subway, but of the quiet woods outside Menemsha.

The next morning Bella Ponder called to say that Dennis had accepted my terms, and the day after that I moved up island.

CHAPTER NINE

THE DAY I MOVED WAS THICK AND GRAY; last night's wind had blown in a canopy of low clouds that promised rain. The drive up island was dun-colored, but the beginning colors of autumn were oddly enhanced by the dullness. The stand of beetlebung trees at the crossroads in Chilmark was beginning to redden a leaf here and there. Livvy had said that in the autumn they were one of the Vineyard's glories. My first New England autumn: I felt as excited as a child going on a vacation in new territory. It was how I would live, I thought; how I would create a new life up here: I would taste as fully as I could each new experience, new sight, new sound. I would leave my baggage at home. I did not want to waste any time on regret and pain. The great stew of unresolved emotion over my mother and my marriage would just have to simmer on the back burner until I got around to it.

Moreover, if I were going to make a fresh life in this place, I had better get on with it right away. For the first time I felt, on that drive, an urgent sense that my time of being was no longer limitless. The sense left a residue of sucking blackness, as if a curtain had parted briefly and let me look into an abyss. "Mortality," my mother used to exclaim. "You can't live until you confront your own mortality." But somehow she had never confronted her own, probably not even when it happened. I dumped the mortal blackness into the stew pot with the rest of my ghosts and slammed the lid down.

The first thing I did when I drove into the glade was to stop by and look in on Dennis Ponder. Get it over with; set up a routine; lay a firm foundation of quick, impersonal, no-nonsense contact. I would, I thought, try checking on him first thing in the mornings and late in the afternoons. That way, if he needed anything, I could get it during the daytime and deliver it to him before dinnertime. Like feeding the swans, I intended that the care and feeding of Dennis Ponder be as efficient and nominal as I could make it. I did not imagine he wanted me hovering over him any more than Charles and Diana obviously did.

No smoke curled from the chimney of the larger camp this morning, though it was considerably cooler than the day before. I walked up the steps and across the porch, and lifted my hand to knock, then saw that the door was ajar. I was instantly uneasy.

"Mr. Ponder?" I called, halfway expecting to hear nothing, as I had before. But a voice called out, "Come in. Back in the bedroom."

I walked through the big living space, seeing that a fire was laid but not lit, and that the stove in the kitchen was unlit, too. There was a wood box beside it like the one in my kitchen, this one filled with neatly hewn logs, and the stove's black-iron door stood open, but no fire burned inside. There was no coffee or tea on the counter, no sign of breakfast. Either he could manage easily after all, and had already eaten and cleaned up after himself, or he was unable to manage at all and I would have to do it. I prayed it was the former. I could not imagine feeding that cold, white man.

I went to the doorway of the big downstairs bedroom behind the living room and looked in. A floor lamp burned there, and he was sitting in an upright chair beside it, dressed and combed. His plaid shirt was buttoned up to the neck and the collar was far too big for his throat. It was the look of the old, or the sick. There were piles of books all over the room: on the unmade double bed; on the floor beside it; spilling off the desk and the one easy chair; still occupying moving boxes stacked against the wall. He had one open on his knee, and was making notes on a legal pad. At first he did not look up, and I stood there, waiting. I was determined not to speak first. Then he finished writing and did look at me.

He looked marginally better. His face was not so waxen yellow, though it was still pale, and the bones still made ridges through the translucent skin. He had not shaved, and there was a dark shadow of beard around his mouth and on his cheeks and chin. His eyes were dark and sunken under level black brows, and his mouth was long and mobile, the pale lips full in contrast to the rest of the desiccated face. If he had been well, it would have been a sensuous mouth. His black hair had damp comb tracks in it, and fell in a shock over his forehead. Forehead and cheeks were cut with deep lines of pain and weakness; I knew those lines from my hospital work. They furrowed what I could see of his brow, too, and bracketed his mouth. I was reminded of someone, and could not think who until I remembered seeing, late one evening the summer before, an old movie with Gregory Peck and Jennifer Jones called *Duel in the Sun*. Dennis Ponder reminded me of the indolent outlaw played by Gregory Peck in that movie, if Peck had been much older and wasted with cancer. Even with the stigmata of the disease on him, Dennis Ponder was a handsome man. Or, at least, had been. The resemblance to his mother was less today, but still apparent, though how that might be I could not have said; Bella was near to being grotesque. But still, in her son's face, you could see what she once might have been . . .

"How are you this morning?" I said when he still did not speak. He stared at me a while longer, then smiled. It was not a warm smile. I thought that his mouth pulled tight in pain would look the same way.

"I'm sorry, I don't mean to stare," he said, and his voice was as colorless as his face. "You really look remarkably like what I remember of my mother. I thought for a minute yesterday you were one of our endless kin; the Miara ones, of course. My mother is very good at importing relatives. But you're not one of us, of course; she wrote me a remarkably thorough dossier on you: outlander through and through, you are, aren't you? No ties at all to this sacred sod. Why you want any is one of God's great mysteries, I suppose, but that's your affair, as is everything else about you, and I assure you it will remain so. I'm sorry I snapped at you yesterday. I'm told I'm not to do it again."

It was not a pleasant little speech.

"That's right," I said. "You're not. So. How are you today? You look a good deal better than you did the last time I saw you."

"How am I?" he said, and smiled, the skeletal teeth flashing white. "I expect you know how I am. My mother's note also said that you work with cancer patients back home in ... Atlanta, is it? She is quite excited about that; thinks it's a sign that *Santa Maria* sent you to us. As you can see, when it comes to *Santa Maria*, no stone has been left unturned."

He gestured and for the first time I noticed that there was a carved black-and-gold crucifix, obviously old, over his bed, and two or three painted statuettes of the Virgin Mary, and a heavy old mahogany reredos against one wall, flowers and candles set out on it.

"I know something about malignancies," I said evenly.

"Then perhaps you'll know what I mean when I say that I have had a stage-four adult soft-tissue sarcoma that made shit out of my knee, found a home in some lymph glands, and headed uptown. By the time we found it there was no way to save the bottom leg and knee, and there's no way now to know if any more of it will have to go. I'm among the elite; it's very rare, especially in adults. It has been treated with radiation and chemotherapy, and I had the last treatment just before I came here. There is not any pain except in the part of the leg that is gone, which I understand is called phantom pain and is quite common. The itching is worse than the pain. The real pain comes next if the chemo doesn't work, which I will not know for a while. Nor will I know where; this baby travels. Mainly I am weak and still nauseated, but I understand this should pass. I still sleep quite a lot. As you see, I have not lost the hair on my head or face, though for some reason I lost all my body hair. I'm as slick as a boiled frog all over; I hope the notion does not appall you, or even worse, turn you on. What I will need from you is for you simply to check on groceries and things like that, and to take me to my doctors' appointments. Those should be minimal, and the first is not for almost a month. I need no help with meals or bathing or household duties."

"Have you had your breakfast?" I said. "I didn't see any dishes, and your stove isn't lit."

His face colored faintly.

"I left my crutches in the bathroom," he said. "I just haven't gotten them yet. I'm still learning my way around this place ... "

His voice trailed off and he looked down at his legal pad. I knew that he had not yet been able to retrieve the crutches, and was trying to put the best possible face on it for me. I knew, too, that he would rather fumble for the crutches, crawl on his knees, do without food and warmth than ask me to help him. For some reason, it made me angry.

I went into the bathroom, got the crutches, and stood them up against his chair. Then I went back into the living room, touched a match to the fire, lit the kitchen stove, and made coffee. I turned on the gas oven, put a couple of slices of bread on a baking sheet, and left it on the counter. I got butter and the ubiquitous beach plum jelly out of the refrigerator and set them beside the sheet. Then I went back into his bedroom.

"I got some things started for you," I said. "For God's sake, tell me when you need help. It takes about five seconds to do what needs doing, and it's one of the agreed-on conditions."

"Ah, yes, the conditions," he said. "Well, thank you, Molly whatever your last name is. From now on I'll remember the crutches, and I'll stay in the bedroom while you minister; you'll find a list of things I need on the table in the living room. That's where it will always be. I won't get in your way; I'll be working in here most of the time."

"Your mother says you're working on a book," I said, I hoped pleasantly.

"My mother is full of shit," he said, "but yes, I am. Do you know anything about publishing, Molly By Golly?"

"I've had a little experience," I said stiffly.

"Wait, don't tell me . . . you edited the Junior League cookbook. Am I right?"

He was, or nearly. It had been the Grady Hospital Auxiliary cookbook. My face burned.

"I'll leave you alone," I said. "If you should need me, just call . . . or no, I guess my phone's not in yet. Maybe you could—"

He gestured at the bedside table, and I saw then that an old-fashioned bronze dinner bell with a carved handle sat on it. Charlotte Redwine had one on her dining-room sideboard, only in silver.

"My mother has provided for all my needs, physical as well as spiritual," Dennis Ponder said. There was color on both cheekbones now, like hectic flags against the pallor. Somehow it did not make him look healthier. "There's even a crucifix in the kitchen, right over the portable toilet, in case I feel in need of a bit of blessing while taking a shit."

"Poor baby," I said meanly, and turned and left the room. This man was odious, dying or no, and I felt neither sympathy for nor curiosity about him. I picked up the grocery list that sat on the split log table in front of the scarred leather sofa, and went out into the gray morning. Down on the pond I caught a whisk of white. The swans were no doubt waiting for their breakfast, too.

"Tough patootie, you stupid turkeys," I said to them. "You can just wait till I have some coffee. Go glom some underwater plants. Eat some algae. Live a little."

It did not help my mood at all that the second man in one summer had compared me to a woman who loomed large in his life. I hated the first comparison and didn't at all care for the second.

"Maybe I'll get my head shaved and my nose pierced. What would you think of that?" I called to the swans as I got out of the Jeep. They had left the pond and were waddling up the bank toward me and, I supposed, their breakfast, lifting their great wings ominously. The larger, Charles I was sure now, began the snaky hissing.

"Terrific way to get your breakfast," I said, moving quickly up on to the porch of my camp. "Really makes the cook feel appreciated. For that you'll wait until I go out for groceries."

I stopped on the porch and looked around. Bella Ponder had been as good as her word. Someone had done some serious work on the smaller camp. From the bronze chrysanthemums in iron pots beside the front door to the swept and scrubbed porch floor and the shining windows, the outside of the little house had been transformed. Two rickety but clean twig armchairs and an old hammock on a freshly painted white iron stand stood on the porch, and there was a sheaf of early autumn foliage in a tin bucket on a twig table. I smiled. I could always spend my time on the porch if the interior was too grim. The real cold would not begin for a month yet.

But when I went inside I saw that there would be no need to do that. It might have been a different room. It, too, was swept and scrubbed; the fireplace was cleaned and laid with logs, ready to light; the two straight chairs had been joined by an old leather morris chair that looked as though someone had polished it; a round table laid with white crockery and a jar of wildflowers sat under the window at the end of the room. Old-fashioned white priscilla curtains, limp from years of wear but clean and ironed, framed the windows. A couple of thick plaid blankets smelling of camphor were draped over the sofa back. In the kitchen, which had been scrubbed, too, the wood box beside the iron stove was filled, and the stove itself looked newly blacked. Cooking stove and refrigerator had been scoured. There were a couple of place settings of age-bleached Fiesta ware, yellow and blue, on the open shelves, and a coffeepot and a tea kettle on the stove, and a new tin of coffee stood ready with a can opener beside it. I opened the refrigerator; it was tiny and stained, but it smelled sweetly of baking soda, and inside it sat a carton of cream and a paper plate with four sweet rolls on it. Crocks on the counter held some odds and ends of table and cooking ware, and there was a big iron cooking pot, an old iron skillet, and a battered baking sheet on an ancient but sturdy little butcher-block table that I had not seen before. A bottle of dish-washing liquid and a tin of scouring powder stood beside them. Even before I went upstairs to reconnoiter, I made coffee in the pot, old but serviceable and electric, and plugged it in. Then I saw, on a top shelf, the little plastic radio, and turned it on. It was set to a classical station, and Pachelbel's *Canon* spilled out into the sunny room. I smiled again.

"Thank you, Bella," I said aloud.

Upstairs was transformed, too. It was largely a matter of cleaning, I saw, but the difference soap and water and wax made was enormous. The long windows were framed in the same white priscillas, and gleamed from a scrubbing with, I thought, ammonia; the sharp, clean smell lingered. Beyond them the pond lay quiet and the sea beyond it glittered like still, silver satin. I could not see the swans from here. Pale, watery light lay in patches on the old pine boards of the floor, which had also been scoured and polished, and a faded rag rug stood in the middle of the room. The narrow iron bed had been replaced by an elaborate maple one, like something out of a turn-of-the-century bedroom, and it was made up with fresh old linen and piled high with quilts. Another bureau had been moved in, this one painted white, and on it stood another jar of the wildflowers that I had seen downstairs. There was now a small, white wicker desk under one of the windows, with a chair, and the two straight-backed chairs had been joined by an old-fashioned slipper chair covered in faded cretonne. The closet curtain was clean and ironed, and the footlocker had been replaced by a big old trunk with a cornucopia of grapes carved on it. It stood at the foot of the bed with a bulbous old black-and-white RCA television set on it. I grinned. There had been one like it in my grandmother Bell's house, before she had come to live with us. I had watched rudimentary cartoons on it for hours.

The other, smaller bedroom was similarly refurbished, and the bath gleamed as much as was possible, given the condition of the enamel. The remnants of old linoleum had been pried up and the floor scrubbed and left bare, and another faded rag rug was laid down beside the shiplike old bathtub. The disreputable shower curtain had been replaced with a new one, a stiff, shining sheet of virulent aqua that smelled of new plastic. Clean blue towels were piled on a table beside the washbasin. A little potted geranium sat on the windowsill, and there was new Ivory soap in the soap dish and an aerosol can of room deodorizer. I squirted experimentally and coughed. Country Lilac exploded violently into the little room. No natural smell could survive here.

I looked out the little window that overlooked a small backyard cleared out of the forest. Beside a tarpaulin-covered woodpile an old blue pickup truck stood, high and bulbous like the bathtub. The promised vehicle. Grinning, I went downstairs to have my coffee. I would stop on my way to take the Jeep back, I thought, and thank Bella Ponder. She had done far more than had been called for. Even the old pickup shone. She must have hired a small army; there was no way she could have done any of this herself.

"I'm going to do just fine here," I told Mozart, who had replaced Pachelbel on the radio. "This is definitely a doable thing."

I drank my coffee and ate a sweet roll; it was buttery and tender and obviously homemade. Then I started out the door to the Jeep. An explosion of hissing white met me on the porch steps. Charles and Diana, obviously not accustomed to waiting, had decided to march on the house and demand their breakfast. I ran back inside and slammed the door in their black-knobbed faces. Exasperation joined the alarm that jolted my heart. I had not taken this enormous step, left all that I knew and come to this wild place, to let a couple of spoiled old birds confine me to quarters every day. Even if they were the size of ostriches and had been known to break forearms.

I stumped into the kitchen and looked around for something to feed them; perhaps they would settle for the rest of the sweet rolls. And then, in a tiny cubicle of a pantry beside the water heater that I had not noticed before, I found two big sacks of the cracked barley that Bella fed them, and a stout stick that must have begun life as a broom handle. I poured the barley into the old tin pail that sat beside the sacks, picked up the stick, and went out to discharge my primary duty. Slowly, like a native bearer beating my way through a dense jungle, I advanced toward the pond, the swans surging and flapping and hissing and grunting around me, keeping always just a step beyond my swishing stick. When I had reached the pond and dumped the barley, and they had snaked their heads out to attack it and abandoned me for the moment, I went back to the camp, my steps measured, my spine very straight, the stick at the ready, refusing to look back. I was both amazed and horrified at myself. The temptation to whack the elegant necks had been almost overpowering.

When I got into the Jeep and started out of the glade, they were both gliding on the pond, looking like an enchanted woodcut out of Sir Thomas Malory.

"Shitheads," I muttered. "Maybe you can beat me up, but I can starve you. You do not have a level playing field here. The sooner you get that through your mean little heads the better."

Bella and Luzia were obviously waiting for me. When I got to the big house, the front door was open and they both called to me to come in. When I did, I found them dressed in fresh, flowery cotton and sitting erect, Luz in the little yellow bed and Bella in a chair beside her, their hands folded in their laps, smiling hugely. A tray with a steaming teapot and more of the sweet rolls stood on Luz's bedside table. The flowers in the room were fresh. The piles of books had been neatened. They stared at me, wordless, waiting, barely able to contain their glee. Even Bella's dark face looked like a huge, expectant child's.

"Well? What do you think? Isn't it pretty? Aren't you pleased?" Luz piped, unable to contain herself.

"I am utterly dumbfounded, and totally pleased," I said, laughing at them. "I never would have thought it was possible. It must have taken some powerful magic."

"No, but it took almost all the money we had for the month. Bella hired six men and a lady," Luz said happily, and I winced and Bella frowned.

"Luz," she said quietly, and the little old woman fell silent, looking from Bella to me in shamed confusion.

"Then I thank you from the bottom of my heart, and I hope that one day I can find a way to do something just as splendid for you," I said, and the little brown face lightened again.

"What will it be?" she cried.

"It'll be a surprise," I said, and she clapped her hands.

Bella poured tea and urged another sweet roll on me.

"They're the only thing I could do for you myself," she said. "The cleaning crew took them down when they went. Is everything all right? Did they forget anything?"

"Absolutely nothing," I said honestly. "I can't imagine wanting or needing anything else. It's miraculous. I love it."

"We knew you would," Luz said. "Bella said it was a good investment. And," she smiled slyly, "I know about Denny."

Bella Ponder rolled her black eyes, and I smiled at Luz.

"I hope we all still feel that way when the winter's over," I said.

"What happens then?" Luz said, and Bella said quickly, "I know I said I wouldn't pry, but can you tell me just a little about Denny? I thought maybe he'd give you a note for me, but I guess not . . . "

I was torn between pity and irritation. Pity won.

"He seems a good bit better this morning," I said. "He was up and dressed and working, and he gave me a list of things he'd like to have when I go shopping. I'll take your list, too, if you have one. Oh, and thank you so much for the truck; I'll be able to take my friend's Jeep back to her house now. And the radio and the TV . . . "

"Phone will be in by the end of the week," Bella said, waving a large, impatient hand. "What about the cancer? Did he tell you about that? Is he hurting? What do the doctors say about it? What do you know about the kind that he has?"

"Not much," I said honestly. "I usually worked with the incurables. He doesn't know . . . no one has apparently said that his was incurable by any means. He goes back for a checkup in a month, but he's through with his chemo. And he says there isn't any pain. Just some phantom discomfort where the missing leg was. On the whole, I think he's doing as well as he could. He seems eager to go on with his work. I'm to pick up his lists from the living room; he's working in the bedroom for now. I don't want to disturb him, but I will insist on seeing him with my own eyes at least once a day. I don't think he's terribly pleased about that."

I did not tell them any more about the carcinoma, or what I knew about it. I saw no reason to alarm these old women yet, even though I knew that eventually they would have to know the worst. As it was, Luz's little chin was quivering.

"You didn't say it was cancer, Bella," she said, her voice thin and trembling. "You didn't say Denny just had one leg now."

"Well, now you know everything, and it's not so bad, is it? Molly says he's doing just fine, and she should know."

Luzia set her mouth.

"So when will we see him?"

"Well," his mother said, looking away, "he can't get around much yet. He's still learning how to use the crutches. And he takes some medicine that makes him real tired. So I expect it will be a while."

"Can he come for Christmas?"

"We'll see. Hush now."

Bella looked at me.

"Did he say anything about his wife and daughter? Are they still out West, does he see them . . . "

"You know we agreed that I wasn't going to get into that," I said as gently as I could, but firmly. "Really, Bella, I just can't. I have a lot of things I've got to work through myself."

I thought of the shining camp, and the old car, and the appliances. She had done so much, even if it was in the nature of a bribe.

"I tell you what, though," I said. "If he tells me anything on his own, and I don't think it's confidential, I'll tell you."

I knew I was safe. Dennis Ponder was not going to surrender one more iota of himself to me than was necessary to sustain life.

"Well, I'll appreciate that," she said, apparently giving up. I rose to go, but she said, "Stay just a minute. Luz has been looking forward to company for days. Luz, do you remember that you said you were going to tell Molly how it was when we were growing up back home, in West Bedford? About the music and the songs, and the wonderful things we had to eat, and the old stories?"

And the little old woman in the bed sat up straighter and, like a good child and with joy in her dark eyes, spun me a glittering story of a life lived, as nearly as was possible, as a Portuguese king's kin among the alien corn of a blue-collar American neighborhood. It was full of exotic color and smells and odd, dark music, and old chants and gilded pageantry, and heroes and saints and bittersweet, perfumed things to eat and drink, and of a provenance so enchanted that even a child could have told it was fantasy; I knew that I would never know what Luz's childhood had really been like, or Bella's, for that matter. I wondered if either of them knew, really. It did not matter. The stories were enthralling. When Luz's head began to droop toward the pillows and I got up to leave, I realized from Bella Ponder's sly smile that I had been as deliberately and skillfully mesmerized as the listeners to Scheherazade's wonderful stories, and for much the same reason: so that Bella's only link to her son would stay alive.

I smiled back at her. My smile said that it was all right, she and Luz might spin their web at will, so long as they knew that I knew. She nodded.

As I went out the door, she called after me.

"Was he more polite this time? Did he treat you better?"

"He was fine," I said over my shoulder. I wasn't going to get into that, either. "And I did fine with the swans, too, although I thought I was going to have to whack them."

"Wish you had," she said, closing the door. "Save somebody the trouble."

I drove Livvy's Cherokee back to Chappaquiddick under the low, gray sky, left it in the garage, and called the Edgartown taxi. Waiting for it, I walked down to the edge of Katama Bay and looked over at the little town, shining like a child's toy village in the shafts of iridescent light that shot occasionally down from the clouds. It looked no more real than a doll's village, either, and I was not sorry, when the taxi finally came, to leave it behind and start back on the

Edgartown–West Tisbury Road, up island. I did not look back toward the town or the sea.

The Ford sputtered obediently into life when I started it, and I drove it gingerly down the rutted, overgrown little lane toward Middle Road. It was tall and ponderous and had, apparently, no springs left; it was like wrestling a tank through the undergrowth. I did not care. This shiplike old truck could, I thought, get me through any kind of weather the Vineyard could throw at me. I felt tough and competent; I whistled experimentally through my teeth, to see if I could still do it. I could.

I went all the way to Vineyard Haven for supplies, hoping not to have to go out again for a week or so. The first of Tee's checks had been duly waiting at Livvy's Edgartown bank, and the first thing I did was to open an account at the Compass Bank on Main Street. I withdrew a reckless amount of cash and bought more pots and pans, cleaning supplies, propane for the lanterns I had found in the pantry, a pin-up reading lamp and a floor lamp, and a score of lightbulbs. All of a sudden it seemed imperative that I not lose the light. At the A&P, crowded even off-season, I bought food and sundries. I would, I thought, look in the want ad pages of the Vineyard *Gazette* for a used freezer; the old refrigerator in the camp had none.

After that I went over to the Black Dog and bought bread and sweet rolls and had a bowl of Quahog chowder for lunch, then treated myself to a couple of sturdy Black Dog sweatshirts. The air, even at noon, had a pinch to it. They would feel good on chilly mornings. Walking back to the Ford I passed the Bunch of Grapes bookstore and, on impulse, went in. I had planned to find a library for my reading material; books were one expense I thought I could forego. But I came out laden with both paperbacks and hardbacks, thinking with delight of the moment when I slipped between my silky old sheets and turned on my new reading lamp and opened a new novel. Home: leisurely reading in bed would always be, for me, one of its cornerstones. Promising myself a modest shopping spree later for lamps and pottery and throw rugs and such, I loaded up the old car and wrestled it out of its parking space, turning it out on to the state road toward home.

I stopped in front of the larger camp and took Dennis Ponder's groceries in. He was nowhere in sight, but music drifted softly from the closed door of the bedroom. I recognized "Vissi d'Arte" and smiled; unless I missed my guess, it was Renata Tebaldi singing. I loved opera, and Tebaldi's *Tosca* had been my first recording. I had seldom listened to it at home, though. Tee and Teddy snorted at it. This would give me something else neutral to talk to Dennis Ponder about at the times when contact could not be avoided. He could hardly snarl at me for loving "Vissi d'Arte."

I put the groceries on the table in the kitchen. A note there said he was sleeping and did not wish to be wakened. He had forgotten to put scotch and wine on his list; if I had some, he would appreciate the loan. If not, I was to get him some single malt and four bottles of a good Merlot tomorrow. He did not specify brands. Here's where I mess up royally, I thought. This could well be a trap. Looking around, I saw that a bowl and spoon and glass stood draining on the sideboard, and a small saucepan sat in the sink. So he had managed some sort of meal for himself. I put away the perishables and tiptoed out, only then realizing that I had been holding my breath. One curmudgeon down, I thought, only two more to go.

The swans behaved no better when I took them their barley. This time they were out on the water, and I thought I might scatter it unmolested, but they were there in full flapping, hissing battle mode before I got the first handful cast on the verge of the pond. I picked up the stick and struck the ground with it so hard that dirt and grass flew. Diana shrank back for all the world like a vaporous Victorian virgin, and Charles advanced, hissing and grunting, almost to my ankles, so I thumped the ground again and he drew back. But one of the great wings connected with my shin, and almost knocked me to my knees. I knew that I would have a monumental bruise there. I whacked once more, and he stopped his posturing and glared at me malevolently with his flat jet eyes.

"You and what army?" I hissed at him. He hissed back, but then turned away and began grandly to peck barley. When I went back to the camp, neither of them followed me. I refused to limp, though my shin hurt smartly, and felt only slightly ridiculous trying to save face in front of a pair of neurotic swans.

"Molly the Swan Killer," I said aloud, and laughed. It struck me then that I was doing quite a lot of talking to myself. Well, so what? Who was there out here to hear me?

That night the low sky began to weep rain. It started as I was heating mushroom soup and Black Dog bread in the gas stove, a soft pattering on the old cedar shake roof. It sounded wonderful, like a magic circle of protection being drawn around the little house. I poured a stiff shot of sherry into my soup and took my tray into the living room. I lit the fire and turned on the little radio, now engaged with something sinuous and symphonic, and ate my supper on the sofa by firelight. I could not imagine ever in my life being lonely again. Contentment almost smothered me.

The spell of the night lasted when I climbed the perilous stairs to my bedroom and slipped into the high maple bed. I had brought a cup of cocoa and a new Anne Tyler, and I sipped and read until my eyes grew heavy and I turned off my lamp and slid into my first sleep in this place. The last thing I remember before the soft dark closed over me was the gentle tattoo of rain overhead.

Two hours or so later, I woke drenched with sweat and choking on my own cry. I had dreamed of my mother, not in her subterranean grotto this time, but sitting on the slipper chair across the bedroom from me. She wore her faded and darned leotard and tights, and she was so knobbed and corded she might have been carved from pale wood. Her arms were outstretched to me, hands curled into imploring claws, and her face was contorted with rage and terror. She was saying something to me, but I could not hear what it was; it was as if all my senses but sight were dead, for I could not move. The dream was in slow motion; my mother formed her poor, monstrous words as if under fathoms of deadening water. She cried, silently and awfully. I only knew that I was crying, too, when I realized I was seeing her through the silvery blur of my tears. What? I tried to say to her over and over, What? What do you want from me? What can I give you?

Then she was up and gliding toward me, slowly, slowly, her hands reaching, her mouth making the silent scream of need, her tears flowing, flowing. I tried so hard to shrink away from her touch that, just before she reached me, I woke myself with an enormous, sickening wrench. My cry of horror and pity still echoed in the room. There was no other sound. Sometime during the dream the rain had stopped.

It was long minutes before I could get up and go into the bathroom and wash my face. My hair was matted with sweat. My T-shirt was soaked. I changed it and drank a glass of water, and then, reluctantly, crept back into my bed and pulled the covers over my ears, leaving only my nose exposed. I did not dare look across the room where my mother had sat. I lay still, feeling so alone in the alien bed that my very skin cried out for touch, for the warmth of living flesh against it.

"Tee," I whimpered silently, but then realized that it was not his touch that I wanted. That warmth flickered and died.

"Lazarus," I whispered aloud, and felt peace and comfort steal over me like warm water. Less than a week now. In less than a week he would lie there as he used to when Tee was out of town, his big, slack, sweet, smelly body giving to me unstintingly its full measure of sustaining warmth. I felt the nightmare recede like a train going away.

I sat up and looked where my mother had sat, and saw now the trail of a white quarter moon on the water of Vineyard Sound, beyond Menemsha Bight. It looked as though you could walk across it, a bridge to somewhere magical, somewhere as remote and safe as the moon that cast it.

I lay back again, put my arms out to embrace the place where Lazarus would soon lie, and went back to sleep.

Thus ended the first day.

Grandma Bell was forever telling us grandchildren that the Bible said not to put old wine into new wineskins. But I found that I was unable to get myself through those first days in the little camp without establishing a routine, making a trellis of sorts for them, and that the routine was nearly identical to the one I had followed all of my adult life. I slept in only on weekends. I woke with the light. I washed and dressed and had my breakfast, then I did my fixed chores: checking on Dennis Ponder, feeding the swans, checking to see if the old women in the big house needed anything, consulting my own lists. Then I would go out in the stately, bucketing old Ford on the business of procuring things: to the general stores at Menemsha, Chilmark, or West Tisbury if the various lists were minimal, to Vineyard Haven if they were longer or at all esoteric. I would come back then and deliver my groceries, usually stopping for tea or coffee with the old women, almost always putting groceries away in Dennis Ponder's empty kitchen, with the strains of Puccini or Verdi drifting from the bedroom.

I would turn my attention to my own nest then. I painted, rearranged furniture, laid down scatter rugs, hung curtains and set out new towels, arranged flowers bought from roadside stands, hung the winter clothes that arrived from Missy in the scanty closet, organized shelves and kitchen cabinets, made lists of things I wanted to add as the little structure came gradually alive. The camp was like a child's playhouse, my very own: no one's needs to be met but mine, no one's taste reflected but mine. I grew as fussy and particular about where to put what, which books should lie where, what cushion should grace what corner as a little old maiden lady. I think that it was partly because there was so little space and I had so few things to mess about with; at home, where the flotsam and jetsam of all our lives and years was as abundant as dust, it was possible only to try and contain it all, never mind arranging it. Here, in this sparsity of space and objects, I found that I cared inordinately what trinket or pillow or vase went where, what color book jacket sat next to another. Toward the end of the day I would find myself adjusting for the fourth time in an hour a new pottery pitcher I had bought at an antique shop, and would snort with disgust and stop and make coffee. Then I would check on Dennis again, determinedly waiting until he showed himself if I had not seen him that day, feed the swans again, and come home to what I had begun to think of as the "real" time of the day, the time when I stopped doing errands and fiddling about and sat down to feel my way into my new life.

I usually lit a fire, for early autumn evenings chilled fast on the pond, and even the great sunset fires burned cold. I put an opera on the little cassette recorder that had been my first purely self-indulgent purchase besides books, and sank on to my sofa and put my feet up. I had it in mind, in these still blue hours, to savor the very particular tastes that made this place itself and none other; to truly and fully bear witness to the slow turn of the season; to try and bring the snarled yarn of the previous summer into some sort of order. I even thought, on those very first evenings, that if I sat very still and summoned my mother from the vault deep inside me where she was stashed in my waking hours, I might begin to come to grips with her death, if not, yet, her life. I might even, I thought once, early on, begin to make some peace with the Tee that had been and the Tee that would, from now on, be.

But I suspect it was too early for those things, and maybe even too early for any sort of interior journeying whatsoever, for I invariably fell asleep on the sofa and woke with a dying fire, a darkening room, a silent tape recorder, and a crick in my neck. In those first days up island, I seemed drowned in an uncharted sea of sleep. The daytime kind refreshed. The nighttime haunted.

My mother came to me for the first four nights that I slept in the camp. It was the same dream, with only minor variations of circumstance: Sometimes I knew she was dead but she did not, sometimes it was the other way around. Wakening from those latter dreams, I would wonder if it was simply what she wanted so desperately from me: simply my knowledge that she was dead. But then I would have the dream again, and her need seemed so consuming, so anguished and ravenous, that I thought it must be life after all that she sought, some sort of life that I could neither understand nor grant her. All the dreams ended in cold sweat and hammering heart and the hopeless black residue that such dreams leave. I grew tired and listless. On the fifth night I slept on the sofa downstairs before the fire, and I did not have the dream. I experimented after that, and found that for some reason I slept relatively dream-free in a nest of blankets in the tiny sleeping nook under the ground-floor stairs, so I dismantled the iron twin bed in the smaller upstairs bedroom and set it up there. The cubbyhole was neither as comfortable as my original bedroom nor nearly as pretty, and I saw no vista of light on sea when I awoke, only old, smoke-honeyed pine walls pressing over and around me. But I stayed, for my mother did not visit me there. Perhaps, I thought on the first morning, she still came nightly to the room upstairs with her silent screams and her weeping, to beckon and implore to emptiness. For some reason it was an awful thought. I found myself reluctant to go into that room at night, for fear that I might see her there.

But my strength and spirits lifted. It seemed a fair trade-off.

Shortly before I was to go to Boston and pick up Lazarus, I stopped in to check on Dennis Ponder. The front door was unlocked, so I went in, as we had agreed, and found him seated on the living-room floor surrounded by open boxes of books and household clutter. He was pale that morning, paler than usual, and there were streaks of dust on his face and in his hair. He was looking down at something in his lap. His legs—or leg—was covered with a thick plaid blanket such as I had in my cabin, and a fire sputtered on the hearth, threatening to go out. There was an empty coffee cup overturned on the sisal rug beside him, and a drying stain on the matting. His eyes were closed and he sat very still. I thought he might be meditating or doing some sort of self-hypnosis, he was so still and seemed so far away. But I did not like the look of his face, and so I spoke, though reluctantly.

"Are you all right?" I said.

He did not lift his head, but he opened his eyes, still staring down into his lap. I saw that there was a framed photograph there, though I could not see what it was, and felt a stab of pity. His wife and daughter?

"Yes," he said.

There was more silence, and then I took a deep breath and said, "The fire is dying and your coffee has spilled. You're paler than death. I know we said I wouldn't hover unless it was necessary, but it seems to me that it is, unless you're willing to tell me why it isn't. So I'm going to stand here until you do that. Then I'm out of here."

Finally he looked up at me. I saw, with shock, that his eyes were reddened, as if he had been crying. But the dying fire was rolling its smoke out into the room, so it could have been that. I went over and piled more logs on it and poked it up, and the chimney did its work and sucked the smoke away.

"Thanks," he said from the floor. "I was about to do that. Sometimes it just seems simpler to choke on the smoke."

It was the first time he had mentioned anything at all about the difficulty of his situation.

"That's why I look in twice a day," I said. "I wish you'd let me tend to things like that."

He made a dismissive gesture with one hand and the long mouth twisted slightly.

"The prostheses they make these days are hardly short of miraculous," I ventured, trying to sound neutral and professional. "I'm sure your doctor has told you that. It would make getting around a thousand times easier. Have you considered it?"

"Is that so, Mollycoddle?" he said and smiled. I would just as soon he hadn't. "Do you just happen to have one out in the car? Want to run and get 'er and let's strap 'er on and have a trial run? Care to dance?"

I was silent. My face flamed.

"I used to be a runner," he said, and handed the photograph up to me. I looked: He knelt there, captured forever on a track in the sun of what looked to be the Northwest, misted mountains and evergreens dark behind the track and a huddle of corrugated iron outbuildings. He was crouched in the classic runner's starting position, one hand ahead of him touching the cinders delicately. His head was up, facing the camera, and his hair hung in his eyes. He was smiling and squinting into the sun, and he looked thin and young and so handsome it hurt your heart to look at him.

"Was this in college?" I said.

"No. That was Harvard. This is after that, when I was first in Seattle. I ran relay then, and I still ran until ... recently. I was an Olympian, in fact. We didn't medal, but we were there. Mexico City. I remember that high, thin air and the sun ... "

"I'm sorry," I said softly.

"Me, too, I didn't mean to yell at you. Are you going to report me?"

"To whom? The paraplegic police? No. I'm not going to tell your mother on you, if that's what you mean."

The "Mollycoddle" had stung me.

"But you are going up there."

"Yes. They need some things from the grocery store."

"Listen, Molly ... would you get something from there for me?"

"If it's okay with your mother," I said prissily.

"She's got ... I think she's got my running stuff. Some shoes, and shorts and things, and the medals and stuff. Loretta ... my wife sent them to her sometime after we separated. If she's kept them, I'd like to have them back. Will you get them?"

"Dennis ... why don't you just pick up the phone and call her and ask her for them? This is ridiculous. You don't have to see her if you don't want to. She can't get down here and you can't get up there. I don't like being a go-between."

His face closed. "It's okay. I really don't need any more stuff lying around here. I don't know what I'm going to do with all this."

I sighed. "All right. I'll ask."

"Thanks," he said gruffly, and went back to his sorting.

"Do you need a hand with that?" I said from the doorway.

"No."

Bella Ponder thought she had the running things in the attic, but she didn't think she could get up the stairs to get them. I offered to go, but she said hastily that I'd never find anything in the jumble up there, and she'd get her cleaning lady to go when she came next.

"Why does he want those old things? Did he say? He sure isn't going to use them," she said, looking avidly at me. She was pale and perspiring today, even though the air outside was brisk. The sitting room was heated to near tropical stuffiness. Her eyes looked like currants sunk in rising dough.

"He didn't say," I said. "I guess he's just trying to get his things all together. He must have been really good, to be an Olympian. It must be hard to be that good and know you can't run again."

She swung her big, dark head away.

"There's worse things," she said.

I got up to go, but she went on talking, looking out the lace-scrimmed window across the meadow and down toward the water. I stopped. She sounded as if she didn't know she was speaking.

"He could always run like the wind," she said. "A lot of Portuguese can do it. I was as fast as lightning when I was little, though you'd never know it now. It was one of the things they never forgave him for, just another sign of his being half-Portuguese. That was the sin, you know. Up here, that's the worst sin there is. Oh, we can do their work, all right, but mix our blood with theirs? They wouldn't have anything to do with me and my cousin and my boy from the beginning, those almighty Ponders and Rakestraws, and so ons. Come from a long line of little old bowlegged, spavined farmers and sheep grubbers, most of them do, and we come from a thousand years of kings, but they didn't know that, or care. I don't reckon Ethan ever told them, either. I'm not sure he ever believed it himself. They weren't talking to him much, not after he brought a Portagee over here to live in their middle and have their grandson.

After a year or two there wasn't any contact between us. I can snub, too, and with a lot more justification.

"So they don't know my son, none of them, and he doesn't know them. Doesn't know his father, either, I don't guess, unless he remembers from when he was two years old. Ethan just . . . left us. For a long time he sent money every month, until Dennis went over to the mainland, I guess, but I never heard directly from him again. I don't know if Denny did or not. So far as I know, I'm still married to him, unless he's dead. He probably is."

"Bella . . ." I spoke, to stem the spate, but it was as if she did not hear me.

"We moved to a little old rented house up on Pilot Hill, Luz and I and Denny, and Denny started to the West Tisbury School, and Luz and I did whatever we could find to do to keep food on the table. I baked for the stores around here. When I feel like it, I'm as good a cook as there is on this island. Luz was a seamstress for a long time. Nobody had hands like those little ones of hers. We did fine, the three of us. The Miaras and Ferreiras can do honest work even if the blood in our veins is blue. But then, when Dennis was about eight, it seemed to me like he was losing his feeling for his Miara people and wanting to be a Vineyarder, and I wanted him to keep his heritage above anything else, so I sent him to my family in West Bedford. I wrote him every day, and they sent letters and photographs, and I sent what money I had, and my father and mother did what they could for him, and the rest of the family—there were lots of us there then—just doted on him. He was smart, and handsome, and such a funny, sweet-tempered little boy. He made all A's in school, and got real big scholarships to Harvard, and worked in the library to help put himself through. But in all that time, he never came back over here. Somehow I wasn't all that sorry. It would have killed me if they'd gotten him, those Ponders. I always meant to go over there to see him, but somehow we just didn't . . . and then he graduated and went out West and started teaching school out there, and later on he married some California woman, and they had a daughter—they call her Claire, I think; I don't imagine his fancy wife cared to have a Portuguese name in her family. Rich, I think they were. Not that I care. I've never met her, nor my . . . granddaughter. I've never even had a letter from them. Not even a picture."

"All that time, and you never saw your son?" I breathed, in pain for her and Dennis Ponder, too. I could not understand. Family; they were family. . . . "All that time, and you were so near each other? It can't be more than . . . what? A hundred miles? Two hundred?"

"A long way longer than that," she almost whispered.

"Does he remember this house?" I said.

"I don't see how he could. I don't think he was ever up here. This was Ethan's mother's and father's house. When the old lady died, a letter came from an attorney in Chicago saying my husband wanted it to come to me and then go on to Denny. The deed was in it. I called his office, but all he would say about Ethan was that the instructions about the house were given to him years before, by letter, and that he didn't know where Ethan was now. So we moved up here, Luz and I, but most of the time we still stayed down in the littlest camp. Well, I told you. Later on we stayed there all the time, till Luz fell. I expect Denny does remember the camps. He stayed with us there until we left, in the littler one. Yours. The bigger one, where he is now, was his father's private property. Ethan used to go down there and stay for days and weeks at a time sometimes. I've never been in it. I didn't know what he did there. I don't think Denny's been in it, either, until now. But he knows the place. He knows the pond and the Bight. He always did love it. Always."

She stopped talking then, and got up and went ponderously into the kitchen. I waited for a bit, but she did not return, so I kissed the dozing Luz on the forehead and left. I felt endlessly, wearily sad for them, and vaguely annoyed, and baffled by the enmity that had led to the estrangement. But I was really not curious. I did not want to know any of this. What a sere, minimal way to live; what a huge, ongoing fee this angry, ridiculous old woman insisted on paying for her life. What a huge fee she exacted from others.

On the appointed day I went to Boston to get Lazarus. He was so ecstatic to see me that he wet the floor of the baggage section, and capered in circles, and howled and barked and panted, and knocked over baggage and me and a dour little man in a bowler hat, who started to protest, then looked more closely at this huge, hairy, grinning maniac of a dog and stalked away.

I hugged Lazarus and rubbed my face into his grizzled coat and inhaled his doggy, disreputable smell that no disinfectant soap could ever completely banish, and cried and cried.

"Old goofy," I sobbed over and over. "You big, stinky, old goofy. What took you so long? Did you walk all the way? Oh, come here, goofball, and let me smell you; you smell like J. Walter Puppy-breath, and I've missed you so much . . . "

It was after dark when we got home, and I had to drag him by his straining leash up the steps of the little camp. He was wild to dash off in all directions at once, to search out the genesis of each new smell and sound, who knew, maybe to slay swans with a joyous vengeance. I would have to be careful with Lazarus and the swans. I fed him and ate my own dinner, and we settled down on the sofa, where he promptly went to sleep on my legs, as he had a thousand times before, making disgusting little snicking, snoring noises, waking every now and then to discharge the duty that had so distressed Carrie Davies: the loving licking of his balls. Home. I was home. Or, rather, home had come to me. I fell asleep, too.

Eventually we stumbled off to bed, Lazarus and I, in the nook under the eaves, but he refused to sleep on the folded blanket I had put down for him beside my bed, and there was obviously no room for both of us in the little bed. So finally, reluctantly, I led him upstairs and we settled into the big maple bed. No sooner had I drifted into a dog-soothed sleep than my mother came.

This time I woke before the dream played itself out, and had no clear image of her in my mind. Only the sweat and the fear lingered. Lazarus's big head was lifted, and he was staring into the corner where the slipper chair sat. Of course it was empty; what had I expected? But his grizzled upper lip was lifted ever so slightly, and the ruff of his neck stood up in little stiff spikes. My own hair stood up.

"I'm not going to put up with this shit anymore," I said to Lazarus, and got out of bed, stomped downstairs, got the black straw hat off the hat rack and brought it up and hung it on the wall over the chair. I hung it with thumbtacks, and impaled the brim every two inches so that it would not fall.

"Come get it if you want it," I said to the corner of the room, and went back to bed. Lazarus waited for me, looking sleep-drugged and put upon. He curled into the curve of my waist, an inert behemoth, and did not wake again until the dazzle of the morning sun lit the long windows. I didn't, either.

CHAPTER TEN

WHEN I WOKE THE NEXT MORNING, I knew before I opened my eyes to the dazzle of water light that something profound had changed about this place. Then I felt Lazarus stir against my hip, and heard the groan that meant he was waking up. I smiled, eyes still closed, and waited. There it was: the sibilant fart that meant the waking-up process was completed. I leaped out of bed before the smell could smite me and ran around it and hugged him.

"Morning, stink-dog," I said into his neck. "Your first fart in your new home. How was it? Did the earth move? Oh, I am so glad you're here! I have so much to show you!"

It is Lazarus's special gift not to be dismayed by changes of scenery. He is amazed, delighted, or puzzled, depending on the circumstances, but he is never afraid when he finds himself in a place new to him. This morning he took off in circles around the room, sniffing everything and thumping his scrofulous tail. Then he worked his way through the upstairs, skidded down the perilous steps, and circled the first floor, his nose and tail working overtime, his tongue lolling out goofily. During the entire tour he grinned his doggy grin, making little busy, cataloguing sounds in his throat. Apparently the cottage was going to be an endless source of enchantment to him. I followed him, as ridiculously pleased as if he were a favored human approving my new nest.

Like most animals, I knew that he would also find his own

special place, the one that would become, if he was not repeatedly ousted from it, the nest he retreated to for sleep, meditation, and the occasional sulk. It was where he would be when he was not doing anything else. After three or four sweeping explorations of the downstairs, he trotted into the little niche under the stairs, sniffed it mightily, and curled up on the single bed there, sighing in contentment. I sighed, but I knew that if I wanted the comfort of his company in my bed, it would have to be down here in this dark-golden cave. I wondered if I could fit a double bed here, and thought perhaps if I gave up a bedside table I might, just. I would ask Bella Ponder if she had another in her resourceful attic. If not, perhaps I could find a used one in the Vineyard *Gazette* want ads. They seemed to harbor everything else.

I fed Lazarus and ate a bagel, then took the bucket of barley and the swan stick and started for the pond to feed Charles and Di. Get it done early, I thought, so they would not storm the porch and start an ongoing territorial war with Lazarus. Somehow I did not think he would win it. I thought I had shut the screen door firmly behind me, but before I was halfway to the water a brindle bullet passed me, nose to the earth, at the speed of a heat-seeking missile. I broke into a run, calling him, but before I reached the reeds that sheltered the verge of the pond I heard contact being made and slowed my steps. What transpired next was in the lap of the beast gods.

The grunting, hissing, barking, and thrashing reached fever pitch, and then I heard a great splashing and thought, Well, what do you know? He's driven them back into the pond. From now on I can leave the stick at home and just take Lazarus. And then I reached the spot where I could see past the reeds and saw, on the bank, the patrolling swans, their great wings spread over their backs in the classic busking display of outrage and choler I had become used to, their serpents' necks darting back and forward, their black-knobbed, orange bills open and hissing like monstrous teakettles.

Lazarus stood, knee deep in the water, head down, growling at them.

"Oh, shit," I said tiredly, and hoisted the stick and went to rescue my dog.

He disappeared into the reeds while I beat the enraged Charles and Di back and scattered their barley, and I thought perhaps he had retreated to the house. I did not see him anywhere, in fact, and so I went on up to the larger camp to check on Dennis Ponder and get his grocery list. I would, I thought, have to warn him about Lazarus, otherwise the barking might alarm him.

I had reached the porch steps when I heard a hoarse shout and a thud from inside, and then a sharp yelp, and a kind of shuddering moaning that chilled my heart. Then I saw that the unlocked door had been pushed open, and I lunged up the steps and into the living room. I saw no one, but I could still hear the odd moaning, and a kind of viscid slurping that could only mean Lazarus, eating or drinking something. Dear God, what had he done to Dennis Ponder? I was so terrified that I could not even speak when I gained the doorway to the kitchen.

Dennis Ponder lay on his back, his hands up to his face, my dog crouched over him, snuffling nose to his exposed throat. Dry cereal was scattered everywhere, and a kettle had shrieked itself dry on the stove. Dennis Ponder was weeping and pushing feebly at Lazarus. I stood still for an awful moment, unsure whether to run for the phone and dial 911 or grab my dog by his collar. I had never seen him go for anyone's throat before, and the thought flashed through my roiling mind that he had gone mad, or berserk.

"Lazarus!" I screamed, and lunged for his collar. "Don't move," I yelled to Dennis Ponder in the same breath. "I'll call for help in a second."

I had the whining, protesting dog dragged out of the kitchen and into the living room and was reaching to shut the kitchen door when I heard Dennis Ponder take a great, gulping breath of air, and say, "No, don't, wait, he's not hurting me," and realized that he was not weeping at all. He was laughing. The wet shine on his face was Lazarus's endorsing slobber; he had been licking Dennis's face with the love-at-first-sight fervor I had seen him display only once before, when he was a puppy and we first brought him home and introduced him to Teddy. I let go of his collar and he skidded back into the kitchen and resumed his licking.

"Jesus Christ, dog, if you don't stop, you'll have to marry me," Dennis Ponder said, choking on his laughter, and I dropped my arms to my side and began to laugh, too, shakily.

"I thought he'd knocked you down and half-killed you," I said weakly. "I thought he'd gone crazy, or something. I'm so sorry, Dennis. I've never seen him behave so badly with a stranger before. Are you okay? Let me help you up . . . "

He sat up, shaking his head. Lazarus sat, too, close beside him, grinning his weak-witted grin and lolling his tongue.

"I can do it," he said to me, and to Lazarus, "Since you knocked me down, you can just help me up, buddy. Sit!"

Lazarus sat, while I goggled. We had been gently asked to leave obedience school, he and I, before he mastered "sit" or much of anything else. Dennis put one arm around the dog and used the other to push himself up. Slowly, with sweat beading his white forehead, he inched his way to a kneeling position, using Lazarus for leverage. Finally he stood erect. Lazarus had not moved. When Dennis Ponder transferred his weight to the kitchen counter, Laz gave a great sigh and lay down on the floor beside him. "There," you could almost hear him say. I simply stared.

"I meant to warn you about him," I said to Dennis. "He just got here yesterday. I was going to keep him at home until he got used to things. He's not a bad dog, but he's as big as an ox, and he never did have any manners. He got away from me while I was feeding the swans, and I never even saw him start up here. I'll make sure he's locked in from now on . . . "

"Don't lock him up on my account," Dennis said. "Just ask him to knock or something before he busts in here. I thought a werewolf had me. Lazarus; is that his name?"

"Yes. He was one step away from the tomb when we got him. He's been grateful ever since," I said. "Look, I can't have him knocking you down every time he gets in here; we'll have to think of another way for me to get in so you can lock your door. Is there a spare key? Never mind, I'll ask your mother if she has one . . . "

"I can't imagine that she doesn't have an extra key to any structure on the island by now," he said neutrally. "No, I'm not going to lock this guy out. He's welcome any time. I had a big dog like him back home. Commander, his name was. I think he was part wolf. I've missed him a lot."

I did not ask what had happened to Commander. Either he was dead or the vanished wife and child had taken him. Either way, it was not anything I wanted to get into.

I pulled Lazarus's leash out of my pocket, snapped it to his collar, and pulled him away from Dennis. He backed up, rolling his eyes at me.

"Where are you going with him?" Dennis said.

"I was going to take him with me while I did the shopping," I said.

"Why don't you leave him with me?" Dennis said. "If he gets loose he's bound to make somebody mad at him, and that's no way to start out on this island. It doesn't take much."

"I see dogs out with their owners all the time," I said. "There's one in every truck I pass."

"Yeah, well, wait a day or two. He doesn't even have his bandanna yet."

I laughed. He did, too.

"I sort of wanted to introduce him to your mother and Luzia. I don't even think I told them about him, and I should have," I said.

His face closed. The laugh was gone.

"You'd do better leaving him here, then," he said. "If I recall correctly, Cousin Luzia is deathly afraid of dogs. I know I could never have one when I was little . . ."

The way he said "Cousin" was neither familiar nor gentle. It spoke of contempt, almost of animosity. Whatever the estrangement between him and his mother, then, it included Luz Ferreira. For the first time, a faint tendril of curiosity prickled at me.

"I will, then, this one time," I said, reaching for the grocery list that lay on the counter. "But from now on he stays with me or at home. I can't have him creating havoc in this heavenly place."

He smiled grimly.

"We certainly can't have that," he said. Then, almost casually: "What do you talk about, you and the Virgin Queen and her consort?"

I looked sharply at him, but he was not looking at me. His fingers were curled in Lazarus's ruff.

I was certainly not going to say, "You," so I said, "Oh, I don't know. Everything and nothing. Mostly they talk and I listen. Luz has been telling me about your family, and about the old days in Portugal, and about growing up in West Bedford, only she calls it 'in America.' What a wonderful heritage you have, all full of kings and knights and soldiers and crusades. King Dinis the Troubadour, he of the thousands of castles . . . "

He snorted.

"My family is no more descended from King Dinis the Troubadour than we are from Vlad the Impaler," he said. "That old charlatan; she's been blathering about King Dinis since I can remember. Our people were probably fishermen, and on other people's boats, at that. Most Portuguese came over here as hired hands on the whalers out of the Vineyard and Nantucket that stopped in the Azores, and we've been hired hands ever since. But my mother can't handle that notion. Her family—and mine—ran a hole-in-the-wall restaurant in Cambridge or worked at the air force base in West Bedford; my mother met my father while she was slinging linguica in Cambridge and he was at Harvard. She's a fake, but at least she knows she is. I don't know if Luz has the sense to know it or not. You ought to call them on it."

I felt a wash of sadness. I hoped old Luzia Ferreira did not know that she was not the spawn of kings; I hoped that she never knew it. Bella, either, for that matter. I thought that they had very little else. I, for one, was not going to take their blue blood away from them.

I unsnapped Lazarus and he loped back to Dennis Ponder and began to lick his hand.

"You must smell like his daddy," I said.

"Your departed husband? That could be a problem," he said nastily, and I looked at him sharply. His face was pinched and shuttered, a kind of fastidious distaste in his eyes. It was as if he were already regretting the moment of shared laughter. The poison in his mother's name ran deep.

"My son," I said briefly, and turned to go.

"I'm sorry," he said, but he did not sound as if he was. He sounded so sarcastic that I said, "Maybe *I* should lick your face."

He only looked at me, cold and distant and untouchable in the fortress of his illness.

"Or maybe I should just kick your gimpy behind," I muttered under my breath as I walked out to the truck. I was suddenly very tired of the Ponders and all their complicated, shape-shifting kin. I regretted leaving Lazarus behind. I did not want to have to go back into Dennis Ponder's house for him.

When I did go back, letting myself as quietly into the front door as I could, Dennis Ponder was asleep on the sofa in front of his dying fire, and Lazarus lay on the floor beside him. I stood for a moment, looking down at man and dog. Dennis looked so white and depleted that I thought I might have imagined the morning's brief moment of rallying laughter. With sentience gone from his long, carved face he looked very near to death, and I wondered once more if he was. I did not know anything about his kind of sarcoma, and did not want to know. But perhaps I should learn more. How awful it would be to come and find him dead, or to have to attend that dying . . .

Fear and anguish stabbed at me and I bid it be gone, down to the place where my other wounds and terrors lay. It went, but slowly. I stood, breathing shallowly, until it was gone.

"Come on, Laz," I whispered, and Lazarus thumped the floor with his tail and got up. He looked for a long time down at Dennis Ponder, sniffing him, and then trotted over to me and sat still for his leash. But when I got him to the door, he looked back at the sleeping man and whined slightly.

"No," I said. "You've got your own walking wounded to look after. This guy doesn't need us."

That night, after dinner, Lazarus and I sat for a while in front of our own fire. I listened to a cassette of *Turandot* I had treated myself to, and he dozed and twitched and sighed and trembled with dreams, and woke and stretched and dozed again. I lay suspended between sleep and waking, swung in a hammock of music and firelight, my hand lying loosely in my dog's rough coat.

"So far so good," I thought drowsily. "I can do this. This really is a doable thing."

With the coming of Lazarus, up island became a different place to me in more ways than one. Without being at all conscious of it, I began to reach out, to venture farther and farther from the camp and the glade, to extend my path past the two small cabins, the big house on the ridge in Chilmark, and my shopping trajectory. My trade route, I had laughingly called it to Teddy during one of our rare phone conversations. Only after Lazarus arrived did I see how constricted was the path I had allowed myself. With his hairy, grinning presence in the truck, I felt empowered to go almost anywhere up island I wanted. It was as if, in some very real way, Lazarus was my permission to roam.

That I needed one was a disturbing notion, when it finally occurred to me. I had spent two or three days forging with him into places I had only wondered about before: wild, boulder-strewn Lucy Vincent Beach, where the wind straight out of Spain nearly knocked us both off our feet; the slick, odorous, time-stopped docks of Menemsha, where Lazarus's busy nose cast him straight up into dog heaven; the breath-stopping cliffs of Gay Head, striped in the sun like a child's cross section of an enchanted earth; the little chapel at Christiantown, deep in the thinning, burning forest, where Thomas Mayhew, bearer of another of the oldest family names, had his early mission to the Wampanoag Indians; the wonderful field of great, cavorting white statues in West Tisbury; Beetlebung Corners, afire now with the thousand scarlets of autumn; down the tiny lanes of West Tisbury, named for what they were in the beginning: Music Street, Old Court House Road, New Lane; down tracks so small and rutted that they seemed impassable, only to find weathered gates barring the way before I could reach the ends.

For those few days I explored in a cocoon of delight and anticipation, never once feeling tentative or unwelcome. Even after Lazarus and I had blundered into one or two private driveways and had to turn around under the level eyes of householders; even after he had scattered the cranky swans on the Mill Pond in West Tisbury and a roving flock of guineas on the lawn of the Chilmark Congregational Church, I did not feel timid or constrained to flee, as I would have before. A woman alone in the places we went would be an unspeakable intrusion; a woman with a great, gamboling dog on a leash was somehow natural and acceptable.

"You're my ticket to ride," I said to Lazarus at the end of one of our days of sightseeing. But that evening, before the fire, in the time when introspection came, I thought that it was not a terribly admirable thing, to have lived my way almost to my midcentury mark, and still need a reason, some sort of permission, to go and see what was around a corner or over a hill.

"Well, at least it's getting better," I said to the dog. I said quite a lot to him in those first days. "Before it was my mother's permission, and Dad's, and then Tee's and Caroline's and Teddy's and the entire boards of directors of half a dozen worthy organizations. Now it's just one dumb dog. Maybe I can do it by myself when I grow up; what do you think?"

It was an autumn of unearthly loveliness, at least to me, accustomed as I was to the humid, muted autumns of the Southeast. Every morning was born scarlet and silver over the pond and the Bight, and the sun was soft and cool on bare forearms and heads in the noons. Blue dusks came quickly and died in incredible conflagrations of rose, purple, orange, and silver over the Sound. Nights were so clear and cold that the stars looked like chips of diamonds, like Scott Fitzgerald's silver pepper. I went often and sat on the little dock with Lazarus, wrapped in one of the hefty blankets, and stared up at the sky, seeing the crystal constellations appear as if out of developing fluid. I kept Laz on his leash, for the swans, bedded down somewhere in the forest of reeds, would often wake and grumble and flap in the darkness, but they never came storming over to see why their tormentor and their serving wench were abroad in the night. Once there was a meteor shower so vivid and close that Lazarus barked and rushed at each luminous, streaking trajectory, and I simply sat still and let them fill me with their cold fire. Everything up here on this New England island was sharp and clear and light-limned, I thought; there was none of the sense I often had back home of slogging waist deep through some allegorical, as well as physical, swamp. Up here, I lived and walked up on the very surface of the earth, almost able, if I stood on tiptoe, to touch the great, open skies.

"The most wonderful thing is," I said to my father sometime that autumn, on his weekly phone call from Kevin's house in Washington, "that the only things you smell are earth and water and sky things. Salt and pine and spruce and smoke and that cold, dark smell that I think is the way the very earth up here smells. You know how, in the winter at home, you start to smell stale air and automobile exhaust and piled-up, rained-on garbage? Up here it's just natural things."

"Sounds okay by me," he said, and I could hear the smile in his voice. "You get some pretty natural smells down here, too, though. I went with Sally to dish up lunch at a soup kitchen the other day;

she does it once a week. Not a deodorant user in the bunch. Couldn't get much more natural than that."

I laughed heartily at this little joke. Kevin kept telling me how depressed our father was, how low he had sunk. But I heard none of it in his voice. On some level I knew he would not allow me to hear it if he could help it, but on another, higher one, I simply put it all down to Kevin's continuing campaign for first place in our mother's heart. Her death did not seem to have stopped that war in the least. I might have seen, had I been more clearly attuned to such things, what message my determined chirpiness was sending my father: Do not disturb this fragile thing I'm building. Do not dare to tell me that you hurt. But I was not attuned, and I did not see it. Anything outside the small, careful circle of my days did not seem real, and I was determined that that would continue.

I kept Atlanta at bay by simply refusing to think about it.

"Later," I would say to myself or perhaps aloud, for I was talking as freely to Lazarus now as I ever did to Tee or Teddy or Caroline. Dear Lazarus; he talked back only with his endorsing tail.

"Later. I know I have to think about it; I know there's a lot I have to deal with. But I don't have to do it now. I've damn well earned the right to heal in my own way, and right now what I need is just to . . . forget it. All of it. Right now is for here and for me."

Eventually, I said it often enough that I actually believed it. I was quite able to keep my stubborn other life at arms' length. I was blithe and flip with Livvy and Missy when they called; I literally never called them. I talked little to Caroline; her litany of pain and outrage at her father never varied and never abated. I listened, I said "mmm-hmmm" and "of course." Often, I thought with irritation, Get a life, my child. Or go and look after the one you've got. A husband and a new daughter and a new house ain't chopped liver. It wasn't you, after all, who got left, literally, without a roof over your head.

That it had not been me, either, not literally, did not occur to me.

I talked even less to Teddy. He was in love with his courses and his life in the Southwest; the few times I did catch him, the burning joy in his voice made me both joyous for him and cold with loss. I told him about the camp and Lazarus and our days in the wild, as it were, but I do not think he heard me. Teddy had gone to

215

live in the arid fire of the sun; the secret forest place I had found for myself could not exist in his burning world. I knew that he would hear me when he could. Until then I would not insist. With Teddy I merely listened and rejoiced.

Tee did not call. Missy could not find him. I did not care.

"But it's getting better and better for our side," Missy said in one of our conversations, at the start of November. "I have it on the word of somebody who was there that the Eel Woman threw a party at your place a night or two ago for her merry band of Cokies. Threw it all by herself, I mean; she was the sole host. The word is that Tee was in Santa Barbara or someplace *way* away. How do you like them apples?"

"Was it trick or treat?" I said, leaning over to pick a burr out of Lazarus's ruff. We had been out on the beach at Squibnocket Point that afternoon, as far east as you could go until you set foot on Madagascar 3,000 miles away. It had been transcendent. My head still roared with it.

She laughed, but she said, "Molly, it's your house. Don't you care?"

"I must," I said. "How can I not? It just doesn't seem real. It's like you're telling me about a movie you saw."

"You're trying to make it go away, I know, and I don't blame you. Whatever it takes is fine, until we can get this thing to trial and you can come home again. But don't drift too far away. You do have to come back, eventually, you know."

No, I don't, I mouthed silently to Lazarus. To her I said, "I'm not trying to make it go away so much as I'm trying to make this stay. This hasn't been easy, Missy. If I've got to be here, then the only way I can do it is to be all the way here. I don't have the focus or the energy to live in two places at once."

"Well, just don't get too comfortable," Missy said.

But in those early days, with the splendid autumn, as exotic as old Persia, unfolding around me, I was as lulled and dreamish as if spellbound. Even Dennis Ponder's overhanging illness and unchanged remoteness did not shatter the dome of contentment around me. Even Bella Ponder's unsated hunger for her son, even Luzia Ferreira's mothlike retreat into childhood, did not penetrate it. Even my mother could not come in. I had found a serviceable iron double bedstead posted on the bulletin board at Alley's and had paid the son of the seller to bring it over and install it in the niche under the stairs, and there I slept now, with Lazarus by my side, arched over with the listing angles of the old stairs, wrapped around with the darkness of old boards and the lingering, piney dust of decades. Not much light of any kind, sun or moon or fire, made its way into my cave, and apparently my mother could not, either. She appeared at the edge of it many times in the lengthening nights, pale and frantic in the cold, but she did not come into my space, and I could no longer make out her expression, or see what her outstretched hands reached for. I hardly marked her coming before drifting into deeper sleep, and Lazarus did not seem to mark her at all. It was as if, like the light, dreams got left at the lip of the cave. I sensed more than I saw her, and the immediacy of anguish and horror she had brought with her were dimmed. I slept without tossing and without waking, and woke without weariness for the first time in many weeks.

But gradually a sense of something missing crept into the days, bringing with it a skulking restlessness, a sly anxiety that sometimes felt almost like guilt, and it was not long until I caught the sense of it. I needed someone or something to take care of. I had done what I could do by myself to the little house, my daughter and son were out of my reach, and my charities at home were, according to Livvy, purring along without me like great, contented cats with open-handed new owners. It was, I supposed, too much to ask that my essential nature would change radically along with my lifestyle; my mother's legacy was too enduring, her conditioning too powerful, for that. The swans took merely minutes of my time, and I wanted no deeper connection to Dennis Ponder or to Bella and Luz; I realized that I knew literally no one else on the island. I was beginning to toy unenthusiastically with the notion of finding some volunteer work to do in Vineyard Haven or Oak Bluffs—surely Edgartown, blessed as it was among villages, did not need volunteers—when Dennis Ponder solved the problem for me. Or rather, Lazarus and Dennis did.

On a gray afternoon in early November, when I was curling up for a nap in front of the fire simply because I could not think of anything else at the moment to do, Lazarus came bounding into the cottage barking as if he had treed all the raccoons in Massachusetts. I had left him off at Dennis's that morning, at Dennis's request, and I thought immediately that Dennis must have tired of his tongue-lolling presence and sent him home. But Lazarus would not stop barking, and finally he put his nose into my ear and gave such a yelp of anxious annoyance that I sat up, then got to my feet. Immediately he turned and ran for the larger camp, and I ran behind him, sure in my thumping heart that something was amiss with Dennis.

Nothing seemed to be at first glance; he sat on the floor in the living room, covered from the waist down with a blanket and dressed in a red-and-black jacquard turtleneck sweater that stained his high cheekbones with color, surrounded by a literal sea of books. All the boxes that had been crammed with volumes and piled against the walls were empty and overturned, and I saw that a few had been placed in the bottom of the bookshelves that flanked the fireplace. The fireplace itself was cold; the fire I had lit that morning had gone out and there was an obstacle course of boxes and books between Dennis and the hearth. The room was cold, and only one lamp burned. Even in midafternoon, it was as dim as dusk. I could see that Dennis Ponder's eyes were closed, and that he was massaging the stump of his leg through the blanket. It was somehow such an intimate moment, a man alone with naked pain, that I closed my own eyes, then I said, "Can I give you a hand? Lazarus came and got me, and I was afraid something was wrong."

He did not open his eyes for a moment, or speak, and I thought that he would dismiss me as brusquely as he usually did, but finally he looked at me, the black eyes dull, and said, "I guess you could make a fire, if you would. I can't get to the fireplace for these fucking books, and I can't seem to get moving until I get warm. I guess you'd call it a conundrum."

I threaded my way through the books and threw logs on the fire and lit them, and waited until a yellow blaze flared up. Then I went into the kitchen and put on the kettle for tea, turning on lamps as I went. The light seemed to banish some of the cold. Then I came back and sat down on Dennis's sofa.

"You're hurting some, aren't you? What have you been doing, heaving these books around? It's too much for you right now . . . "

It was a stupid thing to say; of course he had. How else would they have gotten all over the floor? I flushed and waited for the inevitable sarcastic reply, but he said only, "I couldn't stand them a minute longer. I've been thinking I really ought to get them catalogued and on the shelves before I start my own work; otherwise I'm not going to be able to find things when I need them. I didn't realize I had so many. It would take weeks even with two legs. It's going to take me a year. I fall on the floor twice for every three books I get on the shelf."

It was such a flat, unemotional statement that I looked more closely at him in surprise. Instead of his usual white venom, I saw now simply defeat. The frail energy of anger was gone.

"I could do this," I said, surprising myself profoundly.

"If you couldn't find anybody else you'd rather have do it, I mean," I said when he did not speak.

"I've done it before, for the public library's literacy action program in Atlanta," I went on, aware that I was babbling. He still did not speak. "It was more than just a little charity project; we catalogued and shelved thirty thousand books that were donated for the program. And I had two years of library science in college. I never made under a B plus . . . "

He began to laugh and pushed the gray-shot black hair off his face; the firelight and the laughter deepened the flush of color that the sweater gave him. He looked almost as young as the photograph he had shown me when we'd first met. He did not, for that moment, look ill at all.

"I wasn't doubting your credentials," he said. "I have no doubt at all that you can do a very creditable job at whatever you turn your hand to. I was just thinking that you keep on offering to save my ass even when I'm being as bad a dickhead as I can to you. Are you a Quaker, by any chance? A Jehovah's Witness? An angel of the Lord?"

"I didn't mean to pry," I said stiffly, getting up. My eyes stung and my face burned.

"Oh for God's sake, sit down, Molly," he said. "I wasn't being snotty. I meant it admiringly. I just don't do admiration well. Fix us some tea, or better yet, a slug of scotch, and let's talk about this cataloguing thing. You're right. It *is* too much for me right now, but it needs doing in the worst way. I can't live with my books in a mess."

I saw his color deepen and then recede, and knew without knowing how I did that he had thought, very clearly, that perhaps he would not live at all, and if not, what difference did orderly books make?

I said quickly, "I'd love to help. I could work out here and you could work in your bedroom. A couple of hours a day for a month or two would probably do it. I'd be very quiet, and I wouldn't have to be under your feet at all. Your foot, I mean. Oh, Lord, Dennis, I'm sorry."

He laughed again. "Don't apologize. It's uncontrollable. We don't even do it with the thinking part of the brain; it's something older and deeper. Maybe the cerebral cortex. I met Betty Rollin right after she had those two mastectomies and wrote that book, and promptly told her how much I admired her on the boob tube."

All of a sudden it was all right. We laughed. I brought a tray with tea and scotch and we drank some of both, and listened to a tape of Don Shirley's *Orpheus in the Underworld*, and talked a little about the book project. The fire snickered sturdily behind its screen, and Lazarus snored softly on the rug before it, and by the time the twilight came down and I stood up to go we had decided that I would work a couple of hours three or four mornings a week, and that, as I had suggested, he would begin sorting the notes for his book in his bedroom, and unless he called out to me or left me a note, I need not check on him.

"I wouldn't mind, but I'm not very good company when I'm working," he said. "I've been told that I snap and snarl. That shouldn't come as too much of a surprise to you."

"What's your book about?" I said, and then flinched. I did not think it was the sort of thing one asked a writer.

But he said, equably, "It's about a lot of years spent in the company of kids. About what they really think, as opposed to what we think they do, or wish they could. At least, it's about what I know about that. It's called 'In the Company of Tigers.'"

"And are they? Tigers, I mean?" I said, smiling.

"You bet they are. Don't you know that? You have a son, you said . . . "

"A daughter, too. Yes. I can see what you mean. Often they are, just that. As pure and beautiful and ruthless as that . . . "

"Precisely."

Before I reached the door he called, "Did Lazarus really come and get you?"

"He really did," I said. "Did you send him?"

"No. I guess, after the third or fourth time I fell on my ass, he thought it was time to take matters in his own hands."

"Nosy bastard, isn't he?"

He was still laughing when I closed his door. I walked down the hill in the fresh, cold darkness, Lazarus larruping at my heels, feeling as sated with leftover glee as if I were a child coming home from the circus.

The leftover gaiety held until I stopped at the farmhouse later that evening with groceries for Bella and Luz. I felt, running up the front steps and letting myself in, almost as if I were a daughter of the house, bringing youth and air and sustenance into it. But the room was dark, the lamps unlit, and Bella lay on the sofa, covered with an afghan, breathing windily like a ponderous, beached sea creature, and Luz was crying.

"Don't pay any attention to her; she's just acting up," Bella whispered. Her voice was so weak that I could hardly hear her, and she was white and filmed with sweat. Alarmed, I went over and switched on the lamp and looked down at her. Her lips were blue.

"Bella, I'm calling the nurse," I said, but she shook her head violently.

"It's already going away," she said. "She just provoked me till I yelled at her. Sometimes I think she does it on purpose. But the nurse scares her to death. Maybe you could make us some tea; that's one of the things she's crying for. I've just been too tired to make it."

I made the tea and brought it in. Bella was sitting up by then and did look a little better, though she was still sweating. In her rumpled bed Luz sniffled and cut her eyes at us.

"What's the trouble?" I said, wishing with all my heart I did not have to ask. But the fact that there was trouble hung in the air like rotting grapes.

"Oh, I always tell her a story this time of day, or read to her, and I didn't today," Bella wheezed. "She used to read to Denny this time of day, and we just kept on reading aloud when he left. Then, when she started to fail, I read to her. Or sometimes she told me stories she made up, but she doesn't do that much anymore. Anyway, it just seemed like my voice was too weak to do it this afternoon. I told her that over and over, but she'd forget and beg me again, and after a while I just lost my temper. I'm sorry for that, but she does try you sometimes."

I averted my eyes from her big, white, miserable face. Poor old women, yoked together by decay and failed expectations like two old oxen who had always toiled in tandem, and could no longer do so.

"Maybe I could read to her sometimes," I said, knowing as I said it that I was going to be sorry. But what, after all, was a half hour or so of reading?

"Oh, yes!" Luzia cried, her sulk forgotten. But Bella shook her head stubbornly.

"We don't have any books she hasn't read a million times. And anyway, I don't want to bother you. We agreed that I wouldn't."

But she was looking at me slyly from under her lashes.

"Oh, Bella, please," Luzia whispered, the tears beginning to flow again.

"I'd like to," I said. "I used to read aloud to Caroline and Teddy. I've sort of missed it. I'll get some from the library; what sort do you like, Luz?"

"Oh ... stories. You know. Adventures and things. About places way off that I've never been to. And I like stories about animals ... "

"Maybe I can find some about swans," I said, and left her clapping her hands, and Bella smiling faintly. The morning's benevolence flickered again as I drove home. It felt good to be needed, as long as I could control the precise degree of the need.

The next morning, when I took Lazarus and went to begin the book job, Dennis Ponder was his old self again, remote and chilly and impatient. After I had called into the bedroom a couple of times to ask questions that needed answering before I could continue, I heard him sigh and scramble laboriously to his feet, and heard the thump of the crutches for what seemed a very long time before he stood in the doorway scowling at me.

"I thought you said you knew how to do this," he said. "If you're going to be yelling in there every five minutes about this and that, I'm not going to get a fucking thing done. I should have known there wasn't a woman alive who could resist the urge to chatter."

It was such a consciously, crankily malicious thing to say that I smiled at him. He sounded like Teddy in an adolescent funk. But his words stung, all the same.

"Okay," I said calmly. "I'm just going to sort the books into piles by types today and save the questions for when that's done. Or maybe we could agree to have one small question and answer session at the end of every work day. I could write them down on a piece of paper and slide them under the door to you. Or throw them in with a chunk of raw meat. And I don't chatter. And I asked you exactly two questions."

"Yeah, sorry," he muttered, and shuffled back into the bedroom and closed the door with a small slam.

"Shithead," I mouthed at him. From inside I heard him mutter something to Lazarus, who lay on the rug beside the bed, and heard Lazarus's tail thump in answer.

"Shithead and Benedict Dog," I said, and set about my sorting.

At the end of the morning I had most of the books separated into huge, spilling pyramids, by subject, around the room. I was sitting on the floor, lost in a volume of Isak Dinesen, when I heard him come thumping into the room.

"I got hooked and forgot what time it was," I said. "I'm done for the day. You ought to be able to get through the piles to the kitchen okay . . . "

"Isak Dinesen," he said, looking down at the book in my hands. "Some say the best natural storyteller in the world."

His voice was not so cold now, but tired, a little weak. I realized that it would be a pattern with him, the letting down of his guard to let me in a millimeter, then the hasty withdrawal and the coldness, and then another microscopic thawing. Well, fine. If I scared him that badly, so be it. I wanted no more closeness than that, either. I just did not want any more of the glacial sarcasm. If I was only going to have four living beings to talk to—two ill old women and a dog and Dennis Ponder—I did not want that talk to be constrained and unpleasant.

I had a sudden thought.

"I wonder if I might borrow this book for a day or two?" I said.

"I promise I'd take good care of it. I'm short of books and I don't have a library card yet."

"Take it, by all means," he said aloofly. "I only read science books now."

"What a pity. Why is that?"

"I don't have time for speculation," he said stiffly. "And I'm short on patience with what-ifs."

"I want to read it to Luzia," I said defensively, feeling as though he had condemned me for my frivolity. "She's past the stage where she can read for herself, and your mother is getting too weak to do it."

He said nothing, and then he said, briefly and coldly, "What's the matter with my mother?"

"I think it must be congestive heart trouble," I said. "I don't know any more about it than that. I'm not carrying tales from her, if that's what you're worried about."

"I didn't say you were."

I got to my feet, then remembered.

"Oh, I didn't know what to do with these. I can shelve them along with the others, but some of them seem pretty old and valuable to me. I thought you might want to keep them separate somehow. The damp up here isn't going to be good for them, and they're awfully fragile already."

I gestured to a box I had found at the end of the morning, full of beautiful, crumbling old leather volumes that seemed to be mainly concerned with ships and the sea. After a page had disintegrated into silky dust in my fingers I had not handled them further.

He limped over and looked, then looked away.

"Just leave them there for now," he said. "They're my father's. They came from some lawyer's office after he died last year. I haven't looked at them yet."

"He's dead, then," I said.

"As a doornail."

"Do you remember him at all?"

"No."

I paused, then said, "Do you know that your mother doesn't know he's dead?"

He shrugged.

"Should I tell her?"

"Why?" he said, his mouth curled around the word. "She's done just fine all these years as an abandoned wife. On second thought, though, why not? She could get even more mileage out of being the Widow Ponder. Open up a whole new world for her."

I took the Dinesen book and went home without saying anything else. This was as far as I went with the Ponders, *mère et fils*. If Bella needed to know that her husband was dead, I assumed that the anonymous lawyer would tell her. Or maybe he already had. With her penchant for drama and manipulation, who knew?

That afternoon I opened the Dinesen book and prepared to read to Bella and Luz. It was a happier scene today; the fire burned bright, Bella had managed a tray of tea, and Luz looked as expectant as a child waiting for story time.

"That's a pretty old book," she said, reaching out to touch it. "Where did you get it?"

I hesitated, and then said, "I found it in a box."

I did not want to introduce Dennis Ponder into the day.

"Like lost treasure," Luz said.

"Like that."

I opened the book, cleared my throat, and began to read: "I had a farm in Africa, at the foot of the Ngong Hills . . . "

Thanksgiving Day was wild and windy, with curtains of rain spattering the windows and the last of the leaves whirling wetly to earth. Lazarus and I spent it alone. I had gotten a ready-roasted chicken and some packaged stuffing for Bella and Luz, but had suggested no getting together to share the meal. Luz had a virulent, nose-running cold, and Bella looked strange when I delivered the food on Thanksgiving Eve, as remote as a monolithic statue, gone away somewhere inside herself. Dennis had persuaded me not to look in on him. He was going well on his notes, he said, and did not want to be disturbed. He would call me if he needed me. He did not ask me if I had plans for the holiday, beyond saying that he was willing to do without Lazarus for the day, seeing as it was a family day.

"I'll call you around six, anyway," I said.

"Suit yourself," he said.

I had dreaded the day alone, but it turned out to be a good one. I built a big fire and kept it roaring, and I lay on the sofa before it with Lazarus, reading Oliver Sacks, from Dennis's library, until about four, when I made myself an omelet and fed Laz and the swans. Then I fell asleep on the sofa and dreamed of my mother.

In this dream she was, for the first time in many weeks, back in her subterranean barred room, only this time she did not importune me silently. This time her eyes were fixed on the back of my father's head. He sat in the seat in front of her, staring straight ahead. I knew that he had not seen her yet, but I also knew that he soon would, and would turn to her . . .

I woke myself up sobbing with fear, and got up and called Kevin's house in Washington. I knew that they had all gone to Sally's parents for the day, but thought perhaps they had already gotten back. I needed to hear my father's voice more than anything I ever remembered needing.

When he answered, I was a little surprised. He literally never answered Kevin's phone. I remembered that he would not answer ours, either, when he was at our house in Ansley Park. It was part of his old-fashioned gentleman's code, not to intrude his voice on to another's telephone.

His voice sounded as thick and weak as if I had wakened him from a long sleep, and I asked if I had.

"Caught me in the act," he said. "I was trying to slip in some zees before everybody gets back and the ball games start."

"I thought you were going with them," I said.

He was silent for a moment, then he said, "I really didn't want to, baby. I had some paperwork I needed to catch up on. And I got it done, so I'm that much ahead."

I knew then that they had not wanted him, and he had caught the scent of that as surely as if it were painted on the air. I made some loving, senseless chatter and called Kevin back late that night.

"You didn't take him with you for Thanksgiving," I said without preamble. "What's next, a boardinghouse on Christmas Day?"

"Hell, no, we didn't," Kevin snapped. "And have him sit in Sally's folks' house crying all day? He cries now, you know, Molly. He just sits there with tears running down his face, looking at nothing. Happy Thanksgiving, huh? Sally and Mandy cry all the time, too. You think you can do any better with him, you come do it."

"I damned well can do better than that," I said, my voice shaking with fury. "Put him on."

He sounded his old self, but then he always did, to me.

"Daddy, could you possibly come and stay with me for a while up here?" I said. "There's so much to do to this place that I just can't do; I need somebody who knows something about building, and wiring and things. And Lazarus misses you awfully, and so do I, and there's this pair of outlaw swans I'm stuck with feeding twice a day, and they almost beat me to death with their wings when I try, and they run Lazarus right into the water, and I just don't know what I'm going to do when winter comes . . . "

My father chuckled. It was his old chuckle—wasn't it?

"Swans, huh? I heard they could be mean. Run old Lazarus right into the water, have they? I reckon I'll have to see that."

"You mean you'll come?"

"I reckon I will. For a little while, anyway. If you're sure—"

"Oh, Daddy, I'm sure!"

I began to plan our Christmas the instant I put down the phone, ours and my father's. We would cut a tree from the surrounding forest, gather branches of holly and fir, and string cranberries for the birds; I would show him all of up island, and we would sit before the fire, drink his favorite scotch and eat popcorn, and listen to the old carols, and we would, finally, talk. . . . And it would snow. Of course it would snow.

By the time I went to pick him up at Logan, my fantasy of Christmas had reached towering, tottering Dickensian proportions. It even did, indeed, on the night before he came, begin, ever so gently, to snow.

But it was not my father who got off the plane in Boston and stood, blinking in confusion, looking around for me. Not a father I had ever known, not one I could even imagine. This man wore my father's face, but it was a sagging mask, pale and slack and decades older. And he was thin, so thin, and he shuffled, and his smile when he saw me never did reach his eyes. And though he listened attentively as I prattled of this and that, and showed him the landmarks on Cape Cod and on the road from the ferry in Vineyard Haven toward up island, he did not often speak, and I was not sure he heard me. And when he saw the glade and the pond and the house, with the electric candles in the windows, glowing in the early blue dusk, and the fat, ribbon-tied wreath on the door, and Lazarus leaping with joy at the door, he could manage to say only, "Well, now, this looks homey."

And when I took him upstairs to the big bedroom where he was to stay and he saw my mother's hat on the hat rack, he began to cry.

CHAPTER ELEVEN

I HAVE ALWAYS BEEN INFAMOUS IN OUR FAMILY for delayed reactions. Tee always used to tell Caroline and Teddy to call him, not me, when the grease fire spattered up, the fuse blew, the pipe broke.

"Otherwise we'll be treading water by the time your mom realizes there's a problem," he'd said.

He would have simply shaken his head at me in that awful moment when I stood in my upstairs bedroom and held my sobbing father in my arms. For it was only then that I realized that my mother was truly and finally dead.

I realized on the pulse of the instant that he was gone, though. The man I knew as my father died to me at the instant my mother did, and became, incredibly and grotesquely, my child. I became, in an eye blink, both an old orphan and a new mother. It was as bad a moment as I have ever had. A terrible white, roaring noise filled my head. When it faded, I realized that I was patting my father's back as I had Caroline's and Teddy's, when they were small and in distress. It was pure instinct, and I dropped my hand as if his poor back were burning.

He lifted his head presently and looked at me, and his face was melted and ruined with grief and hopelessness.

"I can't be of any more use to you, baby," he whispered. It was not his voice, not even his whisper. "Something's broken. I can't stop this goddamned crying. It's absurd and obscene and it scares the people I love most and me, too, and I can no more stop it than I can fly. I wish with all my heart that it had been me."

"No!" I cried, knowing what he meant. Terror and desperation took me over. "I couldn't stand that! Don't you ever, ever say that again! I need you any way I can get you! If you never lift another finger, if you cry for the next hundred years, I still need you! Don't you know that? If you say that again, I'll run away; I'll just . . . leave! I promise I will!"

We both stopped, he crying and me shouting, and looked at each other, then began to laugh. Run away?

"As long as you don't hold your breath till you turn blue," he said, and we laughed again, far longer and louder than was warranted. I didn't care. It got us past the moment.

Presently he went over and sat down on the freshly made bed and looked around the room. I had lit the fire in the iron stove, and had brought in armfuls of bittersweet berries and a little pot of blooming paperwhites; the last of the sun stained the long windows vermilion and gold, and struck silver and pewter off the pond's surface and the Bight beyond it. The room looked both lovely and loving, I thought. My house would wrap its arms around my wounded father.

"It's a pretty room," he said. "You've made a real pretty place up here. But I know it's your room; isn't there anywhere else I could sleep? I can't turn you out of your bedroom."

I shook my head.

"There's another bedroom up here if I wanted to sleep in it, but Laz picked us out a little nook under the stairs, and I really love it now. It's like hibernating for the winter. I never could sleep up here, somehow, and Laz won't. You're not putting us out."

He looked around some more, then back at me.

"Do you dream about her? Does she come to you up here? Is that it?"

I stared at him. He smiled faintly.

"Yes," I said finally. "It's not a good dream. I don't seem to have it so much downstairs."

His smile was as sweet and wistful as a child's. Tears dried on his cheeks.

"Maybe she will to me, up here. She hasn't, yet. She hasn't to

Kevin either, he says." He chuckled. "He'd be furious if he knew she'd picked you over him."

"He's going to be furious anyway, just as general policy," I said, taking him by the arm. "Come on downstairs. Sun's over the yardarm. I got you the Macallan."

He followed me down the precipitous steps, pausing to rap his knuckles against a joining or inspect a load-bearing beam here and there, nodding as if satisfied.

"You don't want to be too hard on your brother," he said. "He's mad because it's her he wants and me he got. I don't imagine he even knows why."

"He's a jerk, and I can be as hard on him as I want to," I said.

We had reached the bottom of the stairs, and he turned to me to say something else, but a great battering, hissing, flapping uproar started on the porch. Blows rattled the door. Lazarus sprang at it, snarling and barking angrily.

"Godalmighty," my father exclaimed.

"It's the damned swans," I said, running for the barley bucket and stick in the pantry. "I completely forgot to feed them this afternoon."

As if to illustrate my words, two beautiful, furious heads appeared at the long window beside the door, darting back and forth, pecking at the rippled old glass. Great wings battered and battered. My father sat down on the bottom step and began to laugh.

"Does Walt Disney know about this?" he said.

I opened the door an inch or two and the space was filled with a snowstorm of feathers and stabbing orange beaks. I slammed it again.

"They've never done this before," I said. "Just marched on the house like this. But I've never been this late feeding them, either. What on earth are we going to do? They can break bones . . . "

"Give me the stick and hold the dog," my father said. "And get over there behind that chair."

"Daddy, they really can hurt you; I know a woman who got her wrist broken . . . "

He opened the door and walked out on to the porch, into the sea of whirling white. He slammed the door behind him, and I watched, breath held, through the glass of the window, holding the hysterical Lazarus firmly by the collar.

My father raised the stick and struck the porch a mighty blow.

"Shut up," he said mildly.

Charles and Di did. Not only that, but they stopped the vicious, bullying attack and stood looking at him, tilting their V-shaped heads this way and that. Their wings were still lifted over their backs in the classic busking position that I had learned meant trouble, but they did not flap and hiss and grunt anymore. Very gradually, they lowered their wings and stared. My father gestured for the bucket, and I handed it to him out the door and shut it again.

"Where do you feed them?" he called to me, not taking his eyes off Charles and Di.

"Down on the edge of the pond, right down that path beyond the reeds," I called back.

"Okay," he said to the swans. "Now. If you want to eat, you're going to have to act like ladies and gentlemen. No fighting, no pushing, no hissing, no flapping. Got it? Let's go."

And he turned his back on them and marched down the steps and along the path, into the gathering dusk around the pond. Charles and Di waddled ponderously along behind him like imprinted ducklings. Lazarus stopped lunging and barking and sat down. I simply stared.

"How did you do that?" I said when he got back to the house. "I thought the next step was an AK–47."

He sat down on the sofa in front of the fire, rubbing his hands and grinning. It was the phantom of his old grin.

"Swan psychology."

"No, really."

"I went to the Library of Congress and read up on swans when you first told me about them," he said. "Interesting birds, swans. These are mutes, you know. They don't have caws or cries. They are not, however, your typical swans."

"So I gathered. What *is* typical?"

"Well, sometime when you've got a day or so I'll tell you what I know now about mute swans. Meanwhile, you better let me do KP."

"Why do you think I inveigled you up here?"

We sat sipping Macallan until the sun was long gone and the moon rose, cold and high. I had made a pot of chili, but neither of us was very hungry. It was enough, for me, to sit in my warm little house, wrapped in firelight and the comfort of my father's presence, and hear his voice answer mine. Presently he said, "So tell me about all this," and I did. I told him about the uneasy August on Chappaquiddick, where I could find no shelter, and about the pure solace of finding up island and this small, lost world, and about the colors and tastes and smells of autumn here, and about the deep, clean, pure solitude that so nourished me. I told him about Bella Ponder and Luzia Ferreira, and about Dennis Ponder, and about their place in my new world and mine in theirs. I talked of moonlight on the water off Menemsha, and stars that fell flaming from a crystal sky into my pond, and about the fires that burned in the beetlebung trees and the magic in the old gray stone walls of Chilmark, and about guinea fowl and geese and swans and gargantuan dancing statues, and the clean silver smell of newly caught fish on Dutcher's Dock, and about the rich, silent past that still lived and breathed in the old houses and little gated lanes up island. He listened and nodded, and occasionally he smiled or said, "Mmm-hmmm."

When I wound down and stopped to take a long swallow of my scotch, he stretched mightily and rubbed Lazarus's head and said, "Now tell me about back home. About where it stands with Tee and all that. I gather from Kevin that you don't feel like you can go back and live in your house, but that's all I do know. Teddy's too full of the desert country to be much good as a source of unbiased information, and Caroline's too full of hurt and spite. You got enough money? Made any plans beyond this winter?"

I closed my eyes and looked south in my mind. Atlanta and all that it held for me seemed to pulse and fester there like a red carbuncle. I recoiled from it. I looked over at my father and shook my head, smiling.

"There's nothing that won't keep, Daddy. To tell you the truth, I don't think much about it, and talking about it seems like just plain more than I've got the strength for right now. We have plenty of time. Don't let's spoil this lovely night. You don't know how I've looked forward to having you up here with me."

He nodded agreeably and finished his scotch and leaned back, his long legs stretched out in front of him toward the fire.

"You've got yourself a real magic kingdom up here, haven't

you, baby?" he said slowly. "Complete with a couple of maidens in distress and a fallen knight in need of nursing. Even a pair of swans on the moat."

I looked at him to see if he was being sarcastic, but his face was still and his eyes were comfortably closed.

"It's not like that," I said. "I certainly don't think there's anything magical about it. But what's wrong with feeling happy here? Or at least, peaceful . . . "

He sat up and clasped his hands and rested them between his knees, staring into the fire.

"I worry about you, Molly," he said. "I haven't been so sunk in my own misery that I don't know things are bad for you at home. I don't blame you for not wanting to fool with it. Tee and that little hussy of his haven't cut you enough slack to even stay in town. But, baby, this up here, as pretty and picturesque as it is . . . this is not real. This won't carry you, either. If I'm hearing you right, that's Alzheimer's and heart failure up there in that farmhouse. That's cancer over next door. That's suffering and dying; it's mess and pain and fear . . . "

"Not to me," I said emphatically. "We agreed, Daddy. We agreed that past a certain very particular point, I would not get involved in things here. I made that perfectly clear from the outset."

He shook his head, smiling a little.

"You can't be a little bit involved with pain and death, Molly. It's like being a little bit pregnant. Besides, you're your mother's daughter, no matter how hard you're trying not to be. That's what you're really running from, you know, why you're hiding out up here. You're hiding from her. What she still is, what she's made of you."

"That's just not true. I don't even think much about her, Daddy. I mean to, but somehow I just don't."

"You dream about her," he said. "The deepest, realest part of you is thinking about her."

I felt a wave of cold unease break over me. Could he be right? Could it be that I had buried my mother deep, only to find that she grew more vividly real here in my own soil, more hungrily alive than ever, like Madeline Usher?

Sweat broke out at my hairline. I looked at my father. He was still staring at the fire, and all of a sudden his face was so slack and gray and empty that I was stricken with remorse. He had come a very long way this day.

"It's bedtime," I said. "Why don't you go on up? I'll bring you up some chili."

"Thanks, but I think I'll pass on the chili," my father said. "I could do with another slosh of the Macallan, though."

"Then take the bottle with you," I said, rising and kissing him on the cheek. "Tomorrow I'll start showing you everything, but we've got lots of time. Sleep till you wake up."

"Good night, baby," he said, kissing me on the forehead. I watched him as he climbed the treacherous stairs. Slowly, so slowly . . .

"Good night, Daddy," I said softly into the firelight. "Sweet dreams."

I spent a good half hour the next morning tiptoeing around trying not to wake him before I realized he wasn't upstairs at all, was not, in fact, in the house. When it dawned on me, I felt a cold, still shock somewhere in my chest, and threw my coat over my robe and went out on to the porch. I found Lazarus there, his leash fastened to the leg of the heavy iron hammock stand. He was sitting, but he was as far toward the porch door as he could get, and the leash was straining, and he was whining softly. I ran across the porch and down the path toward the pond, icy dew stinging my feet in my flimsy scuffs, heart in my mouth. I did not even know, on any conscious level, why I was so frightened, or why I was so sure my father had gone down to the water. I did not call out to him, more from fear of what I would not hear than what I would.

I found him sitting on the end of the dock, his legs dangling over the water, regarding Charles and Di. They stood on the bank in their accustomed dining place, heads together, looking back at my father. From the scattering of husks around them I could see that he had already fed them. They seemed at ease, and except for a half-hearted hiss in my direction, they did not flap or fuss or threaten. If I had been at all sentimental about swans, or at least about these two, I might have said that they had been communing with my father. And then I thought, Well, the mere fact that they haven't tried to kill him could be construed as communication.

"What are you guys talking about?" I called softly from mid-way down the path, where I had stopped.

My father looked around at me, smiling. He was pale and drawn, but some of the lax, heartbreaking weakness had gone out of his face.

"All sorts of things. The high price of barley. The shoddy work they're doing on nests now. The scandalous way people let dogs just go anywhere these days. You know, Molly, I think the female has something wrong with her wing. I don't think she can fly. I'll bet that's why they've hung around here all these years. She can't go, and he won't leave her."

"Why do you think that? Her wings seem to flap just fine to me."

"Well, look, while she's still like that. See how one of them just droops, so that the tips drag in the grass? The other one doesn't. His don't."

I looked closer, and saw that he was right. Diana's left wing did seem to hang lower; the snowy tips drabbled on the wet, front-whitened verge of the pond. I realized then that I had never seen them before when their wings weren't drawn back in the horren-dously familiar busking position.

"Come to think of it, I've never seen them flying," I said.

"They don't, unless they're moving on. Too much trouble. Next to the trumpeters, these mutes are the biggest swans there are, almost the biggest bird. It takes them more distance to get airborne than any other bird alive. It would take the whole length of this pond, I expect, and even that might not be enough. They'd have to want to go somewhere a lot more than they do now for them to try to get launched."

"Sorry, guys," I said to Charles and Di. "I misjudged you. I thought it was pure sloth and greed that kept you here. I've been telling everybody you were spoiled brats."

"Well, that's not to say they're not," said my father. "Maybe just not entirely. See there, Molly? Nobody is ever as simple as you think they are."

"I guess not. You want to come with me to check on Dennis and the old ladies? I told them you were coming, but I guess I should introduce you. You won't have to fool with them after this."

"Sure," he said. "I'd like to."

I unleashed Lazarus while my father and I ate breakfast, and when we reached Dennis Ponder's camp Lazarus was waiting for us, as I knew he would be, sitting in the doorway to Dennis's bedroom and thumping his tail. Dennis stood behind him, dressed and balanced on his crutches. I tried to look at him with my father's eyes and almost gasped aloud; why had I ever thought he looked better these days? He looked like a half-melted snowman propped up with sticks. His shirt collar and cuffs stood out a good two inches from his neck and wrists, and it seemed to me that there was much more steel gray now in the black hair that hung over his forehead. It was far too long, too, I saw: It badly needed cutting. Not your problem, a voice in my head said, but my hands itched to get at his hair with scissors. I wondered how it would feel under my fingers.

All my life I have been surprised at the ease and naturalness with which my father meets people. I don't know why I should be, still; I have seen it happen over and over again. I suppose we get used to thinking of people close to us in a certain way: my father, the sweet but not too sophisticated old Irishman from the South Georgia wire-grass country, none too wise in the ways of the world. I was wrong, of course. My father has an innate courtesy, a delicate consideration for others that is almost Navajo in its depth. He is also keenly interested in literally everything and everybody he encounters, or at least he had been, before this awful summer. I watched these qualities reach out to Dennis Ponder now, and watched Dennis respond to them like a half-wild horse under firm, gentle hands.

They spoke in slow, exploratory half sentences to each other, as men will when they first meet, but there was nothing tentative about my father's interest in Dennis, none of the quickly averted eyes that the very ill must come to despise, none of the false heartiness. And there was nothing supercilious or cold in Dennis's response to him, as there had been, and often still was, in his dealings with me. The two men sat on the sofa in front of the fire and drank the coffee that I brought in, and talked peacefully of nothing, even the long silences between their words comfortable. Lazarus slept the sleep of the just on the hearth rug, his nose and toes twitching in his doggy dreams, his two, for now, main men content to be with each other. I fidgeted and sulked. Dennis's behavior toward my father was patently an insult to me, I thought. It was as if he were trying to show me the kind of person he could be when his patience was not being tried by fools.

I roused out of my huff to hear my father laughing quietly, and saying, "Tigers is right. My granddaughter has two earrings in one ear and a white stripe like a skunk's down the back of her head, and looks at you out of those yellow eyes as if she'd like to take a bite out of you. How on earth do you handle the girls? The boys are bad enough."

I knew that they were talking of Dennis's work, and of the book he was writing, and put an interested smile on my face.

"Actually, I didn't handle girls," Dennis said. "Castleberry is all male. It's probably one of the last all-male, private prep schools left in the country, and that can't last. It's just that nobody's filed a class-action suit against it yet. Too busy with the Citadel and VMI."

"Did you like that? Working with just boys?" my father asked.

"Very much. I find them far less distractible. And I've never been good with girls. Somehow we don't connect."

There was a silence, and then he turned to me and said, "And it's not that I have the old Jesuit thing about little boys, either."

"Well, I should think not," I said stiffly. "Why would you think I thought you did?"

"Some people have," he said briefly. I did not reply. I was seething inside. It had been an unwarranted thing to say.

"I do have a daughter," he said to my father, who nodded agreeably. "I don't see her. Her mother thinks I don't care much about her; she says I was always distant from her, and am much worse since the divorce, so she doesn't let me see her at all now. Maybe she's right. I never could think of much to say to Claire. Girls are not the snap to raise that boys are."

My dad winked at me.

"Takes some doing," he said. "Sometimes they turn out okay, though."

"I hope mine did. I hope she does," Dennis said. "I keep thinking I ought to try to see her again . . ."

He did not say, "now that I'm sick," but I heard it in my head.

"How old is she?" my father said.

"Ten."

I was surprised; I had thought his child must be much older.

He was at least my age, and probably more; it was not possible, with the illness, to say. It had been either a late marriage or a late fatherhood. Either way, the separation must be recent. That must still hurt. I wondered how I would feel, separated from Teddy and Caroline and knowing that I was desperately, perhaps mortally, ill. Unwanted pity swept me.

"We need to get on," I said to my father. "Dennis is working, and I've got to get groceries for the ladies. I'll get back to the books next week, Dennis, and I'll stop in with your stuff later today . . . "

"No hurry. Spend some time with your dad," Dennis said pleasantly, and then to my father, gruffly, "I'm sorry for your loss."

My father looked at me, and Dennis caught the look.

"My mother wrote me," he said. "Molly is as closemouthed as a flounder about personal things."

"Well, thank you," my father said.

"A nice man," he said to me as we got in the truck and headed for the farmhouse. "Pity about his sickness. He does well with it."

"I guess so," I said, wishing perversely that he could see Dennis Ponder in the midst of one of his arctic spells. "Of course, he's never once told me he was sorry for *my* loss. I can certainly see why he says he doesn't connect with women. Do you realize he told you more about himself in half an hour than he has me in two months?"

"Well, you said you had an agreement," my father said. "I don't have any agreement. Maybe he just needs to talk. It's usually easier for a man to talk to another man about personal things."

"Oh. It's a guy thing, huh?"

He chuckled. "I guess so. Do you care?"

"No."

But oddly enough, I found that I did, just a little.

I had not told Bella and Luzia that I would bring my father up to meet them that morning, but they were ready to receive distinguished company nonetheless. The fire burned brightly, the teapot steamed on the tea table, there was a bunch of fresh-cut, berry-laden holly in a beautiful old brass urn I had not seen before, and the old women wore what must have been their best, and makeup. Bella's dull black rayon was draped with a magnificent old red paisley shawl shot with gold threads, and her hair was piled on top of her head so tightly that her black eyes slanted like a Chinese empress's.

Indeed, she looked for all the world like a slyly serene Buddha, huge and richly adorned. Luz wore an ivory linen nightgown that buttoned up to her wattled throat, and another shawl, this one in shades of soft rose and green, wrapped her small shoulders. Bella had brushed the thistledown hair until it stood out around her tiny yellow face like a silver nimbus, and put a dab of pink lipstick on her little mouth. She looked like a mummified child, dressed forever in her grandmother's clothes.

"Well, you both look absolutely beautiful," I said, smiling at them. "Is all this for my old pa?"

"Is there a law against a body putting on something decent for a change?" Bella said archly in her deep voice. Her face was flushed crimson, whether from rouge or illness I could not have said.

"Bella said a mysterious stranger was coming to see us," Luzia said and giggled. "Don't I look pretty? I feel like a princess in this shawl. It was my great-grandmother's. She really was a princess. Tell them, Bella . . . "

"Hush, Luz, you promised you wouldn't babble," Bella growled, but she smiled fondly at the tiny woman in the bed.

"I can well believe it of both of you," my father said, smiling and bowing slightly to the old women. He had taken off the tweed hat he always wore outside, and held it in his hands. Bella took it from him and laid it tenderly on the tea table.

"Nice to see a man's hat in this hen's roost," she said. "I always did like the look of that."

She cut her black eyes at him and smiled so archly that I had to stifle a giggle myself. Bella Ponder was flirting with my father! I wondered if he knew. If he did, he did not betray it by so much as the lift of an eyebrow. As I said, Daddy is nothing if not a gentleman.

"Bella, can I tell him about King Dinis?" Luz pleaded. "I'm sure he doesn't know, and I don't want him to think we're just ordinary, normal people."

"Later, maybe," Bella said, glaring at her. "I don't imagine he thinks we're normal, by any stretch."

Again the sly cut of the eyes, and the arch smile.

"Anyone would say extraordinary," my father said and smiled, and went and sat down by Luz. "I'd like to hear all about it sometime when we have more time. I think I have to go shopping with my daughter in a little while. Could I come one day especially to hear about King Dinis?"

"Oh, yes! When? Today? Bella, can he come today . . . "

"Let the poor man have a little time with his daughter before you start rattling in his ear," Bella Ponder said. "Nobody much wants to hear those old tales these days, anyway."

"I do," my father said, and I knew that he did. Luz knew, too. She settled contentedly and watched and listened while my father worked his quiet magic on Bella Ponder. It was no more, really, than his extreme interest, and the mild but total focus of his eyes, but before long Bella was babbling like a teakettle herself. I went in to replenish the coffee and found a fresh loaf of bread on a tray, still warm from the oven. I sniffed; it smelled wonderfully of vanilla and something vaguely foreign. Sweet bread, then. I wondered what it had cost Bella to bake it. She had said she didn't bake much anymore. There was a cake of firm white cream cheese on a saucer beside it, and a jar of homemade beach plum jelly. I put them all on a tray and brought them out.

". . . But he doesn't even speak to me anymore," Bella was telling my father, and I sighed. The saga of Dennis's defection again. "I've always wondered what they did to turn him against me, over there in America. I sent him so he could learn about his true heritage, but so far as I know he hates even the mention of the Portuguese. He wrote me right before he came that he wanted absolutely nothing Portuguese put in his house. I managed to sneak in a little touch here and there, though. It's a proud heritage. He mustn't forget it."

"I don't imagine he will," I said, thinking of the *santos*, and the reredos in Dennis Ponder's bedroom. So far he had not objected violently to them, at least not in my presence. Or maybe it was just that he knew he was stuck with them; he certainly could not move them out.

"You must be wondering why we don't speak," Bella said to my father.

"It's a hard thing when families break up," he said mildly.

"Oh, it is! You don't know the pain that I live with in my heart," she said eagerly. "And I don't mean this silly weakness of mine. My son has been a knife in my heart since the day he left me. I wish I knew why he hates me so, but my family has long since gone back to Portugal, what's left of it, and I will never know unless he decides to tell me. But it had to be something they said or did . . . "

"Denny was the cutest little boy," Luz piped from her bed. I had thought she was sleeping; she had been nodding, her eyes closed.

"He was like my own; we played together all the time. He loved the old stories, and the games. When he gets better, he's going to come and see me. Bella promised. We can't go down there, you know."

Bella Ponder rolled her eyes at us.

"You never know what she hears and what she doesn't," she said. "I never told her that; it would be cruel. He doesn't want to see either of us. Luz is . . . childish, you know. She was always like this. No wonder Denny liked to play with her; it was like playing with another child. She's gotten worse since she fell, but not all that much."

"Does Denny remember me?" Luz said wistfully to my father.

"He hasn't said. I just met him, you know. But I'll bet he does," Daddy said. "He remembers about when he was a little boy here."

Bella Ponder's head whipped around to my father.

"What? What does he remember?" she said. "What did he tell you about that?"

"As I said, very little. He said he remembers his grandmother, and his cousins. He used to go to school with them, and play with them at recess. Not much more than that."

I looked at Bella Ponder. I thought she had said her son never knew his Ponder relations. She did not look at me, but her color deepened.

"What else does he remember about that time? Did he say?" she muttered. Her breath had begun to rasp in her chest.

My father smiled at her, a gentle smile, but I saw something in his face close, and knew that Bella had crossed a line with him.

"He didn't say much else about anything," he said. "We didn't talk very long. He's busy, and I didn't want to tire him. It hasn't been all that long since his operation, and it's not an easy one to get over."

"He's very sick, isn't he?" Bella said.

"I don't know, Mrs. Ponder, but I suspect he is," my father said quietly.

Bella stared into his face for a long time. The black eyes shone with tears abruptly, and she turned her head away. But then she said, very softly, "Thank you. You could have lied to me. Most people would have."

"I'm not going to do that," my father said.

"Will you come again?"

"Of course, if you like."

"Will you . . . tell me about my son? I promised your daughter I wouldn't ask, but if he's so sick, I want to know about him . . . "

"I don't think I can promise you that," my father said. "Not unless he agrees to it. But I'll see if he will."

She nodded. Presently we got up to leave. I collected the grocery list and walked out behind my father, with Bella.

"You bring your daddy back," she said. "He's a nice man. A good man. You're a lucky girl to have a father like that, to come all the way up here to be with you. Mine wouldn't have done that, no more than Dennis's would. You take care of that man."

"I will," I said, and surprised us both by kissing her on the cheek. My father had done it again; I knew more about Bella and Luz Ferreira from this brief meeting than I had learned in all my days with them before.

"Sad ladies," my father said, getting into the truck. "Nice, but real sad. They both miss that boy something awful; it's too bad. It doesn't seem like any of them have a lot of time left . . . "

"You know, it just doesn't ring right when Bella says she never got around to going over to the mainland to see him," I said. "All those years, and she never got around to it? If it were Teddy or Caroline over there and me over here, I'd have swum over there. There's got to be something else . . . "

"Oh, yes. Something really tragic is buried in there somewhere, I suspect. But it's her affair, hers and his. We mustn't pick at it, or pry. I tell you one thing, though, whenever I next feel down in the dumps and sorry for myself, I'm going to remember those three people."

"They seem to be doing all right, though, don't you think?" I said, anxious for him to agree with me. "I mean, considering every-thing."

But he just shook his head.

"It's hard enough, losing to death. It must be nearly unbearable, losing to life. Well, I guess you know about that, don't you, baby?"

"I guess so," I said. But it did not feel like the same thing at all. Somewhere deep down in the middle of me, I knew that my loss of Tee was not on the same scale of pain. Why that was true was a thing that would nag at me, I knew, for weeks to come. I had thought it was the worst pain I could know.

The three weeks before that Christmas were exquisite. Whenever I think "winter," it is not the Southern winters I have always known—landscapes of sepia and gray and fields the color of an old lion's coat, and soft, sulky, wet days—but those short weeks before the turning of the light toward spring up island. Days were cold and dry and clear, and the sun hung low in the south, so that the light, instead of pouring down from overhead, seemed to flow over the fields and the sea like thin silver wine from an overturned cask. The sea glittered in its shallows and the pond was crumpled foil, but it was a dulled glitter, nothing like the glass shards that the sun struck off the sea in August. That up island winter light . . . it still glows in the best of my dreams.

"Another magic light day," I would say to my father as we headed out in the truck with Lazarus to explore Menemsha or Lucy Vincent or Gay Head or one of my little secret up island trails.

"Seems like it," he would say mildly, and smile at me. But I knew that he felt a deep, harrowing stab of pure pain whenever something particularly lovely or remarkable took his breath, because his first impulse was to show it to my mother. I still felt that, too, sometimes, the need to tell Tee about things, even though I almost never wished him with me anymore. Then one morning, after a brief, pristine little snow that was gone by afternoon but left the glade and the pond such perfect silver miniatures that I cried aloud with joy at the first sight of it, I saw the brief slash of pure, burning orange that was the swans' beaks in all that photographic negative black-and-white, and I turned and ran back up the hill and pulled Dennis Ponder out on to the porch of his cottage to see. He did not laugh at me this time, but nodded and limped back into his house and brought his camera and took a few shots, and before he went back to work he said, "Thanks. I'm letting the leg make me miss too much."

I was as proud of myself as if he had given me a good-conduct commendation and it was only much later that I realized that it had been him, and not Tee, that I'd first thought of when I'd seen the swans.

"What does that mean, then?" I asked myself, but there seemed to be no answer except "nothing at all."

We were busy enough those first days so that I do not think my father felt the terrible, bone-sucking depression that he had at Kevin's, though I know that the sadness was still heavy and constant on him. When we stopped, as we finally had to do in the late afternoons, he would fall silent and sit very still, his face blank and empty, looking bleakly at nothing. I knew, though, that for him those nothings were filled with my mother, and I often wondered what he saw. Her presence was as palpable in the little house as if she had just left the room; I felt her everywhere, perhaps brought near by the sheer power of his wanting, and she still came in my dreams, even if she did not enter the niche under the stairs anymore. I wondered if she came to him upstairs. I did not think so. I thought that he would have been happier if she had.

But on the whole he did well. He admired the places I took him with unfeigned interest, and he asked me a thousand questions that I realized I probably should have known by now about up island, and he busied himself around the house with tools borrowed from Bella Ponder or Dennis, so that soon there was not a squeaking board or a drafty knothole or a thumping pipe or a faltering stove in evidence. He made a small split-log parson's table for the living room, found and rewired and hung a reading lamp for me so that I could read in my cave, installed a swinging dog door, and made a splendid insulated doghouse for Lazarus in the backyard so that he could indulge himself in swan-scanning or raccoon-barking far into the nights if he chose. Laz loved it, but he always came in before dawn. I never woke up in that place without his solid, odorous weight snugged softly into the curve of my hip or knee.

My father began gradually to take over some of my chores for

Dennis Ponder, too. He let me do my morning's cataloguing and shelving alone, content to stay behind and putter in the cabin or take the truck and go into Chilmark or West Tisbury. He loved the truck. But he was soon going in the afternoons to take Dennis's groceries to him and do the afternoon check, and then the visits became daily affairs, purely because each man wanted it so. I was vaguely annoyed. I felt proprietary about my father to a degree I would not have thought possible, and did not want him co-opted by the cold, pale man across the glade. We had an agreement, after all. There would be no intimate contact. And I resented that my father needed more than me.

"What do you talk about all the time?" I fumed one afternoon when he came home late, and the hot cheese rounds I had made to go with our scotch had cooled into little rubbery circles.

"Well, just the things that people talk about," my father said. "Books. Music. The weather. How it used to be up here. The old families; that's interesting to me. Being one of them, there's not much Dennis doesn't know about their history, even if he doesn't know the current crop. It's a pity he won't reach out to his kin now. Seems to me he'd want his people around him. But I don't think that's going to happen. Lot of bitterness there, though I declare I can't quite see why, if he doesn't even know them. Like we said, there's something bad there. And we talk about the other folks up here, the ones who've only been here for a generation or so, or less than that. There's a lot of them, way more than the old-timers. A real mixed bag. Storekeepers and fishermen and artists and writers and lawyers and real-estate people—seems to me half the island is trying to sell the other half some land, or buy it from them. Lot of building going on up here; Dennis says there's a lot of anger about that, too. There are more really poor people here than you'd realize, he says, and a lot more folks just making it, and I can see why the temptation to sell any little piece of land you've got is so strong if your family is hungry. On the other hand, nobody, especially not the old families who've still got a lot of land, wants to see happen up here what's happening down island. But the taxes are killing them. It's got a lot of people at their neighbors' throats."

"How does Dennis know all that if he hasn't been back to the Vineyard since he was eight years old?"

"He keeps up," my father said briefly. "He's always taken the

Gazette. Anyway, we talk about a lot of things. You ought to come join us sometime. You know a lot more about books and music than I do. Seems to me that's what he's mostly hungry to talk about."

"Well, let him ask me himself, then."

He chuckled.

"Would you go?"

"No. That's not part of the deal."

"Well, then."

Perhaps, I thought, going into the kitchen to heat up supper, I resented it just a bit that Dennis Ponder needed more than me, too. I had found my carefully structured caretaking routine extremely satisfying; an uninvolved angel of mercy suited me perfectly. Dennis had never once indicated that he wanted more. I guess he really doesn't, I thought. Not from me, at least.

I went by the farmhouse twice a day now, but now my father went with me two or three times a week, and on those days we stayed longer, and Bella put out a tea tray and some of the sweet bread she had baked that first time. *Massa Sovada*, she said it was called: Portuguese sweet bread. The spice I had wondered about was saffron.

"It's Easter bread," Luz said. "We always had it after early Mass on Easter morning. And Holy Ghost soup; Bella, remember how Denny used to love that? He called it HoGo soup when he was tiny, because he couldn't say the whole thing. Remember, Bella?"

"I remember."

On those afternoons my father would tell a story out of his Southern boyhood to Luz, and then she would tell him one of her dark, splendid tales of royalty and battles and gold. Sometimes even Bella would chime in with a story, usually about King Dinis and his times. It seemed to me that the old ladies knew no stories but those that had happened in a distant, magical past. And occasionally, when I came alone, I would read the women something short, a poem or a part of a chapter from a longer book I was reading. That Christmas we were reading T. H. White's *The Once and Future King*, my own college favorite and still, I think, Teddy's, and even old Bella was charmed with the rich, lyrical tapestry of kings and knights and animals who talked, and swords that stuck fast in stones except for orphan toys. I had given a little glad cry when I came upon it in Dennis's library, and had asked if I could borrow it.

He had only nodded.

"It's an odd book for you to have, if you don't mind my saying so," I said. "It's the only piece of out-and-out fantasy I've seen among all your books."

"It's not mine," he said.

Later that evening I had looked at the flyleaf: "To Claire from Daddy, love at Christmas" was written there in Dennis's backward-sloping hand. I wondered why he still had the book, but I was glad. It was soon Luz's favorite of all the things I read to her, and I read it to her over and over far into the spring.

They did not ask again about Dennis, though sometimes when my father was with me he would offer some small tidbit like, "Dennis walked as far as the pond with me yesterday. When he leans on Lazarus or me, there's almost no place around the glade he can't go by himself."

Or, "Dennis and I put up a bird feeder at his camp. We counted seven redbirds there last evening."

And Bella would be content with that. It was as if they had a tacit agreement. She did not wheedle, tease, or hint for more news of her son. But she always said, "Thank you, Mr. Bell," when he offered news of Dennis, and my father always nodded gravely. He never became Tim to her in all the time he knew her, and she never became other than Mrs. Ponder to him. Child of the Deep South, I did not think it strange. Nearing fifty, I still called the parents of my friends Mr. and Mrs.

But he spent the most time with the swans. In the early mornings, and again at sunset, when he took the bucket and went to feed them, he often squatted down on the bank or the dock and spent an hour or so just being with them. Hanging out, he said. He never took the stick now, and he still did not permit Lazarus to go with him, though Laz fairly danced up and down in his eagerness to promise that he would not chase Charles and Di.

"Later, maybe, after you've proved you can hold it in the road," Daddy would say to him.

I would see my father there, hunkered down with his arms wrapped around his long legs as he had done ever since I could remember, his tweed hat pushed back on his head, staring at Charles and Di. Sometimes he spoke; I could see his lips move. Sometimes they made noises back. But they never flapped or hissed at him, and they lifted not a wing at my father. I never knew what passed between them. I knew only that when I crept out to join them, fascinated by his taming of the two big, belligerent birds, they would immediately pull their beautiful, dingy-tipped wings back into the busking position and the grunts and hisses and snaky neck dartings would start.

"They act like I throw rocks at them," I said bitterly to him one night when I had been ousted once again. "I might as well do it. What do you and Luz have that the rest of us don't?"

"Pure hearts and simple minds," he said. "*Real* simple minds. You know I told you I thought Di had something wrong with her wing? She does. There's a break in the bone right where it goes into her chest, or shoulder, or whatever. The edges don't quite come together. She could never fly with that."

"How do you know?"

"She let me feel it. She didn't like it, but she let me."

"Shit," I said in frustration, and then, "I'm sorry, Daddy. It's just that I feel like a washout up here. I'm supposed to be taking care of two old ladies and a sick man and two old swans, and all four of them like you better than they do me."

"They know I'm not going to stir up their lives, make them change," he said. "I'm no threat to anybody. It's not fair, I know. I'm reaping all your good work."

"Well, I certainly am not going to stir them up or change them," I cried indignantly. "I've never done a single thing that would make any of them think that. We have an agreement . . . "

"I know, your famous agreement," my father said and smiled. "I don't care what kind of agreement you've got with who, Molly. There's just something about you—an energy, an impact, a kind of presence—that makes people know instinctively that it's not possible to stay unchanged by you. It's the one part of your mother that's clearest in you, and I think it's the thing about you she just couldn't leave alone. You don't even know you have it, I don't think. But it's there. None of these folks is ready to let go of what's eating them, and so they stay a little shy of you. I think they're afraid you're going to heal them in spite of themselves."

"Why . . . you never said anything like that to me before," I said wonderingly. "I didn't know I had . . . that. I thought Mother had all that in the family, she and Kevin. I thought I was the . . . you know, the one who made things work. The plain one."

"Oh, baby," he said. "That's her doing, too. I could always see when she did it, but she couldn't help doing it and I couldn't stop her. Plain one? Do you ever look in mirrors anymore? When you walk into a room, it's not possible for people to look away. That's not very comfortable for some people. I suspect it's not to Bella or Dennis. They're too busy staring inward at their pains and their hates. As for the swans, who knows? Maybe I smell like Luz and you don't. Maybe you smell like Lazarus."

I laughed and went away cheered. He could always do that. On the way into the kitchen, I sneaked a look at myself in the wavy, speckled old mirror on the hat rack. I looked the same as I always did to myself: tall, filling the entire mirror, having to stoop a little to see the top of my head, tousled by the wind and flame-cheeked from the cold. There *was* a vividness there, though: a pure blue glint from my eyes, the steel-and-silver streaks in my hair, the wash of summer tan that still lay over the bridge of my nose.

". . . an energy, an impact, a kind of presence . . . ," I whispered to the woman in the mirror. She flushed and dropped her eyes.

But all that night I was pleased, and felt pretty.

In the next few days, my father and Dennis Ponder started work on a nest for the swans under the porch of my camp.

"You'll never in the world get them under here," I said, watching as Dennis coiled and formed the dried reeds and grasses that my father cut from the pond bank with an old scythe he had found and restored to brightness in Dennis's toolshed. Dennis sat cross-legged, or what would have been cross-legged, on the cold earth, with a rubber poncho over his lap, and the low winter sun on his head. His black-and-gray hair shone in the slanted light, and the sun was laying faint streaks of color on his cheekbones and forehead. He looked almost well, almost young.

"I'm betting on Tim," he said to me. "If he thinks they need a winter home, then they need a winter home. He might be right. I hear it's supposed to be one of the worst winters we've had in years and years. The pond's apt to freeze right down to the bottom."

"Worst winters? It's been gorgeous so far," I said, looking up at the low, serene blue sky. The winter glitter lay far out on Vineyard

Sound this morning; I was getting accustomed to it now, but it still beguiled me. Only small, puffy white clouds like those of the summer sailed slowly up from the south.

"I remember a winter or two that started out like this," Dennis said, "and ended up with us being snowed in for days and weeks at a time. It seems to me we just plain had worse winters then. Maybe we're starting into another cycle of that. It doesn't usually get too bad until after Christmas, anyway. The water coming up from the Gulf is too warm until midwinter. But the Vineyard *Gazette* had a piece about it, and the weather idiot on Boston TV has been hollering about it. And your dad says the skinny at Alley's is that there's a bad one coming. Lots of talk about caterpillars and acorns and lichens."

"Far be it from me to contradict a caterpillar," I said. "You want anything before I head out? I just made some coffee."

"Got any sweet rolls? Lazarus and I have worked up an appetite."

"Coming up."

I was so delighted to have him hungry that I brought two big slices of the Portuguese sweet bread Bella had sent us home with, as well as the sweet rolls. Lazarus swallowed his in one gulp. Dennis looked at his and set it ostentatiously aside.

"Did she send you some Holy Ghost soup along with it?" he said neutrally.

"No," I said. "If you don't want that, give it to Daddy when he comes up. He loves it. Nobody's trying to force you to eat Portuguese. God forbid."

I took off for Vineyard Haven at rather too high a speed, rattling fiercely down the path through the tangled skeletons of the low scrub and the bare winter woods. There was no way I was going to please Dennis Ponder, I knew. There was always going to be at least one small thing amiss with everything I did for him. I thought that if it had been my father who offered the *Massa Sovada*, Dennis would have eaten the whole loaf and asked for more. I was still fuming when I got back. It was not yet noon, and I thought that they would still be working on the nest, but the yard was empty and piles of rushes and grass still waited to be woven into it, drying in the sun.

My father was not in the house, but came in while I was putting the groceries away.

"Are you done already?" I said.

"Nope. Dennis had a kind of bad turn, so I took him back up. I'm afraid this was too much for him, but he was doing so well . . . "

I put down the groceries and moved toward the coatrack for my coat. "I'm going up and have a look . . . "

"No. He said to tell you he'll be all right. He just wants to lie down. Let him be, baby. He's promised to call if he needs help, and I think he will."

"But I'm responsible—"

"No. Ultimately, he's responsible for himself. Leave him that at least."

"What kind of bad turn?"

"Some pain. A dizzy spell. A little nausea. I don't know. He knows what to do for himself. Let's let it be for now."

"He goes back soon for a checkup," I said. "I think it's next week. I've got it on my calendar."

"I know. Next Wednesday. I'm going to take him. He says he'll go in sooner, if this keeps up. I gather it's the first pain he's had in a while."

I let it go. My father would take care of it. I laughed at myself as I ladled soup into our bowls; how many times in my life had I thought just that: My father will take care of it.

"I'm so glad you're here," I called out to him

"I am, too," he called back. "You're terrific company for an old man, Miss Molly. Young one, too, come to that. Tee is the dumbest ass in six states."

Tee . . . for just a moment I simply could not think who he meant.

The day that he took Dennis to the doctor in Oak Bluffs was the day that the weather turned and my Dickensian Christmas died. The morning had been white and still, with a thick felting of gray-white clouds piling in from the northeast over the Sound. The air felt wet and sharp. By the time my father returned home in the truck with Dennis, the first flinty little flakes of snow were skirling down, and the temperature had dropped twenty degrees.

My father's face was grim. He was quiet for the balance of the morning and spent the early afternoon hours hunkered on the dock in silent communication with Charles and Di. Neither, yet, would follow him up to the nest under the porch, though they trailed him everywhere else. When he came in for our pre-dinner drink, he was still abstracted and closed.

"How bad is it?" I said finally. I had shrunk away from asking before. With the start of the snow my dream of my perfect wood-land Christmas had bloomed like a flower; I did not want anything dark or sharp to intrude on it. But eventually I had to ask.

"He's not doing very well, I don't think," he said.

"Has it come back? Is he going to lose more of his leg? Is he dying?" I prodded.

"I don't think they know yet," my father said. "He's due for some more chemo right before Christmas. I know he was hoping to avoid that, so I guess they've found something else. Or maybe it's just precautionary. He doesn't say much about it. And he doesn't want either of us to come by tonight. He has enough food, and he wants to sleep. Today tired him a lot. The effort to walk with those crutches is exhausting."

"I don't know why in the world he won't consider a prosthe-sis," I said. "He's in good shape; he's an athlete. It would give him back a lot of mobility."

He looked at me.

"There's no sense doing it yet if they're going to have to take more of the leg. And it could well be that he just doesn't have enough time left to justify it."

We had a silent dinner that night, and he went to bed early. I lay before the fire with Lazarus, too lethargic to stir myself to get up and do the dishes. I hadn't gotten around to it yet, but it was in my mind to ask Dennis Ponder to share Christmas dinner with us and Teddy and Caroline and her family. All of them had agreed to come. But now I did not want to mention Christmas to him. It might sound trivial, or at worst, heartless. Some of the enchanted glitter flaked off my dream holiday and drifted to the ground.

At nine-thirty Teddy called. He chattered and beat around the bush until I said, "You aren't coming, are you?"

"Oh, Ma . . . I can still come if you really, really want me to. But here's the thing, see. Dad is spending Christmas in Aspen, and he wants me and Barry to come have Christmas there, and then he's going to treat us to a week of skiing. Everybody out here skis, Ma. I need to learn. And I haven't seen him since . . . well, I haven't seen him. And you've got Granddad there with you, and Caroline and them are coming . . . "

He fell silent. My heart twisted with pain.

"Teddy, I can see why you'd want to go skiing. Aspen sounds wonderful. But the idea of you spending Christmas with them . . . this Christmas, especially . . . "

"I don't think there's any 'them' to it, Ma," Teddy said. "She's not coming. It's just Dad. I think she's going to spend the holidays with her family, or something."

I was silent. Not bloody likely, I thought, not the Eel Woman. Not in that trailer in the Georgia wire grass with those cold, whining people. What should I make of this, then?

"I know she's not in our house any longer," Teddy said, surprising me. I hadn't known that he knew about that.

"Well . . . that's a relief. I'll have to get the fumigators in. So . . . yes, of course, sweetie. I think that sounds like something you'd enjoy. And you're right, Caroline's family is coming, and Daddy's here. We'll miss you, but this will be something really special for you."

If I sounded like I was playing Mildred Pierce he did not notice.

"You're the best, Ma," he said. "How about if I spend part of the summer with you? If you're still there, I mean. And how about if we call you Christmas Day?"

"Summer would be fine," I said heartily. "And sure. We'll look forward to hearing from you on Christmas Day."

I was halfway expecting the next call, and it came an hour later.

Caroline's voice came over the wire, sharp and anxious. I thought for one startled moment that it was my mother.

"Are you snowed in? The weather said New England was having a terrible blizzard," she said.

"Nope. It's beautiful," I said gamely, but I had not looked outside since dinner. Now I could hear that the wind had risen, and was moaning around the chimney. All of a sudden I was cold.

"Well, listen. We're going to have to cancel. The baby has had a fever that will not come down, and I just can't drag her out to some remote island with no medical facilities. Not in a blizzard. I mean, what if you lost power? Didn't you say you only had woodstoves? I just can't take the chance, Mother."

"You're probably right," I said, my heart sinking slowly like a stone in viscid mud. "But the Vineyard has fine medical facilities. There are a lot of quite wealthy people here, Caro. They insist on the best and they get it. If she gets better, she'd be quite safe here. It's not the Yukon, you know."

"I just can't, Mom. Would you have taken me or Teddy there when you were a young mother?"

"I guess not," I said, feeling as though I had never been a young mother.

"We'll call, of course. On Christmas Eve and Christmas Day and everything. Lord, I wish you'd come on home and live like a human being, especially now that Dad's little doxy is out of the house. That's where we all really ought to be having Christmas."

I did not even ask her how she knew Sheri Scroggins had left our house. If Teddy knew, in far-off Arizona, surely the jungle drums had reached Memphis. I hung up and lay for a while thinking how much my ideas of comfort, even of luxury, had changed since I had come up island. To me this place felt more soothing and secure than the Ansley Park house ever had, more totally mine.

Before I went to bed, I opened the front door and put my head out. The bone-chilling wind almost knocked me backward. I saw, in the yellow glow of the security light my father had put up, that the ground was deep with drifted snow, and the branches of the nearest trees were weighted with it. The wind's voice was huge and old and wild, and I slammed the door against it. As I got into bed in the under-stairs cave, my bed lamp flickered, then went out. I got up again, built up the fire, pulled more blankets out of the cupboard and laid them over my sleeping father, and piled more over me and Lazarus. My Christmas dream sank without a bubble.

It took until late afternoon the next day for the power company to get the lights back on up island, though I heard on the transistor radio that Edgartown never lost power. Well, of course not, I thought sourly, dragging more wood. And if they had, they could just burn money for heat and light. When I said as much to my father, he smiled faintly and said that I sounded like a proper up islander.

Dennis Ponder had his first chemo treatment three days before Christmas. By late that afternoon he was vomiting. By nightfall my father and I were taking turns holding his head and wiping his face. I came home when he finally fell into an exhausted sleep, looking waxen white and already dead, but my father stayed the night, dozing on the sofa and listening for Dennis's call. He was better in the morning, but only a little. I stayed in his camp until after lunch, making soup and putting it in the freezer for him, listening to see if he needed me. He did not. He only wanted, he said weakly, to be left alone. Finally I did just that.

I had planned to take Christmas dinner up to the farmhouse and share it with the old ladies, but on Christmas Eve they called to say that they were both down with something that entailed nausea and diarrhea and coughing, and so I went out again, in the teeth of still another nor'easter, with groceries and aspirin and cough medicine, and spent the night making chicken soup and Jell-O and the things that I remembered from Teddy and Caroline's childhood sicknesses, and dozing in the cold guest room. Daddy spent the night on Dennis's sofa once again, with Lazarus on the rug beside him. On Christmas Day we met at our camp about two in the afternoon, red-eyed and scratchy-throated ourselves, looked at each other, rasped "Merry Christmas," and went to bed. I never cooked the turkey I had bought and stuffed, and we never even opened our presents.

"I tell you what," I croaked as cheerfully to my father as I could, "let's open them on New Year's Eve. New Year's Eve is always awful, no matter where you are or how you feel. That'll cheer us up. Maybe Dennis will feel better and he can join us. Let's just call this Christmas a wash and sleep through the rest of it."

"Done," my father said. "You don't know how I've been dreading this day. Now it's almost over. Thank God for small blessings."

"I love you, Pa," I said, tears welling in my eyes, not for my mother but for the maimed man she'd left behind her.

"Love you too, baby. You're my best Christmas present," he said. "You always were."

I crept into bed, intending to think about the Christmases at home with my mother, and of the ones in Ansley Park with Tee and the children, to begin to probe those deep, dark wounds, but instead I fell asleep and slept hard and dreamlessly, and when I woke it was to near darkness and swirling snow and a kind of hard joy that we had, indeed, gotten through.

We did, indeed, get colds, my father and I, and the week between Christmas and New Year's passed in a kind of snow-felted fever dream. Dennis was better, though weak; he did not want us, and we did not dare take our colds into his house. The old ladies had the visiting nurse, complaining bitterly about the intrusion, but insisting that we not bestir ourselves on their account. I could literally hear Bella's lungs filling with fluid as we spoke on the phone, but for once did not rush to check on her. Whatever we had might well kill her, and surely a registered nurse would serve them better than either my father or me. We slept, we read, we sipped soup and tea, my father and I, and we watched endless daytime television. Except for feeding Charles and Di, who still stubbornly refused to come to the nest under the porch and circled mulishly in a smaller and smaller circle of unfrozen pond, neither of us went out for several days. Even though the house was chilly, and I could never seem to build the fire high enough or get the stoves hot enough, I was not cold, and I don't think my father was. We lay about cocooned in camphor-smelling wool, surrendering gratefully and even happily to what could not be helped. I remember being, in those few days, quite content. I think my father was, too.

On New Year's Eve we got drunk. There isn't any other way to put it. Perhaps it was that all three of us were weak and hollowed out by illness, and deliriously grateful to be up and about again. Whatever it was, I, who had not been drunk since college, before I married Tee, got so sodden with bourbon and flown with joy that I did a bump and grind in the middle of the hearth rug to the habañera from *Carmen*. My father, whom I had literally never even seen tipsy before, told stories that, he said, he had heard forever around the fires at night in the fishing camps he loved; they were so childishly and good-humoredly obscene that Dennis and I laughed until tears rolled down our helpless, foolish faces. And Dennis Ponder, whose drinking habits I had no ideas at all about one way or another, sang. He stood propped on his crutch before the fireplace in the little house he remembered from his childhood, his head thrown back to show his corded white neck, and sang opera. He sang "Nessun Dorma" and "E Lucevan le Stelle" and most of the tenor arias from the Puccini operas, and he even sang snatches of Wagner, from *The Flying Dutchman* and *Tannhäuser*. He had a startlingly beautiful voice, and he spilled it effortlessly out over us. For perhaps the hour that he sang, he looked and sounded as well and young and vibrantly alive as any man I have ever seen, and I realized, when he stopped and looked at us almost shyly, that more than anything in the world, I wanted to go over and kiss him. So I did.

"Thank you," I said weepily into his hair, which by now nearly brushed his shoulders. It smelled of shampoo and wood smoke. "It was a great gift you just gave us. The gift of self . . ." only I said "shelf," and he laughed, and so did my father, and then so did I. After that, we laughed at everything.

"Being drunk is the only way," I remember pronouncing. "The only way. We should have done this ages ago."

"We'll do it from now on," my father said owlishly. "There's not enough bourbon on the Vineyard to hold us."

"We don't have to sober up at all," Dennis said. "Not until . . . not until we want to. Maybe never."

This was brushing too close to things under our glee that hurt, so I cried, "I know! Let's tell secrets! Everybody has to tell one thing that he's never told anybody else before. It can be anything, as long as nobody else has heard it."

They laughed and cheered. Encouraged, I poured myself another glass of bourbon and said, "I'll go first. Nobody on earth knows this, now. It's a complete secret. But you know, the night Tee told me about ol' Sheri Scroggins? The very night the Eel Woman entered my life? Well, that night, when Tee came in from out of town, I met him wearing nothing but three rolls of Saran Wrap. Isn't that incredible? Three whole rolls it took to wrap me up. Can you blame ol' Tee for running off with a lawyer?"

I laughed uproariously. No one else did.

"Don't you think that's funny?" I demanded, leaning over to peer into first my father's eyes, then Dennis's. I had to lean quite close; their eyes kept blurring.

"Oh, baby," my father said, softly and soberly, and I saw that there were tears in his eyes. I squinted; was I seeing correctly?

"I think he was a goddamned fool," Dennis Ponder said. He was not laughing, either.

"Yeah, but see, here's this really, really *big* lady with this wild black hair and a psycho-something rash on her butt, wrapped up in three rolls of Saran Wrap, like a big old Christmas present . . . "

"I think I'd like to kill Theron Redwine," my father said tightly.

"I think you're beautiful," Dennis said. "I'd love to see you wrapped up in Saran Wrap."

"Now I know you're drunk," I chortled, pointing a finger at him and almost falling over on the rug.

"Guilty as charged," Dennis said, and we all laughed some more.

"Okay, now you," I said to him, and he closed his eyes as if in thought and finally said, "I stole all my cousin Luzia's underwear once, when I was about seven, and buried it in the Peaks' sheep corral under a pile of dung. Their ram dug it up. Mr. Peak took a photo of him with her brassiere on his horns."

We roared.

"Why did you do that?" my father said.

Dennis looked startled. "I forget," he said. "I think it was something I saw . . ." He stopped laughing and his voice trailed off. Then he shook his head. "I don't know. Something . . . "

"It'll come," I said. "Now, Daddy. What about you?"

"Well, once when you kids were little I took you down to Tenth Street to see an adult movie," he said. "I didn't know it was when we went in, but I caught on pretty soon, and I didn't take you out. Your mother washed your mouths out with soap for weeks, the questions you were asking. I should have confessed, but I never did."

We laughed again, and then I said, "It's all such tame stuff. Now we have to tell something really big. Something that changed things. Dennis, you start; Daddy doesn't have any secrets. I'll tell you what I want to know. I want to know why you don't speak to your mother and Luz."

I paused and grinned around the room slyly, pleased with my daring. I did not see my father's frown, or the cold stillness that ran like a shadow over Dennis Ponder's face.

"I don't remember," he said levelly. I should have dropped it, but I did not.

"Come on, it's New Year's Eve. Of course you remember. You have to tell. No secrets allowed between us."

He looked up at me; I was capering around the living room, too full of bourbon and my own cleverness to sit still.

"It was something I saw. That's all that's your business, Molly. I owe you a lot, but I don't owe you that."

It penetrated even my drunken fog then: I had gone too far. I was not so drunk that I could not feel my cheeks flame.

"I'm sorry. That was really out of line. I apologize. Look, I've got some champagne on ice; let's uncork it. By the time midnight comes there'll still be enough for a toast."

I could tell that he did not want to stay, but my father's face was so stricken by my gaffe that apparently Dennis could not bring himself to leave. He nodded. My father nodded. I raced off to get the champagne, my cheeks and chest and forehead still burning. I knew that I would loathe myself in the morning.

But the champagne did the trick. By the time the little ormolu clock I had found at a flea market chimed twelve, we were laughing again, and we toasted the New Year and hugged each other and threw our hardware-store glasses into the fireplace. Outside the circle of firelight and liquor and hilarity, the world howled, and dark shapes slunk through it. But inside it, just for this one night, we were safe and warm. I would have done anything to keep that circle unbroken, but eventually sleep took me.

I remember that my father helped me to bed, and Dennis Ponder kissed me on the forehead and said, "Good night, Cinderella. I'm going to remind you in the morning of every dance you danced and every song you sang."

I woke sometime later, and heard them still talking before the fire, still laughing, but quietly, now. Sometime even later, I heard a kind of fussing, scurrying noise under the porch and sat up, blinking, and then realized fuzzily that the swans had made their way up from the pond and settled themselves into the nest my father and Dennis had made them. I was trying to rouse myself to get up and tell them about it when sleep took me down for good.

In the morning Dennis was gone, and my father was bustling

around the kitchen cleaning up. He grinned at me when I crept into the room, my head pounding, my mouth and throat furry with thirst.

"If you feel like you look, you should go back to bed," he said.

"Was I just unbearably awful? Never mind. I know I was. I've never done that before," I said. And then, remembering, "Oh, God, I've got to go up and apologize to Dennis. That was just a shitawful . . . sorry, Daddy . . . thing to ask him."

"No. Let him be," my father said. "I put him to bed on the sofa and he woke up awfully sick. I had to literally carry him over to his place. We should never have let him drink. I fault myself on that."

The pain and alarm I felt was quite different from the cringing guilt over my insensitive question the night before. The depth of it surprised me. I was suddenly terrified for Dennis Ponder.

Sometime in the night before, everything had changed. I could not remember much of what we had said to each other, but I thought of him differently now, in a new way. He was not simply the sick man across the way for whom I had contracted to care. He was someone who had poured out a liter of his very essence to me, as I had to him. He was real now. He was a living, funny, gifted, difficult, suffering, perhaps dying person who for one moment had reached out to me. I could have pulled away, as I had done all the weeks before, but I had not, and so I could never again think of him as I had before. For a moment I wanted that back desperately, more than anything. I did not want this whole, real, wounded new Dennis Ponder in my life. But there he was, and there, I knew, he would remain.

I wonder how I seem to him now? I thought. I wonder if I'm different to him? What's happening to us? Are we changing into other people up here, or just into whoever we were meant to be to begin with?

Maybe that's the magic of this place, I thought, going upstairs to take my shower. I stood under the hot water, eyes closed, surrendered to it, until it began to run cool, and then cold, but the strange new reality of Dennis Ponder and me would not wash away.

CHAPTER TWELVE

THE CATERPILLARS AND THE OLD MEN AT ALLEY'S GENERAL STORE were right about that winter. Conceived, the delighted weather-people said, of El Niño and the lingering ash clouds from Mount Pinatubo, great storms rolled east week after week, borne along on the jet stream, which clung to New England like a lover. Snowstorm followed snowstorm or, if conditions were just right, ice blanketed the Vineyard. The snows soon lost the luster of novelty and began to be hardships, but they never lost their power to enchant. A hushed white, perfectly still morning in the glade was still the stuff of held breath. Daily the blue-white yard was crisscrossed with the delicate traceries of whatever hungry animals had come foraging during the nights: skunk, raccoon, deer, an occasional opossum, the lacy evidence of a hundred birds around the bird feeder. Often, at the edge of the front porch overhang, there would be the furious, swooping snow angels made by the swans' wings as they protested the intrusion of their hungry neighbors. We saw, too, the wide, deep spraddle of their webbed feet as they waddled flat-footedly back to the pond. In those bitter early days of January, my father went down almost hourly to break up the ice on the pond so that the indignant Charles and Di could paddle.

"You'd think they'd be glad to give it up till spring," I said, fretting about my father's habit of going out in the bitterest weather in only his flannel jacket and tweed hat. "They don't need to drink it; they've got the water you put out under the porch. I think they just insist on it to jerk you around. Why don't you try leaving it frozen for one night, and see what happens?"

"It's their job," he said mildly. "It's what they do. I don't mind whacking ice. It could get old if this doesn't let up for a while, though."

It didn't. As I said, the snows were tolerable because of their beauty. But the ice was different. Oh, it was beautiful, all right; the rare glitter of sun off the crystal branches along the lanes, the incredible sight of entire forests of curly scrub oak blazing and clicking under an iron-blue sky; the bone-chilling morning when we skidded down to the docks in Menemsha to buy scallops and found the Bight a solid sheet of steel-gray ice—I will never forget those sights.

But the ice brought cold and danger along with the extravagant chandeliers it hung up island. Branches and wires came down and it was often days before crews could get to them. Cold darkness prevailed. People could not flee to the little towns for light and warmth because the roads were treacherous; each storm brought news of an accident that harmed, and once or twice, killed. More than once the governor declared the Vineyard a disaster area, and National Guard trucks rolled ponderously off the ferries with supplies for farm animals and people in the worst-hit areas, only to skid helplessly off the roads and end up, turtlelike, on their sides. In the end, it was neighbor slogging and sliding across fields and down lanes to neighbor with food and firewood or propane that saw up island through. On one of my rare, perilous, crawling trips to the store I heard an old man telling a child, "Maybe the folks up here ain't so kissy-kissy most of the time, but by God they make good neighbors in hard times."

I had not thought that many people knew I was there, in the little camp at the end of the lane, or that Dennis Ponder had come back. But twice, when I went out in the morning to stock the bird feeder, I found that someone had been down the lane with a small plow mounted on the front of a vehicle, and once there was a paper sack full of scallop chowder, crackers and bread, milk, and a bag of apples. There was no note on the bag, and no name. I came very close to tears that morning. My father smiled.

That same morning, because of the plowed lane, I was able to get to Middle Road and down to the lane that led to the farmhouse. I had thought I would have to leave the truck and walk up, but the lane, too, had been plowed. I carried my bag of provisions into the kitchen and found that a paper sack similar to the one left at my door sat on the kitchen table.

"Who's the Good Samaritan who brought your food?" I said to Luz, who was nodding by the smoldering fire. Bella, she said, was still upstairs.

"I don't know. We knew it wasn't you because you'd come in. Bella says we're not going to eat it. We don't take charity. I wish we did. I can smell scallop soup. I don't think I had any breakfast."

I was appalled, and furious with Bella.

"Luz, how often do you miss your breakfast?" I said gently. "Does Bella always stay upstairs this late in the morning?"

"Yes, but I don't mind. I always save my bread from supper. She comes down by lunchtime. It's just that she needs to sleep; I don't think she sleeps much at night. I hear her coughing almost all night long."

I went into the kitchen and heated the scallop chowder and brought it in with a chunk of bread I found under a white dishcloth; there was little else in the kitchen. I had not been able to get there with food for several days. The anonymous offering of soup and crackers would have seen them through two more days if I could not have made it today. I was very angry. I wanted to shake Bella Ponder until her fat jowls quivered. Her arrogant pride was going to kill them both.

At first Luz hesitated over the soup.

"Eat the damned soup," I snapped. "You can always pretend that the peasants brought it as an act of homage."

I was immediately sorry for the sarcasm, but Luz's little face brightened and she tucked into the soup hungrily. She did not speak until the bowl was empty.

"I'm glad you thought of that. The soup was wonderful," she said. "I'm glad you thought of that about the peasants. I'm going to tell Bella, I'll bet she never thought of it."

"You do that," I said grimly. "And you tell her I'll stop by this afternoon if I can still get up the hill. I'll bring some more soup, and part of an apple pie I made."

I kissed her cheek, put another blanket on her bed, and built up the fire.

"Can you believe it?" I fumed to my father when I got home. "She can't even get down the steps to feed Luz; they're cold and they're hungry, and they won't eat hot chowder somebody brings them because they don't take charity! I swear, it's getting to be time to do something about them. Get them into a home, or get a full-time nurse in, or something. I can't let them starve and freeze, and I can't count on getting over there until this weather lets up."

"It doesn't look like their neighbors are going to let them starve or freeze," he said.

"Well, but they won't eat the food. I told you what Luz said Bella said about that. Who should I call? The visiting nurse? It's the only number I've got. Isn't there some kind of organization for the elderly on the island? It seems like I've seen something on a sign in West Tisbury . . . "

"There are a couple of organizations for us old farts, I think," he said. "It seems to me I've heard they deliver hot meals and health care and all kinds of stuff to shut-ins, and I know they've got people who'll take you to the doctor or to the senior center for a meal. The senior center's a nice place; I've dropped by there a few times and played some Scrabble and shot a little pool. Got the pants beat off me the first few times, but I'm getting my game back. I don't think there's much for Bella and Luz if they won't ask, though. As for getting them into some kind of residential place, you're probably right, but that's not your job to do. Only someone connected to the family could do it legally. That's Dennis, I guess. I wouldn't imagine he's up to it right now, and probably not inclined to tackle the old ladies if he was. I think the best and only thing we can do is what we're already doing. The weather can't last forever; I hear from the old-timers around Alley's and the senior center that the Vineyard winters aren't usually much worse than Atlanta's."

I knew he was right. I looked at him with interest. I could no more imagine my father playing Scrabble and pool with the elderly men of Chilmark and West Tisbury than I could imagine doing it myself, but there was no good reason for my surprise. He had always had two or three close friends with whom he had done things; it stood to reason that he must miss that. On reflection, the fact that he had quietly moved to find companionship for himself, instead of clinging to Dennis Ponder, said much about his adjustment, and the lifting of the terrible depression.

"I'm proud of you," I said, giving him a quick hug. "You've done what I should have been doing all along: getting to know some of the other people up island. I think I've just assumed that they were what Bella and Luz and Dennis said they were: tight-knit old families who don't want any truck with anybody else. That doesn't make any sense, does it?"

"No," he said. "But you needed some time to heal and some space to do it on your own terms. I always thought when it was time, you'd stick your nose out and get to know a few folks. If you're ready for that, I could take you with me to the senior center next time I go. Having you around would probably jump-start a lot of pacemakers."

I grinned.

"You got a deal. I've forgotten what it feels like to rattle a chain."

"Pity," my father said. "You need to remember how that feels. And some folks I know need to remember how it feels to get 'em rattled."

"If you're referring to Dennis, that's ridiculous. That's almost obscene."

"Hell, Molly, the man's a long way from dead," he said irritably. "If you hadn't been so squiffed New Year's Eve you'd have seen that Dennis was acting like a rooster in the henhouse around you. You've got to stop burying your men folks before their time. Makes them cranky."

I just rolled my eyes at him. But the conversation lingered. Before I went up to check on Dennis that afternoon, I put on some lipstick and brushed my skunk-striped hair until it shone. I had not done either for a long time. It felt good. By the time I gained the porch of the larger camp, there was a spring in my step that had not been there since the siege of bitter cold had started.

He was lying on the sofa in front of the fire, Lazarus sighing and twitching on the rug beside him. I had only seen him once or twice since New Year's Eve. While he was so desperately ill from the chemo he had seemed to want only my father, and with my new, skin-prickling awareness of him, I was willing to give him that. But by now I found that I wanted to see him; needed to see for myself that he was still there, still alive. Simply that. I knew that he had only two more chemo sessions, and I found that I had been thinking of the time beyond them as a time when I would have back the man who had laughed and sung on New Year's Eve. But now, looking at him, I thought, with a surge of desolation, that I might have seen the last of that man in that first glimpse.

He looked terrible. He was white and still and the thick hair was lusterless and dry now, hanging messily around his collar. His face was sunken and yellow. During the long spells of nausea, he had lost a lot of the weight he had regained, and even his hands, lying still on the blanket that covered him, were thin to bone and white to transparency. I stood staring intently until I saw the blanket rise and fall shallowly over his chest, then I tiptoed into the room.

"You don't have to do that," he said, his eyes still closed. They were ringed in gray-blue, and his beard was thick and blue on his jaw.

"I'm not asleep. Just listening to the tick of ice on the roof. Doesn't sound a damned bit cozy, does it?"

"I brought you some scallop chowder," I said. "I'm going to heat it up and we're both going to have some. It's colder than a well-digger's butt in Arkansas out there, as my dad says, although I could never understand why a well digger would have a cold butt in Arkansas. And then I think I'm going to cut your hair. You'll feel a lot better without it straggling down your neck. I might even shave you."

He opened his eyes and rolled his head on his neck until he could see me. It was a weak gesture, sick and resigned.

"I'll let you cut my hair and shave me if you'll make that scotch instead of chowder," he said. "I'd just throw it up. For some reason, booze stays down. Maybe we could get drunk again. What do you say? Sing a little? Dance a bit?"

The rictus on his white lips frightened me until I realized he was smiling, or trying to. It was dreadful to see, heart-wrenching. I found myself wishing that he would snap at me as he would have before.

I went and got the scotch and poured us both some, and

handed his to him. When he raised the glass to his lips, his hand was trembling so that some of the amber liquid spilled down his chin. I took the glass and held it while he sipped, and presently his hand was steadier, and he took the glass back.

"Where's Tim?" he said, struggling to sit up. I started to help him, then sat still.

"He's down cracking the ice for those damned swans for the thousandth time," I said. "Then he's going to take some soup over to the farmhouse. He needed to go now, before it starts to ice up too badly. He'll stop by on his way back, he said."

He was silent for a while, sipping scotch. I watched the fire and the sleet ticking on the windows, and, when I thought I was unobserved, his face. It looked, in the firelight, a bit like Roualt's head of Christ, stark and tortured and finished. My fingers itched to get at the hair and beard.

"So what's going on at the farmhouse?" he said finally. There was reluctance in his voice, but something else, too. A kind of slackening, a loosening of something that had held tight, like a vise. I knew he was not simply making conversation. He was too sick and weak for that. I wondered whether to put a bright face on the two old women's plight or to tell him the truth.

"It's not very good," I said. "They've gotten to the point where they can't really take care of each other. Your mother doesn't come downstairs until midday; I think she's coughing so badly at night that she simply has to sleep in the mornings. It leaves Luz on her own, with no food and no heat. I'm going to start going first thing, and Daddy's going to take the afternoon trip. That is, if the weather ever lets up. It's getting almost impossible to get up that hill to the farmhouse. I know this isn't what you wanted to hear, but I'm afraid the time is coming when they need more care than Daddy and I can give them, and you're the one who would have to make the arrangements about a nursing home, or something. Or, at least, okay, whatever we can arrange. I'd spare you this if I could, but I'm afraid for them. They won't take help."

And I told him about the food that was left but uneaten.

He shut his eyes again, and let his head roll to the side. His face was pinched and colorless.

"Goddamn that stupid Portuguese pride," he said. "She never

would take what people offered her. She never would. People tried to help when Daddy left; I remember the pies and cakes and covered dishes that came into the house, even if I don't remember him. She dumped them all out and washed out the dishes they came in and made Luz take them back. God knows that bigoted old Gorgon, my Ponder grandmother, made her life miserable enough over being Portuguese, but she did reach out to her after he left. Mother did everything but spit in her face. I don't know if I blame her, but it would have been a start toward some healing. It could have meant a different life for her, and for me, too. But she had King Dinis. What else did she need? Now they're up there freezing and choking on their precious pride. Well, let King Dinis come save them. I don't give a shit. I'm only sorry you and Tim have gotten stuck with them. Let them go. Call the county and dump them."

"I haven't minded until now," I said. "I like your mother. I'm truly fond of Luz. And they gave me the start of a life back when they let me have the camp. I'm not going to just abandon them. But I promise I won't mention them to you again."

He shook his head weakly, and sighed.

"I'm sorry," he said. "You've got enough problems of your own. I'll try not to add my natural sweetness and generosity to them. Keep me posted on the old babes. If it comes right down to it, I'll figure out what to do about them. Provided, of course, I'm still around by then."

My heart flopped in my chest like a fish. He had never come so close to the subject that hovered always in the air over our heads.

"Dennis," I said, "if I can hold your head while you barf, I think I deserve to know what's going on with you and the leg. I'm not going to run on about it, and I'm not going to tell anybody—who would I tell? *People* magazine? I don't talk about you to your mother, if that's what bothers you. But I want to know. I . . . we care about you and the way you feel, Daddy and I. It's hard to think about you over here going through God knows what when we're right over there not doing anything to help . . . "

He turned his head to look at me again. He did that for quite a long time. Finally he said, "I don't know myself. They found some more . . . involvement with the bone in my thigh, that's why the chemo. It was hurting a good bit. It hasn't done that until now, not really. They're going to check after this course of chemo is over, and then they may want to take some more of the leg. I've already told them that's out. I've got some painkillers. I don't use them much, but they're here if I need them. And I've got some stuff to help me sleep. I don't use that, either. But it's here . . . if I need it. So far, scotch is better. I'm not going back after the last chemo treatment. I'm not going to give them any more of my leg. If it gets too bad, I'll decide then what to do. Who knows, this round may do the trick. Either way, I should know before spring. It's not going to prolong your tour of duty. I'm not asking you to re-up."

My eyes stung and I shook my head mutely. He saw it, and said, "I'm sorry again. I didn't mean that the way it sounded. I'm not used to nice women."

It was such a matter-of-fact pronouncement that I laughed, startled. He smiled, too.

"'Thus spake Zarathustra.' It's true, though. I seem drawn to your basic Grendel's mother type. The nice ones I manage to run off before they can apply for sainthood."

"You sound like the hero in a bad romance novel," I said. "A wild, bad boy until he's redeemed by a good woman's love. What decent long-suffering women have you managed to run off?"

"Two wives," he said. "One daughter." He was not smiling now.

"Why is that, Dennis?" I said quietly. It seemed to me that I was very close to seeing past the wall of illness and rudeness now.

"I grew up knowing only one thing about women, and that was that they will leave you," he said. "I made up my mind early on to be the one who did the leaving. I don't think I ever knew that consciously, until I got sick and had to stop and look inside. By that time, it seemed too much trouble to try and change things. I don't think there's that much time left, even if this leg turns out to be okay. I don't have the staying gene in me. I couldn't have. Neither of my parents had it . . . "

"Your father may have left you. But your mother didn't," I said. "She's still here. Right up there where she's always been, still waiting. All it would take is one word from you . . . "

He laughed, shortly and bitterly. "Is that what she told you? That she's waited for me all these years? That old bitch. She doesn't even know what's true and what isn't anymore."

I said nothing. I wanted, suddenly, no more of this. I was tired of the stubborn, senseless little drama of mother and son that had played around my head since the first day I had come up island. I stood up to go, snapping my fingers for Lazarus.

"Wait a minute," he said, and I stopped.

"Could you do one thing for me?"

"Of course."

"There used to be a sled in the woodshed out there. A blue Flexible Flyer. I wondered if it was still there. Would you mind looking?"

"Of course not."

I went out into the deepening blue of the January night. An early moon was rising, huge and white and low. It looked like a disk cut from bone, and polished. It would light the night almost like daylight, I knew. The Wolf Moon, my father said the old men at Alley's called it.

The sled was at the back of the woodshed, covered with a filthy old tarpaulin.

"Still there," I reported. Dennis smiled.

"I got that sled for Christmas the year before I went to America," he said. "It was a winter like this one, cold, with lots of snow. I don't remember any ice, though. We had our Christmas at the little camp, where you and Tim are. After dinner we went out on that hill that goes down to the water on the other side of the dock, and tried it out. I still remember my mother running like a deer, pushing that sled and belly-flopping down on it, shooting down the hill yelling like a Wampanoag. If they yell. I've never heard one. Her hair was in braids down to her waist, and they stood straight out behind her . . . "

I saw it in my mind, a tall, slim woman and a dark little boy, lifted off the earth on a snowy Christmas Day, literally, for a moment, hung between heaven and earth.

"Is she dying?" he said.

"I think so."

"How long?"

"I have no idea. It's congestive heart failure. I don't know much about that. I think the danger would be pneumonia, or something like it. I can find out . . . "

271

He shook his head.

"No."

And then, "She's very fat now, I know. Tim told me. I wish you could have seen her when she was young. She was . . . very beautiful."

"I wish I could have, too."

"There's something of her in you. Something of her like she was then, I mean. I told you that the first day, didn't I? Physically, I mean. There's no similarity in any other way."

"How do you know?" I said.

"I know."

His eyes drifted shut again, and I took Lazarus and went back to the little camp. I felt heavy and thick, freighted with a hopeless sadness, but under it was the beginning of elation. He had let me come close tonight. For just a moment, he had opened a door. . . .

"Looks like it's going to be a pretty night," my father said when I came into the kitchen. "Why don't we go out for dinner? There's a spot I keep hearing about. We ought to try it out before another blizzard hits."

The Red Cat Restaurant sat in the brilliant snow beside the state road in West Tisbury. After the empty, moon-washed snowscape we had traveled through, it looked like the confluence of all the lights and warmth and human companionship in the world. Cars and trucks and all-terrain vehicles were parked around it, and I could hear a little surf of rock music, thumping and cheerful, when I opened the door of the truck. All of a sudden I could hardly wait to get inside, to be part of a community again, even one unknown to me. I felt like a child going to a party, shy and awkward, but with a small fountain of secret glee in my stomach.

"I had no idea I'd missed this so much," I said to my father.

"Missed what?"

"Lights. People. Just going out to dinner."

"It ain't Buckhead."

I laughed.

"Right now it looks better to me than the Ritz."

We went in to the low, rambling, warm-lit building and were ushered to a table in a corner. On the way to it my father nodded to a couple of tables where men and women sat, and they smiled and nodded back. One of the men was pouring something from a paper sack, and he lifted the sack and said, "Evening, Tim."

"Ready for a game sometime soon?" another said.

"Any time," my father said.

It struck me that the men and women looked much as we did, or vice versa: ranging from young middle age to the sturdy elderly, bundled into parkas and scarves and caps or dressed in sweaters and turtlenecks and wool pants. Most wore boots. All looked healthy and weathered and simply glad, like us, to be out at the Red Cat on a snowy night.

"We could almost pass, couldn't we?" I said to my father as we sat down.

"Wouldn't miss it far," he said. He pulled a paper sack from the pocket of his jacket and put it on the table.

"Would madame like a cocktail before dinner?"

We sat and sipped the Macallan and I took a long, fussily elaborate time choosing from the menu. I loved this place and this night. I wanted to prolong it as much as possible. I finally decided on lamb shanks in red wine and sat back and drank some more of the Macallan.

"You could get drunk just from the sheer excitement of being with people, couldn't you?" I said.

"You could get drunk quicker on that stuff," he said mildly. "Don't you go getting cabin fever on me, and turning into a deep-woods lush. I can't have you dancing on tables here."

We talked lightly of things that did not seem to matter much, just for the sensation of doing such a wonderfully ordinary thing as making small talk in a restaurant. But finally we fell silent.

"I think Dennis may be thinking about killing himself," I heard myself say and gasped aloud. I had not known I thought that.

"Why do you say that?" my father asked. He did not seem shocked.

"I don't know, exactly. He's not going back to the hospital for any more surgery, you know. And he won't know for a while if this chemo is working. I don't know what the chances are of that, and he isn't about to tell me. I know a recurrence isn't good. But he said he had painkillers and sleeping pills, and that he would make up his mind how to use them if he needed them. Those were almost his words. It just now struck me that that's what he might have been talking about."

"Does it shock you? Scare you?" my father asked.

I thought about that.

"It doesn't shock me, I don't guess. But I hate the idea. I just hate it, Daddy. A man as young as he is, with such gifts, with so much to live for . . . "

"Maybe he doesn't think he's got so much to live for," my father said. "He's lost his wife and his daughter and his job and his leg. He's estranged from all his people. He's had a good bit of pain and there may be more coming. You can sort of see his point—"

"Daddy! I can't believe you're saying this about Dennis! He's your friend; you act almost like he's a son sometimes . . . "

"I won't wish bad pain on any man, Molly," he said. "I know about that. I wouldn't wish it on my worst enemy, and I certainly am not going to wish it on Dennis. You're right; he is my friend. Only he knows what his limit is. If he reaches it, I hope I can be there with him, but I'm not going to stop him."

"You knew he had this in his mind . . . "

"I knew it was an option with him, yes. There are others, some that I don't think he can see yet. I hope I can help him do that. If I can't . . . "

"If you can't, then you'll help him die. Is that it?"

He looked away and shook his head.

"Molly, there are just some things you don't know about. You haven't lived long enough to get to them yet. Not enough has happened to you. Let's drop this. It's Dennis's business."

"Oh, Daddy . . . hasn't there been enough death?" I said.

"When you get to be my age, it seems like there's never enough death," he said bleakly. "There's always more in the trough, just waiting. You can't stop it. The best you can do is try to deal with it decently."

"And helping a man commit suicide is decent? Oh, Lord, I'm sorry, Daddy. I'm spoiling this night for you," I said guiltily. "I promise to shut up about things I can't change. I love being here with you. I'd rather be here right now than anywhere in the world I can think of."

"You're some kind of daughter, Molly," he said. "Some kind of woman, come to that. Don't ever stop talking to me about what's on your mind."

"Sometimes I think we ought to just go on and jump in and talk about Mother," I said. "And I start to bring it up, and then I just can't. Are you waiting for me to do it?"

"No. I thought I'd be able to do it up here, in a place she wasn't part of, but so far I can't. It's like she's *too* far away. I can't feel her. Maybe I'll have to go back home to do that. I've been thinking that maybe it's time for that . . . "

"No, don't. Not yet," I said. "Please stay. Stay until spring. Until we know about Dennis. I don't think I could go through . . . and what about the swans? You can't leave the swans . . . "

He smiled at me, an amused smile like the ones he had sometimes given me when I was a child.

"Molly, I have to go home sometime. You do, too, as far as that goes."

"Why? I can't see one reason on earth why either one of us should go back to Atlanta right now. Not one."

"Because it's home," he said. "Because it's what we have. Because it's what we are as well as where. It's where all our context is. It's where everything we have left is."

"There's nothing left there for me," I said. "Tee's gone. Caroline is gone. Teddy's as good as gone. You're talking about finding a place out in the country. What's left there for me?"

"Oh, Molly," he sighed, and put his hand over mine. It was weather-chapped from his ice-breaking, and callused from the carpentry jobs around the camp. It felt as warm as a hot-water bottle. I squeezed it.

"Don't you know you're more than the sum of other people?" he said. "If you don't know that by now, what's it going to take?"

"All my life that's what I've been," I said. "I can't just change now."

"I think you can and you'd better," my father said.

We were finishing our dinner—the lamb shanks were rich and melting, cooked with tomatoes and wine and caramelized onions—when a woman came over to our table and stopped. She had fair hair and was small and stocky, dressed in a Fair Isle pullover and gray stretch pants, and her face was tanned and pleasant. Her eyes were clear and pale; there was something about them . . .

"Excuse me, but aren't you Mrs. Redwine?" she said.

I nodded.

"I'm Patricia Norton," she said. "I'm Dennis Ponder's second cousin once removed, or something, and Bella is my some kind of aunt. I just wanted to say that we all appreciate so much what you're doing for Denny and Aunt Bella and Luzia. We've been terribly concerned about them, but we haven't been able to do much for them. I guess you know by now that we don't see them, or vice versa. It makes it hard to know what to do."

"Please sit down," my father said. "I'm Tim Bell, Molly's father. I could have told you were some kin to Dennis. You've got the eyes."

I saw that she did, those ice-gray eyes that startled.

She laughed. "The Ponder eyes. We all look like we can see through solid rock. Straight through the dirt down to hell, my grandmother Ponder used to say. That was Dennis's grandmother, too, his father's mother. A grim old Gorgon if ever there was one born. She hated seeing those eyes in that wild little Portuguese face of Denny's, when he was little. They were the only thing about him that said Ponder, but they said it loud and clear. She couldn't pretend he wasn't at least half hers."

"Please sit," I said. "It's such a relief to meet some of Dennis and Bella's people. We've been wondering who to contact about them. Things aren't very good with any of them. So far we can handle it, but I don't know how long we'll be able to, and we don't have the authority to get any sort of official help for them . . . "

She sat, and ran her hands through her short hair in a gesture of annoyance and frustration; I think women everywhere on the planet do it. My own thatch often stood up in spikes from a similar gesture.

"You shouldn't have to. We're all embarrassed that two nice strangers are having to deal with our own. I was going to come down and talk to you about them when the weather cleared, but it doesn't look like that's going to happen. I should have done it before. Tell me about them. I can tell the others. We'll think of something."

I told her what I knew of Dennis Ponder's plight, and of Bella and Luzia's. Her face softened with real grief. She was, I thought, a pretty woman, though you didn't see that at first. There was something about her of Livvy, something strong, something that would endure. I thought I would like to have her for a friend. If I had been going to stay up island, that is.

"Oh, it's such a mess," she said. "It all started with Grandma Serena. I don't know where all that spite and bile and hate came from, but it corroded the whole family. There wasn't anybody in it that she didn't spill it over. Grandpa Ethan just plain went to sea and never came back because of it; she didn't know for a year or two whether he was dead, or just gone. When she found out he was dead, she didn't miss a step. She had little Ethan, after all. Denny's father. By the time he got away from her and over to America, to Harvard, he was just like her, colder than a dead mackerel and meaner than cat manure. I think he married Bella just to spite his mother. If there was anything Grandma Serena hated worse than the Portuguese, I don't know what it was. And none of us ever knew why; she would just say that they were shiftless and sly and lazy and low class, and would steal you blind if you didn't watch it. Most of us think the only stealing any Portuguese ever did to Grandma was Grandpa Ethan. He spent an awful lot of time around the Azores. Well, anyway, at the end of his junior year here comes Ethan home with this tall, beautiful creature with Portuguese written all over her, and a waitress in a restaurant at that. Grandma started in on Bella the day she got off the ferry. It didn't take Ethan but two or three years to get tired of his little joke and cut out for who knows where, but by that time there was Denny, and I guess Bella just couldn't think how to get him out from under Grandma's hate any other way than to send him off island to her people. That finished him with Grandma. She wrote him out of her will the day Bella shipped him off. None of the famous Ponder land was going to end up with any Portuguese, no sir. Of course, it did anyway, in the end. But it went to Bella, not Denny. I think Grandma's probably still spinning over that. By that time Bella had turned into . . . what she is now. She wanted none of us and nothing from us. I can't say I really blame her, considering how Grandma and Big Ethan treated her and Denny. But the rest of us would have liked to make amends, only she wouldn't let any of us near her. I can't imagine why she's stayed all these years, just her and poor little old Luzia. I was hoping to get to know Denny a little, though, only from what you say there may not be time . . . oh, what a mess it all is! Nobody can hurt each other like family, can they?"

"No," I said past the knot in my throat. Poor old woman, ossified into her bitterness like a corroding statue. Poor Dennis, dying of a coldness next to the bone . . .

"It was you who plowed us out, wasn't it? And left the soup and the apples?" my father said, smiling at Patricia Norton. "And plowed out Bella and Luz?"

She grinned back, and nodded.

"I've got a little plow on my Cherokee. I've been plowing the ladies out every winter since I married Tom Norton and his Jeep. She thinks the county does it, or I think she'd pile the snow back over the road. I know she doesn't eat the food I leave, but I keep hoping Luz sneaks some of it. Now that I've met you, though, maybe we can figure out some way to get them all some help, and get some of the burden off you. I'll call a war council of the others over the weekend."

"Let's wait a while," my father said. "All of them are pretty weak, and it's just so damned cold. I don't want to stir things up just yet. Let's try to go on like we are until early spring. It's not a burden so far; we'll tell you if it gets to be. And we'll give you bulletins along the way. Molly's got a reasonable and decent agreement with Bella and Dennis. It's working fine for now."

After she had gone and we had paid our bill and left for home, I looked over at my father. His profile was calm in the thin silver light of the Wolf Moon, but he was chewing on his bottom lip, and I knew that that meant he was puzzling about something.

"They're not what Bella said," I said to him. "The up islanders. The old families. They're not cold and distant at all. They'd have taken all of them in; they'd have done that years ago. Do you think she knows that? How could she not?"

"Bella thinks what she needs to think," he said. "Don't take that away from her. It's hard, and it's wrong, but it's what's kept her going all these years. She'd have nothing if she lost that."

"Oh, God, it's just so stupid," I said. "So wrong and so useless. They don't think that way about the Portuguese; you can tell that.

Only that awful old grandmother thought that. But all these years . . . "

"They were her years, Molly. Dennis is wrong about the up islanders and about his mother, too, I think, but the hate is what's driving his engine now. When he's done with the chemo, though, I think I'm going to set them both straight. Oh, they won't thank me. But neither one of them needs to die thinking what they think now."

The cold, old sadness came back up into my throat, like bile.

"Maybe they won't die," I said. "That's always a possibility."

"Yes, it is," he said, and reached over and put his hand over mine. Neither of us said any more until we reached home.

In the days that followed things got a little better. Dennis finished the chemo, and if he did not regain the weight and color, at least the terrible, enervating nausea stopped. He began to come out once in a while during the mornings when I was working on his library, and he sat on the sofa and talked while I sorted and shelved. Most of the talk was about the books themselves, and the manuscript that was growing infinitesimally slowly in his bedroom. But once in a while he would let something personal drop, as lightly and quietly as a leaf falling from a branch. And always, when that happened, I would offer him a little chip of myself, another leaf from my tree. When February came roaring in on the shoulders of yet another winter storm, we both had a small, neat pile of each other's leaves.

Once he asked me, out of the blue, if I had ever slept with anybody besides Tee.

"Why do you ask?" I said, my face flaming.

"Because I wanted to know," he said reasonably. "You don't have to tell me, of course. I was just thinking what a waste it would be if you hadn't. What a waste for you and for some guy."

My cheeks burned hotter.

"No, I haven't," I said. "We got married awfully young. You just didn't do that back then, not in my crowd. Now I wish I had. I may never know what I missed."

I spoke lightly, but he said, "I wish I could have shown you. I really wish that. It would have been quite something, I think. From my standpoint, at least."

"Dennis," I said. "Are you making a pass at me?"

"No," he said. "What, a one-legged man making a pass at a woman?"

"I wasn't aware that it was the leg that was necessary," I said, and then blushed so deeply that I could feel it on my chest and arms and forehead.

He laughed.

"You almost make me wish I didn't have cancer," he said, and we both laughed, and the moment passed. I did not know if I was sorry or not.

Things were not good with the old women, though. Luzia caught a cold on one of the nights when her fire went out, and I spent almost all day for a week at her bedside. She needed a great deal of nursing care, and when she got better, Bella caught the cold and it went straight to her laboring lungs. The coughing and gasping were so bad that I finally called an ambulance, but she flatly refused to go to the hospital, and the attendants could not move her huge bulk. So I set up my contagious ward in her bedroom and settled in for another spell of nursing.

My father took over the library for Dennis, and he came every night to read to the old ladies while I got their supper. We both grew pale and worn and more tired than I can ever remember being for any length of time. I would fall asleep on the sofa after dinner; he would fall asleep sitting up in his chair at breakfast. He did that for the second day in a row one bitterly cold, ice-sheathed day in the middle of February, and I roused him and sent him up to bed.

"You sleep all day, and I mean it," I said. "I'll get you up when it's time to go up to the farm tonight. You can take over then, and I'll sleep."

He was too tired to protest, and so it was I who took the truck and went up the hill to the farmhouse in the dusk, to read to the old ladies. The ice was so bad that day that I had to leave the truck halfway up the lane and walk the rest of the distance, slipping and sliding and muttering weary curses. It was, I suppose, the reason that they did not hear me coming. The truck always made a lot of noise.

The door was unlocked, as it always was, so that whoever was expected could enter. But the house was dark. Almost always by this time Bella was downstairs, and had lit the lamps and the fire. I felt a prickle of unease on my forearms and scalp. For some reason, I felt that I should whisper, tiptoe. Do not stir up trouble, my grandmother Bell would have said, and maybe it will go away.

I saw them before I got even partway into the living room. I stopped dead and tried to breathe, but could not; when breath finally came it was so shallow and high in my throat that I almost felt it whistle. My head felt light and my face stung as though I had been slapped, hard. Afterward I knew that it was shock, but I also knew that it was not the sort of shock that I might have expected to feel. There was nothing grotesque about them, nothing obscene. Rather, they simply seemed totally exotic, totally out of any context I had. The first thought that penetrated the still white dome of the shock was that they looked Indian, something from a frieze on an ancient temple in a lost garden somewhere, one of the exquisite little erotic Indian miniatures that the Victorians so prized. They lay together on the bed at the far end of the room, intertwined so that it was hard to tell where Luz's delicate, withered arms and legs left off and Bella's colossus's limbs began. They were naked, and the firelight played over them: ivory, white, black, gilt, gold. They were kissing. It was a kiss of great and complex tenderness and old love, and of simple hunger. I averted my eyes and tiptoed out of the room and shut the door softly. All the way back down the icy driveway I tried as best I could to tiptoe.

By the time I reached home I had begun to shake all over, a very fine, silvery trembling. Everything I did, I did with great, precise care: parked the truck, got out and made my way over the spoiled old snow to the porch, opened the door, laid down my bag of groceries and the book I was reading to them. It was still *The Once and Future King*; Luz had asked again for the scene where the Wart pulls the sword out of the stone. Poor Luz. So in need of empowerment. Or perhaps not. Perhaps that was one of the things she found in Bella Ponder's great white arms. I found myself beginning to cry, silently.

I told my father, of course. I could not keep my tears from him, and I needed the ballast of his mind and voice. He listened while I poured it out, nodding. When I had finished he reached over and took my hand in both of his.

"Molly, baby. What is it that upsets you so about it? Is it because they're women, or they're old, or sick and maybe dying? What?"

"I guess it's that . . . that . . . I just didn't *think* about them that way. I mean, it must be like walking in on your parents when you're little and seeing them . . . "

". . . and you have to change the way you think about them forever after. Is that it?"

"I guess so. Oh, Daddy, I don't care if they're women, or old . . . I guess I care because of Dennis. Don't you see? That's what he saw. When he was just a little boy; that's what he saw them doing, and right after that they . . . she sent him away. I don't think he would have been shocked, providing he understood what they were doing, which I doubt. Small children don't shock easily. It's that she chose Luz instead of him. That's what he's lived with all the time. His mother loved her cousin more than she did him, and she sent him away when he found out about it. After his father, it must have seemed the ultimate betrayal. I'm not angry at Bella for loving Luzia, for God's sake; I'm happy she *has* someone to love. It's obviously a very real and very old love. I'm angry at her for sacrificing her son to it! That's monstrous!"

Somewhere during my outburst the shock had turned to rage; I had felt it happening. Even as the fire of it scorched at me, I wondered at it. What business was it of mine? Why should I care about these three people I had known such a short time and would not, could not, know for much longer? Danger flared with the anger. Beneath all of it I was frightened.

My father sat back and stretched his legs out to the fire. He sighed. He looked impossibly weary.

"I know that's the way Dennis feels about it," he said. "He thinks she was afraid that he would tell somebody, and it would get back to her mother-in-law and the other Ponders, and all the other old families, and they would simply drive Luzia off the island. That she—Bella—couldn't protect her, and that they would hurt her beyond repair. I have an idea it had gone on a long time by the time she married Denny's father and came over here with him; she must have been frantic to get away from that Portuguese Catholic enclave they lived in. What kind of future could she and Luz have had there? Maybe she did use Ethan Ponder, but no worse than he used her. He must have found out when Denny was very small. It was his excuse to leave, even if it wasn't his reason. And by that time they were stuck. They couldn't go back to the mainland. And Bella couldn't take a chance on his telling . . . or that's what Dennis thinks anyway. I don't think that's all there is to it, but he's not ready to listen to any other ideas yet. He may never be."

"If you don't think that, what do you think?"

"I'm not sure. I do know that she loved that little boy, though. And I know that she loves him now, as much as any mother ever loved a son, even if it's in her own grotesque way, and she's torn up about him. Ah, Lord. What a mess of unhappiness. What a swamp of pain and lies."

"Dennis told you, then."

He nodded. I was not surprised at that, but I felt a flicker of resentment that he had told my father and not me. But then I remembered our agreement.

"Do Bella and Luz know you know?"

"No. And they must never know either of us do, unless they decide to tell us. You're not to go telling Dennis what you saw, either."

"Oh, Daddy . . . as if I would!"

"This is a hell of a conversation for a father to be having with his daughter," he said, and I managed a watery smile.

He went to bed then, practically dragging himself up the stairs hand over hand, and I lay down on the sofa and watched the flames. Sadness and bitterness lay in my stomach like a sickness. A terrible pity underlay it all. It seemed to me then that the worst suffering in the world was inevitably born of love.

I am still not sure how I would have handled what I knew, or if I could have made some kind of peace with it, because before the week was out everything changed again, and in the face of the change the love of two sad old women in a farmhouse on a Chilmark hill simply did not seem out of the ordinary to me anymore.

We had an abrupt softening of winter the morning after I saw Luz and Bella together, and when I awoke, head aching dully, bones as sore and troubled as if I had been in an accident, the snow was turning to slush and the icicles that had hung from the trees and porch eaves were dripping, and a weak, repentant sun had come sidling out to bathe the glade in milky light. Even before I opened the front door I could sense the change, and when I did I felt the softness of the air on my face, and smelled, not spring, but a cold, fresh, sweet, faraway *promise* of spring. I stretched, feeling better. I would have a shower and wash my hair and maybe go into Vineyard Haven and buy something unnecessary for the cottage. Perhaps my father and I would have lunch there. Maybe I would go into the Bunch of Grapes and treat myself to a new book, or a pile of them. Later I might, finally, cut Dennis's hair. I looked at my watch. It was very late. I went upstairs to wake my father. How on earth could both of us have slept so late? Except that we were both so very tired . . .

He was not there. His bed had been slept in, but he was not in the room and not in the cottage. Well, of course, the swans. He'd gone to feed the swans. How on earth it was that they had not waked us with their hissing, battering cacophony I could not imagine; they never failed to go into their indignant act of swanly starvation when we were late with their breakfast.

I threw on a coat over my pajamas and went down the path toward the pond. Out over the Sound the sky was a clear, pale, washed blue, and the water was still and streaked in darker shades of blue. The white smoke of spume that the cold wind blew off the tops of the whitecaps on the hard, iron mornings was gone. The Irish had a word for this sort of weather: a soft day.

My father was sitting on the end of the dock. His head was bowed and he was very still; at first I thought he had drifted into one of the little neck-crippling naps that he sometimes took sitting up. But then I saw that he was looking into the water, watching a swan circling in the cleared patch. Circling, circling. And as I came nearer I heard the sound that the swan was making, and I never want to hear it again, awake or in my dreams. The swan's head was thrown up to the sky, the long neck in a fierce, beautiful arch, and it made a great, rusty, desolate cry that sounded as if it were being torn out of the elegant throat. I never heard a mute swan make such a sound again.

I did not see the other swan. I did not know which one this was. I do know that my blood ran cold and thick, an icy sludge in my veins.

"Daddy . . ." I whispered.

He did not turn.

"It's Charles," he said. His voice was small and dry. "Diana is . . . gone. I found some feathers and a few splashes of blood in the reeds, but she's gone. I looked everywhere. Something got her in the night, fox or something. I don't know what their predators are. She couldn't have flown away with that wing. He's been doing this since I got here. It's been almost two hours."

Grief and pity for the two bereaved old creatures at the pond nearly brought me to my knees.

"Daddy, come up to the house now," I said, forcing my voice not to break. "How can it help him if you freeze to death? Let me fix you some breakfast. Maybe she's just hurt somewhere, and she'll come out when you're gone; don't animals hide when they're hurt? Later we'll look for her. Laz has a great finding nose . . . "

"No. She's not here. He would know. Don't you see? He knows she's gone; he doesn't know where she is; he's calling her. I didn't know they could do that."

"Daddy, come on."

He turned and looked at me. His face was absolutely gray and still. There was nothing in his eyes.

"Don't natter at me, Molly," he said, and I heard, incredibly, irritation in his voice. I could not ever remember hearing it before. It was a weak, peeved, *old* kind of irritation.

"But you're going to get sick . . . "

"Then I get sick! Can't you stop hovering for once in your life?"

Hurt flooded me. My eyes filled. I turned and stumbled back up the path. But by the time I had gained the porch, the hurt had receded and pain and dread had taken its place. He had simply had too much; this last hurt was past enduring. He loved those swans; this was too much; this was not right; this had gone over into the realm of pure cosmic malice. Besides, maybe he was wrong. Maybe Diana would come back. Maybe in a little while he would come up and tell me she was back and did not seem too badly hurt . . .

But he did not come back. I went up and got Dennis Ponder and we went back to the pond, he limping and holding on to my arm and Lazarus's head. My father was still sitting there. Charles had stopped the circling and crying, and was riding flaccidly on the water, his head down as if he were about to plunge it under the surface in search of food. He was drifting in idle circles, one black foot sheltered in the sweep of his wing, as I had often seen them both do. He looked like a ship with its rudder broken.

"Will you come up to the house with us now, Tim?" Dennis said quietly. "You need some food and something to drink. After we've had both, I'll come back down here with you and we'll build a fire and wait with him."

My father looked at him.

"Do you know how it feels?" he said. "I do. I know how it feels. I don't know how else I can help him, but I can be here with him."

"Tim . . . just for half an hour. That's all. Just for that."

In the end my father went with him. Somehow I knew that I must not join them. It might have hurt my feelings once, but it did not now. I made coffee and put it into a thermos, and made sandwiches and wrapped them in foil, so that when they went back to their vigil they would at least have some sustenance.

But they did not need the coffee or the sandwiches, and I found them days later, cold and beginning to mold, in the pantry where I had left them. When they went back to the pond, scarcely half an hour later, Charles was gone, and he did not come back.

CHAPTER THIRTEEN

FOR A WHILE AFTER THAT, my father went to the pond several times a day to look for Charles. He did not say that was why he went, but of course it was—in the hope of seeing, yet knowing he would not see, that frigate of white sailing mulishly in the tiny circle left of clear black water.

I went, too, in between trips to Dennis's camp and down to the farmhouse and into town for supplies. I went, as my father did, hoping, but knowing it was a futile hope. Somehow I knew that the silent whiteness that had swallowed Diana could not sustain Charles's life.

Dennis went, too; every now and then when I went, I saw the tracks of his one good foot and the holes made by the crutch, and the paw prints of Lazarus beside them, deeper from taking Dennis's weight.

None of us spoke to the other about going to the pond. It was as if to speak of it would open a gate to more pain than we could bear, any of us.

When my father went, he stayed a while. I know he kept the ice broken up, because when he came back the stick was always black and wet. But I do not know what else he did there. At the very beginning he was obsessed with how Charles had managed to get himself airborne.

"He wouldn't have had enough open water," he said over and

over. "He'd have needed the whole pond to get his momentum up, and there was almost no clear water. But I know he did, somehow, because I'd have found him if something had happened to him around the pond. I've been everywhere. I'd have found him."

Each time he came back, my father was duller and sadder and quieter. I would have given anything I had to take some of the pain, but I knew that I could not. It was not only Diana that he mourned.

"Let him be," Dennis said when I voiced my worry to him. "He's coming to terms with your mother being gone now. I don't think he's really stopped to do that before."

"Do you think Charles flew away?"

"I don't know. No. I think whatever got her, got him. But I'm not going to tell Tim that. This godforsaken place is going to leave him something, anyway."

After a week or so my father went less and less often. One evening toward the end of February, another great storm came down on us on its battering crystal wings, and I watched as he looked up from his newspaper toward the rack where his coat and hat always hung by the front door, hard by the black hat of my mother's that I had moved there. He always put them on before he went down to the pond. I saw him decide, saw his eyes drop to his paper and then lift to the fire, watched as he sat still. He did not seem to see the fire or the room around him; soon he got up and went upstairs to his bedroom. He did not go to the pond again.

I knew that he was not sleeping much in those days. I would wake in the night in my cave under the stairs and hear his footsteps over my head as he wandered around his room. I heard him go into the bathroom, heard the bed creak as he got back into it and creak as he got up again. Sometimes, not very often, I heard him come downstairs to the kitchen and go back up again, and once or twice I found a coffee cup on his bedside table, but more often I found the bottle of scotch. Lazarus heard him, too, and would lift his head and look at me and whine softly, and I would pat his head and say, "Go back to sleep. He wouldn't want us to think he'd waked us."

I asked him about it, finally.

"I'm okay," he said. "I'm fine. I guess I've just slept myself out. You know how good the sleeping is up here; it's almost all I've done since I came. And I'm getting some reading done that I've been wanting to do for years. You ever read Thoreau? 'I went to the woods because I wished to live deliberately.' Now that's a fine thing. Maybe I can do that up here. I never could at home."

He began to sleep later and later in the mornings, and I let him. Often I would hear no sound from his room by the time I was ready to go up and work on Dennis's library, and would tiptoe up the stairs and look in on him, and he would still be sleeping, a motionless mound in a cool, dark room, only the soft rise and fall of the quilt over him speaking of life. In those moments, I did not feel as if it were my father I stood looking at, but Caroline or Teddy, a child loved but strange and somehow imperiled in sleep. The uneasiness of that would stay with me through my day.

He would be up when I came back in the early afternoon, of course, and would have done this or that around the cottage; we would talk desultorily of his day's occupation. More and more often he fell asleep in the late afternoons before the fire, and I could not bear to waken him to go and read to the old ladies, so I began to take that task back over, too. Perhaps it was just as well that I did. Bella and Luzia seemed to me terribly diminished, possessed by winter and illness and fretfulness, steeped in old age and darkness. The acute stage of Bella's flu, or whatever it was, had passed, but the horrific cough lingered, and she was unable to get up and down the stairs, so she had made a bed for herself on the sofa across from Luz's bed, and there she stayed most of the time, a great, bad-tempered, musty black crow in a slatternly nest. In addition to the reading, I now began to air and straighten the bedding and the room when I went in the afternoons, and wash the stale dishes piled in the sink in the cold kitchen, and put on pots of soup and stew for their dinner, and bring wood and build up the fire, and clean out and light the stove against the coming night. The feral winter still held the island in its talons; I would think, as I watched the sleet or snow beginning yet once more to spill from the soiled, stretched gut of the sky overhead, of the first flush of lemon-icing forsythia and the red flowering quince at home, of the frail shoots of daffodils green against the wet, black earth. Bella and Luzia both had told me how transcendentally lovely the Vineyard's spring was, and Patricia Norton had spoken of it, but in those evenings in the dark farmhouse on the lush moor, with only firelight and the dim-watted bulbs in the old lamps for light, spring seemed simply unreal, a fever dream, a madman's sad hallucination. We would, I felt, be stricken into this tableau of cold and lightlessness forever.

Dennis had drawn back inside himself. As if the death of Diana and the disappearance of Charles had severed some tender new cord connecting him to the world, he retreated into his room, working silently and feverishly on his book. I heard the sounds of industry as I worked at the shelves in the living room: the riffling of pages and occasionally the furious tearing as he jerked a page from his legal pad and crumpled it; the slide and splash of pages as one of his tottering piles of reference books fell over; his under-the-breath exclamations of impatience; the constant accompaniment of Mozart or Verdi thrumming away under the muted bustle. But he no longer came out and sat and talked as I worked, or called out to me from his bedroom, and even Lazarus often gave up on him and came clicking out to where I worked, sighing greatly and collapsing against my legs in boredom and abandonment.

"Any old port in the storm, huh?" I would say to him, and he would sigh again, and slide into his disjointed, doggy sleep. But presently he would jerk awake, and look accusingly at me as if I had kidnapped him, and get up and pad back into Dennis's bedroom. Aside from leaving groceries, I did not bother Dennis. It was as if he were engaged in some fierce contest, a race against some immutable deadline, to finish his book. I could not dwell on that. I did not think he felt worse, or any differently than he had for a while; I got no sense of that. It was just that for a little while he had been present to me, and now he was not. I did not know if he saw my father during the times I was in Chilmark or West Tisbury or Vineyard Haven, if Dad came across the snowy glade and sat with him as he once had. If they met, neither spoke of it. It was as if winter had stopped time in its last days, and our life and community had stopped with it.

Tired, my God, I was tired in those bleak, low-ceilinged days. I was so tired that I did not even recognize the feeling as such, just that I seemed mired in a lethargy born of this strange, dingy, gray stasis that held us fast. It did not even occur to me that I needed surcease and could probably have it by calling Patricia Norton or someone for help with the old ladies. Looking back, it seems incredible that I did not realize that our situations were uncomfortable and rapidly growing untenable, but at that time I didn't. It simply seemed that the one important thing was to keep going forward as I had been. Just to keep the minimal routine of our days spinning slowly without their sagging and toppling. Just that. I still do not quite know what malign alchemy held the glade in its grip in those days. I only know that it came with the soft-footed thing that took away Diana, and there seemed at the time to be nothing that could lift it.

Trouble boiled like hot water in the lengthening days. Luz developed bedsores of such ferocious suppuration that I finally had to call the visiting nurse. I had not even known she had them; she had turned as coy and fussy as a two-year-old about letting me help her change her clothing and take her sponge baths, and Bella had backed her up, saying belligerently that of course she could still bathe Luz; she did so every morning. What did I think she was? I only found the sores when I lifted Luz to put clean cases on the pillow behind her and smelled the sick, sweet odor of putrefaction under her clothing.

When I pulled away her nightgown she shrieked and I nearly vomited, and went that instant and called the nurse. When I got back Bella was sheltering Luz in her great arms, glaring at me for making her cry, and when the nurse arrived, Luz's shrieks reached such a crescendo of noise and hysteria, and Bella's shouts of protective rage were so terrible, that the poor, weary woman simply put out some medical supplies on the porch and told me how to clean the wounds, saying that Luz should be seen by a doctor. And she left. Bella finally let me clean Luz's sores as best I could, holding the tiny woman in her arms and crooning to her as I worked, trying not to gag, and watched me as I applied the antibiotic salve and bandaged the wounds.

"But you're going to have to let me get a doctor up here to look at them," I said. "And let the nurse come and change these bandages every day. Otherwise she'll have to go to the hospital."

"No," Bella said, not looking at me. "You do it. You can do it; you did a good job tonight."

"Don't you understand? The infection could get into her bloodstream. She could get very sick. She could die. She's awfully frail, Bella. These sores should have been seen to a long time ago. I can't help either of you when I don't know anything's wrong. You'll have to tell me when you aren't feeling well."

"Oh, I will," Bella said, smiling radiantly at me with her blue lips. I knew she would not.

The sores did soon begin to heal, but one morning Bella fell in the kitchen and could not get up, and I found her there that afternoon when I came, almost unconscious and soiled with her own urine. Luz was wailing thinly and monotonously from the living room. This time I did not try to reason with either of them. I went to the telephone and called Patricia Norton. She was there in fifteen minutes, her strong, pleasant face red with cold. I met her on the steps.

"I'm sorry. I hate to bother you. But they ran the nurse off last week, and I think that if she starts screaming that hard in the state she's in, it will just stop her heart. My father isn't well, or I'd ask him . . . I just need someone to help me lift her back on to the sofa in the living room. I don't think she's hurt or has had an attack. She just can't get up. I'll take it from there if you can help me . . . "

Patricia looked around the dingy living room and her brows drew together. I saw her take a deep breath, mouth closed, nostrils flaring, as if stifling shock.

"I had no idea it was this bad," she said in a low voice. "I don't see how you've managed by yourself this long. Let's get her on the sofa, and then I'm going to call the others and we're going to make a plan and go talk to Dennis whether or not he wants to listen, and get them both into a hospital or a home as soon as possible. This is . . . not acceptable.

"You'd better not tell her who I am," she added under her breath as we went into the kitchen where Bella lay. I had covered her with a quilt, and she looked, in the dimness, like a vast, helpless amphibian cast up on a dark beach.

"Won't she know?" I whispered back. "You look an awful lot like a Ponder."

"I don't think so. I haven't been in this house since I was nine or ten. None of us has."

But Bella did know. She knew, and she began to scream like a banshee for Patricia Ponder Norton to get out of her house. She did not stop screaming all the while we pushed and pulled and hauled and swatted at her, not while we frog-walked her across the kitchen and living room and dumped her on to the sofa, and when she reached that haven she threw a vase and the heavy brass lamp at Patricia. Her lips turned navy blue and her face deep magenta, and she began to choke and gargle and rasp.

"I'll call for an ambulance on the car phone," Patricia said, and ran out into the frigid darkness. The wind was high that night, and crooned around the corners of the house; I almost lost her words in the swell of it.

By the time the tri-town ambulance came hooting and fishtailing up the glassy driveway, I had cleaned Bella Ponder and she lay, pale but calm and smiling, under a cocoon of clean blankets, sipping cocoa. It was obvious to the EMTs that, as she said, she did not need emergency ambulance service.

"My young friend gets terribly excited," she said, smiling her great white shark's smile at the two exasperated young men. "I didn't know she'd called you until you came up the hill. I'd never have let her if I'd known. I have these little spells all the time. My doctor knows about them. It's Dr. Cardin, over in Oak Grove; he's got his offices in the hospital. You can ask him. I'm awfully sorry about this. Can we offer you some cocoa?"

We could not. The men went away, carefully blank-faced, no doubt cursing hysterical off islanders who called for help when help was not needed on icy, dangerous nights.

I looked at Bella. She did not look back.

"If you do that to me again, our agreement is off and I'm leaving," I said, my voice shaking with anger. "And don't think I won't. You have people of your own who can and want to help you. One of them came tonight. Next time I'll let them."

"I promise I won't," she muttered, dropping her eyes. Her eyelashes lay on her waxen cheeks like black silk fans. I had seen Dennis's lashes like that, in the exhausted sleeps that followed his chemo. Dennis . . . She would do it again, of course, if it happened again. But at the moment I was too tired to think ahead. I built up the fire and the stove, heated some stew for them, and went home and fell into bed. I did not wake until past nine the next morning.

All the next day the white blanket of my fatigue dragged behind me wherever I went, and by the time I was to go up and read to Bella and Luz, I did not think I could take another step.

I got up slowly from the sofa, where I had dropped after coming in with groceries for all three houses, and the room took a slow, majestic spin around me. I shook my head and held on to the arm of the sofa and the spinning ceased, but my knees were still watery. I listened for any sound of my father upstairs, and when I heard none, climbed the stairs hesitantly. I hated to disturb any sleep he might find for himself, but perhaps, just this once, he would take the groceries to the farmhouse and read to the old women. If I did not sleep, I thought I would die.

He was sitting on the edge of his bed, staring out at the pond and the Sound beyond it. The evening was very cold, but the sky was clear, a tender, soft lavender that gave back a watercolor wash to the quiet water. The moon was full, or nearly so; later, I knew, there would be a silver-white path down the water to the horizon, and the lingering snow would be flooded with blue-white light. I did not think my father saw any of it. His eyes were fastened on another, different distance.

I went and sat down beside him, and put my arm around him.

"Can't you sleep, Daddy? Want me to make you some cocoa?"

He shook his head, not looking at me. He was still staring at the hat.

"Well, then, maybe a scotch. I'll fix you one and you can have it up here while I run over to the farmhouse, and then we'll have dinner. I got some clam chowder from the Black Dog."

He did not answer, and I was beginning to feel real alarm when he turned his face to me. It was naked with yearning, terrible to see. I tightened my grip on his shoulders.

"She almost came, baby," he said, and his voice was a rasp. "I fell asleep when the sun was going down, and for a minute she was there. Just for a minute . . . and then I woke up. And I can't go back to sleep now; I don't sleep in the nights, and she won't come in the daytime. I brought that hat up here, thinking she might know, somehow, but she still doesn't come . . . if I could just sleep in the nights. Just one night . . . I know she'd come. I know she would."

I put my head down on his shoulder silently, thinking for a moment how wonderful it would be to just give up, let go, opt out, let someone else take over. But there was no one else. I could not ask this wrecked old man to care for anyone else. He could not even minister to himself.

I remembered something.

"I have some sleeping pills," I said. "Charlie Davies gave them to me before I left Atlanta. I haven't taken all of them. Why don't you try one? I don't think they're very strong, but they worked for me. You're right, you do need to sleep at night."

He nodded slowly.

"Maybe that would do it. Maybe it would," he said, and the frail hope in his voice was more than I could bear. I jumped up and ran downstairs and got the pills, for the moment the fatigue forgotten.

When I got back upstairs he was already lying flat in bed, covered with the quilts, and his bedside light was off. I gave him the vial of pills and he shook one out and took it with the water I had brought.

"You want it now?" I said doubtfully. "What about dinner?"

"I'll get some later," he said back. There was almost a merriment in his voice, like a child who knows a secret. I turned away from him.

"Sleep tight, Daddy," I said.

"Thank you, baby," he said back. "Would you pull the door to when you go?"

I did so, leaving him there, waiting to go and meet my mother in the country of his sleep.

I went downstairs in such a fever of anger that I almost forgot the old ladies' groceries as I stumped out to the truck. I knew why she did not come to him in his sleep. It was because, for the last two weeks or so, she was spending her nights with me, and the dreams she brought with her murdered sleep as effectively as Macbeth. Every night she came, usually about three A.M., so that I had only had a couple hours' sleep and would get little more after I woke from the dreams. She came and she raged like a wild beast, a madwoman, from behind her bars. She thrust her hands and arms out through the bars of her subterranean lair and clawed the air with them, and she raged and shrieked and howled out her impotent fury. In my dreams I was no longer afraid of her, but I felt a profound, all-enveloping despair. Whatever it was she so wanted, I could not give it to her. I did not understand her furious pleas. The despair would last long after I woke, until dawn broke, earlier now, and I slid back into the thin sleep of exhaustion. I thought that if my mother did not stop howling at me in my sleep I would go mad.

I stood still, beside the truck, the bag of groceries in my arms.

"I hate you," I said clearly and dispassionately to her, in the cold, silken air. "If that's what you want, then that's what you've got. I hate you for what you're doing to both of us. You're killing me with your furies and your fits, and you're killing him with your absence. Why the hell can't you just go to him one time? God knows you've got enough presence to spread over six states. Put some where it's needed."

I drove carefully up the still frozen hill toward the farmhouse. I was still bone-tired, but I felt a bit better. Perhaps my father would sleep this night. Perhaps I would, too.

But it was not a better night, after all. Bella and Luz had obviously been quarreling all afternoon, and were still at each other when I came in. The house was cold and stale and malodorous with whatever food Bella had not put away in the kitchen, and the fire in the living room was out, and papers and magazines and used tissues were scattered all over Luz's bed and the floor, and all of a sudden I could hardly bear the fusty mess of sickness and age. My temper flared again.

"Whatever it is you're fighting about, just stop it right now," I snapped. "I'm tired to death, and I've got to rake out this place and get you some supper, and I don't feel like listening to you snipe at each other while I'm doing it."

"It's her fault," Bella said stubbornly, sounding like a gargantuan sulking child. "She insists that you're reading *Once and Future* to us, and I can't tell her you've read that twice already and that we're in the middle of *Penrod and Sam*. I'm not going to listen to *Once and Future* again. I'm sick of it. It was my time to choose, and *Penrod* is what I chose, and *Penrod* is what I want to hear. You tell her so."

Luz began to wail. "That's not so! We were reading *Once and Future*. I know we were! She's just mad because I spilled stupid soup on her stupid crossword puzzle. I know we're reading *Once and Future*, and I want to hear about the Wart and the sword!"

"Shut up!" Bella shouted. "You little old baby, you just shut up! You get your way all the time because you're a little old cry-baby! I spend all my time doing for you, and you keep wanting everything . . . !"

"Big old bully!" shrieked Luz. "You're the one who gets her way all the time! You get your way because you're the biggest and you can walk and I can't—"

"HUSH!" I shouted, and they both stopped and looked at me, the whites of their eyes showing.

"Just be quiet. I will not listen to this. I'm not going to read either one tonight. I'm going to straighten this place up and heat your supper, and then I'm going home and get some sleep. You can watch television or scream at each other, I don't care, but I'm not reading to you."

And I didn't. I stalked into the kitchen and washed their dishes and emptied the garbage and heated their clam chowder and brought it to them, and I picked up the room and built up the fire, all in a stony silence. They pleaded and promised, and Luz began to sniffle again, but I held firm. I could not wait to be out of that spoiled-smelling farmhouse and into the clear, cold air.

"Now," I said to myself when I was under way, skidding down the long lane to Middle Road. The rising moon hung low over the Atlantic, and I could see that it left its luminous paths on sea and Sound alike. The whole world was light and shadow: snow drifted on stone walls, woods, moors, beaches, and boulders, the occasional blue bulk of a house, windows lit yellow. Over it all, great clouds of stars swarmed. I took a deep breath and waited to feel better. But I did not. Bullying two sick old ladies had not helped at all. I felt craven and cowardly and ashamed of myself, and I felt a deep, despairing fear for my father, and the fatigue was back in all its sucking power, and under it all there trembled something so akin to red, killing rage that it frightened me. I thought that if it surfaced, something would happen that would change the world forever. Something would die. Something else, perhaps, would be born.

I took a deep breath and pushed the anger back down. I drove on carefully, thinking determinedly of nothing but supper and bed. I remembered that Lazarus was still at Dennis Ponder's cabin, and if Dennis should happen to fall asleep, he would be there all night.

Somehow I could not bear the thought of that. I skewed the wheel and the truck slid into Dennis's yard. I got out and went softly up the steps; he would undoubtedly still be working in his bedroom, and I did not want to talk to him this night. I would just open the front door and whistle for Lazarus.

But Dennis was sitting on his sofa before a leaping fire, sipping scotch and listening to *Nabucco*, and Lazarus was lying on the sofa beside him with his head in Dennis's lap. I stared at them, suddenly wanting to strangle both my traitorous dog and the man who had lured him away from me. Dennis and Lazarus stared back at me.

Dennis had recently shaved, something he seldom did in the evenings. His thin face had a shine to it, of fresh-shaven skin, and just the tiniest wash of color—or perhaps it was only stained by the fire. Whatever it was, he looked better than I had seen him for a long while. He wore the red jacquard sweater that I liked, and khaki corduroy pants which, if they were too large, did not look it because of the enveloping sweater.

"You look like you're going out on the town," I said, purely for something to say. "What's the occasion?"

"I don't know," he said, still looking hard at me. "All of a sudden I realized I hadn't shaved in two days, and hadn't bathed in more than that. It struck me that cabin fever had set in. I don't think I've looked up from that manuscript for a week."

"Is it going well?"

He jerked his head impatiently.

"I really don't know, or care much, right now. It hit me suddenly that what the world really needs now is a pompous treatise on boys from a man who only knows about them because he's afraid of girls. I guess it's been my night for epiphanies."

"How you know about them doesn't matter, only that you do," I said. "I thought it was a wonderful idea. You can't mean you're going to stop—"

He held up his hand and I fell silent. One unwritten rule we had was that I did not ask him about his work.

"Right now I'm more interested in you. It's like I haven't really seen you for weeks. What in hell is the matter with you? You look like you've been whupped through hell with a buzzard gut, to quote a housekeeper from Mississippi my wife once hired."

298

My eyes flooded with tears, and a great, cold salt lump came into my throat. I turned away, afraid I was going to cry in front of Dennis Ponder and loathing the idea.

"Molly, turn around here," he said, and I did.

"How long has it been since you've had any sleep?" he said slowly. "What's going on over there? What's happening to you?"

I shook my head mutely, and he reached over and got the scotch bottle and poured some into his empty glass and handed it to me. He gestured for me to sit down. I sat as if I had been a child bidden to do so. Laz lifted his head, thumped his tail, and went back to sleep.

I took a gulp of the scotch.

"I didn't mean to just walk in on you," I said. "I was on my way back from the farmhouse and I remembered Laz was still here. I was just going to whistle for him. I can't have him just living over here."

"You didn't disturb me. I thought you might come by. I was ready for some conversation, I guess. But it looks more like you're ready for some sleep. Is it Tim? Are you worried about Tim? I knew he hadn't been by, but I thought he was letting me work, like you've been doing."

The scotch burned in my stomach. It felt wonderful. Something loosened just a hitch.

"I am worried about him," I said. "He's not sleeping . . ." And I went on to tell him about my father's deepening depression since Charles and Di were no longer on the pond, and about his terrible nighttime sleeplessness and his days spent in exhausted slumber, and the conviction he had that my mother would come to him in his dreams if only he could sleep at night.

"He's even moved her hat upstairs to his room. He sits and stares at it," I said. "He's nobody I know, Dennis. And the old ladies . . . "

I fell silent. We weren't to talk about his mother and Luz, either, unless he initiated the conversation. That was another rule.

"Tell me," he said, and so I did. I finished with the quarrel and my stalking out of the house without reading to them, and how ashamed I felt about that, and how worried I was about both of them. He said nothing, only stared at me.

"There's more, isn't there? You're not sleeping. Why not?"

So I told him about the nightly dreams in which my mother raged and stormed at me from her subterranean barred cave, and about the terrible feeling I had that she wanted something from me, but I could not understand what it was.

"The dreams happen in the very middle of the night, so that when I do get back to sleep, it's dawn and I have to get right up again," I said. The warmth of the scotch was loosening my limbs pleasantly, and my head felt sinuously furry. "And by the time I go up to read to the old women and get their suppers and clean up, I can hardly move."

He frowned.

"Tim was doing that, wasn't he?"

"He hasn't been, for two or three weeks. Almost since Di was killed and Charles left. He sleeps in the daytime, Dennis. I can't bear to bother him about the old ladies."

"So you just go ahead and do it. Christ, Molly. How long do you think you can keep that shit up?"

"I don't know. I guess until something changes, one way or the other."

I flushed. I did not want him to think I meant until he took a turn for the worse, or died, or until one of the old women did. He grinned briefly.

"Well, we've got to get you some help. What would help most?"

"I think . . . being able to sleep through the night. Just that. Oh, Dennis . . . *What on earth does she want from me?*"

It was literally a cry, torn out of a part of me that I did not know was so close to the surface. I was shocked at my own vehemence.

Dennis considered for a long time. And then he said, "Maybe she just wants her hat back."

We looked at each other for a long moment, and then I spit a mouthful of scotch into the fire-warm air and began to laugh. In a moment he did, too. In the blink of an eye we were laughing so hard that neither of us could get our breaths, and long, wheezing gasps punctuated the insane laughter in the living room. And still we laughed.

Just as suddenly something inside me burst and I began to cry. I cried and cried. I sobbed and strangled and howled aloud like a woman at the Wailing Wall; sounds came out of me that I did not know a woman could make. I gagged and retched and wept some more, and struggled for breath, only to begin to cry again. He sat watching me for a moment, then he moved over on the sofa and put his arms around me and held me while I cried. He did not pat me, or whisper that it would be all right, or offer me a handkerchief. He just held me.

It was a long time before the awful, primitive sounds stopped long enough for me to gasp out, "I hate her! I hate her with all my heart! And I hate him! First she left me—she did that a long time ago, before she finally did it for good, and I hate her for all those times—and then he left me, too! I knew she would do it eventually, and I finally got used to the fact that Tee did it, but Daddy . . . he was never supposed to leave me! He was never supposed to do that!"

"Oh, Molly," he said finally. "He hasn't left you. He's just . . . out of touch right now."

"You haven't seen him," I wept. "You don't know . . . "

"I know what depression is like. I know that. I went that route right after the first surgery, when I knew that I would have to leave the school and come home to my mama because I didn't have a penny left to my name. No family, no job, no money, no leg, and no future . . . I was a mess. I slept all day and stared at the television all night. I was afraid to live and afraid that I was going to die. I was afraid to go to sleep. I was paralyzed in more ways than one. I literally couldn't move. It's a terrible thing. There isn't anything worse. I know that. I'll look in on Tim tomorrow. See what I can do."

"You don't feel that way now, though," I said, heaving myself up out of his arms and mopping my face. I felt as hollowed out and as light as a balloon, a dummy of a woman.

"No. It's funny. Now I seem to be able to function only right in the moment, like a small child. Just in the day I'm in. I guess it's the not knowing . . . what's going to happen. If I knew one way or the other, I think I'd be depressed, or terrified, or angry, or whatever. It's why I've refused to go back to the doctor, I think. But lately I've just been sort of . . . focused inside myself. Time to come out now though, I think. Past time."

He reached over and pushed the damp hair off my hot face. I could not even imagine how terrible I must look. But he smiled.

"Nobody's being good to you, are they?" he said. "Not for a long time, if they ever were. Nobody's taking care of you. It's all the other way around."

"It's okay. I don't usually mind—"

"I mind. We're going to do something now just for you. Something absolutely wacko and off-the-wall. Oh, hell, it's for me, too, of course. You up to an adventure?"

"What?"

"I'm not going to tell you. I'm going to show you. You'll have to do some of it. First, I want you to go out to the shed and get the sled. You remember? Will you do that?"

"Dennis ... we aren't going sledding in the middle of the night!"

"Go get the sled. Are you a total wimp?"

"No," I said, suddenly filled with gaiety that bordered on giddiness. The iron fatigue had lifted. I was floating on scotch and release.

"I'm no more wimp than you are! I'll show you who's a wimp!"

I raced out of the cottage and around back to the shed where the sled still lay, silent and grimy beneath the tarpaulin. Overhead the moon rode high like a white schooner, and the earth leaped and blazed with light from it, and the stars, and the reflection off the deep-creamed snow. My boots scrunched as I hauled the sled around the side of the cottage, and snow flew in little silvery puffs from the laden branches of the evergreens when I knocked against them. The air was cold and so dry that it felt like ginger ale in my lungs. It smelled of cold salt and pine and the peculiar, wet-blue smell of snow at night. I drew in great gulps of it, as if I could never get enough. By the time I reached the porch, I was giggling.

He was dressed and waiting for me. He wore his parka and a scarf and gloves and a dark watch cap like the scallop fishermen who went out of Menemsha wore, and his teeth and the whites of his eyes flashed in the shadow of the porch. He had one crutch and he was leaning on Lazarus with his other hand. I moved up to help him, but he motioned me away.

"I can do it," he said. "We've been practicing."

And he put his hand on Lazarus's back, then together they inched down the steps, Dennis holding on and hopping, Laz carefully taking his weight, waiting until he felt it full before going down another step. They managed the steps and stood beside me in quite a short time. I felt tears prickle again.

"He's a good dog," Dennis said. "I'd forgotten what it was like to have a good dog."

I don't remember precisely how we made it down the path to the dock and up the hill beyond it, but we did, slipping and sliding and laughing. Sometimes Dennis leaned on me and sometimes on Laz, and sometimes he was able to manage with just the crutch. By the time we gained the crest of the long, smooth, snowy hill, we were both panting. I felt my cheeks flaming with exertion and laughter, and I saw the flags of color in his. We stood together silently for a time, looking down the long swoop of white gleaming under the moon, out over the blue and white and black pond and the glittering Sound beyond it, wrapped in the quilted silence that a snowfall gives to the world. I don't think I have ever seen anything lovelier than that night of late snow and moonlight up island. It still burns silver and black sometimes, when I close my eyes.

"Okay," he said presently. "This is how we'll have to do it. I don't think it'll be too hard on you. We'll get the sled right there on the very edge of the slope, and I'll lie down on it, and you run along behind, pushing, and then, when it takes the crest, you just belly-flop down on top of me."

"Dennis, I'll mash you to a pulp! I must outweigh you by twenty pounds."

"Not anymore," he said. "Come on, Molly. That's the way everybody does it when they want to go two on a sled. You won't hurt me. I've got a ton of clothes on."

And that's what we did. We maneuvered the sled to the lip of the hill that ran steeply down to the verge of the pond, and he lay down on it on his stomach, with Lazarus dancing and barking beside him in the snow. I took a deep breath, and reached down and put my hands on the back of the sled and gave a tentative push. Nothing happened.

"Give it everything you've got," he shouted, and I pushed with all my might, and the sled shot forward, creaking on the snow, and I bounded after it, and half-leaped, half-fell on top of him as it shot off down the hill.

Somewhere halfway down, in the cold rush of the wind and the flying, stinging spume of snow, I became aware that I was laughing and crying at the same time. My ears were full of the *whushhh* of the sled's runners and Dennis's laughter and Lazarus's manic barking as he capered and floundered and slid after us. As soon as the tears left my lower lids, they froze on my cheeks and hot, new ones took their place. I did not care. I was not crying for grief, but for joy. This was what it was, then, to be airborne. This was what it was to be free.

The sled flew down the last sharp segment of the hill and shot out on to level ground and down to the edge of the pond, and hit the ruff of reeds where Charles and Di used to lurk, snow-mounded now, and turned over, toppling us both off into deep, soft snow. I fetched up, lying directly atop him, struggling for breath, hair in my eyes, laughing, laughing. His face was directly beneath mine, but I did not realize it until I felt his breath warm on it and realized that he was laughing, too. He reached around me and pushed the hair out of my eyes, and I lay looking down at him.

For what seemed a very long time we simply lay there. I could feel our hearts beating together through the heavy clothes, and feel his warm breath. His eyes were very close, and wide open, and dark. Unreadable eyes. His mouth was soft and slightly open, like a child's nearing sleep. I felt my laughter slow and die, and his did, too.

He pulled my head down to his, then, and kissed me. It was a very long kiss, complex and searching, seeking hard, and seeming to find what it sought in my own mouth. I felt myself slacken into the kiss, going more deeply into it, more deeply into his arms. It felt strange, to be held by arms that were not Tee's, to be kissed by a mouth that did not taste of Tee's. But not that strange. Soon it no longer felt strange at all. The kiss went on and on.

In a little while I felt the hard, muffled surging of him against me, and laughed in pure delight.

"Hello," I whispered into his mouth. "What's this?"

He pulled his head away and looked up at me. His face in the moon and snow light was beautiful. He was grinning.

"Good God. I can't believe it," he said, beginning to laugh. "Do you think it's possible for a one-legged man to fuck in a snowbank?"

As it turned out, it was.

CHAPTER FOURTEEN

I STAYED AT DENNIS'S ALL THAT NIGHT and for much of the next day. I slept and slept. It was the sort of sleep you think you remember from childhood or adolescence but really don't: silent, sweet, voluptuous, bottomless. It seemed a separate element to me: I would dive and glide and turn and roll in it as a seal might, in beneficent water; I would sink deep and soar up to the very sunlit surface of it, stretch and dive down again. I was conscious of no need at all to surface except satiety. When I had had enough, far past noon the next day, I woke up.

Sunlight was pouring into the bedroom, but it did not fall where I was accustomed to seeing it, and for a moment I simply lay, slack-limbed and rested in all my parts, looking at the pale rays with dust motes dancing in them, falling on a quilt and a rug and an armchair I did not know. I started to smile out of sheer well-being, and then I remembered where I was, and why, and sat up with my breath huffing out of my throat.

"Oh, God," I whispered to myself, eyes squeezed shut. "I made love to Dennis Ponder in a snowdrift and spent the entire night in his bed. Oh, shit! What does this mean? I don't know what this means!"

And then I looked at my watch and vaulted out of bed as if catapulted, tangling myself in the bedclothes and falling to my knees on the rug. I scrambled up again, searching for my clothes. It was nearly two-thirty in the afternoon, and nobody but Dennis knew where I was. My father would be frantic, the old ladies would be cold and hungry and possibly worse. I found my clothes, still damp from last night's snow, on the floor beyond the chair and skinned into them, grimacing slightly at the unaccustomed but not unpleasant soreness in parts of me where no soreness had been for a very long time. I glanced in Dennis's filmy old bureau mirror and saw a madwoman with tousled hair and a flushed face, raked my fingers through my hair, and ran into the living room barefoot, looking for my shoes.

Dennis Ponder had not been in the bedroom, but he was in the living room. He stood with his back to the room, looking out the window at the sun striking light off the snow, holding a cup of coffee. He wore a black turtleneck and chinos and a work boot, and he balanced on the back of the sofa as he stared out. Lazarus lay beside him, and he turned and thumped his tail at me when I came in the room, but Dennis did not turn. I stood stock-still, feeling my face beginning to flame, unable to think of a single thing to say to him. So far as morning-after etiquette went, I had had need of it only once, long ago, and in that instance I had married the partner. I had no casual postcoital talk.

I cleared my throat to speak, and he said, "If you want to forget it ever happened, we'll say no more about it. If, on the other hand, you enjoyed it as much as you said you did, let's go back in there and do it again. It's your call."

"I . . . oh, Lord, Dennis, I have to go! My father doesn't know where I am . . . "

"He knows. I called him last night after you'd gone to sleep," he said. He still did not turn his face to me.

"But Bella and Luz . . . "

"I went," he said.

"You what?"

"I didn't want to wake you, so I went over there and built up a fire and heated up some soup. Don't make a big deal out of it, Molly. You were half dead and it's past time I stopped letting you carry the whole load. The truck's got the oldest automatic transmission in the Commonwealth of Massachusetts, but it has one. The county's gotten to the road and somebody's plowed out the driveway. It was no problem."

"Dennis . . . my God . . . "

He turned then, and I could see that his eyes were rimmed with red and his nose was pink. There was no doubt that he had been crying. I felt shock and hope and dread collide in my chest.

"Can you tell me about it?"

"No. Not now. Maybe in a little while. The thing is there's nowhere you have to rush off to, so let's have some lunch and a glass of wine and see where things go. Last night was . . . more than I thought I was going to have again in my life."

I felt the flush on my cheeks flood down over my chest. I saw my shoes beside the door and went and got them and sat down on the sofa, busying myself with them. My whole body felt on fire. Every place he had touched me last night seemed limned with light and flame.

"I . . ." I began, and choked, and cleared my throat. "I enjoyed it, too," I said, stupidly and primly.

He laughed.

"Can you look at me? Okay, that's better. Now. Tell me what's on your mind. Did my magnificent hairless body turn you on? Did my one-legged state repulse you? Did the earth move? Should I have lit two cigarettes and handed you one? What?"

"I . . . you know, Dennis, I've never done that with anybody but my husband before. This wasn't anything like that, and thank God for it, but I don't quite know yet how to act. Did I like it? You must know I did. But I don't know, I just don't know . . . if I can jump right in bed and do it again. I mean . . . I hardly . . . "

"You hardly know me?"

He laughed again but there was not so much warmth in it this time.

I nodded. That really had been what I meant and even in my addled state I realized how utterly ridiculous a notion it was. I might never know Dennis Ponder any better than I did now.

"I guess I mean maybe we should talk about what sort of relationship we're going to have," I said miserably. I could not seem to make myself sound any way but absurd.

"What relationship?" he said. "What relationship could we have but the one we do?"

"I sort of thought we needed to let things develop, see what common interests we have, get to know one another in . . . other ways, too. We already have a lot in common . . . "

"Molly . . . "

He sighed, and came and sat down beside me on the sofa.

"Listen. We made love. We screwed, to put it another way. It doesn't mean we're engaged. It doesn't mean I won't respect you tomorrow. You don't want any other kind of relationship, I can promise you. What would be in it for you?"

"I don't just screw, Dennis."

"I know you don't. I didn't think of it as just screwing. It was . . . something else entirely for me. But I'm not exactly a prime candidate for a long-term relationship, to use a New Age term I loathe only slightly more than 'special.'"

"You mean you think you're dying?"

"I mean I don't know. But I know I'm not dying this afternoon, and all I'm proposing to you is a suitable occupation for the rest of this afternoon."

"Dennis, I just don't know if that's enough," I said softly.

"It's all I have," he said.

We sat looking at each other, seeing no quarter in each other's eyes. And then he said, "I won't hassle you about this. If you feel like it, you let me know. The offer stands."

I laughed in spite of myself.

"What do you want me to do, just tap on your shoulder in the middle of some afternoon and say, 'Please, sir, can I have some more?'"

"That, or 'Let's fuck,'" he said mildly, and I laughed again. The awkwardness went out of the air. I felt absurdly good, young and lighthearted and sensuous and admired. I could remember that feeling from the very earliest days of Tee's and my courtship, that delicate, flirtatious, breath-held time when all things seemed wonderful and possible but there was no hurry about anything. The sense of delectation was high. I wish I had had a lot more of that feeling before I had what came next. I wanted, suddenly, to tell it to Teddy: Don't rush into anything, take that long, delicious, teasing time that's your due before you settle on someone. I wished I could have told it to Caroline, too. I wondered if Dennis Ponder had ever had it. Somehow, I did not think so. It presupposed too much self-delight, too much sheer playfulness. I thought Bella might well have murdered any capacity he had had for those things.

Bella . . .

"Dennis, your mother . . . how is she? Physically, I mean. It must have been an enormous shock for her, not to mention old Luz. Do I need to see about them? Or . . . do you want to go again? I don't intend to pry, but I have to know how to play this now."

"I don't think I'm going to be able to tell you much about my mother, Molly," he said. "I went, she was surprised, she cried, she carried on, she prayed, she got to coughing and gasping. I gave her a shot of scotch and calmed her down and stayed until they'd eaten and were about to drop off to sleep, and then I came home. You probably ought to check on them in a little while, but I think they're fine. She's too old and sick to make much of a fuss, and Luz is too out of it. Luz didn't turn a hair, by the way; she just looked up and said, 'You may be tall, but I know you're Denny. Where's your other leg?' And I told her I left it in Seattle, and she just nodded. Luz is exactly the same as she was when I left, except wrinkled. But my mother . . . my God, she's grotesque, isn't she? And a real wreck physically. Well, I guess neither one of us is much of a prize. And that's it. That's all I know about it right now. If there's any more, maybe I'll tell you about it. Or maybe not."

"All right," I said faintly, and as it happened, that was all I ever did learn about that first meeting of Dennis Ponder with the terrible, sad old woman who had thought she could only have one love.

But after that, he went frequently to the farmhouse on the Chilmark moor. He went a couple of times in the mornings so I could do other errands, but mainly he went in the evenings, because that was when Bella was strongest and most alert, and when Luz was most focused, and when his own carefully husbanded energy burned highest. Once or twice he went alone in the truck, but usually I drove him so I could have the use of it, and picked him up again when I was done with whatever I had to do. We did not specifically agree on it, but gradually he took over the late-afternoon reading.

"It's not that we don't like the way you read," Luz told me sweetly on one of the first days Dennis read, "but this is our Denny, and when he reads about kings it's nice because he's descended from one, just like we are. It's the same king, you know, King Dinis. It's like hearing about family."

And Bella nodded, her black eyes flaming with joy.

I did not look at Dennis when she said that. From the very beginning, we all pretended that there was nothing in the least unusual about the fact that Dennis Ponder, son of this house and this huge old woman, sat reading to her in the dusk of a place from which he had been banished more than forty years before. I don't think to Luzia there was anything extraordinary about it; in the tapestry of her shadowy mind it was little Denny, to whom she had read only a heartbeat ago, who sat with her in the lamplight now. But it must have been an unimaginable effort for Bella to conceal her radiant pride. Yet she merely sat quietly, looking interested and appreciative, like a lady to whom a well-bred youngster is tendering a special, small social favor. I don't know how she managed it. Her florid mind must have been roiling with the sort of baroque maternal passion she had not been able to indulge for many decades. I wondered if Dennis had laid down any ground rules about how they would all behave, and decided not. Whatever there was in his heart for his mother and Luzia Ferreira now, I knew it could not be simple love, not in any ordinary filial sense of the word. Perhaps the pretense that all was as usual was necessary for him to go into that house at all. Perhaps Bella's facade of mere pleasantry was in the nature of a child's pretending not to see a wild little animal so as not to frighten it away. It was an infinitely delicate and careful balancing act that the three of them conceived. I would not have asked about it for words. Bella never told me how she felt, and Dennis did not until much later.

On the first evening that I dropped him off to read to the old women, I said, "The books they like to hear are on the table by Luz's bed. We're in the middle of *Penrod and Sam*, but Luz is going to beg for *The Once and Future King*. It's Bella's turn to choose. Don't let them start fighting about it; it makes Bella sick, and it takes forever to calm Luz down."

"I brought my own book," he said. "They'll get it or nothing."

"What? The Marquis de Sade?" I teased.

"*Mother Courage*," he said dryly. But he did not show me the book.

When I came back, in the clear green light that you get on the twilight moors of Chilmark every now and then in the earliest spring, the house was quiet, and I let myself into the living room softly so as not to disturb the old women if they had fallen asleep. But they had not; they sat in their familiar little tableau, Bella sprawled back in the big recliner that by now bore the indelible shape of her great buttocks, Luz snuggled into her tattered linens. Dennis sat opposite them in a spavined old morris chair, his leg outstretched on a hassock. The fire whispered, and Palestrina trickled from Dennis's cassette recorder. A single old milk-glass lamp shone down on the book he was reading from, and in its light I saw that Luz wore a smile more of the air than the earth, and the nacreous tracks of tears traced Bella's blank moon of a face.

"'I went to the woods because I wished to live deliberately,'" Dennis read in his deep voice. Or perhaps he was reciting; I could not see his face in the shadows. "'. . . to front only the essential facts of life, and see if I could not learn what it had to teach, and not, when I came to die, discover that I had not lived.'"

He let his voice trail off, and sat for a moment with the book in his hands.

"That's enough for now," he said. "A little Thoreau goes a long way."

The old women did not beg for more, but sat quietly, turned inside themselves. I turned away and moved softly into the kitchen so that none of them would see that I, too, like Bella, was crying.

On the way home we were silent, and finally I said, "My father was reading that, too. He quoted just that passage to me not long ago. I wish . . . I wish he would go with you sometime when you go up there to read. He used to do it all the time. They loved hearing him. Oh, I wish . . . I wish." I fell silent. There was no use talking about it.

"Do you know the rest of the quotation?" Dennis said after a moment. "'I did not wish to live what was not life, nor did I wish to practice resignation unless it was quite necessary.' Maybe for Tim it's quite necessary right now. I know from experience that you have to get down to the resignation, to get done with everything that isn't life, before you can begin to see what is. I think that's where he is right now. You can't go there with him. Nobody can. He's the one who decides when to go on from there."

"*If* he decides to go on from there."

I had hoped that Dennis would rush to allay my worst fear, but he did not.

"If he does," he agreed.

We did not speak again until he got out of the truck at his camp, and held the door open so that Lazarus could come bounding into it. I did not go in with him; I had not done so since that first day. He was as good as his word. He had not pressed me to stay, or for anything else. Often, like that evening, I wished he would. I needed his warmth and his touch, but I could not bring myself to ask. In my mind I could hear my mother on a long-ago Saturday when I had been thirteen and called my friend Dickie Hembree up the street to come over and go to the movies with me: "You never, *never* ask a young man to take you anywhere, Molly. It's cheap. It sounds desperate. It sounds like you can't get a date any other way. With your height and those big breasts, you're always going to have to be careful not to look desperate. A real beauty can get away with it, maybe, but the rest of us ordinary girls have to be very, very careful not to look desperate."

And she had given me her brilliant, quicksilver smile to show that she included herself in the pantheon of ordinary girls. But I had long known that she lived in that other world, and felt even larger and more graceless than usual. I called Dickie back and said never mind, and never asked a boy or a man for attention again. I could no more have asked Dennis Ponder to make love to me than I could have asked him to grow a new leg, no matter how badly I wanted to. Somehow, I realized that night, I had expected him to know that. I was obscurely angry with him because he apparently did not. I was irritated with his homilies about my folks, too. I wanted him to feel my fear, not quote Thoreau at it.

The day after that, everything changed.

In an odd way, my father was better. He was sleeping well, he said, and suddenly felt like an outing for the first time in months. After that, he was out and about once more, as he had been before the awful deadness sucked him down. On the first day or two he took the truck when I wasn't using it, but a day came when both old ladies had doctors' appointments and I had to drive them into Oak

Bluffs, and the truck was not available to him for a full day; that evening he came home from Menemsha with a disreputable old blue Toyota that he had bought from a sign posted in Poole's Fish Market.

"You need the truck, and I thought I might do some exploring down island, go check on some of the old farts at Alley's and the senior center," he said. "See how they wintered over."

I simply stared at him. It was an enormous change from the terribly diminished man he had been, of course, but somehow he seemed even stranger to me now: abstracted, oddly exalted, with a kind of luminosity about his face that had never been there before. He seemed to be constantly listening to something just out of my hearing range, and often he smiled at it.

"It's a fine car," I said heartily when he brought it home. "And you'll never know how glad I am to see you feeling better. Why don't you take it up and show it to Bella and Luz? They've been asking about you. And take Dennis with you, why don't you? Do you remember that I told you he was seeing his mother again? You go and tell me what you think about that; I can't tell what's going on with them, and he sure isn't talking about it. He misses you, too . . . "

"I'll look in on them in a day or two," he said. "And Dennis needs to get on with his work. Later on I'll spend some time with him. Yes, I recall that you did tell me about him getting back together with Bella. That's fine, isn't it? You tell him I'm happy for him."

And he would kiss me on the cheek and go out to his old car and lurch away down the lane, hideously rutted now from the deep freezes and melting snows of the hard-dying winter, and I would not see him again until after dinner.

"What did you do today?" I would ask, heating up the food I had saved for him.

"Oh, sat in on a game of pool at the center," he would say. "Took three dollars off of Martin Golightly. Went over to the big hardware store in Vineyard Haven and looked at some roof tiles. We're going to have to do something about this roof when the weather warms up a little. Cost about twice what they do back home; maybe I'll do a little comparison shopping. No thanks, baby, I had something to eat at Back Alley's. You wrap that up in foil and I'll have it tomorrow."

And he would climb the stairs to his bedroom and prepare for bed. Oh, perhaps he would sit for a half hour or so and watch some television with me, but never more than that, and though he smiled and replied to my chatter with his old banter, I could tell that he was tired and wanted only to go to bed. And because he had so very much sleep to make up for, I did not object when, in a very short time, he kissed me on the cheek and climbed the narrow stairs. I should have been reassured with the change, and on one level I was, but underneath the relief something did not seem right, and I pushed the strangeness as deep as I could simply because I did not think I could stand any more worry.

One noon I ducked into Alley's to pick up a jar of mayonnaise and turned when I heard someone say, "Molly? Molly Redwine?"

It was Martin Golightly, the man to whom my father was closest up island, the one whose snooker expertise was legendary at the senior center and around the stove at Alley's.

"Well, hello," I said, smiling at him. "I hear my father finally beat you. He must have drugged your root beer."

He looked at me oddly.

"How is Tim?" he said. "We've missed him. We all thought you must have been so wintered in down there on the pond that you couldn't get out, but it's not like him to let a little weather keep him away from the snooker table. Is he okay? You tell him there are at least three guys waiting to whip his tail."

My face felt stiff.

"I'll tell him," I said. "The roads have been pretty bad down our way, but they're softening up now. He'll probably see you in a day or two."

"Glad to hear it," Martin Golightly said, and turned back to the stove and his coffee. I went home and waited for my father. When he came in, long after dinnertime, I called him on it. My heart was beating violently. I was terrified without quite knowing why.

He sighed and sat down beside me on the sofa.

"She comes every night now, Molly," he said, his face translucent with the strange joy that had played over it for the past week or so. I stared at him. When had he gotten so thin? He looked as if he were being consumed by something inside him as fiery as a nebula.

"Oh, Daddy," I said, my voice trembling.

"Every night. At first I thought it was just a fluke, but she comes closer and closer every night. I knew it was just a matter of being able to sleep at night. And now that I can . . . now that I can . . . Molly, she looks beautiful. And she's happy. I can tell that. She stays longer and longer; it's like she's playing, teasing me like she used to do when I first met her. I know I shouldn't have lied to you, but I was afraid that it wouldn't last, and it would have been worse if she didn't come back and I'd told you about it . . . "

"But where do you go if you don't go to Alley's or the center? What do you do all that time?" I said, my voice quivering.

"I drive around. I walk. I walk for miles. I've been places I never knew were on the island; this afternoon I spent hours and hours on Lucy Vincent, and yesterday I went up on the Gay Head cliffs. It's all so beautiful. It's like I'm seeing it through her eyes, showing her the Vineyard for the first time . . . "

"Daddy . . . "

"Don't start on me about this, Molly," he said fiercely. "I have her back. I never thought I would. I love you like the light in my heart, but I'm not going to let you meddle with this."

And he turned and went upstairs. I sat looking after him, drowning in his strangeness.

After that I left him alone, and he slept through his nights in the company of my mother and wandered alone in the soft gray days, and a morning came when it was finally spring.

It was a time of glittering white frosts in the morning, and clear, pale, earlier dawns, and the silvery clatter of the cardinals and redwings in the scrub forests. The lyrical pinkletinks called and called, in the brushy swamps. There was no green yet on the tracery of the wet black branches, but you could feel it was down there, deep, pushing slowly upward like blood toward a beating heart.

On one of those first soft evenings, Tee called.

I was alone. My father was out on God knows what wild hill, and Dennis and Lazarus had gone down to the pond, Dennis to throw sticks and Laz to retrieve them. I had seen little of Dennis since I had learned where my father went in the daytime and how he spent his nights; somehow I simply could not tell Dennis about that. To voice it would have made it too real. Like my father earlier, I found myself increasingly consumed by a need to sleep, and now that I had more free time on my hands, that is what I did. I slept in the afternoon while my father roamed and Dennis worked or went up in the truck to read to the old women, and I slept longer in the mornings. Whenever I think of the coming of that spring, I think of it through a haze of sleep as tender as the first flush of pale green on the lilac bushes up island.

I was dozing when Tee's call came, and for a moment I could not think how to respond to the voice on the telephone that was at once strange and as familiar as my own heartbeat. It seemed to come out of a time and place as far away as my childhood. For weeks now I had heard no voice from Atlanta. Missy and Livvy both had finally told me, in annoyance, to call when I had some idea of what I was going to do; they were tired of calling and getting the same hedging answers from me.

"How you doing?" Tee said, his voice warm with his old, intimate interest, and I said, stupidly, politely, "I'm just fine. How are you?"

"Well . . . you know," Tee said. "Not so fine. Stewing in my own juice, having fucked up yet again."

He laughed, the deep, lazy laugh that had been the first thing I had loved about him. Suddenly I had a flash: Tee at twenty-four, sitting in the sun on the beach at Sea Island, his hair bleached gilt, laughing at me and lighting the world up with it. It had been the first time after our marriage that we'd gone there. In the background Charlie and Carrie Davies laughed about something.

I blinked, and the vision went away.

"What have you fucked up, Tee?" I said. For a preposterous moment I could not think what he might mean. It was an expression he used a lot, capable both of charming and disarming.

"What haven't I?" he said. "Listen, I just wanted to see how you were doing. Nobody has heard from you. I got your number from Missy, who, incidentally, is about as pissed at me as it is possible for one human to be at another, closely followed by my mother. I've been thinking about you. I missed the family at Christmas."

I said nothing, thinking that he had been with Teddy then and wondering if he didn't count his son as family.

"So when do you think you might come home?" my husband asked.

"Why on earth do you care?" I said, almost amused at him. "Is this about the house? You-all can have the house. I told Missy to tell you that. Did she not?"

"Yeah, she told me. Moll . . . there's not any more us-all, I don't think."

He waited for an answer, and when I did not, he said, "She isn't here anymore. Sheri. I'm not seeing her anymore. She's trans-ferred to marketing in New York and asked for Europe and will probably get it. It's with my total blessing. I'm the one who, I guess, broke it off."

"Hmmm," I said. "And just what is it she'll be marketing in New York and Europe?"

There was a silence, and then he said, "I deserve that, of course," but I could tell that he did not think he did.

"What I mean is, I'm not going to marry her," Tee said. "It . . . turned out to be just what my mother called it, a bad itch in the pants. You probably called it worse than that, and I don't blame you. I think that I was just plain and simply afraid of getting old, and she came along just at the time I was most vulnerable."

"Poor baby," I said.

"Okay, okay. There's a lot more you need to say to me, and that I need to hear. I don't blame you for that, either. I called to see if we could start to talk now. I'd hoped you'd come on home now that the house is empty again . . . that was a stupid damned thing, I know . . . but I could come up there one weekend. I've already checked about planes and ferries. We could talk face-to-face . . . "

"No, we couldn't," I said, my ears ringing with what really was, now, suppressed laughter, and put the telephone down.

It rang again and again and finally stopped. By that time my laughter had exploded and waned and stopped, and I sat in the dusk feeling that all the sleep in the world would not be enough, and knowing that I would never drop off. I got up and went into my bathroom and opened the medicine cabinet to take one of the sleep-ing pills that Charlie Davies had given me. This was one night I did not intend to toss and turn like a hagridden mare.

The pills were not there. I knew suddenly where they were. I ran up the steps to my father's bathroom so fast that I stumbled twice and almost went headfirst down into the living room. The vial of pills was there, but it was empty except for two. There was another bottle, full, beside it, with my father's name and the name on the label of a doctor I did not know in Oak Bluffs. I knew now where my father's sleep came from, knew on what wings my mother came to him in the nights when he went down deep.

I was at Dennis's camp pounding on his door before I even realized what I was doing.

I spilled it all out, with him sitting on the sofa before the fire watching me but not moving to touch me as I jabbered frantically in my fear and anger, or when the tears of despair started down my face.

Finally, when I stopped simply because I was too drained to talk or weep any more, he said, "Leave him alone, Molly."

"Dennis! Leave him alone? What if he . . . you know . . . "

"Leave him alone. It's his business. If pain gets too bad, there ought to be an out. Everybody deserves that much. Even an animal deserves that much."

Rage flared deep in my chest where the awful fear had been.

"Oh, good, Dennis. Very good," I cried. "That's just what he said about you when I told him about the pills you had, and what you said about them. He said for me to let you alone, that I didn't know enough about pain yet to know what I was talking about. Well, fuck him and you both, because I do. I know as much about pain as either of you ever will, and I'm goddamned sick of both of you, with your contingencies and your neat little plans for getting out when your famous pain gets too bad. What about the ones of us you leave behind? What are we supposed to do for our pain?"

"Who do *I* leave?" Dennis said coldly.

"Oh, God, I am so *sick* of hearing that! Your daughter! Your family! Don't you know what that *means*?"

He got up and limped to the window and pulled the curtain aside and looked out into the night. The window was raised just a little, and I caught the smell of fresh, wet earth and soft, sweet salt from the Bight, smells to break the heart. Eliot had said it: "April is the cruelest month . . . "

"How many times do I have to tell you what I am?" he said in a lifeless voice. "I'm stone-broke. I'm probably flat out of time. I have one leg and a dick that works part-time and seventy-five pages nobody wants to read by a man scared pissless of women, who only knows the little boys he's paid to know. Some book. Some expert. Some legacy for my so-called family."

"You have your mother," I said. He turned and looked at me, but said nothing. His eyes were as dead as his voice.

"I knew about it, Dennis," I said. "I saw them one night. I saw what I guess you saw. I know that I can't even imagine how awful it was for you for a long, long time, but you have her back now . . . "

"For how long, assuming that I did have her back or even wanted her? She's probably going to kick off before I do."

I was very angry, but under it there was pain as fresh and red as new blood.

"You have me, goddamn you."

"They hired you," he said.

For a while I simply said nothing, and then I said, my voice shaking, "You are behaving just horribly. Just horribly. What is the matter with you?"

"I have the exquisite, unassailable excuse of probably being about to die," he said. "The question is, what is the matter with you?"

"My husband called me tonight," I said, beginning to sob. "He isn't getting married after all. I don't know how I ought to think about it . . . "

He laughed and walked away toward the kitchen, hopping on his one good foot, balancing on furniture.

"Congratulations," he flung at me over his shoulder. "But I really must refer you to Ann Landers. She is, I think, more your style."

I blundered out of the camp, treacherous tears beginning. When I got home, my father was already upstairs asleep. In the light from the slightly opened door I could see that he had a small, secret smile on his face.

I was still crying, softly and hopelessly, when I got into bed, but the two Halcions I had taken kicked in quickly, and I was asleep in my cave under the stairs even before Laz got up off the hearth rug and came wagging and padding to bed.

When the telephone rang, deep in the night, I woke swiftly and cleanly and reached for it, so sure that it was Dennis apologizing for

319

his behavior that I was already framing my reply: "I quite understand. Let's say no more about it."

Restrained, noncommittal, dignified. Altogether better than he deserved.

But instead of Dennis's contrite voice, I heard a breathy, small gulp, as if a child were sucking in air, and then a soft, bubbling, frantic spill of sound that I listened to in consternation for about half a minute before I realized it was Luz, and that she was speaking Portuguese.

"Luz! It's Molly. English. Speak English, please," I said, and she stopped and drew a long, sobbing breath, and said, all at once, "Bella is making funny noises. Like a duck, quack, quack! Molly, come! I don't like this! She won't get up!"

I bolted upright, already reaching for my blue jeans.

"Listen, Luz. Call 911. Can you do that? Hang up the phone and then dial 911, and when somebody answers, tell them you need help at the Ponder farm off Middle Road. They'll come right away. I'm right behind. Do you understand? Hang up and dial 911."

"She looks funny," Luz whimpered, and put the telephone down. I could hear her rustling around in her bedcovers, making small, mumbling sounds, but she did not pick up the phone again and she did not hang up.

I called 911 myself and ran out of the house and across the glade to Dennis's. A light in the living room still burned, and when I hit the porch, running hard, he was at the door, looking out. He still wore the clothes he had had on, and he was pale and red-eyed.

"Come on," I said before he could speak. "It's your mother. Luz called and I can't be sure what's wrong, but something is. I've called 911."

"Shit," he said softly. And we did not speak again until I had helped him into the truck and was jerking it around to make the hard left into the lane. Then he said, "I've been expecting this for a while. I guess you have, too."

"For some reason I really haven't," I said. "I don't know why. I've always known she was very ill. But it could be nothing; you can't depend on Luz, and I've had some false alarms with Bella before. Let's don't jump to conclusions."

"Good old Molly," he said between clenched teeth. "Ever the voice of reason. By all means, let us not jump to conclusions."

I whipped my head around at him.

"Don't you dare start on me again, Dennis," I said. "I don't know what's wrong with you tonight, and right now I don't care. Just don't you speak to me again that way."

He was quiet for so long that I looked over at him. He sat with his head down, his hair falling partly over his eyes, and his hands on the dashboard were clenched and white-knuckled.

"You're hurting, aren't you?" I said, my chest contracting with fear. Were any of us going to be spared on this horrible night?

"Not so much. A little. It's not the bad stuff, I don't think. I banged my stump the night we went sledding, and it's gotten sort of inflamed. I was going to call the doctor in the morning and see if he could give me a shot, or something."

"Why didn't you tell me? I could have put something on it for you. I've got stuff at my house . . . "

"I really don't think our relationship has progressed to the point that I'd feel comfortable showing you my stump," he said prissily, and I blinked incredulously before I realized that he was teasing me. Before I could even smile, he said, "I'm sorry, Molly. I've been a prick tonight. I guess . . . I really didn't want to hear that about your dad or your husband. My mother, either. The world is just shit-full of things I don't want to deal with tonight, but there's no reason for me to take it out on you. I'd start this day over if I could."

"I don't mind," I said. "It's okay. It really is."

So much for dignity and restraint. If I had not been so frightened for Bella, I might have grinned like a Cheshire cat at Dennis Ponder. But I was frightened, and so was he. I could feel his fear in the soft darkness, smell it, like acrid smoke.

There were no lights in the farmhouse but the struggling fire, but it was enough to see that Luz was crouched on the floor beside the overturned recliner with Bella Ponder's big head in her lap. Forever after I wondered how Luz had gotten herself out of bed and across the floor. She herself did not remember. In the fire-flicker her little yellow face was as serene as that of a seraph high on a cathedral, eyes closed, and she rocked Bella's head back and forth and sang to her a little Portuguese song in a minor key that sounded like a child's song, a nursery air. I ran to them and knelt down, leaving

Dennis to make his way into the house with his crutch. I wanted to be the first to see Bella Ponder. If it was too bad, perhaps I could make her look a bit better before her son saw her.

It was bad, I could see that at once. Bella lay on her back where she had fallen from the recliner, her great arms crossed and her fists pressing into her chest, her face absolutely colorless, the white of dead narcissus. Huge, pearled drops of sweat stood on her forehead and at her hairline. Her eyes were closed. Her lips were slate blue, working silently.

"*Ajudar-me*," she whispered. "*Ajudar-me. Papa, ajudar-me . . .*"

"Bella," I said, and she opened her eyes. They were flat and black and focused on something beyond me. The pupils were pinpoints.

"Mama?" she said, and I knew she had gone into a far country where I could not follow.

"It's Molly," I said, dabbing at the sweat on her forehead with the tail of my shirt. Luz smiled and rocked, smiled and rocked, sang and sang.

Behind me I heard Dennis's voice slip into the little nursery song along with Luz. I was surprised somehow that he knew Portuguese, but it stood to reason. He had heard it for the first seventeen years of his life.

Dennis came then, flopping awkwardly down on the floor beside his mother.

"Bella," he said tentatively, and then, "Mother. Mama. Can you hear me?"

Bella's eyes came back from the far country and saw him. They widened, and a small smile curved the terrible blue lips up. "*Papa*," she whispered. "*Magoar. Papa . . .*"

"It's Dennis, Mama," he said. His voice was hardly stronger than hers.

"*Dennis! Ah, Dennis, obrigado . . .*"

I closed my eyes briefly. I did not know if she thought she was addressing king or son. I did know that she would not stay long in the farmhouse, one way or another.

Dennis Ponder looked at me, wildness in his gray eyes.

"An ambulance . . ."

"I called from home. Let me get a blanket. We shouldn't move her . . ."

322

The tri-town ambulance came howling into the yard then, and I ran to the door to let the crew in, switching on lights as I went. Just before I jerked the front door open, I heard Dennis, whispering, "Don't you dare die on me. Don't you fucking dare leave me again, old woman . . . "

He went with them in the ambulance to the hospital in Oak Bluffs. I stayed behind with Luzia, wondering what to do next, wondering what on earth, now, my role was in the farmhouse and on the pond, what the right thing to do was. It seemed to me that there would certainly be an immutable up island ritual for this, but I did not know it.

One of the young EMTs, a square, sandy-haired youngster who looked vaguely familiar, had helped me get Luz back in bed. He did it tenderly and respectfully, saying, "Let's get you back where you belong, Miss Luzia," and I thought that he must somehow know Luz, but could not think how that could be. Bella had not let medical help come into this house for years. Luz, mumbling and vague, let us tuck her in, and lay there smiling expectantly, as if waiting for a treat.

"Thank you," I said to the boy. "I don't quite know what to do next . . . "

"Somebody's coming," he said. "Just hang on. We'll take care of them."

And he was out the door and into his vehicle before I could ask who. When it had screamed away toward Middle Road, I drew my chair up to Luz's bed and took her hands.

"You mustn't worry. Dennis is going to take good care of her, and we aren't going to leave you alone."

"I know," she said sleepily. "She told me. Would you read to me, please? I haven't heard *The Once and Future King* in ages and ages." And I picked up the flaccid book, which fell open to a point near the middle, and began to read as the sky over the sea to the east began to lighten infinitesimally: "'A white-front said, "Now, Wart, if you were once able to fly the great North Sea, surely you can co-ordinate a few little wing-muscles here and there? Fold your powers together, with the spirit of your mind, and it will come out like butter. Come along, Homo sapiens, for all we humble friends of yours are waiting here to cheer."'"

I had not gotten far before there was a quiet knock at the door and Patricia Norton let herself into the room.

"I'm so glad to see you," I said simply, not wondering, at that moment, how she had known to come.

"My oldest son is one of the EMTs who took the call," she said, laying her coat on a chair and coming over to sit down beside me. "He called me just after they got your call. I've been sort of waiting for this; Jeremy knew to call if he was on duty if and when it happened. Do you know anything yet? Does Dennis know?"

"I don't know what it is; Luz called, and when we got here Bella was almost unconscious, but I'm nearly sure it's a heart attack. Dennis went with her to the hospital. I stayed with Luz, of course . . . "

"Well, I've come to sit with her if you want to go on to the hospital. I expect you do. You've been the closest thing to family Bella has had for a while, and Dennis won't know anybody over there. He'll need some backup. How is he doing about it, by the way?"

"It's hard to say. You probably know they've been sort of reunited for a little while, but it's hard for me to tell how he feels about her. It's been wonderful for her, of course. I know that he was . . . singing to her in Portuguese just before the ambulance came . . . "

Patricia's gray Ponder eyes filled with tears and she smiled. "Then she'll be okay whatever happens. But he may not be. You go over there, now. I've called some of the others and there'll be somebody along to spell me directly. Come on back here when you can; we'll be here. If there are . . . plans to make, we can help you do that. We'd go on over to the hospital, but none of us knows if Dennis would want us or not. I'll let you be the judge of that. But we'll be here."

"I don't know why," I said, my own eyes at last beginning to fill with tears. "She's frozen you out her entire adult life. And Dennis has simply . . . written you off."

"I remember him so well," she said softly. "He was my best friend for a year or two; I never had another quite like him. He was all laughter and mischief, the best of the Ponders, before his grandmother's cold spite could kick in. We all remember him, and some of us remember Bella, too, when she first came to the Vineyard. I barely remember, but I know I never saw anybody so beautiful, or so vivid and full of life. It was a Ponder who brought her here and a Ponder who made her what she is. Seems to me Ponders ought to hop to now and see if we can help fix things for Denny. There aren't enough of us left that we can afford to lose one."

I pressed her hand with mine; it was warm and rough and felt somehow like my father's, though she could not have been much older than I.

"I'll let you know the minute I know anything," I said, and went out into the just-born morning. Behind me, I heard Patricia Norton begin to read, taking up where I'd left off: "'The Wart walked up to the great sword for the third time. He put out his right hand softly and drew it out as gently as from a scabbard . . .'"

Isabel Miara Ponder died in the hospital at Oak Bluffs at 6:14 that morning. She was dead when I got there. When I came hurrying down the corridor, Dennis Ponder was sitting in the dim, scruffy waiting area off the elevator lobby, his hands folded in his lap, looking down at his lone foot in a boot to which the rich black mud of spring still clung. When he heard my footsteps, he looked up, and I saw in his face, white and still and oddly formal, that she had gone. But still I formed the words with my lips, though no sound came: "How is she?"

"Gone," he said in a neutral voice. "About fifteen minutes ago. The doctor's in there now doing . . . whatever you do. Then I have to do . . . whatever you do. Thing is, I don't know what you do. Do you? I guess you do; you just went through this with your mother, didn't you?"

I nodded slowly. I felt numb and so tired that I did not think I could stand up any longer. I sat down on the cracked Naugahyde sofa beside him.

"Bad year for mothers," he said.

"Dennis, I'm so very sorry."

He reached over to my hand and patted it absently. I don't think that he knew he held it.

"I know you are, Molly. She was a lucky old woman, to have you to be sorry for her. She just as well could have had nobody."

"She had you. You'd have been here whether or not I was."

"No," he said slowly. "I really don't think I would have. Listen, are you hungry? I'm starving. Do you think there's somewhere around here to get a bagel or something? I guess it's okay to leave. She's sure not going anywhere."

"Let's go back to the farmhouse," I said. "There's somebody waiting for us there you're going to remember, and she'll make us some breakfast. Just tell the nurse at the desk. Bella . . . your mother . . . I think she's supposed to stay here until the, you know, funeral home people come and get her. The nurse will know that."

"I don't know any funeral home people, not here and not anywhere," Dennis said, hopping beside me down the hall. His crutch made a rubbery, squelching noise on the dirty white tiles.

"Your people know. They'll take care of it. They already know about your mother."

"I'll bet they do," he said. "Ding dong, the witch is dead."

"They're not like you think, Dennis," I said. "They never were. They're nothing like your mother taught you they were. If you don't know anything else about this island, you need to know that."

He was silent until we got into the truck and headed out of Oak Bluffs. I cut through the fabled camp meeting grounds, silent like a Victorian Brigadoon in the still, chilly morning, and drove along the beach road through Hart Haven into Edgartown and onto the Edgartown–West Tisbury Road, heading up island. The morning sea was like a silver-pink mirror except for an early ferry wallowing west toward Woods Hole. The main street of Vineyard Haven was just coming to life. Over everything the sharp, cold air of early spring breathed quietly.

"Do you know what she told me in the ambulance?" Dennis said.

"What?"

"She told me that after that time—that I saw them together, you know about that—that after that, I was over at the Peaks' sheep farm playing with the little Peaks like I did sometimes, and we were playing around the corral with some of the grown-ups watching us, and Mr. Peak's old ram mounted one of the ewes, and I laughed and pointed and yelled, 'My mama and Aunt Luz do that!' And old Mrs. Peak asked me, 'What do you mean, Dennis?' and I told everybody what I had seen them doing. Mrs. Peak must have gone straight to my grandmother, because Mother said that that night Grandmother came to the house on Music Street and told her that she knew about her and Luz, and that she was going to take me away from her and raise me herself, as a proper Ponder, and see that Mama never set eyes on me again. Mama said Grandmother threatened to run her and Luzia right off the Vineyard. I was sent off island less than a week later."

He fell silent, and I simply drove, numbed and stupid with pain. Then he said, "She said she sent me because she knew they'd take me away, that they could do that, and so that at least, if I was with her family, I'd stay part of her. But it was the wrong thing to do if that's what she wanted, Molly, because if I'd stayed on the Vineyard, at least I'd have seen her now and then. I'd have *had* to at least run into her . . . "

"She did the only thing she knew to do to keep you," I said around the aching lump in my throat. "Maybe it was wrong, but she didn't know any other way. You have to remember that in spite of being a married woman, she was still very much a girl, and a pretty simple one at that."

"She could have sent Luz away and kept me with her."

"No. She'd have lost you to her mother-in-law anyway, and then she'd have been totally alone. And if she'd gone back to her people, what sort of life could she have had? Having to pretend Luz was nothing to her but a nice, accommodating cousin . . . and you'd have grown up and gone out into the world anyway, and there she would have been, growing old without you *or* Luz, with only those fanatic old Catholic royalists around her. By then she'd gone too far beyond that, don't you see? You can't ever go back to what you were before you've loved somebody . . . "

"That time at the sheep farm," he said, as if he had not heard me. "That was when I buried Luz's underwear in the sheep manure and the ram dug it up. You remember, I told you about that New Year's Eve? I don't mind so much that they told her what I said about seeing her and Luz, but I hope before God they didn't tell her that I made a joke of it . . . "

"I hope so, too," I whispered. It was all I could think to say.

Back at the farmhouse, Patricia Norton met us at the door, looked at our faces, and held her arms out. After a long moment, it was Dennis who walked into them, not I. They looked at each other, he and Pat, out of the same rain-gray eyes, and after we had eaten Pat's pancakes and drunk her coffee and looked in on Luzia, who slept peacefully in a clean gown under clean sheets by a newly built fire, he reached out and tweaked the back of Pat's sandy hair, where it straggled over her collar.

"It used to hang down almost to your waist," he said. "You wore it in two pigtails."

"And you dipped the ends of them into the inkwells at school," she said. "My mother had to cut five inches off it. She was furious, but I was delighted. I hated those damned braids."

"It's been a long time, Pat," he said. "I wonder if it's just plain been too long."

"No," she said. "Not to us. We've all wondered if we'd ever get to know you. Whether or not we do now, we'll at least get a look at you. The eyes are all Ponder, of course, but the rest of you is her. It'll be nice to have that of her still."

"I'm not real sure what happens next," he said.

She laughed. "That's one thing we Ponders do know, how to bury other Ponders. Unless you want to take her back to America and bury her where her people are, we'll take it from here. With your approval, of course. There's a whole tribe of us in the Chilmark cemetery. We outnumber John Belushi about three hundred to one, but of course he gets all the press."

He smiled then.

"I've missed you, Pat. I wonder why I didn't know that," he said.

"About Luz . . ." I began.

"My sister Hannah is coming in to sit with her in a little while," Pat Norton said. "And some of the others will spell her. Luz seems okay, considering. I don't think she comprehends, do you?"

"I don't know. It doesn't seem that way so far," I said. "Thanks, Pat. When I've looked in on my father and cleaned up, I'll be back to take over."

"Molly," she said, putting an arm around my shoulders, "let us do it. God knows we did little enough for them while Bella was alive. Maybe they wouldn't have let us, anyway, but we could have tried harder. This is ours to do now."

Then what is mine to do? I thought desolately, but did not say it aloud. It seemed an almost unimaginably selfish thought.

On the way back to the pond, Dennis laid his head against the back of the seat and, despite the truck's drunken lurching, slept. Or I thought that he did. But just as we reached the cutoff down to the Ponder camps, he said, eyes still closed, "They weren't what she told me. I don't think they ever were. Just my grandmother, and I guess my father. In the long run they could have accepted her and Luz; maybe they knew anyway. They've accepted more than that in all the hundreds of years they've been in this place. She could have had some kind of life here. I could have . . . "

"You still can," I said softly, but he did not answer.

Though it was nearly nine-thirty when I got home, there was no sound from my father's room upstairs. Lazarus lay quietly on the rug in front of the dead fire, waiting for me. He thumped his tail and rose to meet me, and went with me up the stairs to wake my father and tell him about Bella Ponder. But the curtains were still drawn, and he was still asleep. I shook him gently.

"Let me sleep," he murmured, not opening his eyes. "She's here. Let me sleep."

I went back downstairs and shucked off my clothes and slept, too.

They buried her in the old cemetery on a day so warm and still and tender that you could almost feel the leaves pushing out of their woody prisons, the first flowers stirring and fretting to be born. The sky over the Sound was a fresh-washed blue, and small, puffed, silver-limned clouds sailed slowly in from the south. From all the moist places up island the pinkletinks chimed. Every now and then the querulous honk of a returning goose broke the late-morning silence, and up at the edge of the cemetery one of the small roving herds of guineas darted and gabbled and dipped their ridiculous pinheads into the grass.

There were perhaps twenty assorted Ponders, plus their spouses and progeny, on hand, standing quietly around the newly-dug grave as the young minister from the Congregational church in Chilmark read the simple old service for the burial of the dead. I stood alone at the back of the small crowd; Dennis stood in the middle, obviously uncomfortable in a dark, rumpled suit that hung on him like a scarecrow's. I had helped him pin the left trouser leg up that morning, so that it did not flap. There were no hymns sung, and no one said the elegiac words over the dead that I had dreaded. It would have seemed a sacrilege. No one seemed to expect Dennis to say anything, either, and he did not. When the short service was over and the concluding prayer done, the Ponders who remained up island shook his hand gravely, and some of them patted him awkwardly on the back, and Pat Norton, who stood beside him, said, "We didn't think a get-together back at the farmhouse would be a good idea, with Luz there and all, but all of us will call you in a day or two. You'll have more dinner invitations than you ever had in your life. And there are people lined up to sit with Luz in eight-hour shifts for two or three days, until you can decide what should be . . . you know, done about her. I guess you don't know any more than we do about any family she might have left in America. If you want to see about nursing homes on the island, or some other kind of facility, I think we can help you there. There are one or two state-supported places. You just let us know. I'd bet that there's enough cash in Bella's account to see you through the first few weeks and get Luz settled somewhere. Molly, you know where she banks, don't you? Banked, I mean? They'll know. Nobody will hassle you about getting into her account, I don't think, Denny. After probate, you'll have the farm, of course, but we can certainly help out some . . . "

"Go home, Pat," Dennis said, kissing her on the cheek. "You're going to drop in your tracks. If you've left anything undone, I can't imagine what it is. I'll think about Luz and let you know. I don't have to say thank you, do I?"

"No. But 'I'm sorry about the pigtails' would be a good start."

Back at the farmhouse, after the Ponder cousin who was sitting with Luz had made us coffee and cut one of six or seven cakes that had come tiptoed out, we sat down in the living room and looked at Luz Ferreira. She looked back, alert and sweet-faced, smiling her joy at seeing Dennis again. The Ponder cousin had combed her hair into a silver halo and put a dab of lipstick on her little mouth, and there was a cloud of something that smelled like old-fashioned rosewater in the stale air. Dennis and I looked at each other. She could not have weighed ninety pounds, but she loomed as large in the dim old room as Bella ever had, as massive as an anchor. What on earth was going to become of her now?

"We need to talk a little now, Luz," Dennis said finally. "We need to talk some about Bella, and then about . . . what we're all going to do later. We need to make some plans."

The sweet smile deepened. It was obvious to me that she did not comprehend that Bella was gone. I wondered if she ever would, and when she did, who would be there to help her bear it.

"All right, Denny," she said, like a good child. "And then you can help me pack. I have a suitcase all my own; it's blue. Bella gave it to me for Christmas . . . sometime."

My heart contracted with pity.

"Where are you going, sweetie?" I said softly, pushing the spindrift hair off her face.

"Why . . . home with Denny. I know I can't stay here. I can't climb the stairs. Bella said I was to go with Denny now. I guess I'll stay until she comes for me. I don't remember what she said about that."

I could feel pure pain twist my face; I buried it in her hair so that she would not see it.

"Oh, honey," I began.

"Who wants some ice cream?" Dennis said loudly. "I saw some Chunky Monkey in the freezer. It seems a shame to let it go to waste."

"Oh, I do," cried Luz, clapping her hands.

I just looked at him.

"Come on in the kitchen and help me, Molly," he said. "You can carry the bowls."

He was halfway across the floor before I got up and followed him.

"We can't put this off forever," I whispered. "We were halfway there. Why didn't you just go on with it? There's not going to be a better time to tell her . . . "

He was fumbling in the freezer.

"Can you get her ready? Pack up some things, and all?" he said over his shoulder.

"Ready for what?"

"Ready to come back to my place with me."

"You have got to be kidding," I said, slowly and fervently.

He turned to look at me.

"No. It makes sense. You wouldn't have to be running up here every five minutes, and no one else would either. No one would have to stay. You'd have both of us right down there at your doorstep. And there's a lot I can do for her, more than you think . . . "

"Dennis, she just needs so much . . . "

"It would kill her to put her in some kind of home, Molly," he said.

I was quiet for a long time, trying to think it out, trying to feel how it would be. The dwindling old woman, the very sick man, there in the glade with me. With me and the father I was, ever so slowly, losing. With only me and a dog and a place of straw under the steps where two swans had been but no longer were . . . could I feel that?

Could I do that?

Yes, I could.

"You know you'll probably have to do it eventually," I said slowly.

"But not now. Not today. By God, Molly, not yet."

"Denny?" Luz called from the living room.

"Coming. Just getting your stuff together, toots," he called back.

I went upstairs to find Luzia's blue Christmas suitcase and pack her things.

It took a long time to get her moved into Dennis's camp. Patricia Norton and her son and a friend carried Luz's tiny body and her few possessions—scuffed, old-fashioned children's things—to the friend's Explorer, where the backseat had been removed. I went ahead with Dennis and together we moved his things out of the downstairs bedroom and I put fresh linen on the bed that would, now, be Luz's.

"Where will you sleep?" I said, shaking out quilts and fluffing pillows. I had brought them from the farmhouse, new ones that Bella had obviously put away for a rainy day. Oh, God, Bella . . . they smelled of camphor and lavender, but they still bore their tags, and the creases of newness. Somehow, they turned the rough, masculine room into the bower of a young girl.

"On the sofa in front of the fire," he said. "You have no idea how often I fall asleep there anyway. Don't frown, Molly, it'll be much better. My books will already be where I am and I won't have to get up and stump around in the dark looking for them, and I can get at the scotch a lot easier, and if you should just happen, one fine day, to come around saying, 'Please, sir, can I have some more?' I won't have to throw old Luz out of her room, and nobody will have to worry about corrupting the morals of an old lady."

I looked at him, startled. Was he teasing me? He had been quiet and withdrawn all day, gone inside himself, I thought, against the weight of whatever it was he felt as he watched his mother lowered into the earth of up island. I realized that I was not likely ever to know what that was. I realized, too, that I was probably not ever going to be able to tell when he was teasing me.

How long, for Dennis Ponder and for me, was "ever" going to be?

He was not smiling, but something in his eyes was more alive, more present, than I had seen all day.

"We couldn't have that," I said, and bent to pick up the pile of used bedding.

"Molly."

"What?"

"Are you? Going to ask?"

I straightened up and looked at him.

"Am I going to be around *to* ask, Dennis?" I said.

He frowned.

"Why wouldn't you be?"

"My contract was with your mother. I have to assume it's void now."

"Your contract, if you want to call it that, was with me. She was just an agent. I don't see any reason to void it unless you want to. Luz and I still need some looking after. I've gotten better about what I can do, but I don't know . . . how long that will last. I'd have to get someone for Luz whatever happens. Why can't it be you? Do you . . . are you thinking of going home?"

I shook my head impatiently. I had not been thinking of anything. Too much had happened too fast. Now, though, I saw just how profoundly our situation had changed. He *was* better, or at least had learned the parameters of his small world so well that he could operate in it almost unaided. Whether it was healing or mere adaptation, I did not know, but it was real. There were resources, now, to help with Luz; his Ponder kin stood ready, if he should ask. And the powerful chord that held me to the glade had always been, I knew now, Bella Ponder. Without her presence looming from the farmhouse on the moor, my hold on this small world felt flaccid and tenuous. I hung in the air of the glade, unable to touch earth, unable to fly away.

And, of course, there was my father. I could see it so clearly, all of a sudden. What had I been thinking of? I needed to get help for him and I needed to do it quickly. Why had I not seen it before?

On the other hand . . . Atlanta. I saw it clearly, in a split-second crack of clarity: the anonymous tiled clinic for my father, with the daily visits and the drugs and the steps forward and the slides back, and the needless, endless "family therapy." And then the "long-term facility . . ." I had volunteered at enough mental health facilities to know where clinical depression in the elderly generally led.

And the sessions with Missy and Tee and some smooth-visaged, feral lawyer, in Missy's ridiculous Laura Ashley office. Endless, endless . . . Or else, the talks with Tee alone, in the Ansley Park house he had wanted to give to Sheri Scroggins and now wanted back; the dull rehashing of hurt and anger and guilt where before there had been laughter and easiness and old, warm love. Could I do that? Could I sit in my own library or on my own terrace with Tee Redwine and try to reconstruct a life he had blown to smithereens? Did I want to?

And if I didn't, what did I *want*? And who? Was there anything at all available to me that could possibly last?

"Dennis," I said, "I don't even know where home is."

"Then stick around until you figure it out," he said, and turned away to finish pushing a box of books out of the room with his crutch.

From my own camp the silent pull of my receding father was as strong as that of the moon on the tide.

"There's the little matter of Daddy," I said. "It seems to me neither of us has given that much thought. I don't think it can wait, now."

He did not speak. When finally he started to, we heard the crunch of the Explorer's tires coming into the glade, and it was time to bring Luzia Ferreira home.

It was late, after dark, when I finished at Dennis's and walked home across the glade. The moon path lay thick and satiny on the Sound, and though there was still no green on the branches of the hardwoods, there was the foreshadowing of it in the pervasive wet, cold greenness that shimmered from the earth and water. I was very tired. Luz had been as giddy and overwrought as a child in a new place, and had had to be soothed and read to and fed by hand. She remembered the swans when she saw the glade, and cried out so frantically to go and see them that Dennis had finally said, rather sharply, "Hush. It's past the swans' bedtime. Tomorrow will be soon enough for the swans," and she had subsided, and soon forgotten them in the shower of words from *Anne of Green Gables* that he was reading to her. It must, I thought, have been his daughter's book. I did not know what he would tell her about the swans, but I was determined not to be there when he did it.

I called out to my father, but got no reply, and went up the dark stairs to look in on him. It was barely eight o'clock, but he was already deep in sleep. Whether or not the pills had taken him no longer mattered; night and sleep were his world now. I saw, with my new clarity, that he was already more than half gone from me, half down there with her.

I knew then that I would have to take him home. The weight of the knowing almost bent me double.

My mother came to the edge of my cave that night. Free of her subterranean bars, she fluttered there for a long time, and for some reason I could not see her clearly, but the sense of her was terribly strong. In my dream I literally willed my eyes to see her and finally they did; she was smiling. It was a small, curved, kitten's smile; I had seen it many times before, when she had made her point, won her game. As I stared, she turned away and then she faded.

"No, you won't," I said to her in my dream, between clenched teeth, and I struggled so hard to reach her that I could feel, in sleep, the sweat start on my face. But I could not reach her, and I could not wake.

Beside me, on the floor, I could hear Lazarus begin to growl, softly and eerily, and then I heard him spring up and scrabble across the floor and out the dog door, and heard his great, booming barking begin. Still I struggled in sleep, caught in the tendrils of the dream. When the barking did not stop, I woke abruptly.

He was still barking. There was a purposeful note in it: It was not the barking that meant he was bored and simply wished to start a commotion. I sat up in the damp, tangled sheets, aching all over from the force of my struggle to wake, feeling thick and heavy and mindless. The barking went on and on. Outside, the morning light was pale and new.

I knew Lazarus would not stop until I stopped him, so I got up and pulled on the clothes I had left in a pile beside my bed—my funeral clothes; what a long time ago that seemed—and started heavily for the door. I heard Dennis then.

He was shouting hoarsely from down by the pond, over and over. I could not make out what he was saying. My heart literally stopped. Daddy . . .

But then I heard that he was saying, "Get Tim! Get Tim! Molly, bring Tim!," and I turned and scrambled up the stairs and into my father's bedroom and shook him hard. I knew without seeing why Dennis wanted my father. I will never know how, but I did.

He did not want to wake, and he did not want to come with me when he did, and was petulant and then quite sharp with me; I simply grabbed him by his shoulders and pulled him out of bed and jerked him to his feet. I remember being shocked that he was so light; he seemed, now, all hollow bone, like a huge bird. But I did not dwell on it; I would deal with it later. When I had him on his feet, swaying and fussing in his too-large pajamas, I bent and literally jammed his feet into his slippers. Then I pulled him down the stairs so fast that we both nearly tumbled to the bottom.

"What are you doing?" he kept demanding, in a sick child's whine. "Where are we going? What is the matter with you?"

We were halfway down the path to the pond when we saw them. I stopped abruptly, and he did, too. He stopped struggling with me and slowly, very slowly, his arms came down to his sides. Then he lifted them slightly, as if he might be about to stretch lightly after sleep.

The two swans were waddling awkwardly up the path toward

us. Behind them, Lazarus capered, barking and barking, keeping his distance. Behind him, Dennis ran and fell and got up and ran again, laughing. Laughing. The swan in front was smaller than the one behind, obviously newly grown, and so white that she shone in the pale sun. There seemed to me no doubt that it was a pen. She was frightened and angry, and she kept stopping and turning around and darting her beautiful, sinuous neck at the larger swan and at Lazarus, and once or twice lifted her wings into the busking position. They glistened as if they had been dipped in liquid crystal. But the big swan behind her would hiss and grunt and thrust at her with his beak, and she would start forward again. Charles. There could be no doubt, either, that the big, dingy cob was Charles, and that he was bringing his new pen to see my father. I sat down on the path and began to cry.

My father stood still until Charles had prodded and flapped and hissed the young pen to a position directly in front of him. Both swans stopped then, and Charles stationed himself behind the pen so that she could not bolt, and simply settled himself into his great, battered wings, tucked up a black foot, and looked up at my father. The pen settled herself, too, though she kept darting her head around, and her wings stayed in constant slight motion, like voile blowing in a spring wind.

Slowly, slowly, my father sank down on his heels into the crouch that I knew from a thousand days of my childhood, the one that he could maintain for hours. He looked at the swans, and then he said, in the voice I had not heard for a long time, my father's voice, "You old fool. Where the hell have you been?"

CHAPTER FIFTEEN

EASTER WAS AS LATE THAT YEAR AS I CAN REMEMBER, and it came in on the wings of a great nor'easter that seemed to say to the Vineyard, after we had basked gratefully in a string of perfect spring days, "Gotcha!"

Afterward, the old men at Alley's said that there had not been such a spring storm since most of them could remember, though a few of the very oldest claimed they had seen worse. I didn't see how there could be worse.

We had known it was coming, and I, as well as most of the up islanders who could drive, had stocked up on tinned food and sterno and wood and propane and candles.

"Will you be okay?" said Pat Norton, whom I had run into at the A&P in Vineyard Haven. "You're sure to lose power down there."

"I've got all the stuff for both camps," I said. "And Daddy has tightened some shingles, and I left him and Dennis trying to decide whether to board the windows. Dennis wants to do it, but Daddy is afraid he can't keep an eye on the damned swans if they do. I think I know who's going to win that one. There's not a one of us who can stand up against those swans."

"I'm so glad he's better," she said. "All I was hearing at Alley's for a while was how much everybody missed Tim Bell. It seemed to me you just plain had more than you could handle, but I didn't want to pry—"

I hugged her impulsively, and she smiled shyly, though she flinched away from the hug. I laughed.

"I keep forgetting I'm not in the South," I said. "Yes. He *is* better. Oh, Pat. What on earth would we have done without you?"

She shook her head impatiently, but then she said, "Stay, Molly. We've gotten sort of used to you. All us Ponders have."

I drove home in the stiffening wind, feeling as if I had been given the keys to up island.

The storm hit in earnest early in the blackness of Easter morning, and by dawn the glade had indeed lost power. I had cooked a ham the day before and made a drunken, lopsided coconut cake from scratch, and bought potato salad from Back Alley's deli counter, and I put it all out on the back porch to keep. The wet cold that came back with the storm would keep it better than the dead refrigerator. At ten A.M. I heard a crash that meant the telephone pole that served the glade was down, and shortly after that Dennis, swathed from head to heels in oilskins, knocked on the door and shouted above the roar of the wind and rain that he wanted to bring Luz down to our camp.

"It's warmer down here," he yelled. "I can't keep her warm up there; the fire won't reach into her bedroom, and for some reason the living room confuses her, and she cries for Bella."

His concern was real, although it was hard to gauge the meaning of it. His relationship with Luz was complex, but it seemed comfortable to both. Whatever it was, I knew it was born, as he had been, of Bella Ponder, and that she was with him still, every day. He did not often speak of her, but she lived in the camp with him as surely as Luz did. She lived in my camp, too. Bella was vigorous and palpable in the glade.

My father put on his foul-weather gear and went out into the gale with Dennis, pausing to look under the porch, where the swans were huddled in their straw bower, fussy and miserable. Charles had one great wing fanned over Persephone, who had her head and neck tucked almost completely into her own shining feathers. The straw was wet, but the wind did not reach in so badly. Together, Daddy and Dennis brought Luzia, completely wrapped in blankets and oilskin, back in a fireman's hold. I have no idea how Dennis managed it; I could not bear to look. Both men were drenched when they came in, but Luzia was snug and dry, and so enchanted to be back in the little camp she remembered that she forgot to fuss constantly for the swans. I put her on the sofa and covered her and built up the fire, then sent Dennis and my father up for showers in the remaining hot water, and dry clothes. They were my father's, and they hung loose on both men. It did not matter. I was absurdly glad to have them here. I had planned to take Easter dinner up to Dennis's, but this . . . this was better.

The storm raged all afternoon. We could hear occasionally the crashes of trees going down in the woods, but it was impossible to see through the solid curtain of howling silver rain. When I did look out, the air was full of flying green as the wind stripped the new leaves from the oaks and hickories and hurled them aloft. The pounding of the waves over on the Bight and the Sound was audible, even through the wind, when the door was opened. We didn't do that often, needless to say. For some reason, I was never worried. It simply never occurred to me that we might lose our roof, or suffer a direct hit from a tree.

At two in the afternoon I served the ham and potato salad before the fire, and we had cake and coffee made in the spatterware pot over the flames. I brought out a bottle of Napoleon brandy my father had brought from Atlanta and we opened it. We had made a considerable dent in it when there was a great, furious flapping at the door and my father rushed to jerk it open and Charles and Persy literally blew into the room, wet and truculent and aggrieved. After a skittering skirmish with Lazarus, my father herded them into a pile of old blankets behind the sofa, and there they settled, fussily, to wait out the storm. My father put barley and water there for them, and occasionally went and crouched down and talked softly to them, and from time to time we all heard the great, liquid splatting that meant swan excrement.

After the first splat, I simply closed my ears to it.

"Relax," Dennis grinned. "Pat will surely know what gets swan shit out of chintz."

By late afternoon the wind was beginning to drop, as it often did when darkness fell during a nor'easter, and though we all knew it would pick up again with the coming of the next day's light, we stirred and smiled at one another, and I passed the brandy again, and threw a log on the fire. Dennis had put Pachelbel on his little battery-powered cassette recorder, and he and my father sat at the crooked table in the corner playing chess and sipping cognac. Luzia snored softly on the sofa, murmuring every now and then in Portuguese. Lazarus slept on the hearth rug, groaning deliciously, one ear cocked toward his feathered adversaries behind the sofa. They had not fussed or rustled or splatted for some time now.

I sat in the wing chair drawn up to the fire, nearly gone into sleep and cognac. I thought that I could sit there, just so, forever.

A log burned in two, then collapsed in a shower of sparks, and Lazarus twitched; behind the sofa a swan grunted crossly. The smell of pent-up swan was beginning to curl ripely into the warm room. I did not care about that, either. I sat up and stretched, and walked to the front door to look out at the storm. It seemed to catch its great breath for a moment before shouting on.

"It you're going into the kitchen, bring us back some of that Chunky Monkey," Dennis said lazily from the chess table. "I packed it in dry ice, but it's going to melt if we don't eat it."

I was suddenly pierced through with such a blade of pure knowing that I literally doubled over with it. Then I straightened up and began to laugh, softly.

Right now, I thought, just for this minute right now, we are a family. A six-foot Southern Betrayed Wife and her widowed father and a senile old Portuguese lesbian and a one-legged schoolteacher and a mongrel dog and two aberrant swans—we are a family. That is what we have made together. For just this moment, we are as real as any family anywhere in the world. Maybe one of us is dying. Maybe more than one. Or maybe not. Maybe one or more of us will fly away. Or maybe not. It doesn't matter. Right now, we are us and we are here.

Still smiling, I went to the hat rack and took my mother's black hat from it and opened the front door. The wind howled hungrily. I looked at my father, and he looked back at me for a long time, then nodded slightly and smiled.

"What the hell are you doing?" Dennis Ponder said.

"Throwing my hat in the ring," I said back.

I opened the door and walked to the edge of the porch and stopped.

"It's not forever, Mama," I said aloud. "Just for right now. It was never really mine, anyway."

And I gave the hat to the wind, which took it and whirled it away over the lashing trees, toward Gay Head, all the way up island.